DEAD OF

BARBARA
NADEL

DEAD OF NIGHT

headline

First published in 2012 by
HEADLINE PUBLISHING GROUP

1

. Cataloguing in Publication Data is available from the British Library

ISBN 978 0 7553 7164 8 (Hardback)
ISBN 978 0 7553 7165 5 (Trade paperback)

Typeset in Times New Roman by Palimpsest Book Production Limited,
Falkirk, Stirlingshire

Printed and bound in Great Britain by
Clays Ltd, St Ives plc

Headline's policy is to use papers that are natural, renewable and recyclable
products and made from wood grown in sustainable forests. The logging and
manufacturing processes are expected to conform to the environmental
regulations of the country of origin.

HEADLINE PUBLISHING GROUP
An Hachette UK Company
338 Euston Road
London NW1 3BH

www.headline.co.uk
www.hachette.co.uk

To the great city and great people of Detroit. Also for
Jim Reeve and his big, beautiful view of the Shard of Glass

Cast of Characters

Çetin İkmen – middle-aged İstanbul police inspector
Mehmet Süleyman – İstanbul police inspector, İkmen's protégé
Commissioner Ardıç – İkmen and Süleyman's boss
Sergeant Ayşe Farsakoğlu – İkmen's deputy
Sergeant İzzet Melik – Süleyman's deputy
Dr Arto Sarkissian – İstanbul police pathologist
Tayyar Bekdil – Süleyman's cousin, a journalist in Detroit
Lieutenant Gerald Diaz – of Detroit Police Department (DPD)
Lieutenant John Shalhoub – of DPD
Lieutenant Ed Devine – of DPD
Sergeant Donna Ferrari – of DPD
Detective Lionel Katz – of DPD
Officer Rita Addison – of DPD
Officer Mark Zevets – of DPD
Dr Rob Weiss – ballistics expert
Rosa Guzman – forensic investigator
Ezekiel (Zeke) Goins – elderly Melungeon
Samuel Goins – Zeke's brother, a Detroit city councillor
Martha Bell – urban regenerator, Zeke's landlady
Keisha Bell – Martha's daughter

Grant T. Miller – man Zeke Goins suspects killed his son, Elvis

Marta Sosobowski – widow of deceased Detroit cop, John Sosobowski

Stefan and Richard Voss – undertakers

Kyle Redmond – an auto wrecker

Downtown Detroit

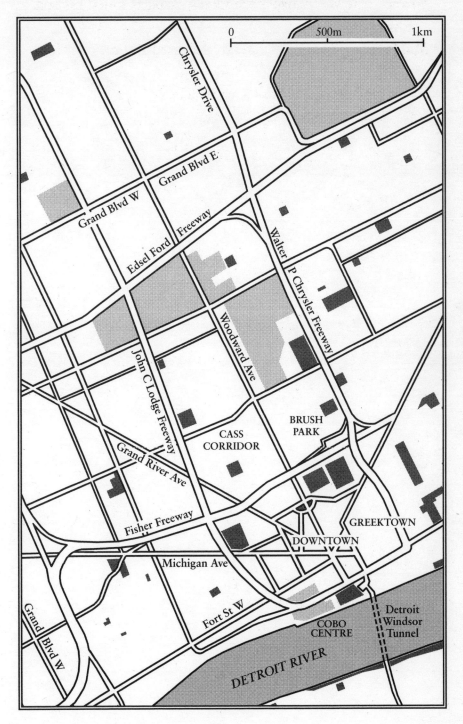

1 December 1978 – Detroit, Michigan

His breath came in short, spiky gasps as his face was pushed hard into the unyielding brickwork in front of him. There was a gun jammed against the side of his head. It was wielded by the same unknown person who had twisted his arm up his back so that his hand nearly touched his head. He was afraid, but also angry. In spite of not being able to breathe properly, he yelled, 'You fucking Purple motherfucker!'

But there was no reply, none of the usual murmurs of approval from the other gang members that generally accompanied hits of this kind. Was there anyone else with whoever had grabbed him? He began to feel the blood drain from his face as he considered the possibility that his assailant was alone. Apart from the shame he felt at being somehow disabled by possibly just one person, he also knew what this could mean on another level. Every so often kids like him just got taken. Generally it was by some sort of wacko freak who wanted to have sex with them – or with their body after they were dead. He'd seen that movie *The Hills Have Eyes*; he knew what went on.

'Listen, man, I ain't gonna let you have my butt!' he said, and then instantly regretted it. His ma always said his mouth was way too big for his head. The pressure on his arm and then from the gun against his temple increased. Either he'd hit on the truth, or he'd just enraged his attacker still further. After all, if he wasn't homosexual,

1

he had just insulted him. Then it got worse. 'But if you gonna rob me, then that's cool,' he blurted. 'Or . . . no, it ain't cool, but . . .'

But he didn't want to be robbed either! Again, he panicked.

'Not that I'm sayin' you're a faggot or nothing, man,' he said. 'Maybe you just want my stuff. I dunno!' Then his voice rose in terror and he yelled, 'Just tell me what you do want, you crazy freak!'

There was snow on the ground underneath his feet. He looked down at it, knowing with a certainty that made his head dizzy that his blood and brains were going to colour its city greyness red. He began to shiver. The gunman, his weapon pointed at his head, pulled the muzzle back just ever so slightly. 'Why are you going to kill me, man?' the boy cried plaintively. 'I ain't nothing special. What I ever do to you?'

But he never got an answer to that or any other question. His assailant pulled the trigger at just short of point-blank range, and as the boy himself had imagined in the last moments of his life, his blood and brains turned the Detroit winter snow red.

Chapter 1

27 November 2009 – İstanbul, Turkey

Inspector Çetin İkmen's office was cold. The police station heating system had developed a fault, and so everyone was having to make do with tiny, weak electric heaters. Also İkmen was not actually in his office, which always made it, so his sergeant Ayşe Farsakoğlu believed, even more dreary and cheerless.

She leaned towards the tiny one-bar heater and thought about how badly her week without her boss was starting. So far, since İkmen and another inspector, Mehmet Süleyman, had left to go to a policing conference abroad, first the computer system had thrown a tantrum, and then the heating had broken down. It was almost as if the fabric of the building was protesting at their absence. Ayşe herself always felt lost without İkmen, and whenever Süleyman was out of town, she worried. Some years before, she'd had a brief affair with the handsome, urbane Mehmet. She still, in spite of his so far two marriages as well as numerous affairs and liaisons, had feelings for him. Where the two officers had gone, representing the entire Turkish police force, was a very long way away, to a place apparently even colder than İstanbul. As she leaned still further in towards the fire, Ayşe found such an idea almost beyond belief. Then a knock at the door made her look up. 'Come in.'

The door opened to reveal a slightly overweight dark man in his late forties.

'Sergeant Melik.'

İzzet Melik was Mehmet Süleyman's sergeant, and like Ayşe Farsakoğlu, he was not finding the absence of his boss or the bitterly cold November wind easy to deal with. He was also, Ayşe noticed, carrying a paper bag that appeared to be steaming. He held it up so that she could see it. 'Börek,' he said, announcing the presence of hot, savoury Turkish pastries. 'If the heating's going to be down for a while, we need to eat properly and keep warm.'

Ayşe smiled. İzzet, in spite of his tough, macho-man exterior, was a kind and rather cultured soul who had held a romantic torch for her, in silence, for years.

'That's a very nice thought,' she said.

He took a tissue out of his pocket and then picked a triangular pastry out of the bag and wrapped it up for her. 'Mind if I join you, Sergeant Farsakoğlu?'

He was always so careful to be proper and respectful with her. As she looked at him, in spite of his heaviness and lack of physical grace, Ayşe felt herself warm to him. Like her boss, Çetin İkmen, İzzet Melik was a 'good' man. What you saw was, generally, what you got. No subterfuge, no hidden agendas, none of the fascinating mercurial scariness that could surface in Mehmet Süleyman from time to time. She pointed to the battered chair behind İkmen's desk and said, 'Bring that over.'

He smiled. For a while they both sat in companionable silence, eating their börek, İzzet pulling his coat in tight around his shoulders. Then Ayşe said, 'So this conference our bosses have gone to . . .'

'*Policing in Changing Urban Environments*,' İzzet said, quoting the conference title verbatim.

'What's it . . .'

'About?' He shrugged. 'I think it's about gangs and drugs and migration and how those things, and other factors, affect life in a modern city.'

Ayşe bit into a particularly cheesy bit of her börek and was amazed at just how much better it made her feel.

4

'Officers are going from all over the world,' İzzet continued. 'But then changing urban environments affect us all. You know this city, İstanbul, had only two million inhabitants back in 1978? We're now twelve million, at least.'

'More people, more problems,' Ayşe said.

'Yes. And a lot of those problems are global now too,' he said. 'Kids from New York to Bangkok sniff gas, shove cocaine up their noses and make up rap tunes about inner-city alienation. The internet allows terrorist groups to reach out to men and women on the streets of cities everywhere. Everything's expanding, complicating, getting faster.' He frowned. 'If we don't either take control of it, try to understand it or both, we could find ourselves in the middle of an urban nightmare, a real futuristic dystopia.'

İzzet was way cleverer than he looked. Sometimes he was too clever. Ayşe knew what a dystopia was, but she never would have used the word herself. She finished her börek and then wiped her fingers on the tissue. 'Well, whatever comes out of it,' she said, 'Inspector İkmen and Inspector Süleyman are getting to go to America. Çetin Bey was a little nervous, you know. Such a long flight!'

'They're changing planes at Frankfurt,' İzzet said. Then he frowned again. 'One thing I can't understand is why this conference is being held in a city that is actually shrinking.'

'Shrinking?'

'Since the US motor industry started to go into decline at the end of the 1950s, Detroit, where the conference is taking place, has been contracting,' he said. 'As I understand it, anyone with any money left years ago. Those that remain are largely poor and unemployed. Detroit has one of the highest murder rates in America.'

Ayşe, suddenly cold again, shuddered. 'İnşallah the inspectors will be safe in such a place!' she said.

'With hundreds of officers from all over the world around them, not to mention the Detroit Police Department?' İzzet smiled. 'It'll be OK.'

5

Ayşe looked unsure. 'With one of the highest murder rates in America?' she said. 'One has to ask what the police there are actually doing.'

İzzet looked away from her and into the depths of the electric heater and said, 'Maybe Detroit is what cities become when they get beyond the mega-city stage. Maybe eventually everyone will just leave.'

'İstanbul?'

He shrugged again. 'We're still growing. But it has to stop some-time. When no one can stand it any more, when the infrastructure breaks down, when there aren't enough jobs for everyone.' He looked across at her. 'That was what happened in Detroit. Maybe it's what will happen here too.'

Air travel wasn't Çetin İkmen's favourite form of locomotion. Not that he'd done a lot of it. Until this trip, the furthest he had flown had been to London, which had taken all of three and a half hours. Now he was on what he considered to be an eight-hour marathon from Frankfurt to Detroit, and less than sixty minutes into the flight, he was already uncomfortable and bored.

Mehmet Süleyman, his one-time protégé and now colleague, had managed somehow, already, to drop off to sleep. Quite how he had achieved that, İkmen didn't know. Maybe it was some sort of defence mechanism against the craving he knew the younger man would be experiencing for a cigarette. There had been no time to find some-where to smoke when they'd changed planes at Frankfurt airport. No one let anyone smoke in peace any more! Even his own office had been out of bounds for smoking since the previous July. It made İkmen miserable. Now that the weather was cold, trudging out to the back of the station was a chore. It was, he felt, ridiculous too. Almost everyone he knew was outside more often than they were in! Except, of course, his sergeant. Ayşe Farsakoğlu had given up when the ban on smoking in enclosed spaces had first been imposed. He was proud of her for that, even if he had no intention of following her example. He thought about his destination, about how rabid, or seemingly so, Americans were against smoking, and it almost made him wish that the plane would crash. At least death would end his nicotine cravings, as well as his fear of being a long way away from the ground in a sealed metal tube.

He took one of the boiled sweets his daughter Çiçek had given him out of his pocket and put it in his mouth. Recently married to a Turkish Airlines pilot, Çiçek had been a flight attendant for twelve years, and so she knew a thing or two about air travel and its risks and problems. She'd met her father at the airport armed with a bag of boiled sweets, a neck pillow, some sort of headache-preventing thing consisting of a strip of cold gel one placed on one's forehead, and a pair of long, tight compression socks.

'The flight socks will stop you getting deep-vein thrombosis,' she'd said when she'd made him sit down and put them on in Departures. 'Long flights increase everyone's risk. And someone who smokes as much as you do is a prime candidate.'

Mehmet Süleyman, who didn't get a pair of flight socks, had smirked. Now, watching him asleep and apparently motionless, İkmen wondered whether it would be the younger man, and not he, who would get deep-vein thrombosis. Çiçek had said that as well as wearing flight socks, it was also a good idea to move around, or at least keep your feet moving. İkmen idly rotated an ankle, and then reached forward for the Lufthansa flight magazine in the pouch in front of his seat. As he did so, Mehmet Süleyman first frowned, then shuffled uncomfortably in his sleep. Economy seats were problematic for tall people like him. But then the İstanbul Police Department could hardly be expected to pay for their officers to travel in business class, especially at a time when the entire world seemed to be falling into recession.

For İkmen, space was not too much of an issue. Short and thin, he had no problem with his leg room, or even with the fact that the

7

person in front of him had now tilted his own seat backwards. İkmen flicked through the magazine, which fortunately for him was in English as well as German. English and French plus some German was what he spoke. Süleyman spoke English too, but was far more fluent in French, which reflected his decidedly privileged and Ottoman background. The old royalists had all spoken French, which they considered very cultured. Süleyman's father, the son of a prince, albeit a deposed one, had been no exception.

The articles in the magazine ranged from cookery to the architectural delights of the German capital, Berlin. But the beautiful photographs of cafés and cathedrals made İkmen frown. Where they were headed wasn't going to be anything like that. His youngest son, Kemal, who was turning out to be quite a computer geek, had shown him some websites about the city he was going to visit. Detroit, it seemed, was characterised by urban decay. Once the 'Motor City', an industrial giant, geared up to providing sustenance to the US's endless love affair with the automobile, it was now apparently in decline. As far as İkmen could tell, it was full of poor, unemployed people living lives blighted by gang warfare and drugs in houses and apartments that were on the verge of collapse. An urban nightmare with a history of civil unrest and a reputation for being almost impossible to police, Detroit provided a vision of a post-industrial future that could spread across the western world – and that included the Turkish Republic. İkmen baulked at this at the same time as he accepted that it was a possibility. Even cheap Turkish goods couldn't compete with cheaper Indian, Chinese or Korean imports. New players were emerging on the world stage, players whose efficiency and expertise could leave the more traditional industrial nations high and dry. But then if Detroit had been chosen as the best place to host a conference about policing changing urban environments, there had to be more to it than just pointing out the city's failings.

'It seems Detroit is coming back to life,' his boss, Commissioner Ardıç, had told him when they had first discussed the conference back in June. 'Don't know how. You have to find that out. Policing remains a challenge. There have been numerous corruption scandals in the past. But the Detroit Police Department have already gone where some of us have yet to imagine. They're finding solutions, it seems; the people of the city as well as the police.'

Ardıç wanted İkmen and Süleyman to find out how the Americans were dealing with their gangs, with the drug culture that seemed to go with that phenomenon, and with the reality of mass unemployment and the resultant poverty. Officers were coming from all over the world to observe, ask questions, listen and learn, and also to share their experiences with each other. It would, İkmen felt, be a full and interesting week, if not a particularly pretty one.

The old man sat so still in that battered garden chair of his that for a moment, the girl thought he might be dead. It was snowing, and she was cold and didn't really want to be outside at all. But her mother had told her to.

'Go out and get Mr Goins inside,' she had said when she'd seen the old man sitting motionless in amongst where they grew the vegetables. 'He's too old to be sat out in the snow like that.'

The girl, Keisha, had put her coat and snow boots on and run out of her apartment and down the stairs to the gardens outside. From her kitchen window, three floors up, her mother watched in case anyone approached her daughter. Antoine Cadillac Project had been turned into a place of peace, of self-sufficiency and urban beauty, but that didn't mean that the boys with knives, the gun-toting drug-dealers and muggers didn't pay them a visit once in a while. Kids were particularly vulnerable, and Martha, Keisha's mother, had already lost one child, with a second almost gone to crack cocaine, in spite of her best efforts to steer her children away from drugs and gangs.

Keisha nudged the old man with one gloved hand. 'Mr Goins!' she said, her breath turning to ice as she spoke. 'Ma says you gotta come in now!'

His eyes closed, he didn't move. Only the very faintest of mists coming from his mouth gave Keisha any indication that he was even alive. His face was a very weird colour – blue. She shook him again. 'Mr Goins!'

This time he grunted, sniffed and then opened his eyes. Like Keisha's, the old man's eyes were as black as crude oil. He looked around him without seeing the girl, and then said in that southern accent, just like Keisha's grandpa Wally had had, 'Where in the name of the Lord is that boy? Where he about?'

Keisha knew some of what this meant.

'Mr Goins,' Keisha said, 'your boy ain't here! You gotta come inside now. It's snowing.'

He turned and looked at her, as if seeing her for the first time, and said, 'What you doin' here, child?'

Keisha sighed. Mr Goins forgot things. Sometimes it was where he was, sometimes it was who people were, sometimes it was his own name. There was only one thing that he never seemed to forget, but Keisha, young as she was, knew that she should never, ever start that subject up with him. Most times he raised it himself, as he had just done when she woke him.

'Ma's made some hamburger. Come inside,' Keisha said as she put one of her small hands underneath his arm and began to pull him up on to his feet.

From her kitchen window three floors up, Martha Bell wondered yet again how and why she'd come to take some mad old white-looking man into her home. But then she knew the answer to that question just as surely as everyone else on Antoine Cadillac did. Somebody'd had to.

Chapter 2

'It started coming down about five hours ago and it hasn't stopped since,' the hotel receptionist said with a smile. 'But that's winter for you.'

İkmen looked at Süleyman, whose face was, if anything, whiter than the snow they had just come in out of. It had only taken seconds for the two officers to get out of the taxi, pay and enter the hotel, but it was enough to freeze them both almost solid. On top of the almost empty streets, the ghosts of buildings hinting at urban desolation, the shock of the frigid temperatures was intense.

'Yes.' İkmen attempted to smile.

The Lakeland Plaza was an old hotel in the grand tradition of early-twentieth-century Detroit buildings. It was huge, almost Soviet in its four-square functional facade, while inside it was not unlike some of the grander nineteenth-century İstanbul palaces. High ceilings, vast gilt mirrors and heavy, dusty chandeliers projected a feeling of venerable, if faded, worth. İkmen rather liked what he had seen so far, although Süleyman, chilled to the marrow and beyond, just wanted to have a wash and get some sleep before the conference began in a little under three hours' time.

'You're in Suite Twelve, sir,' the receptionist said as she handed a swipe-card key across to İkmen.

'Thank you.' Suite Twelve sounded very grand indeed, and İkmen, glazed and dazed after the flight, began to feel slightly dizzy. In the last twenty-four hours he had not only entered a new continent; he had also, after nearly fifty-eight years on the earth, taken possession of the key to his first hotel suite.

The receptionist pointed to a couple of doors way, way across the vast wastes of marble flooring and said, 'Elevators over there, gentlemen. Floor fourteen. Have a nice day.'

Süleyman, at least, had expected some sort of help with their luggage, but no bellhop or porter materialised. The two men picked up their suitcases and walked towards the lifts through a crowd of people who all sounded American. Although grand, there was a slight dustiness about the reception area that İkmen, at least, had not expected. The United States, he had always believed, was a country that had the highest standards of hygiene in the world. They got into a lift that had a few bits of litter in one corner, and İkmen pressed the button marked 14. The lift, however, had a mind and will of its own.

First stop was floor three, which, though dimly lit, was heavily carpeted and had an ornate, rococo feel. Floor seven was rather plainer and brighter, and a couple of besuited men stood and stared at the Turks for a few moments before the lifts doors closed again.

'Obviously going down,' İkmen observed. Süleyman, tired beyond patience, didn't answer. The lift started again; this time it stopped at floor eleven. This was somewhat different from the floors the men had seen before. When the doors opened, they found that they could barely make out anything much through the gloom. If the doors hadn't got stuck as they attempted to close again, they would have seen nothing. As it was, the temporary malfunction in the lift allowed them not only to smell an odour that was a mixture of cigarette smoke, cooking meat and urine, but also to see that the floors were uncarpeted, and that just across from the lifts, against one stained, gloomy wall, was an old, abandoned fridge.

As the doors closed, this time successfully, Süleyman, who had been silent up to that point, said, 'May Allah protect us.'

İkmen smiled. Undecided himself when it came to divine entities, he said, 'Well, at least that wasn't our floor.'

Süleyman, a thunderous look on his pale face, retreated back into silence.

When the lift did finally reach a juddering halt at floor fourteen, the Lakeland Plaza had clearly regained its mojo. The floors were carpeted, the walls clean and the only smell was that of air-freshener mixed with the very faintest tinge of tobacco. The latter, in a world that was becoming increasingly hostile to cigarettes, made İkmen smile. America's fearsome reputation as an enemy of smoking had made him wonder how he would cope, and even whether he would be arrested for smoking at some point during this trip. But then maybe Detroit was an exception to this rule.

İkmen and Süleyman got out of the lift and looked for a door marked Suite Twelve. It took them several minutes to find it, mainly because the numbers on the doors were so small. All the while they looked, Süleyman groaned with weariness. İkmen ignored him. As soon as they'd landed and the younger man had seen the snow, he'd descended into exhaustion and despair. He had not, apparently, brought very thick clothes with him. He had not, as İkmen – or rather his wife Fatma – had done, packed thermal underwear. But then the twice-divorced Süleyman no longer had a loving woman to do that or anything else for him.

İkmen opened the door to Suite Twelve and walked inside. It was a plain, again vaguely tobacco-scented suite of rooms that looked clean and adequate. After all, if the İstanbul Police Department was paying for a hotel suite, it would not be elaborate, at least not for the likes for İkmen and Süleyman. İkmen walked into the smaller of the two bedrooms and put his case on the bed. The slightly dusty window at the end of the bed allowed him to see a range of skyscrapers capped with snow and in some cases decorated with long, witch's-finger-shaped icicles. Buoyed up by the prospect of new and possibly exciting sights and experiences, he had just started to smile again when he heard Süleyman, from the next room, mutter, 'I can't believe it! What is this?'

13

İkmen, his face unsmiling now, went to see what the problem was. He found his friend and colleague in their shared bathroom, pointing at something above the bath.

'Fingermarks!' he said furiously. 'Red fingermarks!'

'You mean blood?'

'Who knows? Maybe it's just hair colouring!' Süleyman shrugged. 'Fridges in the corridors, blood, maybe, on the walls, dust! What kind of place is this?'

'It's Detroit.'

'Yes, I know . . .'

'A city with problems,' İkmen said. 'That's why we're here. No point in talking about urban issues in a city where everything is perfect. We've come to talk about gangs and drugs and drive-by shootings and—'

'Talk, yes, experience, no,' Süleyman said as he angrily put a cigarette into his mouth and lit up. 'I knew I should have taken Tayyar up on his offer! I knew it!'

Süleyman's cousin Tayyar, a journalist, had worked in Detroit for two years and had a very nice house in the smart Grosse Pointe district. When Süleyman had told him that he was due to come to the city for a conference, Tayyar had offered both him and İkmen rooms in his house. But as İkmen had pointed out, it was a long way from there to the conference centre downtown where they were obliged to go every day for nearly a week. Now, however, although quite happy with the hotel himself, İkmen did rather regret having said no to Tayyar's offer. Süleyman was furious, and was already on the highest of very high Ottoman horses. İkmen watched as, in an attempt to rail about the state of the suite to reception, his colleague wrestled with his bedside phone, which did not, it seemed, work.

The bullet had gone clean through one ear and clean out the other. It was probably just a fluke, but Gerald was nevertheless impressed.

14

If he carried on being impressed by the details, then maybe he'd forget how young the kid was – and how dead.

Brush Park district looked even more spooky than it normally did in the snow. Jagged ghosts of houses pushed up through the whiteness, their glassless windows like gouged-out eyes surrounded by the tatters of once-luxuriant ivy. Gerald knew it as a place where rich motor executives and industrialists had once lived. Now, although bits of it were being restored, for the most part Brush Park, at least in its northern quarter, was a place of spectres, of grand, dying buildings, of coteries of crackheads in what were once someone's servants' quarters, and, just occasionally, of the odd weird kid exploring. Had the fifteen year old Gerald now knew had been called Aaron Spencer been one of them? He'd had his school bag with him, pens and books flung out everywhere as he fell, now stained with snow and with Aaron Spencer's blood.

One of the youngsters in uniform came over, looked down at the kid and said, 'Drive-by.'

'Maybe.' Gerald shrugged. He was much taller than the young officer, much darker too.

'You know it, Lieutenant,' the officer said as he slouched away, going back no doubt, Gerald guessed, to the warmth of one of the squad cars. But then who could blame him? It was fucking freezing, and besides, it wasn't as if anyone could do anything for Aaron Spencer now. They probably wouldn't even find who had killed him, or be able to tell the kid's parents why their son had died. Gerald hadn't verbally agreed with the young officer's assessment of the situation, even though he knew in his heart that the boy had been right. This was a drive-by shooting. One young black kid, all smart for school and with well-thumbed books, killed for kicks or, if anything, for the little bit of cash he may have had on him for his lunch. Blasted out of existence by crackheads or junkies for not even the price of a fix.

The smashed-up doorway where Aaron's body had fallen led into a mansion still known as the Royden Holmes House, named for some early Detroit lumber baron. Gerald recalled that as a kid in the sixties he'd been told that an old woman lived there all alone. He'd imagined that she was probably a descendant of the lumber baron, and he and his brother Ronaldo, both under ten at the time, had staked the place out in the hope of seeing her. They'd succeeded. But rather than discovering some romantic reclusive gentlewoman, the last of a once-noble line of luminaries, all they'd actually found was a wild old junkie who cawed like a mad crow when she saw them. More than forty years on, Gerald still shuddered at the thought of it. But then, as he was all too painfully aware, he was not the sort of person for whom time healed. He'd seen his first dead kid with a bullet hole in his head over thirty years before, and he could still recall it in minute detail.

'Lieutenant Diaz?'

He looked away from the child's body and towards the pretty young woman at his side. 'Addison.'

'Sir, you supposed to be at that conference downtown,' she said.

Policing in Changing Urban Environments. Yes, Gerald Diaz knew. But, he thought grimly to himself, I have my own, sadly most decidedly unchanging urban environment to deal with right now. Kids killing kids; was there ever any way that was going to stop? One thing was for sure as far as Gerald was concerned, and that was that no amount of talking in overheated rooms with a bunch of foreigners was going to make a jot of difference to situations like poor dead Aaron Spencer.

'Sir, you gotta take some of those foreign cops out to Cadillac Project this afternoon,' Rita Addison said.

'Yeah, I . . .' Gerald put his head down as he looked once again at the prone, snow-spattered body of the schoolboy.

'This a drive-by,' Addison said. A tough Detroiter, at twenty-six she had already seen her share of death in the city, just as Gerald had done at her age. 'You know it's so.'

Gerald Diaz looked at her and smiled. Just very faintly, he saw her cheeks colour. Tall, slim and loose-limbed, even at fifty-three Gerald Diaz was a very handsome man. Women were attracted to him, even young women.

He shrugged. 'Leave you with it?'

'To tell the parents?' She looked sad. 'I'm used to that shit.'

'Sorry.'

She shrugged.

'Oh, and get the guys to try and find the slug,' Diaz said. 'Could be embedded in the house, the ground, who knows.'

'Sure.'

Gerald Diaz took one more look down at the dead child and then made his way towards his car. Addison was right: there was nothing more he could do for Aaron Spencer. The boy's body would be dissected, the bullet hopefully recovered from somewhere on the scene, the parents told and sympathised with. Then one newspaper report, max, a funeral, a burial and a statistic. End of.

During the first coffee break, İkmen and Süleyman kept themselves to themselves. Everybody, or so it seemed, was staying in ethnic groups. One female officer, a Brazilian, looked across and smiled at Süleyman, but there was nothing new about that, whatever the context. She was a woman and so she fancied him. He had that effect upon them.

At lunchtime, though, things changed. While Süleyman looked down at his plate of chilli with a mixture of horror and incomprehension on his face, İkmen stirred his food around and made conversation with a Detroit lieutenant called John Shalhoub.

'We came here from Beirut back in the early fifties,' Shalhoub said. 'I was just a baby. We're Arabs, Christians. Although I'm an all-American boy myself, with ex-wives and kids at university and a mortgage. I guess you guys, being from Turkey, you're Muslim.' He smiled. 'You know we have some great halal restaurants here in the city.'

17

İkmen smiled back. 'That's very kind of you, Lieutenant,' he said. 'But there is no need on our account.'

Shalhoub was joined by a woman, this time a sergeant. 'Donna Ferrari,' she said as she offered her hand first to İkmen and then Süleyman. 'Sorry you people have to eat this slop.' She looked around the vast, cop-filled convention-centre restaurant and continued, 'You'd think Detroit's finest would be able to get a bunch of caterers to cook properly!'

İkmen, in diplomatic mode, said, 'Oh, please, Sergeant Ferrari, this is perfectly adequate. It's—'

'So why isn't he eating it?' Ferrari asked as she pointed over at Süleyman. 'It's disgusting, right?' she said to him.

'Well, um . . .'

'Listen, you don't have to be polite,' Ferrari said. She got up and began to walk over to the service counter. Catching one of the server's eyes, she said, 'Hey! You!'

John Shalhoub noticed the Turks' embarrassment immediately. Making a fuss in a foreign land was something he knew polite Middle Easterners didn't do. He tipped his head towards Ferrari and said, 'The sarge, she's a little bit, you know, ballsy . . .'

İkmen, who knew exactly what this meant, smiled. 'Ah.' Far more expert in the fine art of idiomatic English than Süleyman, he turned to his confused colleague and said in Turkish, 'Sergeant Ferrari has spirit.'

'Clearly,' Süleyman replied.

'So you're in the group out to Cadillac Project this afternoon,' Shalhoub continued after a pause. 'Should be interesting for you, I hope.'

'Yes, although I am a little confused,' İkmen said. 'A project here in America is a public housing block, isn't it? And yet Cadillac is I think something quite revolutionary.'

'Antoine Cadillac Project was, just as you said, Inspector, standard public housing,' Shalhoub said. 'Like many of these urban projects it was started in the 1960s, and due in part to the poverty of the people living in it, it soon became crime-ridden. Drugs, alcohol, weapons, gangs. Man, we were in and out Cadillac every day until it began to turn around five years ago.'

'What happened?' Süleyman asked.

'Well, you'll hear more about it when Lieutenant Diaz leads you out there this afternoon,' Shalhoub said. 'But in a nutshell, eight years ago, a woman called Martha Bell moved into Cadillac. She had three kids, and when one of them died in a drive-by, she decided to create a garden in his honour. Then, that not being enough for Martha, she decided to grow food there. Then she roped in her neighbours. She is one remarkable lady.' He leaned forward and looked at the two Turks very seriously. 'But I'll let Lieutenant Diaz fill you in on Cadillac. He's its greatest supporter. To him, Martha Bell and Cadillac are the future of this city.'

Chapter 3

If anyone could look after herself, it was Ayşe Farsakoğlu. Intellectually, İzzet Melik knew this. Just because Ali Kuban, the infamous serial rapist of Edirnekapı, was due to be released from prison later on that day didn't mean that Ayşe, or indeed any other woman for that matter, was immediately at risk. Kuban had exercised his reign of terror over the women of Edirnekapı back in the early 1970s, when he was in his late thirties. Now in his seventies, he was hardly a threat to anyone, and had actually been released on compassionate grounds because he was physically ill. But İzzet still fretted about it. He fretted about Ayşe, and anything that might adversely affect her, a lot.

As he walked past İkmen's office, he saw her leaning over her computer terminal. She didn't see him. The station heating system was working properly again, and so she was getting on with her paperwork. Just looking at her stirred him. Not that his obsession was completely about sex. Yes, he desired her, and thinking about her made him aroused, but he really cared for her too. She was a good person, and he hated considering how spurned he knew she had felt after Süleyman rejected her. The rumour was that years ago she had loved the inspector, completely given herself to him. But then he'd thrown her over for the woman who then, for a while, became his wife, and Ayşe, on the rebound, had got involved with a fellow officer who mistreated her.

İzzet knew that he would never do such a thing. He would only love her, only do nice things for her, never make her unhappy. Not that such a thing could ever happen. In his fantasy, the two of them

20

married, went to Venice for their honeymoon and then set up home in some nice apartment in Beşiktaş, where they had sex every night and during the daytime too on occasion. It was all sentimental, vaguely pornographic nonsense. He continued walking until he came to his own office, and then went inside and closed the door behind him.

Antoine Cadillac Project consisted of four low-rise blocks of apartments arranged in a square around a large open space. It was in an area known as the Cass Corridor. It had been, and to some people remained, a notorious district given to drug abuse, lawlessness and prostitution.

'Originally this area between the blocks was all car parking and two ball courts,' the tall, dark, slightly stooped officer said. He was called, İkmen recalled, Lieutenant Diaz. Unlike the Turk, Diaz was not shivering. Thermal vests aside, İkmen's clothes were not really up to Detroit, and Süleyman was visibly shaking. The rest of the group, Mexicans and some British officers, all looked a bit cold too.

'But then, as can happen with open spaces, it got hijacked,' Diaz continued. 'Kids playing ball were hassled by dealers until most of them didn't want to play ball any more and just spent their time screwing up their brains. This lot was just burned-out cars, broken furniture, kids playing music fit to burst your eardrums, junkies, crackheads, hookers, you name it.'

It was snowing hard as they all stood on the edge of the open space, which was now under at least a quarter of a metre of snow. All that could be seen were seven, maybe eight, small garden sheds dotted about apparently at random.

'It stayed like that for years,' Diaz said. 'Then, in the summer of 2004, a sixteen-year-old boy called Luther Bell was gunned down in a drive-by shooting just over there.' He pointed to an anonymous snowy area in front of one of the blocks. 'Automobile full of cracked-out gangsters came sweeping in here and took out anyone and anything in their path. Classic drive-by. Luther Bell, luckily the only victim, was dead before he hit the ground.'

Bell, his family claimed, wasn't part of any gang himself, and so his death was a meaningless act. The gangsters, Diaz said, had done what they'd done just because they had guns and they could. It had even, possibly, been part of some gang initiation ritual. If it hadn't been Luther Bell, it would have been somebody, anybody, else. The boy's mother, Martha, brother Marlon and sister Keisha had been distraught. But in Martha at least this tragedy eventually led to something else, something far more positive. While Marlon dealt with his grief by disappearing into the arms of crack cocaine, his mother and little sister began to build a garden.

'First off, what I wanted was a garden to dedicate to my boy Luther,' the attractive black woman at Diaz's elbow said. Martha Bell, İkmen thought, was probably in her forties. Wrapped up tight in a long tiger-print coat, she reminded the Turk of a picture he'd once seen of the exotic dancer, and toast of Paris, Josephine Baker. Martha Bell was altogether a far bigger woman, but she had that kind of leonine style that Josephine had possessed. She wore high-heeled patent leather boots in the snow and she didn't give a damn.

'The dealers just kicked over whatever I made,' Martha said. 'If it wasn't them, it would be some junkie dropping needles all over, kids just wrecking stuff, hookers doing who knows what all over it. But every time it got kicked down, I just built it straight back up again.'

The apartment blocks were grey, poorly maintained and depressing. When İkmen's son Bekir had died, at least he had been able to mourn the boy in the relative comfort of his Sultanahmet apartment. Often he had salved his emotional wounds by looking out across Divan Yolu at the great mosques and monuments that surrounded his home: Aya Sofya, the Blue Mosque, Topkapı Palace. He hadn't had to deal with all the things this woman had been up against.

The snowfall began to intensify, and Martha Bell and Lieutenant Diaz took them inside one of the blocks to what they were told was the 'community centre'. It was a large grey room filled with chairs

22

and tables that had seen better days, but it was warm, and there was coffee provided by a group of young men and women, mostly black, many of whom were very heavily tattooed. As they sat down at a table with two of the British officers, Süleyman spoke to İkmen in Turkish. 'This is like Ümraniye used to be at its worst,' he said, referring to what had once been one of İstanbul's most troubled districts.

İkmen, who wasn't fond of anyone speaking in a language no one else could understand unless he just couldn't help it, didn't comment. Süleyman, he felt, had taken against Detroit as soon as they had landed. He'd never been a lover of the cold; it had to have been the snow that had prejudiced him.

'By the middle of 2005, I was almost ready to give up,' continued Martha Bell, now hunched over a large mug of coffee. 'And, I'll be honest, I would have done so if it hadn't been for one old lady. She dead now, but Imelda Blois, she come out one day as I was putting back some flower bulbs and she said to me, "Martha, if you stop putting in them silly bits of nothing and grow something a person can eat, I'll help you."'

And so Martha, the old woman and then a few other people began a vegetable garden. They called it the Luther Bell Food Patch, and anyone who agreed to work on it or help keep it safe was entitled to a share of its produce. The first year they grew potatoes, carrots, onions and collard greens, and for some families this meant that their food bills went down. Working in the garden became fun, especially in the summer, and the following year more people and more land produced even more food. People who had never talked to each other before became friends, and when Martha suggested they all get rid of the burned-out cars and the old broken furniture, a lot of them were willing to help her do that. The dealers and the gangsters stayed, but began to get pushed into more and more distant parts of the space. Unspoken was the knowledge that the dealers and the gang bosses just helped themselves whenever they felt like it to the now many vegetables that grew in the garden. But they didn't oppose it any more. There were too many people who liked it and worked at it, and anyway, no one actively opposed the gangs. People just got on, ignoring them and slowly growing things. Some of the gangsters, if a little reluctantly at first, even helped out themselves. Funding came in too. From local council officials, from the city, and eventually from the police.

'Then, one day about two years ago, the dealers not involved in the garden just weren't on the ground out there no more,' Martha said. She looked down for a moment as if to collect herself. After all her struggles, to finally triumph like that had to be almost unbelievable. But then Martha looked up again and she smiled. 'Lieutenant Diaz saw what we done; he been involved from the start, helping us, fund-raising. PD do us proud now. So we help them too, it's mutual. And that's why you're all here today.'

'Things like the Luther Bell Food Patch are what will bring parts of this city back to life,' Diaz said. 'I am a Detroiter born and bred, and it offends every bone in my body to see what unemployment, gangs and drugs have done to this city. But this is one way forward, and it's things like this that the Detroit Police Department are actively engaging with and supporting. And the Luther Bell Food Patch doesn't just grow food any more, does it, Martha?'

She told them about the groups that ran out of that dingy one-room community centre. Art classes, rap for the kids, mothers' groups, therapy for the bereaved, the mixed-up, the repentant gangsters, the addicted. It was impressive. She, Martha Bell, was impressive. İkmen looked over at her and smiled, but she didn't smile back. There hadn't been so much as a whisper about any sort of male partner helping her to bring up her three kids in this rough, dour project. She had the look of a woman who had done with men. Men, or boys, had killed her son. Men, or boys, had probably had a hand in getting her other boy addicted to crack. Only when Martha looked at her daughter, a pretty young girl İkmen reckoned to be about twelve, did she smile.

But then the girl, Keisha, was her baby, the precious child who had helped her with her garden, and probably her last hope of a genetic footstep into the future.

Lieutenant Gerald Diaz told them that if the police wanted any say in or influence over what happened in communities that were blighted by poverty and lawlessness, they had to engage with them.

'Folk talk about a war against drugs,' he said. 'But it's a war we're going to lose unless we start getting real. We've got to stop cuffing people and start trying to see the world from where they are.'

İkmen saw several of the Detroit officers who had come along to support Diaz look at him in a somewhat less than approving manner, Sergeant Donna Ferrari in particular. But then Diaz was not, as far as İkmen could tell, sticking to the US government-approved zero-tolerance line on illegal drugs.

'If people don't feel hope, if they don't see themselves having a stake in their own future, they will go with their instincts and settle for short-term instant gratification,' Diaz continued. 'Ask yourselves: why wouldn't they?'

Marisa was a woman of no more than forty who looked more like a sixty year old. She'd been on heroin since she was fourteen, had worked as a hooker for fifteen years and had given birth to three drug-addicted babies that had all been taken away from her within days of their birth. At one time she'd been a dealer herself. Now she was on a programme, and although not yet 'clean', she was trying. She told İkmen that the first time she'd eaten vegetables from the garden, she'd thought she was hallucinating.

'It was a head-fuck, you know?' she said. İkmen didn't, but he smiled anyway. 'I wasn't tasting anything. When you're on junk, you don't care. You stick junk in your veins, put crap in your mouth, when you think of it – burgers, French fries, any old shit. It don't matter! But . . .'

'The vegetables . . .'

25

'Everyone working on that ground, and then that taste.' She smiled. 'Onions was what it was. An onion, raw and sweet and . . . I hadn't never tasted nothing like that. I didn't think that anything could taste like that.'

The residents had wanted to talk to the foreign police officers. Whether or not they had been addicts themselves, they wanted the foreigners to know what had been achieved at Antoine Cadillac, what they had done and how hard it had been. Something else İkmen noticed was how much they all spoke to Lieutenant Diaz. Not only did he support these people; they liked and respected him too. It was more than could be said for Sergeant Donna Ferrari. If looks could have killed, Gerald Diaz would have dropped where he stood after his speech about the unwinnable war on drugs. Süleyman, he saw, was talking to Sergeant Ferrari now.

'So where you say you come from again?' Marisa asked.

'Oh, er . . .' İkmen was briefly distracted by the sight of Süleyman with yet another attractive woman. 'From İstanbul in Turkey.'

'Turkey?'

Someone grabbing his arm was accompanied by the sound of an old, cracked voice somewhere to İkmen's left. 'Turkey?'

'Yes?'

The old man, who had been sitting almost asleep in a chair, pulled himself up on İkmen's arm and looked deep into his eyes. Not only was he very old; he was also very dark and very troubled-looking too.

'You a Turk from Turkey?' he said.

'Yes, sir,' İkmen said. 'My name is Çetin İkmen. I am a police officer from İstanbul.'

The old man continued to just stare at him for a moment. Then a single tear tracked down his face and he said, 'A police officer. From İstanbul, Turkey. Praise to God. You don't know how long I have been waiting for this, son. You and me, we's kin. Now everything'll come clear! Now the criminal'll finally come to justice!'

26

Chapter 4

'*Meraba!*' the old man said in very bad Turkish as he threw his arms around İkmen's neck and gave in to deep, aching sobs. İkmen didn't know what to do. This elderly American seemed to be unduly impressed by the fact that he was a Turk. It was entirely a mystery to him why that should be. But although somewhat taken aback, he wasn't uncomfortable with the old man's embrace. The American seemed gentle enough, and no one was pulling him away, as they certainly would if he was known to be dangerous in some way. In fact Lieutenant Diaz and the formidable Martha Bell were looking on with something approaching approval.

Not so the fiery Sergeant Donna Ferrari. 'Come on now, Zeke, that's enough,' she said to the old man as she pulled his arms away from İkmen's shoulders.

As he disengaged, he looked at her, and the expression on his face changed from benign to malicious. 'Get your hands off of me, you fucking bitch!' he snarled.

'Ezekiel!' Martha Bell came over and put her arms around him. 'No need for that,' she said gently. 'No need, old man.'

Everyone in the room was watching. Now apparently focused on Martha, the old man's face softened instantly as he looked up into her eyes and smiled.

'It's been a long day,' Martha said. 'Come on, I take you home for a rest.'

She began leading him towards the door, while people round and about spoke in small groups. İkmen, still rather taken aback, heard the old man say as he left, 'We go to see Elvis now, do we?'

The poor old character had to be mad. Süleyman, now at İkmen's side, said, 'I'd heard about Americans still believing that Elvis Presley is alive. But I never thought I'd actually see it.'

'It was as if my being Turkish meant something to him,' İkmen said. 'Something special.'

'Ezekiel Goins is nuts,' Donna Ferrari said as she came over to offer the two Turks some more coffee. 'How Martha looks after him, I'll never know. She's a saint.'

'Mrs Bell takes care of the old man?'

'Four years, to my knowledge,' Ferrari said. She poured them both some more coffee and then went off to other groups. İkmen watched her. Although she was polite and smiling to the foreign policemen, she looked as if she barely tolerated the residents of Antoine Cadillac. But then from the looks on some of their faces as she approached, the feeling was clearly mutual.

Going outside to smoke was something that Çetin İkmen had become accustomed to. Turkey had taken the plunge into smoke-free work-places the previous July. Even so, venturing out into the snow was something of a mission, and it was one that he found he couldn't interest his colleague Süleyman in.

'It's far too cold,' Süleyman said, when İkmen finally managed to take his attention away from Sergeant Ferrari for more than a moment. It was, although in truth Süleyman was probably lining Ferrari up for a romantic conquest at some point too. Now single yet again, he was rarely if ever without some sort of female in his life, however casual that might be.

İkmen went outside and lit up. The snow was falling so hard that he could barely see the apartment block opposite. Shivering underneath someone's battered concrete balcony, he thought he was alone until he heard a voice say, 'Another sinner. I like that.'

28

Gerald Diaz had a Lucky Strike hanging out of the corner of his mouth, and he smiled broadly at the Turk.

'Lieutenant Diaz,' İkmen said. 'I didn't know you . . .'

'You think all Americans are health freaks?' He shrugged. 'This isn't California, Inspector. Motor City folk make up their own minds.'

He moved across to stand next to İkmen. 'You got some attention in there,' he said as he nodded his head back towards the community centre.

'The old man,' İkmen said. 'I think he's one of those people who really likes Elvis Presley.'

Gerald Diaz drew on his Lucky and let the smoke out on a long, low sigh. 'Not Elvis Presley, no,' he said.

'No? But I heard him . . .'

'Elvis is, or was, the name of Ezekiel's son,' Diaz said. 'He died back in the 1970s. Shot in the head.'

'Oh.' Another child lost to a gunshot. Like Martha Bell's boy, like his own dead son, Bekir. The only İkmen child to go 'bad', Bekir had been a drug trafficker. He'd been shot dead by jandarmes in the eastern Turkish town of Birecik less than eighteen months before. He'd been trying to escape into Syria. In spite of what Bekir had been, every part of İkmen still mourned him.

'Poor old Zeke never got over it,' Diaz continued. 'Left his wife shortly afterwards. Spent years on the street until Martha took him in. Went crazy.'

'The death of a child is not something that one can get over,' İkmen said.

Diaz clearly saw at least some of the pain in the Turk's eyes, and he looked away until the other man had composed himself. Then he said, 'You being Turkish brought a smile to Zeke's face.'

'Yes. He tried to say "hello" in my language.'

Diaz laughed. 'Oh, Zeke does try out Turkish! God knows! Whacked-out people from the south, you know, Inspector! Ezekiel Goins comes originally from Georgia, Virginia, some place like that,

I don't know exactly. But they have some racial types down there, I can tell you.' He put one cigarette out and then immediately lit another. İkmen was impressed. 'You ever heard of the Melungeons?'

İkmen hadn't.

'Dark folk, but not Hispanic, not like me,' Diaz said. 'Mainly Protestant; they're mountain people, hillbillies, some would say. But unlike most hillbillies, they don't claim origin in Scotland or Germany or England. Some say they're gypsies, some Native Americans; some even claim to come from Portugal. And there are some say they're actually Turks.'

Lighting up a second cigarette too now, İkmen frowned.

'Reckon they're descended from the crew of a Turkish ship that got wrecked off the eastern seaboard,' Diaz said. 'Back in the sixteenth, seventeenth century. Zeke Goins' family, according to him, was one of them. He believes it. And even if you and I think it's so much bullshit, it has to count for something, even if it is only in old Zeke's head.'

It was rather extraordinary and strange, but İkmen said, 'Yes.'

'He saw you as kin,' Diaz said, 'family.'

'Yes.' But then İkmen recalled something else that Ezekiel Goins had said to him, about a criminal being brought to justice.

Diaz sighed. 'Ah, well, you see, he doesn't trust the Detroit Police Department with regard to that,' he said.

'With regard to what?'

The snow, if anything, was coming down still harder, and İkmen, at least, was shivering with cold. But what Diaz was saying was fascinating. Also, rightly or wrongly, he felt that the American would not be so forthcoming about the old man if he were with his colleagues back inside.

'There's an old white guy, lives in one of the rotten mansions over in Brush Park. Zeke reckons he killed Elvis.'

'Is there any evidence for that?' İkmen asked.

'No. Not that I know of.' He sighed again. 'What you have to understand is there was a lot of unrest here back in the sixties and seventies. Racial stuff. And being a Melungeon . . .'

'Being a Melungeon?'

Diaz smiled. 'It's a bit like being Hispanic; it depends on who you talk to,' he said. 'To the Anglos, Melungeons, like Hispanics, are just short of being black. Not black, but definitely not white, mixed race. And to blacks, it's the same. Melungeons aren't black but they aren't white either. It means a double dose of prejudice and without the backing of the numbers that we Hispanics have. I feel sorry for them. They're a real minority in this country, and they're a minority without even one consistent identity.'

'But if Melungeons come from the south, what is Mr Goins doing all the way up in the north here?' İkmen asked.

'Oh, he came, like all the southerners did, for work,' Diaz replied. 'Goins' family, and Martha's, and my own people all came to the Motor City a long time ago, for work.'

The internet was a wonderful thing. İkmen didn't have any idea about how it worked or why it had come into being, but he approved of the instant access it could afford to information, even if his views on social networking were somewhat jaded. His younger children spent far too much time communicating on line about basically, in his opinion, not very much.

As soon as they'd returned to their hotel suite, Süleyman had wanted to go straight to bed. Jet-lagged and exhausted, he'd nevertheless got it together enough to clean the bathroom, and had then had a shower. In the meantime, İkmen had availed himself of his colleague's laptop computer.

Lieutenant Diaz had told him something about how Detroit had come to be home to so many migrants from the southern states. Almost as soon as the motor plants were first built at the beginning of the twentieth century, they had needed more workers than the local area could provide. To make up the shortfall, labour was recruited from the poor southern states, where segregation of whites and blacks was still harshly enforced. And so white 'hillbillies' and the black descendants of slaves came north to work in factories that were not strictly segregated and which paid more money than anyone from south of the old Mason-Dixon Line could ever have dreamed of earning. But money wasn't always everything to everyone, and some of the new arrivals from the south were loath to work with each other. White and black, the 'hillbillies' and the 'niggers', began to clash. Acts of cruelty and discrimination and riots ensued. And yet still the 'Big Three' motor companies – General Motors, Ford and Chrysler – kept on recruiting from the south well into the 1960s, when Ezekiel Goins and his family had arrived.

İkmen looked up the word 'Melungeon'. To his surprise, there were lots of entries. One of these told him about a delegation of Melungeons who had visited Ankara. Another told him about some genetic research that 'proved' that the Melungeons were in fact Turks. It was a whole new world to him, and, what was more, it seemed to be one based upon few facts and a lot of speculation. Of course the story about the shipwrecked Ottoman sailors could be true. İkmen knew that because he was aware that anything was possible. But he doubted it. Melungeons, as far as he could tell, were or generally had been illiterate mountain people. Originally centred around the Appalachian Mountains, their communities claimed many and various heritages, as Diaz had indicated. The only thing they had in common was their status as Melungeons, which made them all outcasts. And as İkmen ploughed through the available literature, he discovered that things hadn't improved when they'd moved north. If anything, racial differences had become even more important, even more visible, in the factories of Detroit.

Süleyman came out of the bathroom with a towel on his head and told İkmen that he was going to bed.

'Have you ever heard of a people called the Melungeons?' İkmen asked as his colleague began to make his way to his room.

Süleyman turned. 'The crazy Americans who think they're Turks?' he said.

'Yes.'

'Why?'

'The old man who embraced me at Antoine Cadillac Project is a Melungeon,' İkmen said. 'You think they're crazy?'

'Of course,' Süleyman said. 'It's a total fiction. Had Ottoman sailors ever been shipwrecked on this godforsaken coast, they would have taken their own lives rather than live alongside Spaniards and pagans.'

So spoke a descendant of the Ottomans. But İkmen the decidedly un-Ottoman wasn't so sure. That Melungeons were actual Turks was virtually impossible. But those sailors could have been shipwrecked all those centuries ago and people like Ezekiel Goins could be their distant descendants. He searched the web for more and more Melungeon facts long after Süleyman had gone to sleep and long after he too should have gone to his bed.

Grant T. Miller. It was a little while since Gerald Diaz had thought about him. In general he tried not to, even though he'd known him for ever. Even though Miller was part of his world.

Diaz had been a rookie back when all that business with Elvis Goins had gone down. Seeing Elvis's dad on the same day that he'd had to look at that kid's dead body in Brush Park had brought it all back. Not that it was ever really far away. Young Aaron Spencer had been killed in front of the Royden Holmes House, which was just two blocks down from the house that Miller still lived in. A great big redbrick pile with a tower at one end and a rickety Gothic-style veranda at the other. Miller called it the Windmill – in honour, he said, of his ancestors' noble profession of flour-making. But as Diaz recalled only too well, he had said that, as he said everything, with a note of cynicism as well as self-mockery in his voice. Miller's father had been a poor, illiterate German Jew, and Grant T. had hated everything about him, his people and their way of life.

'I'm exactly like my mother,' he was wont to say to even kid cops like Diaz, 'a WASP to my marrow.'

It was midnight by the time Diaz parked his car and walked over to the gate that led to what remained of the Windmill. The tower had fallen in on itself years before and the veranda, even by moonlight, was obviously in very many pieces. Miller's mother had been a white Cajun lady, a faded southern belle in the Tennessee Williams mould. But it had been his illiterate father, a tailor to America's most famous anti-Semite, Henry Ford himself, who had kept her in the style to which her parents had hoped some man might one day make her accustomed. Grant T. had been virtually born in the Ford plant, a child of the automobile, with gasoline for blood and a heart of toughened steel. A man of action rather than intellect, he had run production lines and the men who worked them with the precision of a clockwork martinet and the cruelty of a Nazi stormtrooper.

Gerald Diaz remembered the day he'd been called to Miller's house as if it were yesterday. That was unfortunate. Miller had dialled 911 because, he said, he was being assaulted. Diaz, then just twenty-one years old, had answered the call along with his partner, John Sosobowski. Forty then, John was now long dead, but neither he nor Gerald himself, for very different reasons, had ever forgotten what had gone on in that house. Grant T. Miller screaming in agony as Ezekiel Goins attempted to bite his way through his arm. Blood everywhere. As they pulled Goins off, he screamed, 'You killed Elvis! You killed my boy, you filthy bastard!' And although Grant T. was howling in pain as they dragged Goins away, all of Diaz's sympathies had been with the Melungeon. Everyone knew that Miller hated the Goins family; he hated all the 'blacks'. Everyone had thought it was possible that Grant T., or one of his 'boys', had killed Elvis. And when Miller didn't press charges against Ezekiel Goins, it seemed to bear that contention out.

There had been no proof. Zeke lost his mind, left his wife and hit the road because he just couldn't bear it. Miller, meanwhile, when he wasn't at work, stayed in his house, which was where he was now if the light in the top right-hand window was anything to go by. It was said that Zeke occasionally came to Brush Park and stood outside the Windmill, like a malignant statue. People said that Miller would occasionally appear too – a vision in filthy pyjamas and stinking carpet slippers – and hurl abuse at Goins. Gerald had seen it with his own eyes a couple of times, when circumstances had taken him, always reluctantly, up to Grant T.'s fiefdom.

But even his anger at Grant T. was nothing to the crazy way Zeke had reacted when he'd heard Inspector İkmen say he was from Turkey. Zeke had had that whole Turkish thing going ever since Gerald could remember. But after Elvis had been shot, and especially since he'd been living with Martha, it had intensified. If only he could either get to Turkey or find someone from Turkey, everything would be OK. Miller would be found out and punished and the people he felt had let him down back in the seventies, the Detroit Police, would be made to look like fools. In a way, Zeke deserved just that.

Gerald couldn't put himself in Zeke's shoes. Melungeons, wherever they came from originally, were a people apart from mainstream life. Back in the old days, when Detroit automobiles were conquering the world, life on the production lines had been difficult for them. Separated from their mountains and their own people, they were welcome nowhere and with no one. Even in the twenty-first century, some people still criticised Martha Bell for taking such a person into her home. Zeke Goins, quite apart from the still unsolved murder of his son, was a bit of an unfinished Detroit story, a remnant of a time of plenty that was nevertheless racist and ugly. It wasn't something Gerald wanted their foreign visitors to have too much exposure to. He didn't want to have any more than he needed to do with it himself. Detroit city was big enough to fess up to the demons from its past, but it also needed to move on. Confrontation was no longer the way forward, whatever people like Donna Ferrari might think. Organisations like Martha Bell's were where the future lay: tackling gang problems by talking to those involved, treating addiction as a medical rather than a criminal matter. But Gerald also knew that for all the fine rhetoric around these new ways of addressing urban issues, people like Ferrari still represented what was the national orthodoxy. The 'War on Drugs', just as surely as Zeke Goins' hatred for Grant T. Miller, continued unabated.

Chapter 5

Martha thought that he had forgotten about the Turkish policeman. But Zeke Goins didn't forget a thing – not permanently. This was especially so when it came to the subject of Elvis.

'Martha, I'm going out,' he said once he'd washed the dishes from breakfast.

It was no longer snowing, but the ground was very icy and Martha was concerned. She turned the stereo down, even though it was playing one of her favourite songs, 'Dancing in the Street' by her namesake Martha Reeves. 'You could fall and break your leg,' she said. 'Neither you nor me can afford that. Where you want to go anyway?'

'Down to the river,' he said.

Martha frowned. 'What you wanna go down there for?'

He shrugged. She was used to him being contrary and odd, but to go out into the thick snow for no apparent reason was crazy, unless . . .

'You wouldn't be lying to me, would you, Zeke?' Martha said.

'Lying?'

'Going up to Brush Park and yelling at Miller,' she said.

'No!'

She looked at him with an expression of doubt on her face. 'Because it don't do no good,' she said. 'One day it'll get you into trouble. You know how he is!'

Zeke lowered his head and said, 'I know it.'

'And anyway, Samuel wouldn't like it,' Martha said. 'And you don't want to make no trouble for him, not after all what he done.'

Zeke lowered his head still further. Then he said, 'But I ain't going to Brush Park, Martha.'

'Ma! I'm late for school! Can we go!' Keisha ran into the kitchen in a whirlwind of thick scarves, school bags and gloves.

Martha raised her eyes to the ceiling and then quickly put her coat on and grabbed her car keys. 'I have to go,' she said to Zeke. 'Go to the river if you must, but be careful.'

'Ma!'

Keisha was running to the front door. Martha followed her.

'Don't you even think about going to Brush Park, old man!' Martha yelled just before she followed her daughter out into the snow.

'I won't!' Zeke called out after her. Then he said softly to himself, 'I promise, no Brush Park, honest injun.'

The convention centre where the police were doing all their talking and entertaining of foreigners wasn't in Brush Park. It was indeed down by the Detroit River. Zeke took a can of Coke and a sandwich from the refrigerator for the journey, and then put on his coat, hat and gloves. Downtown things were expensive, and he didn't want to spend any money on fancy food.

'Here in Detroit we call it "white flight",' the tall and imposing black officer said as he looked up at the PowerPoint statistics displayed on the screen above his head. 'But when the manufacturing base moved out of the city of Detroit and work shifted to the suburbs, it wasn't just white people who deserted the centre. White flight is a catch-all term that covers all the mainly skilled auto workers who came to constitute Detroit's middle class. They wanted to be near the new car plants and they wanted to move away from neighbourhoods that had become colonised by gangs and drug-dealers. But this isn't just a feature of Detroit.'

Çetin İkmen shifted rather uncomfortably in his seat. There were few advantages to having a very thin behind. Süleyman, now rested and no longer jet-lagged, looked by contrast finally at his ease. He'd told İkmen that morning at breakfast that now he was accustomed to it, the snow didn't seem to fill him with so much dread. But İkmen suspected that he was probably happy because he was in pursuit of a woman. Sergeant Ferrari had most definitely caught his attention.

'In New York City, parts of Manhattan had become almost no-go areas because of escalating crime rates. People moved out of areas like SoHo and Tribeca, now very fashionable places, because they just weren't nice. Then the NYPD instituted their policy of Zero Tolerance, and all that changed. Now we've got other areas coming into line: Queens, the Bronx. Cities can come back to life, but law enforcement must play its part, and that part must be based on Zero Tolerance.'

Çetin İkmen had heard about Zero Tolerance. Some forces in Turkey, albeit patchily and not in name, applied it. Zero Tolerance was a policy whereby even the most minor infringement of legislation was punished to the full extent of the law. This meant that people would be booked for dropping litter, vagrants would be moved on without regard to their condition or state of health, every cannabis joint would be confiscated and the offender punished. Zero Tolerance meant no hiding place. It also meant, so İkmen had read in newspapers back home, that the criminals and their activities simply moved location. Around New York, in parts of New Jersey, those who had originally operated in Manhattan had set up new and sometimes even more successful criminal operations. Shifting the problem was not, as far as he could see, any kind of real solution to anything. Besides, one had to look at every situation case by case, surely!

İkmen clearly remembered the policing around the European Cup Final football match between AC Milan and Liverpool that had taken place in İstanbul back in 2005. There had been some rowdy behaviour by both sets of fans, but unless violence had ensued, they had been left alone. The police had been visible and clearly serious, but they hadn't punished people for walking along with cans of beer, or even for being drunk, unless they were causing a nuisance.

39

Zero Tolerance in that instance would have resulted in police cells full to bursting.

And what about 'white flight'? Applied to İstanbul, he could see a trend in some districts that could be equivalent. But it was nothing to do with class or colour. Some native İstanbullus were moving out of districts like Ayvansaray and Balat because migrants from the countryside were moving in. Those areas were still relatively cheap, and so migrants were fetching up in such places because they could afford them. In addition, because of migration, such places were becoming more religiously conservative, something that native İstanbullus didn't always appreciate. In İstanbul, the split was town and country as opposed to black and white. Although in a rather curious parallel, some people did actually talk in terms of 'white' and 'black' Turks. The white Turks were the sophisticated urban dwellers, while the black Turks were the country folk. If İstanbul followed Detroit from boom into decline, it was a sobering thought to consider that one day the city might be almost exclusively given over to 'black' Turks.

'And of course, complicating the issue of "white flight" still further,' the officer at the podium continued, 'is the presence of those people who don't fit anywhere. People of mixed race and . . .'

İkmen thought about Ezekiel Goins and the Melungeons, and wondered how many of them, if any, had 'flown' Detroit's broken centre.

Ayşe Farsakoğlu didn't often stop off on her way home from the station to have a drink. She most especially didn't stop off on her own. But the Kaktus café in Beyoğlu was a casual, freewheeling sort of place, beloved of writers and journalists and not the sort of bar where a woman on her own would attract attention. Ayşe didn't want to go home to the apartment she shared with her brother, not yet. A small beer was needed, she felt, to try to wash away some of the things she had been learning about at work.

Now that he had been released, Ayşe had been reading about the 'career' of the Edirnekapı serial rapist, Ali Kuban. Back in 1973/4, he had raped seven women, ranging in age from eighty down to twelve. Although none of his victims had died, allowing Kuban to escape the hangman's noose at the time, he had attacked them with staggering brutality. It had made sobering reading. Although Kuban was now seventy-three years old and apparently way beyond picking up where he had left off in 1974, the fact that he was out again was something Ayşe's superiors were taking seriously. He was to be monitored and watched, and the slightest piece of inappropriate behaviour would see him brought in for questioning very quickly. The world had changed a lot since he had been incarcerated. Now sexual predators had so many more tools at their disposal, pornography online and the miracle of the mobile phone being only two of them.

Ayşe had ordered her small glass of Efes Pilsen when she realised that İzzet Melik was sitting at the opposite side of the café. Nursing what looked like a cappuccino, he was staring blankly down into the depths of his cup like a lost soul. With the knowledge in her head that he desired her, Ayşe wondered whether he had either followed her or engineered this coincidental meeting in some way. But when she went over to him, he seemed genuinely shocked to find her there.

'I was reading some of the old arrest notes and statements on Ali Kuban,' she said as she sat down opposite him. 'I understand why we need to know about him now. But you can't carry that around in your head all the time and feel OK, can you?'

'So you came for a beer.' İzzet smiled.

'I live with my brother, and he wouldn't approve,' Ayşe said.

'He's religious, your brother?'

'No, just protective of his sister,' she replied.

İzzet knew better than to ask her anything more. Family life was, to some extent, private or 'walled', as it had been in Turkish society since time immemorial.

'Ali Kuban is probably too old to be a problem to women now, I

41

hope,' İzzet said. 'I understand the last few years of his incarceration have been tough for him. He had cancer back in 2006, which weakened him considerably. Now he's sick again.'

'Didn't kill him last time,' Ayşe said.

'Maybe it wasn't his time. Or maybe he got lucky and had a good doctor.'

'Inspector İkmen told me just before he left that he remembered Kuban,' Ayşe said. 'He was very young at the time, the inspector, but he said that when Kuban was caught, a great wave of relief broke across the city.'

'It must have done,' İzzet said. 'He'd terrorised Edirnekapı for eighteen months. His behaviour was escalating – little girls, old women.' He frowned. 'To be honest with you, Sergeant Farsakoğlu, it isn't Kuban as such that worries me now he's out. It's . . . well, it seems he achieved something of a legendary aura or status with certain people during his time in prison. Those of a misogynistic type; boys aroused by too much internet porn, too much information.' He laughed. 'Listen to me! Complaining about the age of information as if I can do anything about it! Like an old man!'

But Ayşe agreed with him. High-profile offenders like Kuban, and even more sensationally like Mehmet Ali Ağca, the man who had tried to kill Pope John Paul II back in 1979, attracted both those who wished to follow in their footsteps and sometimes also those who wished to love or even marry them. The idea of someone copying Kuban's crimes, possibly in a bid to attract his attention, did not bear thinking about. And so İzzet changed the subject. 'Would you like to have some food here?' he asked, his voice just wavering a little as he did so. He did not, after all, want her to confuse his offer with some sort of date. He didn't want to scare her. 'It's quite good, the food here.'

Ali, Ayşe's brother, was, she knew, dining with a client. If she went home, it would only be her and a bowl of the soup she'd made and put in the fridge. İzzet wasn't bad company, even if he did have feelings she would rather he didn't have for her. But even with that as a consideration, what did she have to lose? She'd seen several very nice plates of food come out of the Kaktus kitchen since they'd been there. 'OK,' she said after a moment. 'That would be nice.'

İzzet Melik beamed.

There were shades of Elvis Goins' death that hung around the murder of Aaron Spencer. Both kids had been shot, both of them young, both in Brush Park. In both cases no one had seen or heard anything, and so the likelihood of any justice coming along for Aaron Spencer was slim, as it had been, for different reasons, for Elvis Goins.

Back in the seventies, when Elvis had died, there had been people apart from Grant T. Miller living in the area, and so it was possible that someone could, even now, claim to know who had killed him. But Aaron Spencer had almost certainly been alone up there outside the Royden Holmes House. That part of the district, with the exception of Miller's place two blocks away, was almost entirely empty.

A curious, rather bookish kid according to his mother, Aaron had gone to Brush Park to explore, as boys could and should be able to do. But someone had killed him, and now Aaron's curiosity was stilled. Gerald Diaz walked towards the Cobo Center slowly and in a decidedly unenthusiastic mood. In spite of real strides towards community engagement, with involvement around organisations like the Luther Bell Food Patch, and with cannabis use for medical purposes legal in the state of Michigan, the old police orthodoxy was still there. Don't talk, arrest with Zero Tolerance as the ultimate Holy Grail. But that, to Gerald's way of thinking, was one of the things that was perpetuating the gang/drug lifestyle. Popping up elsewhere when the heat got too strong was becoming a game with some of the gangs. To take back the inner city, everyone needed to be on board, and that included the gangs, the crack dealers and the junkies. It was the only way to prevent 'godfathers' of drug supply from rising to prominence as they had done in the past; as they continued to do.

Engaging with local people, even users and gang thugs, was possible. Martha Bell had her own way, and it worked. Or rather, it could work. Gerald pulled his Lucky out of the corner of his mouth and breathed out smoke into the frozen air. Inside the Cobo, Leonard Crosby had just taken a session preaching his gospel of Zero Tolerance. All the foreign officers would be talking about it. From a policing point of view, it was easier than doing it Gerald's way, Martha's way.

Gerald walked up the steps towards the glass and concrete building and saw that Crosby's session had already ended. A big group of officers were braving the sub-zero temperatures to have a smoke. They were all talking and laughing, most of them swinging their arms around or stamping their feet in an attempt to keep themselves warm. Over to one side, alone except for his compatriot, was the Turk, Inspector İkmen. Gerald was wondering why he and his colleague were set apart from the others when he saw that they were not actually on their own at all. Ezekiel Goins was with them, and he was speaking very earnestly.

'Grant T. Miller was a foreman on the line,' the old man said. 'In actual fact he was *the* foreman on the line. Him and his boys, they called theirselves; they was like to the Ku Klux Klan. You know who they are, son?'

İkmen did, but he had to explain it to Süleyman. 'The Klan were . . . well, they saw themselves as sort of white Christian knights,' he said. 'They intimidated and killed black people in the south of America.'

'Here they called theirselves the Black Legion. They didn't like the Jews neither, nor the Hispanics nor us,' Ezekiel Goins said. 'If anybody tells you that all stopped back in the 1930s here in Detroit, then they're lying. Miller, in spite of having a Jewish pa, was at the base of it. The blue-eyed boy whose daddy made suits for Henry Ford. Imagine! A Jew making clothes for that Jew-hater! Everyone turned a blind eye, everyone. Them riots in '67, they was about that kind of stuff. People'd had enough.'

44

It was all very interesting in terms of Detroit history, but because İkmen knew that it was leading up to a request to find out who had killed his son back in the seventies, Ezekiel Goins' story was rather anxiety-provoking. The old man was clearly obsessed, for obvious reasons: his son had been killed. But that didn't make the Turkish side of it any easier for the two officers. Ezekiel Goins had approached them with 'You Turks, you kin, you gonna make it all right now.'

'But then after '67 and into the seventies, Miller went easy on the blacks. He had to. Mayor Young was black hisself and not any understanding of white folk. No one was playing the white game, Miller's game, no more, you understand?' Goins said. 'But us? My boy couldn't get no job, no one'd touch him. Blind prejudice, see. So he set up this gang, the Delta Mavi in your language; the Delta Blues in ours. It all buying, selling, jacking up heroin. Kids do that when they ain't got no future.'

It happened all over the world. Both İkmen and Süleyman had seen it or things like it before. One of the reasons why İkmen was so bitter about his lost son Bekir was because the boy hadn't had to get involved with drugs; he had had a future.

'But Miller and his boys was running drugs too,' Goins said. 'My son got in the way. I know he did. The Delta Blues took some of Miller's business. Elvis was shot in the head over Brush Park at point-blank range. Miller done it! I know it was him!'

'Zeke, you can't go around making accusations.' Gerald Diaz's voice cut across what the old man had been saying with a firm rebuke. 'There's no evidence to connect Grant T. to drug-running of any kind. If Miller finds out, he will—'

'Miller taunts me with it himself!' Zeke Goins said, his eyes beginning to water with the cold and his misery. 'If I go up there to the Windmill, he's always hanging outta his window, laughing at me, telling me how his boys took my son away from me!'

'Don't go up to Brush Park! There was never any evidence to connect Miller to either narcotic supply or Elvis's death,' Diaz said.

45

'And anyway, Zeke, you shouldn't be bothering our guests from overseas with that.'

'Oh, it really is quite all right . . .' İkmen began.

'No it isn't,' Gerald Diaz said. He looked at the two officers. 'Zeke has a belief that because you're both Turks, like he believes he is, you can help him.'

'They can!'

'No they can't,' Diaz said. 'They have no jurisdiction here, Zeke. They don't know the city, the case, anything. It was a long time ago; I was only a rookie when it happened myself!' He put a hand on the old man's shoulder and began to lead him away. 'But I remember it, and the lack of any solution still gets me. I'm not saying that you have to forget, that you must move on or any shit like that. But Zeke, you gotta work with what you got, and that's Martha and her family, the food garden and Samuel. That's a lot.'

The old man stopped, frowned, and then looked back at the Turks before he said, 'You think so?' His voice was bitter and broken, and as he spoke, he threw what remained of the sandwich he had brought from Martha's fridge on the ground. 'How'd you like it if someone had killed your child and was never brought to justice? How'd you like it to know that that person is out there, every day, free?'

İkmen turned away. The old man had been speaking directly to him, he felt, and in that moment, he just couldn't take it. His own son had been killed and he knew exactly who had done it, and why, yet still it hurt like an open wound inside.

Chapter 6

The food was familiar and comforting, and Tayyar Bekdil, Süleyman's cousin, was a very convivial host. Reflecting what Lieutenant Shalhoub had told İkmen and Süleyman, he said, 'There's a big Lebanese population in Detroit, mostly out at a suburb called Hamtramck. Cafés and restaurants with names like the Cedars and Beirut all over that area. It's easy to get foodstuffs. Tahini, köfte, börek, baklava, you name it.'

Çetin İkmen put another square of baklava into his mouth and savoured both the sweetness of the dessert and the warm comfort of Tayyar's massive home. For a man who lived alone, a four-bedroom house with a double garage seemed, to İkmen, excessive. But then apparently, if one was just reasonably well off, that was the American way. Property prices compared to Turkey, and particularly when measured against western Europe, were cheap. And that especially applied to Detroit.

'This place would probably sell for around three hundred thousand dollars,' Tayyar had said when he'd showed them around his home. 'But this is a suburb. It's clean, it's bright, there's no junkies. In areas like Brush Park, which is where a lot of old auto-executive mansions sit mouldering in the street, you can't give property away. I've heard of old houses with gardens selling for a dollar.'

'A dollar!'

'These places are ruined,' Tayyar had added. 'Full of junkies, crackheads and rats. Who wants places like that, even if they were the height of style back in the 1920s?'

He'd prepared them a fabulous meze featuring such dishes as pickled squid, Russian salad and warm home-made hummus. This had been followed by a delicious roasted trout served with a pilaf, and then the scrumptious, glutinous baklava. All of this comfort food had been washed down with a lot of Turkish rakı. Now they were drinking coffee, smoking and grazing on whatever was left of the dessert.

'This is a lovely house, Tayyar,' Süleyman said. 'But I don't know how you could have swapped Bebek for Detroit.'

'You don't?' Tayyar was a couple of years older than Süleyman, and quite a bit shorter and darker. The eldest son of one of Süleyman's father's sisters, he was another one with royal blood in his veins. 'But then I suppose, as cops, you wouldn't,' he continued. 'This is a tough town. Makes İstanbul look like a crime backwater. A village like Bebek, well . . .' He smiled. 'For a journalist, Detroit is great. As a profession, we live off the pickings from the bones of the dead.'

'What a gruesome analogy!' İkmen said.

'But it's true!'

They drank, ate and smoked some more. Tayyar put a Bruce Springsteen CD on, and they all took their drinks and ashtrays to comfortable chairs arranged around a blazing log fire. Once they'd settled down, İkmen talked about Ezekiel Goins and the Melungeons. In spite of what Lieutenant Diaz had said about forgetting the whole thing, he was finding that he couldn't.

'If we think it's bad now, there were some terrible things that went on in the sixties and seventies,' Tayyar said. 'Way beyond '67 it was open race warfare in parts of the city. In those days, the drug of choice was heroin, and there were endless turf wars between gangs of what were basically drug-dealers.'

'This old Melungeon's son got mixed up in it.'

'If he was young and unemployed, it was almost inevitable,' Tayyar said. 'It still goes on, except now the main drug of choice is crack cocaine. The difference these days is there's a will to at least try and put the city back together again. In the sixties and seventies, the

48

whole fabric of the place was just atomising. Corruption was endemic. Cops were, figuratively, getting into bed with gangsters; so was City Hall. The big three car manufacturers wanted to move the plants to the suburbs. Black civil rights versus, in some quarters, continuing white desire for segregation. It was chaos.'

'And yet for Ezekiel Goins it was just yesterday,' İkmen said. 'But when your child dies, clocks stop.'

They all went quiet for a moment. Tayyar as well as Süleyman knew what had happened to İkmen's son, and he didn't know what to say. In the end it was İkmen himself who was obliged to continue the conversation. 'Mr Goins believes that a man called Grant T. Miller killed his son,' he said. 'Have you heard of him, Tayyar?'

'As far as I know, Grant T. Miller was a foreman in the old Ford plant,' Tayyar said. 'He's well known because his father was a tailor who used to make suits for Henry Ford. Why would he have killed this man's son?'

'Mr Goins seemed to think that he was some sort of white suprema-cist,' İkmen said.

Tayyar shrugged. 'I don't know about that.'

They sat in companionable silence for a few minutes while Bruce Springsteen sang 'Born in the USA'. When he had finished, Tayyar said, 'You know the Republican Party here in the US thought that song was some sort of patriotic anthem? Stupid George W. Bush. It's a protest song, the voice of unemployed blue-collar America. This country and especially this city are not what people think they are.'

'I know,' Süleyman said as he lit up another cigarette and then breathed out smoke on a sigh. 'I thought our hotel would be pristine. Real American super-clean!'

Tayyar laughed. 'What, the Lakeland Plaza? Are you serious?'

'Yes. I'm appalled,' Süleyman said. 'The place is not filthy, but it certainly isn't what I would call clean.'

'Well no, it wouldn't be,' Tayyar said. 'The Lakeland is only half a hotel.'

'What do you mean?'

'Some of the floors are given over to people on welfare. The city put them in there.'

Süleyman and İkmen looked at each other. All of a sudden, old fridges in some of the corridors made sense.

'Oh boy, did the İstanbul Police Department get you a cheap deal!' Tayyar continued. 'People have been mugged in the elevator in the Lakeland. Watch yourselves!'

'We will.'

Tayyar did make several offers to them to stay over. But, reluctantly, İkmen and Süleyman both declined. The Lakeland Plaza, for all its drawbacks, was very close to the convention centre, and they did have an early start the next morning. A British officer was down to talk about a method of riot control called 'kettling'.

As ever the perfect host, Tayyar helped them to put on their coats and then walked with them out to the taxi he had called to take them back downtown. As he was walking beside İkmen, he suddenly clicked his fingers and said, 'Goins. I knew I knew that name! Is this Ezekiel Goins anything to do with City Councillor Samuel Goins?'

Martha didn't often call on Samuel, but this time she'd felt that she had to. Lieutenant Diaz had brought Zeke home midway through the afternoon. As promised, the old man hadn't gone to Brush Park to hassle Grant T. Miller. He really had gone down to be by the river. While he was there, however, he'd hung out outside the Cobo Center and then rattled on to that Turkish cop again about Elvis. By the time Keisha came home from school, he was agitated fit to burst, and so Martha had had no choice but to call out Zeke's little brother.

City Councillor Samuel Goins was fifteen years younger than Zeke. He was smart, rich, good-looking and successful. He had also become, after years of hard work and campaigning, the poster boy for Melungeon achievement. His campaigning slogan, 'Not black, not white, not hillbilly – Detroiter!' was delivered in an accent that was

50

very far from his brother's deep southern patois. The youngest of eight Goins boys, Samuel had worked in the Ford plant for a while, but he'd also gone and got himself an education.

'Zeke, you really mustn't hassle people like this,' Samuel said as he took his brother's hand gently across Martha's kitchen table.

'But he's a Turk, Sam! He understand *meraba, gül, mavi, kismet,* all the words I learned!' Zeke said through tears of anger and frustration. How dared that Martha go and bother Sam with all this! 'Like us.'

'Mmm.' Samuel Goins nodded his large grey head and said, 'Zeke, we may be kin to this man in one sense. But we aren't like him and he isn't like us.'

'But he's a Turk!'

'Yes, which means that he's a Muslim,' Samuel said. 'That's a long way from being a Baptist.'

'I don't mind he's no Muslim, Sam,' Zeke said. 'We being Melungeon, we can't be prejudiced who we talk to and who we don't.'

'No, and neither should we be,' Samuel said. 'But Zeke, the poor man's only here for a conference. He knows nothing about Elvis or Miller or any of the things that you talk to him about. You have to leave him be.'

'But he's a Turk. Türkiye! A Turk!'

'Lieutenant Diaz—'

'What Diaz know!' Angry now, Zeke Goins' eyes flashed with spite. 'Motherfucking Detroit police! In Grant T. Miller's pocket! That's why nothing never done to avenge our Elvis! Miller hates our kind. Miller ran drugs, and Elvis, one of us, he was like a thorn in his side!'

'Ssh!' Samuel put his finger up to his lips and lowered his voice. 'You don't want young Keisha to hear you cussing, do you?'

Suddenly ashamed of his outburst, Zeke muttered that no, of course he didn't want Keisha to hear him.

'Zeke, your Elvis was not some sort of great gang godfather,'

51

Samuel said. 'I know he started the Delta Blues. But they were all small-time players. And anyway, there's only ever been rumours about Grant T. Miller and drug-dealing. There's never been any concrete evidence, has there?'

'No.'

'Richie McLennan, a black man, was Elvis's enemy. Richie headed up the Purple Mobile Crew, the Delta Blues' main enemies. Zeke, it was a Purple Mobile who killed Elvis.'

'We don't know that!' Zeke said. He'd had this conversation with his brother before. 'All them gangs dead now!'

'Exactly! They all ended up killing each other or dying from their addiction to heroin. Elvis just died early on in all that. I don't know why! Nobody does!'

There was silence. Just for a moment, Samuel actually thought that he might have got through to his brother. But then Zeke said, 'No, Miller killed him! He killed him, because when I tell the other men on the line that Elvis died, he laughed.'

'Miller is a monster,' Samuel said. 'But that doesn't mean that he killed Elvis.'

'He dealed drugs all that time.'

'Maybe, but we can't really say that—'

'Then why he don't have me arrested when I go up Brush Park that first time and sink my teeth into his flesh? Eh? Diaz and Sosobowski pull me off him, throw me outta the house, and then Miller, he does nothing! Why he always run out after me when I goes up there? Like a crazy man he is shouting out he killed my boy.'

'Zeke, you shouldn't be going up to Brush Park,' Samuel said. 'Miller could have you arrested.'

'Let him try!'

'He may well do that,' Samuel said. He ran an agitated hand through his thick grey hair. 'Zeke, Miller taunts you because you attacked him, and because you're a Melungeon. You have to leave him alone.'

'You just worried about your job!' Zeke Goins said bitterly. But then just as quickly as his anger had arisen, so it subsided, and he took one of Samuel's hands in his. 'I'm sorry, Sam. I didn't mean that,' he said.

'It doesn't matter what you say to me,' Samuel Goins said as he looked at his brother's bowed head with tenderness. 'And contrary to what you sometimes think, I'm not worried about my job. Grant T. Miller has no power over me. But he can make life unpleasant for you, Zeke, if you keep going on with these accusations. He can have you arrested. You have to keep away from him, and you have to stop trying to drag other people in too. Promise me you'll do that, Zeke. Promise me.'

The younger of the two Turkish officers was just like him, in some ways. Divorced, not happy about it, paying for a kid. Gerald Diaz put a carton of Chinese noodles in the microwave and pressed the button for it to cook. He sat down at the kitchen table and lit up a cigarette while he waited. More fucking plastic food!

The older Turk, İkmen, would smoke all the time if he could. Like Gerald, he was quite open about that. But unlike Gerald, he was also, in part at least, happy. Married with a huge number of kids by all accounts, he was a respected man back in his own country, at the top of his profession. But he'd lost a child. Something to do with a drugs raid. His kid, like Zeke Goins' boy, had died by a bullet.

It had to be hard to take. Gerald thought about his own son, Ernesto, and his stomach tightened. Carmen, his ex-wife, had taken the boy back to her native Mexico when they got divorced. Ernesto was seventeen in a country that was torn apart every day by drug-gang warfare. Luckily his son had a very clear and certain goal. He wanted to be a doctor. But that didn't magically make him invulnerable to harm. Anyone could get caught in crossfire. Anyone. Narcotic supply wars did so much harm! If only narc addiction really were a public-health issue. Then, if the state controlled the addicts' supply, as they did for those who needed the drug medicinally, the men with the guns would be put out of business. Simplistic maybe, a dream maybe, but . . .

The microwave pinged, telling Gerald that his noodles were ready. But he didn't get up immediately. He just sat and smoked and looked down at the table with blank eyes. He could understand why Zeke Goins wanted the Turks to help him. Not that he would or could tell the old man that. Everybody needed something or someone to believe in, and with Zeke that was Turks, or rather his notion of them. Those Melungeons who identified with the old Turkish sailors story were completely convinced of its authenticity. Those among them of a more intellectual nature pointed at how similar some of their words were to Turkish; some even claimed actual DNA evidence. People like Zeke believed all that completely. Not so his brother. While Zeke was all about history, heritage and arcane connections, Sam was concerned only with the future of his people and with their integration into the mainstream, their little corner of the American Dream. But then unlike Zeke, Sam had not lost a child, his wife and, some would say, his mind. In a way, Gerald was sorry that İkmen and Süleyman couldn't help Zeke to find out who had killed his son. If they, as Turks, found out, Zeke would believe them, whatever they discovered. As it was, if Gerald himself or any other Detroit cop came up with anything, the old man wouldn't believe it on principle. If the Turks had a shot at the 'who killed Elvis Goins?' story and discovered a solution, they could actually put it to bed and give Zeke some peace. But that wasn't possible. They only had four more days in the city and then they had to go home. Besides, who actually had killed Elvis Goins wasn't that hard to work out, not really. Making anything stick was, however, quite another matter and also quite impossible.

Chapter 7

'What do you mean, Kuban has got a Facebook page?' Commissioner Ardıç said.

Ayşe Farsakoğlu, standing to attention in front of his vast wooden desk, said, 'It's not his, sir. It's a fan site. It's where people who admire Ali Kuban and his "work" go to talk about his crimes and, well, fantasise and—'

'It's everything I hate about the internet!' her superior roared. His large jowly face wobbled with indignation. 'Criminals having "followers". It's appalling! Should be shut down!'

'It's difficult to control, sir.'

And that, if she was honest, made Ayşe sad too. She'd found the rapist Ali Kuban's admiration site easily. It was full of accounts of his acts and suggestions for further action. In reality, those involved in it were probably bored kids who did it for a laugh. But in common with a lot of internet material, the legality surrounding the expressing of such sentiments was tenuous. Ayşe had not liked what she had seen on that site, and so she'd brought it to the boss of her boss. The Commissioner could, in theory, act upon such information. Although quite what he might do was open to question. The Ali Kuban fan site wasn't even written in Turkish. Constructed in poor English, it was in all likelihood the brainchild of some rich kid.

'The world gets madder every day,' Ardıç said gloomily as he chewed upon the end of an unlit cigar. 'Inspector İkmen travels thousands of miles over to America, and there he finds a man of

Turkish ancestry who claims he has been waiting for İkmen to arrive to help him gain justice.'

Ayşe frowned. 'Sir?'

'Something about this man's son getting killed in a gang dispute.' Ardıç shrugged. İkmen had told him about the crime over the telephone, but he couldn't remember anything about it. All he could really recall was that the American in question had been a Melungeon. A deputation of those people had turned up once when he was in Ankara. They had met with council officials and had been greeted by them as long-lost brothers. An odd and at times almost incomprehensible artefact, the visit of the Melungeons had nevertheless been a touching affair. They all believed with a passion that they were Turks. The Turkish government, for their part, apparently concurred. Ardıç didn't know.

'I'll get the cyber-crime boffins to monitor Kuban's fan site,' he told Ayşe after a pause. 'See what they can find.'

'Yes, sir.'

'I'm glad you brought it to my attention.'

Ayşe left Ardıç's office. Before the smoking ban, it had always smelled of rather sweet cigar tobacco. Now it just simply stank of the Commissioner's feet. Mercifully out in the corridor once again, she breathed in deeply and began to make her way back to her own office. As she walked past Süleyman's office, she looked in and saw İzzet Melik. They smiled at each other, but neither one of them spoke. They'd talked for hours the previous evening in the Kaktus. For the first time in a long time, Ayşe had actually enjoyed herself.

Çetin İkmen was completely partisan, and he knew it.

'I'm only interested in programmes and solutions that include the criminal or the criminalised addict,' he told Süleyman as they both slipped out of the morning session. It was being led by another advocate of Zero Tolerance, this time from the UK. 'I think we've both just about finished with Zero Tolerance for now, don't you?'

When they got outside the Cobo Center, they lit up cigarettes and only then considered what they might do for the rest of the morning. Or rather Süleyman did. İkmen knew exactly what he wanted to do.

'I think we should get a taxi to that place that Mr Goins spoke about, Brush Park,' he said.

Süleyman frowned. 'You can't get involved, Çetin,' he said.

'I'm not. I just want to see the place. Now, are you coming or are you staying here?'

Gerald Diaz had spotted the two Turkish officers leaving the auditorium and had followed them when they went outside. He had meant to just go out and have a cigarette with them. But when he heard İkmen use the words 'Brush Park', he changed his mind and decided to follow them.

The small amount of snow that had melted the previous day had hardened into ice overnight. As it insinuated in around the frame of his bedroom window, Grant T. Miller was reminded of the thin, chilly fingers of Jack Frost. Another mythical being from his childhood who lived in the stories that his mother told him and in his subsequent dreams.

His mother hadn't even known who Jack Frost was until she moved to Detroit. In her home town there was never any snow, and people chilled to tales of voodoo queens and zombies and the ghosts that haunted Spanish Creeper-encrusted cemeteries. In her head, Rose Miller had never left the Deep South, and so all the stories she told with a northern theme were as new to her as they had been to him. Downtown, his illiterate father had sewed in his basement shop and had never come home until the early hours of the morning. To him, not to work was to be dead, and to be dead was something to be feared. Grant T. could understand that. Although why the old man had always had to do everything for himself, always play by the rules, always be the big man's bitch was beyond him. Had he wanted, Gustav Miller could have really fleeced boss Henry Ford. But he hadn't. Like a fool, he had only ever taken what was offered. He'd been too frightened to go for any more. A whipped Jew from Europe! Grant T. turned his nose up at the thought of his father, and shook the ice from off his counterpane. Snow from the hole in the ceiling had dripped down on to the bed. It wasn't the first time. It wouldn't be the last. The house was falling in on him, folding up like a picture in a pop-up book. Eventually it would entomb him and he'd become like an Edgar Allan Poe character, a premature burial.

He swung his thin white legs over the side of the bed and slid his feet into his damp, slimy slippers. Everything was rotting, and that included him. He'd been left to rot. One day, he'd just stopped, and everybody else had waved him goodbye as they headed blithely off into the future. He didn't know why – or rather he did, but he just wouldn't see it. That was far more dangerous than some disintegrating old roof. He put on the robe that had acted as an extra blanket on his bed and forced his curved spine to straighten. Stiff he undoubtedly was, but considering how he lived, he was very well for his age. There weren't many men of eighty-five who could survive in an unheated barn of a house with holes all over it. That was something to be proud of.

Grant T. picked his false teeth out of the glass beside his bed and put them into his mouth. If only his teeth had been like his hair! That, long and grey and thick as a horse's tail, hung down to the middle of his back. Like Samson, he felt that his strength was in that hair, and also in common with the Biblical character he hated the thought of having it cut – even if it did make him look a little girlie. He knew he was a man; that was all that really mattered.

But then suddenly the peace of Grant T. Miller's morning regime was broken. Unusually, there were voices outside. He didn't like that at all.

Neither İkmen nor Süleyman was shocked by what they saw. That a man lived in a house that was falling down around him was not

58

something out of the ordinary. New migrants into İstanbul often ended up squatting in semi-derelict houses. But for an apparently wealthy person to do such a thing was strange.

'If this man did kill that old Melungeon's son, then maybe he punishes himself by living here,' Süleyman said as he shivered on the pavement.

'Maybe,' İkmen said. The taxi-driver hadn't wanted to bring them to Brush Park, much less to the house of Grant T. Miller. He'd suggested some apparently pretty island somewhere, but İkmen had been adamant. If the place was indeed crawling with junkies and crackheads, they would, he told the man, deal with it. As it was, Brush Park was eerily silent. İkmen looked up at the house in front of them and frowned. At one end, what looked like the remnants of an old balcony melted into the snow that covered the extensive garden. On the other side, what seemed to have been a tower had collapsed. The roof of the tower, a pointed cone of tiles, lay in front of the house like a casually discarded hat. All around, other houses languished in similar states of disrepair and neglect. In some cases, whole blocks had disappeared completely, the houses bulldozed, replaced by empty, litter-strewn lots. It was, İkmen felt, almost as if the district had been bombed. He went up to the front gate that hung limply between two almost uprooted posts and stared.

'This city was almost another place when the man who owns this house worked in the car industry,' he said. 'When I was a child, you know, Detroit was the absolute centre of the car world. Can you remember when the dolmuşes[1] were all old American cars?'

In spite of the cold, Süleyman smiled. 'Just,' he said. 'Mainly Chevrolets, weren't they?'

'Many of them, yes,' İkmen said. 'Emissaries from the Motor City.' He laughed, and it was at this moment that the door to the Windmill

[1] Dolmuş: Turkish shared taxi. In the fifties, sixties and seventies, dolmuşes were usually large American cars. These days they are generally minibuses.

creaked open and a man in a pair of filthy pyjamas came out carrying a handgun.

'Ah, what . . .' İkmen and Süleyman both stepped back and raised their arms in the air. Received wisdom back home was that all dealings with anyone with a gun in America necessitated absolute and total surrender. People shot first and then thought afterwards, apparently. A bit like some parts of rural Anatolia.

'I don't know what you want,' the old man said as he cocked the handgun and took aim. 'But I'm telling you that this is no place for spics. Get back to the barrio where you belong!'

Neither İkmen nor Süleyman knew what he was talking about. 'Mr, er . . .' İkmen began. 'I apologise if we—'

'You don't need to apologise; just go!' the old man said. And then he fired the gun so that the bullet flew over their heads.

Both İkmen and Süleyman dropped to the ground. Was this old lunatic going to kill them? İkmen saw Süleyman reach instinctively inside his jacket for his gun. But of course it wasn't there. He heard the younger man swear. He saw the old man advance upon them, and although he wanted to say something to at least make him stop and think, he found that he couldn't utter so much as one English word. But fortunately he didn't have to.

'Miller!' The voice came from behind where the Turkish officers had sunk to the ground. 'What the fuck are you doing?' Gerald Diaz said.

İkmen saw the old man sneer. 'Huh!' he said. 'Another fucking spic!'

Diaz walked forward and took the gun out of Grant T. Miller's hands. 'Give me that!' he said. Then he looked around at the two Turks. 'You OK?'

Süleyman helped İkmen to rise to his feet and said, 'Yes. I think so.'

Diaz turned to Miller. 'Grant T., I am going to take you—'

'What for?' the old man said. 'Shooting at a couple of your Latino—'

'They're not Latino!' Diaz roared. His face was red and blotchy from the cold and his anger. 'These are foreign police officers. They're from Turkey. They're our guests!'

'Oh.' The old man didn't look ashamed, but he was nevertheless taken aback.

Diaz turned back to the Turks again, and looking straight at Çetin İkmen, he said, 'You, Inspector, have to leave this alone.'

'My son Bekir left home when he was fifteen and went to live on the streets,' Çetin İkmen said. They were back downtown in an almost deserted café. Over behind the counter, two bored baristas looked out at the snow in the street with blank expressions on their faces. 'He got involved in drugs,' İkmen continued. 'With trafficking, with gangs and with some very dangerous criminals. Before he was shot by one of our jandarmes, he killed an unarmed and wholly innocent man. He would have killed Inspector Süleyman, who was at that time his hostage, had other officers not intervened.'

Lieutenant Diaz looked down into his coffee cup and sighed. 'I can't imagine what that must have been like,' he said. 'Your own son . . .'

'And bad as Bekir was, I still mourn him,' İkmen said. 'I miss him. It is why I can and do empathise with Mr Goins. I know for certain who killed my son, and why. But to not know that . . . It must eat away at your soul.'

Süleyman drank his coffee in silence. He could remember all too easily that night back in the Anatolian town of Birecik, where they had traced the drug-traffickers, including Bekir İkmen. When the jandarma officer had shot him, Süleyman had tried to do what he could to save the boy. But nothing had worked.

'It was wrong of me to seek to find Mr Miller,' İkmen carried on. 'As you say, Lieutenant, there is no real evidence against him beyond the taunts he makes to Mr Goins.'

'No,' Diaz said. 'You know you could still prosecute for attempted homicide. You'd have to stay in Detroit.'

For a moment, Süleyman looked horrified.

İkmen shrugged. 'What would that achieve?' he said. 'Nothing for Mr Goins, certainly.'

Süleyman visibly relaxed.

'You're right.' Gerald Diaz folded his arms across his chest and looked down at the floor. 'Got a Beretta out of it. But then Miller's probably got a whole arsenal in that place.' He looked up. 'You know, most people think that Zeke Goins is crazy.'

'That doesn't make him wrong,' İkmen said.

'Inspector İkmen has a . . . an instinct for such things,' Süleyman said. It was well known back in İstanbul that Çetin İkmen possessed what some liked to call a supernatural tendency to be right about people. His mother, an Albanian woman who came from a long line of seers and soothsayers, had been famous as a neighbourhood witch.

Gerald Diaz frowned. All cops had hunches from time to time, but to have a hunch about a thirty-year-old homicide in a country not your own was stretching it. He looked up at İkmen. 'So you feel that Grant T. Miller . . .'

'Oh, I don't know whether Mr Miller actually killed Mr Goins' son or not,' İkmen said. Then his face dropped. 'But what I do know is that I want to help Mr Goins. I feel that very strongly.'

Diaz drank some coffee. 'But you can't,' he said. 'You've no jurisdiction here. Goins may well want that, but . . . Inspector, you go home at the end of the week.'

İkmen put his head down. 'I know.' Then he raised it again. 'But what if I didn't have to? What if I could stay?'

Süleyman was aghast. 'You can't stay here!' he said in Turkish. 'We go home on Saturday!'

'What did he say?' Diaz asked.

But İkmen didn't answer. 'Lieutenant Diaz,' he said, 'I have annual leave I must take.'

'Oh, no, no, no, no, no! No, Inspector, you can't do that!'

62

'Çetin, this is madness,' Süleyman said in Turkish. 'Leave it!'

'But Mr Goins is a Turk,' İkmen said.

Both Süleyman and Diaz looked at him with shocked expressions on their faces.

'Well, he and quite a few other people believe that the Melungeons are Turks,' İkmen said. 'We have a duty to help our fellow countrymen.'

'By upsetting the American police!' Süleyman said in Turkish. 'Çetin, you must not intimidate these people!'

'What did he say?' Diaz asked again.

'Nothing.' İkmen smiled. 'Lieutenant Diaz, I do not wish to tell you your job or do anything to undermine or . . . You know, in my country these Melungeon people are honoured.' He knew that because Ardıç had told him about visits Melungeons had made to Ankara. Not that Ardıç knew that İkmen actually wanted to stay in America and try to help one of their number. İkmen himself had only just decided that that was what he wanted to do.

'Prosecute Miller for firing at you and stay that way?'

İkmen shook his head. 'No.'

'OK.' Diaz shrugged. 'But you know that even if you were to stay, the chances of finding out who killed Elvis Goins after all this time are slim, don't you?' he said.

'Yes.'

'It'll be a waste of a vacation.'

'Maybe.' But İkmen had to know. Ever since he'd first seen Ezekiel Goins, he'd been intrigued. An old white man living with a black woman engaged in social renewal. A man belonging to an ethnic mystery whose son had died at the hands of a person unknown. Even before he'd heard the full story, İkmen had been struck by how vulnerable and yet at the same time how furious Ezekiel had been. So much so that, İkmen felt, the old man would not be able to rest, let alone die, without knowing what had happened to his son. And İkmen, as a man and as a father, could fully understand that.

'The Elvis Goins case is closed,' Diaz continued after a pause. 'Been closed for years.'

'But Lieutenant,' İkmen said, 'don't you want to know who really killed that boy?'

'Of course.' He'd said as much to Zeke Goins when the old man had tried to speak to him, İkmen and Süleyman outside the Cobo Center. He smiled. 'But it's gone. It was all a very, very long time ago.'

'Yes, but . . .' The look on Diaz's face made İkmen stop what he was saying and descend into silence.

Diaz finished his coffee and got up from his chair. 'If you want to stay on when the conference is over,' he said to İkmen, 'I can't stop you. But I can't and won't help you with Zeke Goins. I have other work I need to do.' And then, just briefly, the hard-arsed facade dropped and he said, 'Listen, Çetin, give me your cell-phone number and I promise I'll let you know if anything comes up about Elvis Goins. I'll even call you in Turkey.' He knew that he would never really do that.

But to İkmen, although it wasn't much, it was something. He shrugged and gave him the number, which Diaz entered into his telephone.

Then Diaz said, 'Come on, I'd better take you guys back to the Cobo. You shouldn't miss the programme. I'm sure you didn't come thousands of miles just to see some ruined mansions in old Brush Park.'

Çetin İkmen felt suddenly very lonely and very crushed.

Chapter 8

Tayyar Bekdil had been sent to interview Councillor Samuel Goins shortly after he joined the staff of the *Detroit Spectator*. In an act of flagrant racial stereotyping, the paper had assumed that Tayyar, being a Turk, would want naturally to speak to one of his own. But Samuel Goins wasn't anything like his brother Ezekiel, who, according to Tayyar's cousin's colleague, was utterly convinced he was a Turk. Sam Goins' conception of his own ethnicity had been that he was most definitely mixed race.

'No one really knows where the Melungeons come from,' he'd told Tayyar. 'And it isn't that important anyway, in my opinion. What I've always directed my efforts towards has been counteracting the racism and the stereotyping that my people have suffered. Getting Melungeons educated, into decent jobs and housing has been my passion for most of my life.'

And it had. When Sam Goins had worked in the motor trade, he'd spent time making sure that all his Melungeon brothers and sisters knew their rights. With them, generally with himself in the lead, Sam had fought for what he believed his people needed and deserved. For such a controversial firebrand, he'd got into politics comparatively easily. But then some of Tayyar's colleagues said that his rise had probably come about because certain other politicians of a liberal bent who'd been around at that time had been reluctant to put their heads above the racial parapet themselves. The late sixties and early seventies had been dangerous times.

Tayyar hadn't known about the murder of Samuel Goins' nephew

Elvis until Çetin İkmen had told him. It had piqued his interest, and now he was looking at old press cuttings from December 1978. Elvis Goins had been shot in the head sometime on the night of 1 December 1978. When police had found the body, outside the old Unitarian Church in Brush Park, there had been heroin both on it and in it. Elvis Goins had been a minor godfather and a user, and had almost certainly been killed because of the gang that he ran, the Delta Blues. The Deltas had had enemies. Chief amongst these was a black gang known as the Purple Mobile Crew. Like the Deltas, the Mobiles had southern roots and were therefore well versed in the reality of racial segregation. In spite of being north of the Mason-Dixon Line, these kids, on all sides, kept that iniquitous separation alive. The Purples were black, other gangs were white and the Delta Blues were neither. Elvis Goins could only have belonged to a federation of the outcasts, which was exactly what the Delta Blues had been. Melungeons, Native Americans, kids that were half Chinese – Elvis, on behalf of the Deltas, welcomed them all provided they would either run drugs, fight or kill, possibly all three. Tayyar, who would have been around about the same age as Elvis Goins had he lived, couldn't help but contrast the Melungeon's upbringing with his own. The nearest the comfortable İstanbul suburb of Bebek had had to a gang was probably the school chess club. Detroit had been a massive culture shock to a privileged person like Tayyar. But that was why he liked it: it challenged him. And he liked the people. They had a lot of problems and could really talk a tough game, but they were also resilient and warm, and he liked that.

Tayyar looked for reports pertaining to Elvis Goins' funeral, which had taken place a month after his death. There was just one, but it contained a surprising detail. Elvis Goins, a drug-user and dealer from a poor Melungeon family, had been buried, with some pomp, in the very beautiful and historic Woodlawn Cemetery. Woodlawn was where the Ford family were interred, and where Aretha Franklin's father and siblings were buried. A Baptist minister called Dennis

Hamilton had officiated, so the report said. It also gave the names of some of the attendees, who included Ezekiel Goins and his wife Sheila, Samuel Goins and representatives from the Detroit Police Department. It had been an elaborate funeral, which Tayyar initially assumed had to have been paid for by Sam. But then Samuel Goins hadn't been anyone special back in 1978. He'd been just like all the other working Joes back then. In 1978, Sam Goins had yet to become 'someone'.

'Counselling, my friend, is for middle-class people with more money than they know what to do with,' Çetin İkmen said to Mehmet Süleyman. 'If I want or need to talk about Bekir, I will go to a nargile salon with . . .' there was a pause, 'with someone and—'

'Who?' Süleyman asked. 'Who will you take with you to the nargile salon to talk about Bekir? It certainly isn't me, and as far as I'm aware, it isn't Dr Sarkissian either.'

Dr Arto Sarkissian, police pathologist, was Çetin İkmen's oldest and dearest friend.

'Well?'

İkmen lowered his head. Now back in their hotel suite, Süleyman had started on him the minute he had closed the door behind them. İkmen's apparent obsession with a delusional old American who had, coincidentally, also lost his son was embarrassing.

'Lieutenant Diaz is going to think you're mad,' Süleyman continued. 'Offering to investigate an old crime in a country you don't know anything about!'

'I know it must sound arrogant . . .'

'Arrogant! Imagine if Diaz had come to İstanbul and offered to use his vacation to help us with some ancient, almost certainly unsolvable crime!' İkmen opened his mouth to speak, but Süleyman cut him off. 'And don't talk about DNA evidence and how it is so useful in solving old crimes. You don't know if any evidence that could possibly conceal DNA is still available, you don't know whether anyone apart from the man who shot at us is a suspect, you don't know how investigations proceed in this country!'

'I know that I feel for that man,' İkmen said. They both sat in plastic-covered armchairs in front of one of the dusty windows, which was open to allow their cigarette smoke to escape into the frigid Detroit air.

Süleyman hadn't wanted to make his friend and colleague feel bad. But his apparent identification with Ezekiel Goins had caused him to embarrass both of them in front of foreigners and almost get them killed. Like it or not, what İkmen needed was grief counselling, or at the very least someone to offload his feelings on to.

'It is generally we old Ottomans who have difficulty talking about our feelings,' Süleyman said as he flicked his cigarette ash into a saucer they'd found underneath a radiator. 'You—'

'Yes, I know that the peasants usually express themselves very effectively,' İkmen cut in bitterly. He looked across at his friend, whose head was now bowed, and said, 'You only think like this because you were married to a psychiatrist.'

Süleyman did not reply. İkmen was right, of course. It was only since his marriage to Dr Zelfa Halman that he had even considered the possibility of talking about one's problems as a form of cure. He also knew that by beginning to refer to İkmen as something other, and lesser, than himself, he had insulted him. But what had been said had needed to be discussed. İkmen couldn't carry on projecting his own feelings on to someone who was a complete stranger in a totally foreign land. 'Çetin, you—'

'I will cease and desist from any involvement with Ezekiel Goins from now on,' İkmen said. He threw his hands in the air as he spoke, as if batting the entire subject away from him. It was a bad-tempered and resentful gesture.

'And when we get home, you must seek some help,' Süleyman said.

İkmen shrugged. 'Maybe.' He was furious. Süleyman knew the signs and so he stopped talking at that point. In many ways, Çetin

İkmen was one of the most accommodating and easy-going men imaginable. But angered or crossed, he was a formidable force, and Mehmet Süleyman was very aware of the value of not becoming his enemy. In all likelihood, come the following day, he would be back to his usual affable self once again. But as İkmen rose from his seat, went to his bedroom and closed the door behind him with a bang, Süleyman did wonder whether he'd pushed his friend too far.

Grant T. Miller had all the right paperwork for the very handsome Beretta PX4 Storm Pistol he'd let off at the Turks and which Diaz now had in his possession. And if Inspectors İkmen and Süleyman were failing to press charges – Diaz strongly suspected that the younger one, Süleyman, just wanted to forget it all and go home – Miller was within his rights to ask for it back. When, however, it was to be returned to him was another matter.

'You don't shoot at people like that,' Diaz said into the telephone on his office desk. It was nearly nine p.m. but Grant T. Miller had known he'd still be at work. Diaz's colleagues were aware that he rarely went home unless he absolutely had to.

'It's a US citizen's right to defend what is his. I know the constitution's in English, which might be a problem for you!' Miller laughed, a bronchitic, sickly liquid sound. 'But if those Muslims aren't going to press charges then you need to return my property to me, Diaz.'

Gerald Diaz knew that in theory, the old man was right. He'd shot at the Turks but he hadn't wounded them, and they hadn't wanted to take any action against him. Diaz had taken the old man's legally held gun off him more out of spite than anything else. Grant T. Miller was a nasty racist bastard, but any proof beyond what would amount to word of mouth of current or indeed past law-breaking by him was non-existent. So he was the son of a Jewish father who was an anti-Semite. So he continued to openly discriminate against blacks, Jews, Hispanics and anyone else who didn't conform to his racial-purity standards well into black Mayor Coleman Young's administration.

So what? Grant T. Miller was well known and feared, and that had changed little in spite of his apparently reduced circumstances. But then Miller knew people, significant people. He always had and he probably always would. That was one of the big problems about trying to pin anything at all on him. He was, as Diaz knew very well, extremely effectively protected.

'Your Beretta'll come back to you when I have time to get up to Brush Park,' Diaz said wearily. He was tired, gagging for a cigarette and needed to be outside if only to blow away the sound of Miller's wheezing. 'I do have a job I have to do.'

'Don't you just.'

Diaz squirmed.

'Weren't you up here for that drive-by on that nigger kid the other day? That was you and your little black girlfriend over in front of the Royden Holmes House, wasn't it?'

Diaz felt his mouth curl in disgust. The old bastard had watched them as they went about their work on Aaron Spencer's death. He had picked up straight away on Officer Rita Addison, young, pretty and black.

'You banging that, are you, Diaz?' the old man said, laughing through mucus as he did so. 'You doing some race relations of your own with her?'

The things he wanted to say to that toxic old man! The abuse he wanted to hurl at him! But Gerald Diaz took a deep breath before he let himself speak, and then he said, very quietly, 'Mr Miller, I do not have to listen to racial abuse. The city of Detroit has standards.'

'What, with niggers taking over every neighbourhood, dealing crack cocaine and knocking up every woman under the age of forty? What kind of standards are they? Eh?' Miller laughed. 'City of Detroit has standards, my ass! That's like saying that a whore has got her virginity! Stop talking horseshit, Diaz, and bring me back my gun. You can drop it off when you and your little girl come up to look at your crime scene again.'

This time Gerald Diaz didn't take a calming breath; he just leaned in as close to the receiver as he could get and said, 'Fuck you.' Miller was just starting to laugh again when he slammed down the phone.

It was only later, when he was getting ready to go home, that Diaz remembered that it wasn't possible to see the Royden Holmes House from Miller's place. In addition, as far as he was aware, Grant T. rarely if ever actually ventured out beyond his front door and on to the street.

Diaz made a detour to the ballistics lab before he drove home.

Ayşe Farsakoğlu sat on the edge of her bed and put her head in her hands. Now that the morning had come, she felt completely ridiculous. Only nervous children got rattled by noises in the night, and she was a very competent (or so she'd thought) adult.

Her brother Ali had left İstanbul to go to Azerbaijan on business the previous morning. Travelling for his company was something he'd done many times before, and so Ayşe was accustomed to it. As usual, she'd got home from work in the early evening, fixed herself some supper and then settled down to watch TV until eleven p.m. She'd gone to bed tired and had fallen asleep almost immediately.

Then, at just gone two a.m., she had woken with a start. Unusually cold and yet sweaty, she'd immediately felt her ears straining into the darkness, scanning for sound. Quite what sound she was trying to detect, Ayşe didn't know. But what she *felt* was a definite notion of intrusion. There was someone or something in her apartment, the lizard brain that existed at the back of her rational mind was screaming at her. And so, because she was alone and because İkmen was out of town, she'd called İzzet Melik, who had come from his place in Zeyrek across the Golden Horn to Gümüşsüyü immediately.

Although she had left a window open in the kitchen, no one had been into the apartment as far as either of them could tell. But in spite of that, she still couldn't shake the conviction that she'd been observed, her space violated in some way. As soon as they'd

71

investigated every room of the apartment, Ayşe had tried to persuade İzzet to go back home. It was very late and they both had to get up and go to work in the morning. But he had insisted upon making her tea first, and they had then talked and drunk, and he had smoked, until just after four in the morning.

It was of course quite possible that some unknown person had been observing Ayşe for some reason. But it was, they both agreed, unlikely. Everybody who lived in her block and in the surrounding streets knew she was a police officer and treated her with both respect and a good deal of reserve. People from outside Gümüşsüyü were obviously unknown quantities, but Ayşe didn't think that anyone she could call an enemy was free and on the streets at the present time. Such offenders' relatives were, of course, another, if unlikely, matter. If she were honest with herself, Ayşe had to eventually concede that what had probably unnerved her had come about as a result of her recent contact with Ali Kuban's Facebook fan site.

Commissioner Ardıç had decided, in his wisdom, to monitor closely the traffic into this site. Kuban had been out of prison for less than a week and the fan site was already, if without his apparent participation, doing a very great deal of business. It was Ayşe that the Commissioner chose for this task.

Not only praise for Kuban but also fantasies woven around his old crimes, as well as some new and even more inventive suggestions for further offences, flooded in. Ayşe, though aware of how important her part in monitoring the site was, felt sickened. In reality the majority of those involved were probably just stupid kids mucking around. But what of the minority? What about those who were taking Kuban's release and a possible resumption of his 'career' very seriously indeed? In spite of Atatürk, of women's suffrage, of more educational opportunities for girls, there were still a lot of men who believed that females were only good for housework and for sex. Any woman or girl active outside the family home was a slattern and a whore and was therefore fair game for any passing pervert. In spite of all her

72

efforts to leave her work behind her whenever she left the station for the day, this particular task had stayed with her and infected her sleep.

'Such opinions strike at women more than men,' İzzet had said as he passed her the glass of tea he'd made for her in her kitchen. 'Ardıç should have given that job to a man. It is after all Vice who will take any action that is required, not us.'

'Maybe he thought that my extra female empathy would make me more sensitive and attend to the material more closely,' she'd replied.

They'd talked. Then she'd started yawning and he'd suggested that they both get some sleep. She'd agreed. She'd thanked him, apologised and then told him to go home and try to rest before work. But he'd insisted upon staying. She was still obviously rattled and might wake again in a state of agitation. This was quite possible. She wasn't entirely comfortable about İzzet leaving her. But she was also very far from comfortable about him staying. She knew how he felt about her, even if they had never actually spoken about it.

He'd looked away from her then and said softly, 'Of course I will sleep in your living room, in a chair.'

She'd let him stay. She feared she might have insulted him by locking her bedroom door, but she'd done it anyway. Now it was morning and she needed to go to the bathroom. But how to do that without having to pass by the living room?

Ayşe eventually rose, unlocked her door and then very tentatively put her head outside to look into the living room. İzzet, as far as she could see, had already left. His departure left her feeling odd. In a way she was relieved that he had gone, but in another way she wasn't.

Chapter 9

The conference downtown was taking up too much of the lieutenant's time. He was supposed to be taking the lead on the Aaron Spencer homicide, but in reality it was Lieutenant Shalhoub who was doing most of the work. Rita Addison got on well with Shalhoub, but he was no Gerald Diaz. People liked him but they didn't trust his judgement in the same way that they trusted Diaz. Diaz could get people to talk to him. Over the course of many years, Diaz had made it his business to get to know Detroiters in all walks of life. He knew politicians and gang members, charity hostesses and junkies, urban activists like Martha Bell, fences, forgers, mad people and crack-dealers. He knew them all, and to the extent that they could, they all trusted him. Had Diaz had his mind fully on the case, Addison knew that he would already have picked up at least a whisper about who might have hit the young boy. But he was the key speaker down at the Cobo that morning.

'He's talking about managing drug-addicted informants,' Rita told Officer Mark Zevets as they continued to search the grounds of the old Royden Holmes place for the bullet that had killed Aaron Spencer.

'Well he should know,' Zevets replied as he sifted through a pile of earth with one plastic-gloved hand. 'Diaz is the only person I know can communicate with a junkie on a comedown without getting a knife at his throat.'

'Trick is, I think, he likes them,' Addison replied. Then she straightened her back and said, 'You ever know a slug so difficult to find as this one? Went clean through that boy's head and into another dimension!'

Zevets shrugged.

The search for the bullet that had killed Aaron Spencer had taken on a strange, almost mythical quality. Usually bullets that had passed through people's bodies were found within hours. But not this one. The search for this bullet was stretching out into days and, according to John Shalhoub, for a very good reason. Although they were still mounting searches of the garden and the waste ground surrounding the house, the most logical possibility was that the bullet had actually entered the property after it went through Aaron Spencer's skull. The problem was that the Royden Holmes House was filled with rubble, old furniture and any number of dumped auto parts and cans of used sump oil, and clearing that had to be a job for the forensics people. In a house that had been left derelict for so long, they could find anything, even dead bodies. Junkies died in such places; gangs dumped their victims in them. The bullet, as far as the ballistic scientists were concerned, could very easily have passed into the body of the house. The boy had fallen with his head just leaning against the half-open front door.

'You know, I heard that the subject of that old bigot Grant T. Miller came up when Diaz was out at Antoine Cadillac with his foreign guests,' Addison said as she pushed a small bush to one side and looked at the soil around the plant.

'The old fuck who lives in that house with the ruined tower?' Zevets asked.

'That's him,' Rita Addison replied. 'Only resident left in this part of north Brush Park. Anyway, over at Cadillac, Crazy Zeke Goins was making a commotion about how he still believes that Miller killed his son back in the seventies.'

Zevets straightened up and breathed deeply for a moment. It was tough work rooting through rough garden, bent over double. 'Diaz worked that case, I heard.'

75

'When he was a rookie, yeah,' Rita said. He had told her all about it some years back. She was, she suspected, one of the very few people he did communicate with. Somewhere deep inside, she suspected, Diaz believed that Miller had killed Elvis Goins. 'Old Zeke Goins got himself all excited about a couple of Turkish cops Diaz took out to Antoine Cadillac. Reckoned his "kin" could prove Miller's guilt.'

Zevets shook his head and laughed. 'Some of those hillbillies, man, they are nuts.'

'We all know that we can't actually do anything to change the behaviour of our drug-addicted informants,' Süleyman said to İkmen as they stood outside the conference centre, smoking in the snow.

'Yes, but what I think Lieutenant Diaz is saying,' İkmen replied, 'is that if you want to build a proper working relationship with an addict, you must make him feel safe. You must avoid judging his behaviour or threatening him with prosecution because of his habit.'

The bad feeling between them over Ezekiel Goins had evaporated, as Süleyman had known it would. Now, apparently, İkmen was focused only on the conference.

'But we don't stop them using,' Süleyman said. 'We ignore what they do.'

'Yes, but as a last resort, to force an informant to give us what we want, we can threaten to prosecute,' İkmen said.

'Of course!'

İkmen frowned. 'You say that,' he said, 'but what Diaz is proposing is a more co-operative and yet at the same time more business-orientated relationship. Trust and money are the keys. The addict is an employee; we, the police, facilitate his habit, but we get a return on our investment in the form of reliable intelligence. Our addicts trust us, they may even like us, and also we provide them with very badly needed money. Everyone is happy.'

This time it was Süleyman's turn to frown. 'And yet isn't there a danger here of overstepping the line?' he said. 'If we make friends with addicts, if we, as you say, actively facilitate their habits, then aren't we laying ourselves open to charges of collusion? Could we not be manipulated by those we seek to use?'

'Those are very real risks, as Diaz outlined,' İkmen said. 'But if the payoff is a closer view of criminal gangs, increased rates of solution in murder cases, more access to the criminal classes, then that is a price that might be worth paying. It appears to be a model that Diaz has some belief in, as well as some evidence of small-scale success.'

'But this city still appears to me to be out of control!'

İkmen threw his cigarette butt down on the ground and then lit up another smoke. 'They're taking small steps,' he said. 'Diaz I believe works like this. I don't know if many of his officers follow suit. I think that most of them use the Zero Tolerance approach. But then even they seem to be behind these community projects, which are unconventional but which seem to be having some effect in Detroit.'

'Mmm.' Süleyman pulled a face. 'But Çetin, this place is like Tarlabaşı, don't you think? Falling down, full of users, thieves and madmen.'

İkmen smiled. His friend could be so precious at times! 'The other day you thought that Detroit was like Ümraniye used to be,' he said. 'Which is it?'

'Oh, you know what I mean!' Süleyman threw a hand petulantly into the air. 'It's like any broken-down İstanbul district. It's shabby and full of jobless people, criminal gangs, drugs . . .'

'Who are all fascinating individuals who often need help,' İkmen said. He had most definitely joined the police to protect his city and help his people. In some ways it was all about him as well, and his need to understand desperate or divergent behaviour, working on the 'why' behind the crime. Süleyman, on the other hand, had, he felt, other motivations. True, he wanted to protect the city, but he didn't always seem as interested as İkmen was in the reasons behind people's actions. There were times, İkmen felt, when policing for Süleyman – the guns, the danger, the women – was just one big adrenalin rush. But he didn't say anything about that to him, and once they'd finished their latest cigarettes, the two men went back into the building to have lunch.

Miller, smirking, told Diaz that he would invite him in but his place was in a bit of a state. That was putting it mildly. Behind the old man's head, all Diaz could see was a yellow-lit chaos. Apparently random pieces of furniture were stacked up everywhere, refugees, in all likelihood, from the now collapsed tower on the east side of the building. In that regard, as well as in so many others, the Windmill was not unlike the Royden Holmes place, where, apparently, his officers were still searching for that missing bullet.

'I have to be downtown as soon as I've finished here,' Diaz said. Snow had entered under Miller's front door and was covering the old man's sagging slippers.

'You bring my gun, did you? My paperwork?'

Diaz didn't answer. 'How did you know that Rita Addison was with me out at the Royden Holmes place?' he said.

'Because she's your partner, isn't she?' Miller said. 'I mean professionally, not . . .'

'She could've been sick that day. Could've been in court.'

Miller looked down at the snow on his slippers, then looked up again and smiled. 'But she weren't. She was with you.'

Miller was well known for his mind games, the type he played whenever he could with poor old Zeke Goins.

'You can't see Royden Holmes from here.'

'I went out.' He smiled again.

'Out?'

'Into the great outdoors, yes,' Miller said. 'Felt like a stroll that day.'

'Felt like a stroll?'

'Yeah. Out in the snow in my jimmy-jams for a morning constitutional.'

'I never saw you.'

Miller's pale-blue eyes widened. 'Oh, you too busy with a dead nigger kid to look at some old white man.'

'I would have noticed you,' Diaz said as he moved a little closer to the crack in the door in front of which Grant T. Miller stood.

Miller shrugged.

'Anyone else see you?' Diaz asked. 'Because my officers certainly didn't. They would have told me.'

'No one lives around here any more,' Miller said. 'You should know that. Now do you have my property for me, Officer?'

For a few moments Diaz held the old man's gaze. Miller was clearly amused, very obviously playing one of his games. But there had to be some truth in what he was saying, because clearly he had seen Rita Addison with Diaz on the first day of the investigation. That or he'd just made a lucky guess. Either way, Gerald Diaz didn't trust him, and was therefore very reluctant to hand the Beretta back to him, even though he knew that he had to.

Diaz put his hand in his pocket, took the pistol out and pointed it at Miller. Even then the old man laughed. 'Oh, you gonna kill me, are you, Pancho Villa?' His voice cracked with age and with the damp that seeped into everything around him. 'Bet you'd love to,' he whispered. 'I saw how you looked at me all them years ago when Zeke Goins come here and bit me like a rabid dog. It was what attracted me, as it were, to you. All your heart was with him, weren't it? All your soul crying out to his in sympathy for his stupid dead junkie son!'

'If you—'

'Oh, boy, you will never know for sure who killed Elvis Goins any more'n anybody will,' Miller said. 'Now stop pointing my gun at me, give it over and make nice. Remember just who and what you are. Weapon was clean, I take it?'

79

Diaz slapped the pistol into the old man's outstretched hand and gave him his paperwork back. 'Ballistics told me it'd been fired,' he said.

'At?'

'The Turks.' He shrugged. 'It's not wanted for any other crime.'

As Diaz walked down what remained of the garden path, Miller pointed the Beretta at him and said, 'I got my eye on you, Diaz.'

Diaz turned briefly, looked the old man hard in the eyes, and then continued on down the broken, litter-strewn path.

'Decriminalising cannabis, prescribing it only for conditions like multiple sclerosis, is not enough. All, at present illegal, narcotics should be decriminalised, up to and including heroin. The more you criminalise, the more young people turn to other things that may be even more dangerous. I have seen people little more than children in my clinic who had poured neat vodka into their eyes in order to get high.'

The speaker, an elderly female addiction specialist from Italy, was making some very radical statements. The war against drugs, she was saying, was not being won on any level. More and more people were becoming addicted to an ever-increasing range of products, some of which, like alcohol in the eyes, were immensely hazardous.

'Many of these young people become temporarily blind,' she said. 'In order to get high without being arrested, they are putting themselves at what could be even greater risk. Decriminalisation of cannabis, particularly, would allow people to get high without fear. It could also, more cynically, provide another revenue stream for governments. At the moment, criminals are the only ones benefiting from this trade. Drugs also feed into their other activities, like prostitution, extortion and people-trafficking. The war on drugs makes no sense.'

Çetin İkmen looked across at Gerald Diaz and saw that he was smiling. Opinions like this were totally in line with his philosophy of social understanding and engagement. What the Italian said also struck a chord with İkmen himself. Although there was no way the Turkish government, just like the US administration, would ever decriminalise narcotics, as an officer on the street he could see that it did make sense. Billions of lire were poured into the war on drugs every year, and every year the problem grew still bigger and more intractable.

In Mehmet Süleyman's opinion, education was the key. Young people needed proper information about drugs in order to make informed decisions about whether to use or not. But there were more radical solutions too. In so far short conversations with Sergeant Donna Ferrari, İkmen had learned that in her opinion, religion was the answer. If kids could just find God, then everything would be fine and they wouldn't need drugs. How that would play out with uneducated youngsters with no prospects, İkmen didn't know. But he was aware that it wasn't just a Christian perspective. Some of his colleagues back in Turkey had similar beliefs about the efficacious employment of Islam in the war against drugs.

Discovering that Sergeant Ferrari was what she called a 'born-again' Christian was interesting on another level too. Much as she might flirt and flutter her eyelashes at Süleyman, actual sex with him, unless İkmen was very much mistaken, had to be out of bounds. Delayed or even sometimes completely frustrated pleasure was something that İkmen automatically associated with fanatically religious people of almost all stripes. In the same way that he couldn't understand promiscuity, he couldn't get his mind around painful self-denial either. Sergeant Ferrari was an attractive woman who was aware of her own allure, and yet apparently she did not act on the effect she clearly had upon men. Süleyman, as far as he knew, had so far failed to so much as take Ferrari for a coffee.

He looked across again at Diaz, who was, rather hurriedly, getting up from his seat and pushing past Donna Ferrari. He had his mobile phone, which must have been in silent mode, pressed to his ear and was obviously listening to something. From the expression on his face, what he was hearing was both important and rather grave.

A line had been crossed and Ayşe didn't know what to do. It was almost twelve hours since İzzet Melik had crept out of her apartment without a word. Like her, he'd gone into work and they had spoken, if a little stiltedly, about matters relating to their jobs when they'd met outside their respective offices. He had said nothing at all about the events of the previous night, and when she'd left the station to come home, he hadn't attempted to stop her or ask her to go elsewhere with him. Since she had arrived at her apartment, he hadn't called her. And yet he had spent the previous night if not in her bed, in her place alone with her. If any of her neighbours had seen him either arrive or leave, they could, at that moment, be gossiping about her. Even in rather upmarket, modern Gümüşsüyü, people could be judgemental about such things.

Not that Ayşe was any kind of innocent. In the past, she'd had affairs with two of her male colleagues, as well as with a lawyer she'd once met at a meyhane[2] in Beyoğlu. However, that had been some years ago, and besides would she really want anyone to even imagine that she was 'with' İzzet Melik? But then, in a way, that was the whole point. She wouldn't want anyone to think she was with İzzet even if in her heart of hearts she didn't seem to have a problem with that any more.

In recent days she had come to rather enjoy İzzet's company. She still didn't respond to him romantically or find him actually physically attractive. But he was bright, he could be funny and he had been very kind and yet at the same time very respectful to her. It was obvious as well as widely known that he had feelings for her. She had thought she had no feelings at all for him. Now she knew that she was wrong in that assumption. She liked İzzet a lot. Without

---

[2] Meyhane: traditional Turkish drinking establishment.

Süleyman around to distract her, she'd actually taken the time to listen and pay attention to the sergeant. He was a good man.

Not that his goodness was the point. The fact remained that somewhere, somehow, a line had been crossed, and Ayşe was confused. The thought of sleeping with İzzet still made her cringe, but the notion of spending a lot of time with him was beginning to appeal to her. As her late mother most probably would have said had she ever met İzzet Melik, 'you could do worse, girl'. And at her age, Ayşe Farsakoğlu had to admit that that was probably true.

Chapter 10

Officer Mark Zevets found the bullet that had killed Aaron Spencer embedded in the back of an old chest of drawers. He'd had to clear out literally hundreds of used junkie needles in order to get at the back of the chest, but once there, he'd seen the bullet easily. Rita Addison, right behind him, had rung to let Diaz know immediately. Then they'd called over the forensic team and Lieutenant Shalhoub. Everyone had whooped with delight as forensics examined the site and bagged up the slug. It had been an unusually long haul, and everyone was buoyed up by the success. When Gerald Diaz arrived later, he found the officers on the scene in almost celebratory mood.

'Now maybe we'll get somewhere,' Rita Addison said as she took her plastic gloves off and threw them on to the passenger seat of her car.

'Where's the slug?' Diaz asked as he lit up a cigarette.

'On its way to the lab,' Addison replied.

'Good.' Although he would have liked to have taken a look at it first himself. 'Lieutenant Shalhoub see it?'

'Yeah.'

Mark Zevets joined them and, as was his custom, took a couple of quick drags from Diaz's cigarette.

'Do either of you remember seeing any civilians about the place the day we found Aaron Spencer's body?' Diaz asked.

The two younger officers shrugged. 'Like who?' Addison asked.

'There was the usual obligatory one white kid and one black kid came out of nowhere, as they do in places like Brush Park,' Zevets said. 'I questioned the both of them.'

'Nothing?'

'Lieutenant, I would've told you if I'd thought there was anything going on,' Zevets said. 'Kids were eight years old at most, and although I know that shit happens at all ages here in the Big D, these boys were obviously freaked. But if you want to have them in and talk to them yourself . . .'

Diaz shrugged. 'We'll see.'

'We'll see what?' A voice smoke-scarred in a similar way to Diaz's own came from behind.

'John.'

Shalhoub smiled. 'See what?' he asked again.

'Oh, Zevets interviewed a couple of kids hanging out around here the day Aaron Spencer's body was found. I think it's probably a dead end, but . . .' He shrugged.

Shalhoub had only recently been assigned to the Spencer case, while Diaz was down at the Cobo Center, and so he hadn't been in attendance on that first day.

'Why?' Diaz looked over at Addison, who was frowning. 'You hear anything about something?' she asked. 'Other folk come forward about the boy, maybe?'

'No.' Diaz smiled. If no one had spotted Grant T. Miller near the crime scene at the time, then he didn't want to lead their trains of thought in case anything significant occurred to someone spontaneously sometime later. Besides, Miller was so well known that if any of Detroit's finest had seen him that morning, they would have mentioned it. 'No, I just want to make sure that all the bases are covered,' he said. He walked back towards his car. He had to be at the Cobo Center for two thirty, and it was already almost two.

When Diaz had gone, Addison said, 'He's just dying to get back to doing some real work.'

Like Zevets and Shalhoub, Rita Addison knew that Gerald Diaz

85

was a workaholic. She knew how frustrated his attendance at this conference business was making him. As well as being colleagues, they were loosely friends too. They spoke most days on the phone. His absence wasn't doing her much good either. John Shalhoub had just as many years of experience as Diaz and was nothing if not a very knowledgeable and respected officer, but Rita was comfortable with Diaz, and she liked him. Also, for an old guy, Diaz, unlike Shalhoub, was hot.

Even though the city was still covered with thick snow, making walking outside sometimes hazardous, Martha knew that to be indoors all day long was not good. It was also very unlike Zeke Goins.

'You should go out and get some fresh air,' she said to the old man as she attempted to dust the coffee table at his elbow. A half-rolled cigarette as well as an overflowing ashtray needed some dealing with, and although Martha smoked herself from time to time, she found this disgusting. 'What you doing indoors all day anyway watching *Sally*, *Jerry Springer* and *Ricki*?' Martha asked, listing the hysterical chat shows that old Zeke usually avoided. 'We usually listen to Motown together. You depressed or something, Ezekiel?'

'Even when Turks come, nothing don't happen,' he said as he looked down at the floor. 'Maybe it's kismet.'

Martha turned the TV down and sat beside him on the sofa. 'About Elvis?' she asked. He didn't reply. But Martha knew what the score was anyway. She sighed. 'Zeke, man, you gonna have to let your boy go sometime,' she said.

Ezekiel Goins looked up. Suddenly his face was hard, angry almost. 'Like you've let go of Luther?' he said. 'I heard you, Martha Bell, crying into the night, even now.'

Martha shook her head impatiently. 'So what if I weep now and again?'

'All the time.'

She threw her hands up in the air. Her eyes were beginning to mist, and she wanted to make sure the old man was distracted from that. 'So what if I weep all the time!' she said. 'That's my business. I also still work, I garden my patch and I watch out for you and for Keisha all the time! I don't sit in no chair watching big fat girls shout at their boyfriends on *Ricki*!'

Suddenly angered, Zeke said, 'Neither do I!' Then he put his head down again and added softly, 'Usually.'

Martha put her duster down on the floor and took her cigarettes out of the pocket of her apron. 'Come on,' she said as she opened the packet and offered it to him. 'Forget about that sad thing you made there. Have a Winston.'

He took a cigarette from her packet and they both lit up. Martha and Zeke very rarely disagreed about anything, with the exception of the subject of his dead son. Turks or no Turks, Martha just couldn't see how anything could be done to bring whoever had killed Elvis Goins to justice. Not now.

'If I just thought that Grant T. Miller would get his one of these fine days . . .' Zeke said.

Martha dragged on her Winston. She'd heard all this many times before. 'But you don't know for a fact that Miller killed Elvis,' she said.

'Yes I do.'

'No you don't, Zeke! Miller taunts you with it all the time, but you think if he was really guilty he'd keep doing that? No, he'd be afraid some time, some day someone might take him seriously.'

'He's protected by everyone!' The old man was close to tears. Martha reached over and took one of his hands in hers.

'No he ain't, not now,' she said soothingly. 'Miller's nothing now.'

'Miller was in the Legion,' Zeke said, fear in his eyes at the mention of the white supremacist organisation the Black Legion, which had once blighted race relations in the Detroit auto industry.

Martha smiled. 'Lord above, old man, the Legion was put down back in the 1930s! I'm not saying we don't have problems, even now, but the Legion ain't one of them. Anyway, how old was Miller when he was part of all that? Six? Seven?' She laughed. 'Grant T. Miller would like to have been in the Legion is the truth. But not even he so old he could've been.'

She had a point, of course. Grant T. Miller, even at eighty-five, would have been just a kid when the Legion was terrifying black workers on the various auto production lines across the city. But Miller had told Zeke about his old Legion days so many times . . .

'Miller's full of shit,' Martha said. 'He says these things to rattle your cage.' She picked up the television remote control and switched the TV off completely. Gently she laid the old man's head on her shoulder. 'Miller is a badass, but I don't believe he killed your son,' she said. 'He's an evil old bastard, but I don't think he ever killed no one.'

'You don't think so?'

'No.' She stroked the side of his head and Zeke closed his eyes.

'Martha,' he said, after a moment, 'why you think it is that God allows bad people to run free all the time like this?'

Martha shrugged. 'I don't have the answer to that any more than anyone else,' she said. 'I guess the sons of bitches just have to wait to go to hell before they get what's coming to them.'

They were only halfway through the conference, and Süleyman was already talking about going home. İkmen had always imagined that his younger colleague would enjoy the USA more than he would. But in fact the reverse was true. Even out at lovely Grosse Pointe in company with his cousin Tayyar, Süleyman had been a fish out of water. Rather uncharitably, İkmen wondered whether it was because, so far, no young woman had actually succumbed to his charms.

That evening they were to be the guests of the Detroit Police at a dinner given by the department in honour of their out-of-town and foreign guests. For İkmen, it meant putting on a half-decent suit and ironing a shirt, while for Süleyman it was a full-on style and personal-grooming mission. Even if the dinner had been for men only, he would have done exactly the same. Women being also present just added an extra frisson of excitement.

Thoughts about women brought İkmen's own wife, Fatma, to mind. He'd called her a couple of times since he'd arrived in the US, but because neither of them ever really knew what to say to each other on the phone, they had been short conversations. Everything back home was, apparently, fine. His daughter Çiçek was relieved that her father hadn't as yet succumbed to deep-vein thrombosis, and his son who worked over in England was apparently marrying someone called Penny Stevenson. Sınan and Penny were, it seemed, going to live in a town called Clitheroe. According to Fatma, it was somewhere up near the border with Scotland.

İkmen looked at the three ties he'd brought with him and wondered which one might be appropriate for a semi-formal cops' dinner. There was the blue one that was tattered at one end, which he wore every day and which had belonged to his father. Then there was a rather feminine-looking one his son Bülent had bought him for his last birthday, and finally there was the awful beige thing he kept because it had been the tie he'd worn on his wedding day. Realistically he could only wear the effete, highly coloured thing that Bülent had bought him. But that was nevertheless irritating. Although he would never have told his son in a million years, the tie was horribly loud in colour and he found even being in the same room with it an embarrassment. That said, the fact that he had no choice but to wear it was clearly kismet, and so there was nothing he or anyone else could do.

İkmen tucked the tie underneath his collar and then began to knot it. Although he had now stopped talking about the old Melungeon, Ezekiel Goins, he had far from forgotten him. He knew that he couldn't get involved in any investigation into the death of the man's son, even if such an investigation did exist. But that didn't mean that he didn't still feel the man's pain and disappointment acutely. Delusional though it was, there was no denying that Goins had waited patiently for many years for a Turkish policeman to arrive. And now that one had, he had let him down. Although İkmen knew that Lieutenant Diaz would roll his eyes as soon as he so much as mentioned Ezekiel Goins again, he would talk about him one last time. If he could at least get Diaz, who was sympathetic to the old man's plight, to look at the case again, then he would have done something.

İkmen looked down at his watch and wondered how much longer Süleyman was going to spend in the bathroom.

Gerald Diaz had no appetite for dinner. Making small talk with a load of other cops wasn't really his style. Most of the official conversation would be about the orthodoxy of Zero Tolerance as applied in conjunction with the community projects and the junkies' needle exchanges that he championed. Not a huge number of US cops were on his wavelength, even if some of the foreign officers were. His superiors used projects like Antoine Cadillac as a kind of window-dressing: 'Look how liberal we are here!' Diaz, by contrast, saw Martha Bell and her work as solutions in themselves.

He looked at himself in the hall mirror and decided that he didn't scrub up too badly. His hair was more grey than black now, and his face was thin and heavily lined. But he knew full well that women still got hot for him. The British, he knew, called older men who still had their mojo 'distinguished'. He could live with that. Gerald Diaz put his car keys into his jacket pocket and was just about to pick up his cell phone when it rang.

He propped it between his shoulder and his ear as he lit a cigarette. It was always best to get one in before a long-winded function. There was nowhere anyone could smoke indoors except in their own home these days. 'Diaz,' he said, and then he smiled when he heard who was on the other end. 'Good,' he said. 'Thanks for calling so soon. I appreciate it.'

But as the person on the other end of the phone carried on speaking, so Diaz's smile faded and he felt his face and his body go very cold. When the party at the other end of the line finished, Gerald Diaz said, 'Very interesting. Thanks. I'll . . . I'll get back to you.' And then he tapped the key to terminate the call. Phone in hand still, he stood in his hall, smoking and wondering what the hell he should do next. The implications were huge. For a moment it made him feel quite sick. And then it came to him: first of all, send a text. Make sure that word was out even before he was. One thing was for certain, however, and that was that going to some dinner in these circumstances was not going to be possible. He'd have to make his apologies, hopefully pick up Addison and then get on with it.

Diaz opened his front door, sent his text, threw his cigarette butt on to the ground in front of him and looked across at his Ford Focus, which was on the street. The bullet hit him right between the eyes and killed him instantly. The cigarette butt, un-stamped-on, continued to smoulder long after Gerald Diaz had hit the ground.

Chapter 11

'Rita Addison,' the attractive young black woman said to Çetin İkmen as she took his hand and gave it a vigorous shake. 'I work with Lieutenant Diaz.'

Diaz had told her to look out for the Turks and to take care of them until he arrived. It seemed the lieutenant had taken a bit of a shine to poor old Zeke Goins' 'chosen' people.

'Çetin İkmen.' İkmen shook back as hard as he could, but Addison was much younger, fitter and a lot taller then he was. He wondered what Süleyman, who had just slipped out for a cigarette, would make of this Amazon.

'From Turkey, right?'

'Yes,' he smiled. 'İstanbul.'

'Ah.'

It was obvious she knew nothing about the city, so İkmen gave her a few facts.

'Unlike Detroit, İstanbul is a growing city,' he said. 'Our citizens are now so numerous, nobody really knows how many we are. Thirteen million? Fourteen? So many migrate from the countryside these days, it's almost impossible to tell.'

Rita Addison's eyes widened. 'Wow!'

'So we have a lot of problems,' İkmen said. 'Like Detroit, we have gangs, drugs, weapons on the streets. We also have foreign gangs, as well as, of course, offences of terrorism.'

'Tough crowd.'

'You could say that.' He smiled again.

Addison looked at her watch.

'We're supposed to eat at seven thirty, I think,' İkmen said.

'Yeah.' She looked up. 'Our Chief is coming, but he's leaving it a bit snug, if you know what I mean.'

It was already seven fifteen, and as far as Addison could tell, Detroit's Chief of Police had still not arrived. Then, within seconds, the sound of sirens directly outside seemed to indicate that he had finally turned up. İkmen saw Süleyman, across the reception area, go up and look at the dinner seating plan. Fortified by nicotine, he was probably looking forward to his food. What Sergeant Ferrari called the 'slop' that was served to conference delegates during the course of the day was really quite inedible, and so a lot of people, including the Turks, were hungry.

Minutes later, the Chief of Police, a broad, handsome black man, strode in, and for a moment, İkmen saw a grave if not frightened expression pass across his features. Why he should be frightened around so many cops, people who were basically his 'own', İkmen couldn't imagine. For a few seconds, İkmen saw the Chief speak very earnestly to Lieutenant Shalhoub, and then the toastmaster for the evening called for everyone to take their seats for dinner.

İkmen offered Rita Addison his arm. 'I believe we are sitting together,' he said.

She smiled and then laughed. Men didn't offer her, or any other woman she knew, their arms very often. It was old-fashioned, could be construed as sexist and just didn't happen any more. But this man was a foreigner, and in his culture, she thought, it was probably normal behaviour. So she took his arm and said, 'Thank you.'

They began to move towards the entrance to the dining area. İkmen was aware that John Shalhoub was moving the other way, in their general direction, but he didn't know that he was actually coming over to speak. When he drew level with them, he said, 'Rita, I need to talk to you.'

Just like the Chief's, Shalhoub's face was grave, his eyes shining with what looked like fear. Rita Addison frowned. 'Can it wait?'

'No.' He was very sure about that. It was a certainty that made İkmen feel a little cold.

Rita unthreaded her arm from İkmen's and made her apologies. 'I'll see you at the table,' she said. As İkmen made his way towards the entrance to the dining room, he looked back once and saw her gasp in what looked like horror.

Where most non-blacks had fled the downtown area of Detroit years before, Gerald Diaz had stayed. There were a few people, like him, of Mexican descent in the old Irish district of Corktown. And so he had stayed near to where he'd grown up and back in the late 1970s had bought what was then a ruined Victorian worker's cottage. Now he lay across its front step, his blood and brains splattered across his doorstep and his small, neat front lawn.

An anonymous caller had alerted the Detroit PD to the body in the front yard of the pretty old house. But no one locally had seen or heard anything. Two officers named Warwick and Kowalski had been first on the scene. When they'd realised who the victim was, they'd called police headquarters. The Chief of Police, who had just been leaving his home to go to the international conference dinner, had ordered the scene secured, personally called out the forensics team and immediately contacted Diaz's next of kin, his brother Ronaldo. Of course there was also Diaz's ex-wife and his seventeen-year-old son Ernesto too. But they lived in Mexico City, and so the Chief and Ronaldo agreed that Ronaldo should take the first flight down there and tell them in person. Such news should not be given to a child about his parent over the phone.

As soon as he'd found out what had happened, John Shalhoub had immediately volunteered to head up the investigation. He and Diaz had not been friends exactly, but they'd always respected each other. Rita Addison, still in her party dress and quite naturally unable to eat in light of the news about her boss's death, left the Cobo Center with Shalhoub. By the time they arrived at the scene, the place was crawling

94

with forensic investigators as well as a group of uniformed officers that included Sergeant Donna Ferrari. Addison glanced over at Diaz's house beyond the incident tape, and her eyes were caught and held by the tent the forensic investigators had now erected over the entrance. Gerald Diaz's body was in there. She felt sick.

'OK, Officer,' Donna Ferrari said to her, 'let's clear these bystanders out the way, shall we?'

People had gathered, materialised somehow from the boarded-up streets and the waste ground round and about. Attracted, as people always were, by blood and disorder, they all stood in front of the tape and tried to see what was in the forensics tent.

'Unless they can tell us anything, they can all take a hike,' Ferrari said. When Addison didn't move, she shoved her. 'Now, Officer.'

'Oh, er . . .'

For Rita it was like a dream, a hideous fantasy land from which, try as she might, she just couldn't escape. Donna Ferrari pulled her to one side, away from the gawping crowd as well as her fellow officers. 'Look,' she said, 'we all liked Diaz, OK? He was a good cop, a decent guy, and he always had your back. But there's nothing any of us can do for him now except catch the moron who killed him.'

Rita Addison looked at Donna Ferrari with tears in her eyes. 'I know.'

'So get on with it,' Ferrari said. She walked over to the tape and shouted at the people outside it: 'OK, this isn't a sideshow, move on!'

According to Lieutenant Shalhoub, the Chief was going to make Diaz's killing number one priority. That was good, even if it didn't necessarily mean that they were going to discover who had killed him. Even cop-killers got away with it sometimes.

While Ferrari did what was turning out to be a very good job clearing people away from the scene, Rita made her way to the tent that the forensics team had set up over Diaz's body. When she pulled the door flap to one side, she found herself looking right into Diaz's shocked, smashed, blood-soaked face. She felt her stomach turn immediately. Diaz had been her boss, her mentor, and at times her friend too. There had never been anything romantic between them, but Rita at least had always hoped that one day that might change. She put her hand over her mouth and breathed deeply. In spite of being appalled by what had happened to Diaz, she nevertheless couldn't stop looking at him. Maybe it was because she knew it could be the last time she ever would.

One of the forensics team, a woman called Rosa Guzman, looked up and said, 'Hey, Addison, you know what Diaz was working on?'

Rosa could see that Rita was shocked, and she adopted a deliberately casual tone in an attempt to take the horror of it all down a notch or two. It was something she'd done quite a few times before.

'Oh, well . . .'

'Lieutenant Shalhoub says he was on that drive-by over in Brush Park.'

'Yes, he was. I am.' Rita inhaled deeply again and then made herself look away from Diaz and over at Rosa Guzman.

'Anything else?'

Rita, fighting the rising tide of sickness in her stomach, made herself think. 'Well, he was talking at that conference at the Cobo,' she said.

'Don't think a bunch of out-of-towners would do this. Anything else?'

'Yeah. There was one thing. He was looking into some old gang murder thing back in the 1970s.'

Something had been wrong at that dinner, but neither İkmen nor Süleyman knew what. Their host, the Chief of Detroit PD, had been late, and then Rita Addison and Lieutenant Shalhoub, who were both supposed to have been on the Turks' table, had disappeared. Lieutenant Diaz hadn't turned up at all.

'They were kind of tense about something,' Süleyman said as he lit up a cigarette and sat down. They were back in their hotel suite after what had been a very nice meal, if one marred by a strange atmosphere. 'To me it felt rather similar to times when we've been waiting for some anticipated terrorist attack. You know, when it might or equally might not happen, when you begin to question the quality of the intelligence that led up to it.'

'Indeed.' İkmen also lit up a cigarette and sat down. 'But then for all the new initiatives and development, this is still a city with a lot of problems. If Detroit is indeed the future of post-industrial cities, then it does send a bit of a shudder down the spine.'

'Which is why, unlike you, I see a place for Zero Tolerance,' Süleyman said. 'Slum clearance . . .'

'Slum clearance doesn't work!' İkmen said. 'You know that! Look at what has happened since Fatih municipality demolished Sulukule district. You, of all people, should know about that!'

Süleyman shot İkmen a furious glare. He had known the old gypsy quarter of Sulukule well because his ex-mistress, Gonca, had been born there. Recently dismantled to make way for new housing, Sulukule's once vibrant streets were now empty. The gypsies who had danced, hawked and told fortunes there had moved on to sterile apartment complexes in the suburbs or, even less fortunately, on to the streets. In spite of the death of Sulukule, the gypsies still danced, hawked their wares and told fortunes – they just did those things elsewhere, often to the chagrin of İstanbul's many tourist visitors.

'Zero Tolerance just moves the problem on,' İkmen said. 'It also criminalises addiction, which should be a public-health issue – in my opinion. I thought this conference was going to provide rather more alternative solutions than it has done, I must say.'

'Maybe, in spite of these gardening projects, clinics for junkies and what have you, Detroit has had to revisit Zero Tolerance simply because of the size of the problem they face.'

İkmen sighed. 'Maybe.' Apart from Lieutenant Diaz and the

Antoine Cadillac initiative, he was rather disappointed in the conference so far. But then as he would have been the first to admit, and for all their good intentions, police officers were generally fairly rigid in their thinking and in the range of solutions they were prepared to employ.

İkmen put his hand in his jacket pocket and took out his mobile telephone. He'd switched it off just after they'd left the hotel to go to dinner. Now he wondered if anyone back home had left any messages. He turned it on again.

Süleyman stretched, relaxed and then said, 'I'm going to bed.'

It was only eleven thirty, but he was not dealing well with the jet lag or the cold and was still feeling almost as groggy as he had done when they'd first arrived in the city.

'OK.'

As İkmen peered at his phone, Süleyman got up to leave. 'Good night.'

'Good night.'

Süleyman went to his bedroom. İkmen's phone beeped to let him know that he had a text message. He didn't recognise the number it had come from, but what he did know was that it was a local, US number. He scrolled through the menu to read the message. When he got to it, there were only two words: 'Got him.'

Got him? Got who? He called the number back and found himself talking to a Detroit Police Department Forensic Team officer called Rosa Guzman.

Chapter 12

'Sergeant Farsakoğlu!'

'Sir?' She turned.

Ardıç didn't often leave his office specifically to talk to individual officers – not unless they were of much higher rank than Ayşe Farsakoğlu.

'A moment in my office,' he said.

She walked back down the corridor, entered his office and shut the door behind her. Although Ardıç, like everyone else, hadn't smoked in his office since the ban the previous July, a very faint whiff of tobacco smell suddenly caught Ayşe's attention. For just a moment, she wanted very desperately to start smoking again. But then the feeling passed, and once Ardıç had given leave for her to do so, she sat down in the chair in front of his desk.

'About your continuing interest in the movements of Ali Kuban,' he said.

'Yes, sir.'

'As you know, he has been under surveillance since his release. But due to the information you discovered on the internet, we, or rather your colleagues in Vice, have identified some people of possible interest in his immediate vicinity. It would seem that some like-minded creatures have managed, very recently, to arrange to lodge close to Mr Kuban.'

Ayşe frowned.

'We are aware of the phenomenon whereby paedophiles like to group together and exchange pornography, information and sometimes even victims, but a rapist?' He shrugged. 'A very famous and at one time violent rapist, I will grant you. Don't know yet if that is indeed what's going on.'

'No.' Ayşe, still frowning, looked across at him. 'I suppose, sir, we have to remember that when Kuban was imprisoned back in the 1970s, the internet didn't exist. But now that everything you can imagine, as well as a lot of things you cannot, is readily available on there, new people are maybe discovering these old monsters now.'

'I accept it could be just hero-worship,' Ardıç said. 'Violent criminals all over the world attract weird and probably inadequate people. But some of the men physically around Kuban now have police records. Not necessarily for attacks on women; some have convictions for burglary or theft.'

'Right.'

'I'm telling you because it was from your initial intelligence that we became aware of what could be a dangerous phenomenon,' he said. 'I'm an old man; I don't think to look at the internet too often. Either everyone on it is telling the world everything about themselves, whether that is wanted or not, or it's just full of subterfuge and deceit.' He looked at her without smiling. 'But yours was a good call.'

'Yes, sir.' She smiled at the compliment, just a little. Ardıç, she knew, would be appalled if she grinned.

'Of course,' he said, 'it is unlikely we will know whether Kuban and/or these men possess malicious intent until they show their hand.'

'By attacking a woman?'

'That is certainly what Kuban does, or rather did,' Ardıç said. 'All we can do at the moment is watch them. Luckily, due to your efforts, we now have some idea about who, along with Kuban himself, we should be watching.'

'Yes, sir.'

Ardıç dismissed Ayşe Farsakoğlu as quickly as he had asked her to come in. She left feeling partly proud of what she'd done, but uneasy too. What, if anything, were the one-time Beast of Edirnekapı and his fans planning?

'I have to wonder whether the message was even meant for me,' İkmen said as he handed his cell phone over to Rita Addison. When Rosa Guzman had picked up the call from İkmen on Diaz's phone, she'd told him that someone would be over to look at the text message and take a statement from him. Addison had volunteered immediately. Now she sat in the Turks' hotel suite opposite İkmen and a very bleary-eyed Süleyman.

Rita made a note of the date, time and content of the message, as well as the make and serial number of İkmen's phone. The message had definitely come from Diaz, although it wasn't addressed to İkmen or anyone else for that matter. The dead man had, it seemed, fired it off very quickly as he left his house. 'Lieutenant Diaz received a call just before he sent that text to you,' Rita continued.

'From?'

'From a guy who works in the ballistics lab,' Rita said. 'Lieutenant Shalhoub has gone around to his place to find out what it was about.'

'Do you have any idea?'

'I imagine it was the results on the bullet we found in a house in Brush Park,' she said. 'A young boy was killed in what we think was a drive-by shooting. Did the lieutenant ever talk to you about that?'

'No,' İkmen said. But of course Brush Park itself was not unknown to him, and so he told Rita Addison, a little shamefacedly, about his involvement with Ezekiel Goins and his subsequent visit to the place.

'Grant T. Miller shot at you?' Rita Addison shook her head, not in disbelief – she could all too easily believe that Miller had shot at complete strangers – but in sadness. Miller had thought the Turks were 'spics' or Hispanics. The fact that this racial shit was still going on and on just made her furious.

'Lieutenant Diaz took the pistol Miller shot at us with,' Süleyman said.

'Did he take it downtown, do you know?'

'I imagine he did,' İkmen replied. 'But when or whether he gave it back to the old man, I don't know. I believe that Mr Miller had the correct papers to hold the gun.'

Rita frowned. 'I'll check it out.'

'Do you think Miller could have killed Lieutenant Diaz?' Süleyman asked.

'We don't know.' Rita shrugged. She was still wearing the dress she'd selected for the dinner, and looked very glamorous, if tired. 'There's a lot to check. Lieutenant Diaz didn't always tell anyone what he was doing. I didn't know about Miller shooting at you.'

'I know that Sergeant Ferrari knows about Ezekiel Goins,' İkmen said. 'She was at the Cadillac Project when Mr Goins originally approached me.' He explained how he'd come to the old man's attention, and why it had piqued his interest and his sympathy. Outside, through the blackness and the neon flickering of the Detroit night, sirens of all sorts punched holes in the sounds of ordinary transport and human voices. 'I was sorry for him and so I became a little involved,' he continued. 'It was not a good thing to have done.'

'Everyone knows Ezekiel Goins,' Rita said. 'A lot of people feel sympathy for him. I know that the lieutenant did.' İkmen saw her eyes fill with tears, which she very quickly brushed away. 'He went out to help separate Goins and Miller years ago, after the old man's son died.'

'Do you think that Miller killed Elvis Goins?' İkmen asked her.

Rita sighed. 'I don't know,' she said. 'I wasn't born when that happened. I know Miller is a racist. I heard he was in the Black Legion years ago. That was a white power organisation like the Klan. He wouldn't have any more time for Melungeons than he would do for me. But whether he killed Elvis Goins or not is something else. As far as the department is concerned, that's a dead case.'

And yet İkmen felt that Diaz had intimated to him that he had it in mind to follow the old Goins case up. He'd even said that if he ever found anything out, he'd let him know. If that two-word text he'd received just before Diaz died had indeed been intended for him, it could, surely, only refer to one person: Grant T. Miller. It just couldn't be anyone else.

The man who'd run the tests on the bullet from the Royden Holmes scene was old. He'd been with the department since the mid-1960s and had identified more bullets, as he put it, than Hollywood had put stars up on the silver screen. At seventy-three, Rob Weiss was well beyond retirement age, and so he didn't take too kindly to Shalhoub turning up on his doorstep in the early hours of the morning.

'Where the fuck's the fire, cowboy?' he asked a very wired and white-faced John Shalhoub. The lieutenant pushed past the old man and went and stood in his living room. Shuffling in after him, Weiss muttered, 'So don't tell me!'

'Did you speak on the phone to Gerald Diaz earlier this evening?' Shalhoub said without preamble.

'Diaz?' Weiss ran his fingers through his thick grey hair and said, 'Yeah, think I did.'

'What was it about?' Shalhoub asked.

Weiss sat down. 'About? Well, about ballistics. It's what I do. What's this all about? Why can't you ask Diaz?'

'Because he's dead,' Shalhoub said baldly.

The old man cocked his head to one side as if trying to hear something. 'Dead?'

'Shot dead, yes,' Shalhoub said. 'Shortly after he received a call on his cell phone from you. I need to know what it was about.'

'The call?'

Shalhoub didn't answer.

'Diaz asked me to let him know the results on the slug recovered from the Royden Holmes place in Brush Park as soon as I could. That's what I did.'

'Was that it?'

103

'Yeah.'

'Did he say anything else?'

'About the slug?' Weiss shrugged. 'Nah.' Then he frowned. 'He was jazzed, though.'

'What?'

'Diaz isn't . . . wasn't a man given to a lot of emotion, as you know,' Weiss said. 'But this time . . .'

'He was angry? Animated? What?'

Weiss smiled. 'Like I said, he was jazzed. I told him that slug had come from the Beretta PX4 he'd asked me to take a look at late yesterday evening, and he thanked me like I'd just saved his child's life.'

Although Süleyman went back to bed after Rita Addison had left, İkmen stayed up. Watching what appeared to be a clear and golden dawn come up over the snowy streets of Detroit, he stood by the window, smoking, for hours. Steam from the vents underneath the road poured up into the lightening sky.

In spite of the fact that he'd only known him for just a few days, he couldn't bear the idea that Gerald Diaz was dead. As far as İkmen had been able to tell, Diaz had been a straight, thoughtful, proactive cop who didn't just like to take the soft shifts and easy ways out all the time. Like İkmen himself, he'd been both in love with and scarred by his city. Diaz had policed a city that was unrecognisable from the place of his birth. That showed commitment and courage, and İkmen liked people who had those qualities. He looked down at the message that Diaz had sent him via his cell phone, and yet again he thought about what it meant.

If 'Got him' did indeed refer to Grant T. Miller's alleged involvement in the death of Elvis Goins, he wondered what evidence Diaz had uncovered that had led him to that conclusion. No doubt his colleagues would find that out as they unravelled the details surrounding his last day alive. Not that it was any of İkmen's business. The conference would go on as before and his life would return to normal. But even so, he was glad that he'd managed to speak to Officer Addison and bring up the subject of Ezekiel Goins and his dead son. If in some way Diaz's death was connected to that old crime, then the text message could prove to be key.

İkmen didn't know what else Diaz had been working on when he died apart from the drive-by killing in Brush Park. A young boy out exploring a derelict house had been gunned down for no apparent reason. Such things happened with, to İkmen, alarming regularity in Detroit. Gangs fought gangs and also the police, and people either got in the way or they looked 'wrong'. But then the logical conclusion to every system or organisation was chaos. Turf wars never stayed turf wars; they spilled out into other areas, involved other people and ultimately brought those who sought to propagate them down. The trouble was, that sometimes took a while.

Çetin İkmen didn't sleep at all that night. When he and Süleyman went over to the conference centre, he felt exhausted and wired in equal measure. After a while, he left, telling Süleyman that he was going back to the hotel.

Chapter 13

'It was Diaz as told me to git,' Ezekiel Goins said as he sat sadly on his old chair in the middle of the snow-covered garden. Although still weak, the sun was out and it wasn't as cold as it had been. 'When I went up Brush Park to Miller when Elvis died, it was Diaz as got me out of there.'

'You were chewing on Miller's arm, yes, I know.' Martha Bell had heard this story a thousand times before. She brushed some snow off the chair beside Zeke's and sat down.

'Diaz knew that what I done was 'cause of my grief and because Miller *did* kill Elvis. He told me to git. Him and Sosobowski knew as Miller wouldn't bring no charges.'

Martha put a hand on the old man's shoulder.

He sighed. 'I know Diaz weren't never going to do nothing about my boy now,' he said. 'But with him gone, it's like everyone who knew Elvis is dead.'

'I know.' Martha hugged him to her. Gerald Diaz's death had been a big shock to everyone at Antoine Cadillac. The lieutenant had supported the community work right from the start, and it was he who often smoothed things over for the tenants when they had issues with Detroit PD. Everybody liked Diaz, even if he could be distant at times. Martha couldn't think who'd want to kill him.

'Maybe it was a drive-by?' she said out loud.

Zeke nodded in agreement. 'Maybe,' he said. 'In spite of all you do, Martha, there still kids want to do that.'

'I know.'

'Diaz couldn't do nothing about it either.'

'No.'

They sat, in Martha's case wrapped in fake fur, amongst the snowy gardens of Antoine Cadillac, listening to the sound of the ice melting in the welcome winter sun. As it thawed, the ice creaked, reminding Zeke of the sound his old front door had made when Elvis used to sneak out to peddle drugs back in the old days. Both of them felt like sleeping. They'd been woken early that morning by one of the women down the corridor who called to say she'd heard that Gerald Diaz had been shot. She'd learned it from the little white junkie, Belinda, who'd spent some of the previous night down at PD headquarters reporting her bag stolen. She'd had all the money she needed for her next fix in the bag and so she'd been howling for justice. But even through that she'd picked up about what had happened to Diaz.

'I guess sometime you have to accept that a thing is at an end,' Zeke said.

Martha, who had been trying to get the old man to do just that ever since she'd met him, said, 'I guess.'

'Elvis is dead, his mama too. John Sosobowski died years ago; now Diaz. Only Miller . . .'

'You have to let Miller go, same as everything else,' Martha said. 'In fact you have to let Miller go more'n anything or anyone else.'

But the old man didn't appear to be listening to her any more. His attention had been caught by something way across the gardens. For such an old man, he stood up quickly. 'It's him!' he said, and then he laughed.

Martha, who had needed glasses for at least ten years, tried to peer through the fog of her short-sightedness. All she could see was a blob. 'Who?'

Ezekiel Goins looked down at her and smiled. 'My Turkish cop,' he said. 'Now he's here, everything'll be all right.'

Martha Bell put her head in her hands and groaned. 'Oh, sweet Jesus,' she said. 'Not this again!'

There was nothing. Not on or in Gerald Diaz's desk, not in his brief-case or even on his computer. Beyond his request for a ballistics report from Rob Weiss, there was nothing in Diaz's effects that linked him in any way to the gun he had supposedly confiscated from Grant T. Miller. There wasn't even a copy of the paperwork that had belonged to the weapon. And yet Rita Addison knew for a fact that Miller had taken a shot at the two Turkish officers. They'd told her. There had been no reason for them to lie.

What really bothered her, however, was Diaz's history with Miller. Rumour had it that back in the 1970s, when Diaz and John Sosobowski had attended his house after Ezekiel Goins attacked him, the two officers had persuaded Miller to drop the charges, rather than Miller himself making that decision. Had Diaz, she wondered, been setting Grant T. Miller up in some way? The two Turks had decided not to press charges against him. Had the fact that Miller had, in effect, got away with it again made Diaz mad enough to try and frame him for that Brush Park drive-by? But if that was the case, then how?

Although he would never have openly admitted it, Diaz could very possibly have believed that Miller had killed Elvis Goins. The boy had been dealing heroin at a time when gangs of all different kinds across the city had been competing to get as many people on to the drug as they possibly could. By the seventies, the long Motor City dominance of the car industry was most definitely on the wane, and a lot of people were unemployed and without much hope for the future. What else was there to do *but* get high?

Most of the dealers who'd dominated the streets at the time were long dead. However, those who many in the city believed had manipu-lated and covertly controlled the gangs from behind the scenes were another matter. Several prominent local politicians as well as members of the Detroit PD itself had been, at various times, suspected of involvement in the drugs trade back in the day. But there had never been any sort of proof against any of them. The old Detroit story, as far as Rita was concerned: of corruption, abuse of power and the exploitation of the poor.

Then again, had that Beretta even belonged to Miller? None of its paperwork apparently existed, apart from Weiss's report. But that didn't say anything about who the owner of the piece might be. That Diaz had taken the weapon from Miller was a matter of fact. Where it had gone after Weiss had tested it was unknown. As far as Rita could tell, the ballistics man had tested the weapon late and in a hurry. His report had been thin and sketchy. However, according to that same ballistic laboratory report, the gun had been handed back to Diaz once the tests had been completed. But it was no longer in Diaz's possession. Had he maybe given it back to Miller?

The shot that had killed Gerald Diaz had not come from a Beretta, and so the weapon was not in the frame for his killing. But according to the Turks, Diaz had believed that Miller had other guns apart from the Beretta. That said, why would Miller kill Diaz anyway? So Diaz had been snooping around! Ever since Elvis Goins' death, certain members of Detroit PD had been looking with suspicion at Grant T. Miller. It was nothing new. The only thing that was novel was the fact that the arrival of the Turkish police officers had apparently agitated Elvis's dad, Ezekiel, again. He'd gone back to shouting his mouth off about Miller, and Gerald Diaz, Rita knew, had become very worked up about that.

One thing was for certain: if the text message Diaz had sent to Inspector İkmen had actually been intended for the Turk, it could only refer to Grant T. Miller. 'Got him' in that context, to that person, could only mean that. And yet, got him how? For Elvis Goins' murder? For what?

Diaz's office phone rang then, and Addison picked it up.

*   *   *

109

According to one 'fan', Ali Kuban's greatest 'hit' had been a night-time assault on a sixteen-year-old gypsy girl in the lee of the city walls at Sulukule. Apparently he'd kept up a sustained attack on her for several hours, and raped her three times. Two years later, her parents had found her dead body hanging from the rafters of their home, which was not even five minutes away from where she'd been attacked. In the note she left behind, she'd said it was the nightmares that made her do it. She just couldn't stand to see her rapist's face any more.

'It is said that psychologists can tell whether someone who enjoys the idea of a certain type of crime is capable of actually committing an offence similar to it,' İzzet Melik said as he stood next to Ayşe Farsakoğlu at her office computer. They were looking at Kuban's fan site, which made, apparently, ever more disturbing reading.

'I think the one who calls himself "Monster" could be escalating,' Ayşe said. 'To me, what he writes signals a heightening of excitement. Here.' She quoted: '*Just imagining the fear makes me hot. I wish I had a girl here with me now.* You see?'

İzzet shrugged. 'Sort of. But Sergeant, you know that men, particularly young ones, can put on the most ridiculous shows of bravado.'

'Yes.' But about rape? Surely that had to be a step too far?

'Also, some men and even boys get off on violent sex, as we well know,' İzzet continued. 'Whether this "Monster" really is one of them, I'm not qualified to say.'

Monitoring Kuban's fan site was not actually their job. Ayşe had been all but told by Ardıç that she should stop doing it. But because she was so uneasy about it, she couldn't. İzzet, although he didn't actually support her in this activity, did provide her with a listening ear. In a way he hoped that talking to him whilst looking at the site would help her to exorcise some of the fear she felt because of it. A lot of men, it seemed, admired Kuban's 'work', and he could easily imagine that for a woman to contemplate such a thing was disquieting.

110

'These men move around amongst women and girls all the time. Every day!' Ayşe said. 'They could be teachers, doctors, police officers, anything!'

In spite of her mounting anxiety, he only tentatively put a hand on her shoulder. He was in love with her, but he didn't want her to know that. That would be unprofessional and quite wrong, and besides, she didn't reciprocate his feelings.

'And I hate to think of that terrible old creature encouraging these men!' Ayşe said.

'Ali Kuban?'

'Well, I imagine he's getting off on all this praise!'

Whether she'd even noticed his hand on her shoulder, İzzet didn't know. Probably not. In all likelihood she looked upon him no differently from the way she viewed her own brother. But that, he told himself, was OK.

'I just wish I didn't feel so helpless to do anything about this,' Ayşe continued. 'I mean, it's all very well to say that we can't do anything until an offence is committed . . .'

'If we did, our prisons would burst,' İzzet said. 'Having potential for something is not the same as actually doing it.'

'Oh!' Ayşe shook her head impatiently, and then sighed. This calmed her a little and she said, 'I know. Intellectually, I know. But in my heart . . .' She shrugged.

İzzet took his hand off her shoulder and sat down beside her. 'It's mostly fantasy, I think,' he said. 'Everyone fantasises. Not everyone, fortunately, fantasises about violence. But a lot do. Young boys in particular, especially now.'

'Because?'

'Because of images they are exposed to online, on television, on news broadcasts. Look at how violent that *Valley of the Wolves* series is! That directly taps into the perfectly reasonable patriotic feelings that many people have, and makes being a Turk synonymous with being some sort of bigoted super-soldier!'

111

Ayşe too was far from keen on the hit series *Valley of the Wolves*, with its graphic violence and heavily nationalistic message. But she was surprised to see that it upset İzzet Melik so much. Men like him generally lapped up such programmes. But then İzzet was no ordinary mustachioed macho man. Brought up in the liberal city of İzmir, he had been educated by an Italian-speaking Jew who had imparted to him a love of all things Latin.

'But people very rarely act on their fantasies,' İzzet said. 'Or if they do, it's something that they do alone or through books or films. Again, our prisons just wouldn't cope if all these people were punished for their unhealthy desires. Sexual assault, if you look at the instances that take place outside the family, is very rare. Rape still makes headlines because it's so unusual.'

Ayşe knew that. And yet because sexual assault within families was known to happen, if only according to unreliable anecdotal evidence, there was, she felt, still an undercurrent of approval amongst some men. And if her occasional reading of some English-language newspapers was to be believed, such attitudes still held sway abroad too. Large numbers of men, it seemed, remained wedded to the idea that women only existed to do their bidding and bring them pleasure. She looked at İzzet and smiled. With other men he had a reputation for being a rough handful. But with the women in the department he was always very sympathetic and polite – especially to her. Ayşe knew that İzzet had been divorced for a number of years, and wondered why that had happened. In a strange sort of way, although heavy and rather ugly, he was really quite a catch.

'You can turn the place upside-down,' Grant T. Miller said as John Shalhoub and a group of officers that included Rita Addison walked into his house. 'You'll only find what remains of an old man's life.'

They didn't have to tell Miller what they were looking for, only that they needed to search the place. But Shalhoub had told Rita and the other officers that they were looking for firearms. Shalhoub it had been who had first discovered that the Beretta that Weiss had tested for Diaz could have come from Miller. Shalhoub had learned something else from Weiss too, which he had also passed on to his team. It was that the bullet that had been found at the supposed drive-by shooting of Aaron Spencer had almost certainly come from the self-same gun.

'I've never done drugs in my life,' Miller said as he followed Rita into his dust-covered living room. Every surface was piled high with old newspapers, even the ancient harmonium that his mother had liked to play on Sunday evenings. On the floor, what had once been a very fine Persian carpet melted into the wet and rotting floorboards underneath. The whole place stank of mice and of mould. 'And as for pornography,' he continued, 'what would I do with that?'

Rita looked around at him and saw the leer that crossed his face as he viewed her from behind.

'I'm an old man,' he said. 'What would be the point?'

Rita didn't reply. In her experience, a lot of old men could and would look at porn, some of it hard-core. Some of them would even act on their fantasies, or try to with their unfortunate wives or with prostitutes. She set about lifting up a pile of papers, the top edition of which was dated 1987. Shalhoub and Zevets were upstairs, while two other officers were in the room that Miller used as a kitchen. Once he'd finished looking at Rita, the old man headed down there to make himself some coffee.

Officers Smith and O'Reilly were making quite a mess of Miller's provision cupboard by the time he arrived. Unopened but now broken packets of Oreo biscuits lay scattered over the floor, together with boxes and boxes of old cube sugar.

'My mother used to use this as a sewing room,' Miller said as he flicked the switch on his kettle and then spooned some cheap instant coffee into a cracked bone-china cup. 'But when the tower rooms went, back in the eighties, they took the kitchen with 'em and so we decamped here.'

Smith pulled open the doors of an art deco gramophone cupboard and began removing saucepans and cake tins. O'Reilly wondered what a badass old racist like Miller would feel about having Smith and Addison rooting through his stuff. The old man, it was said, used the 'n' word very freely when the mood took him.

'Shame, really,' Miller continued. 'This was an elegant room when my mother was young. She'd sit here and sew, listen to Brahms on the gramophone. She was a very cultured southern lady.'

Smith looked across at O'Reilly, who very gently shook his head. No one really knew whether Miller's old 'southern gentleman' thing was really part of his personality or not. It was certainly, in his mind at least, a part of himself that he valued very highly. Maybe it actually took him away from all the vile and unjust things he'd done to people over the years. Perhaps it was, if a person was feeling charitable about it, something of a defence mechanism.

Miller tapped Smith on the shoulder. The police officer looked around into a pair of brilliant blue, seemingly amused eyes. 'You looking for weapons, are you?' Miller said.

O'Reilly stopped what he was doing and made to stand up. 'Mr Miller . . .'

''Cause if you are, then I got a nice little Glock 18 you might like,' Miller said. 'Had it years. These days, given my financial embarrassment, it's the only piece I retain. You boys like to see it, would you?'

114

Chapter 14

Çetin İkmen didn't tell Ezekiel Goins anything he didn't already know. Diaz was dead, and no one, as yet, knew who had killed him or why. He didn't allude in any way at all to the text the dead man had sent him. His motive for going to see Zeke Goins was more to do with just being there as a fellow man who had lost his son. For the Turk, this, his first trip to America, had been upsetting. He hadn't expected that. He'd imagined that by distancing himself from Turkey for a while, he might actually get some relief from thoughts about his dead son. But because of the old man and now also because of Diaz's death, he felt more intimately connected to his grief than he had done for a while.

'In Gerald Diaz we had a good friend and ally up at the department,' Martha Bell said as she put a cup of coffee in front of İkmen on her kitchen table. 'Now?' She shrugged. 'Too many Detroit PD want to punish the kids that hang on these streets, criminalise their habits, send them crazy so they drive around shooting people. Don't need to be like Gladys Knight and hear it through the grapevine to know that's true.'

Because she was so strong, it was easy sometimes to forget that Martha had lost a son too. Ezekiel Goins, who had come inside with them, said, 'Sam'll help us keep the gardens going, Martha. He knows people.'

'Oh, I ain't afraid for Antoine Cadillac so much,' she said. 'Everyone knows what we do and why we do it. No, I had plans and Diaz knew it and he was open to supporting me.'

115

'Plans for more community organisations across the city?' İkmen asked.

'Yeah.' She sat down and drank her coffee. 'You get enough people involved, you teach them how what we do can benefit them, you can start to tame the streets. Going around busting everyone all the time ain't gonna get you nowhere.'

'For some time, and certainly since my son Bekir died, I have been thinking that the problem of drug use is really a health rather than a judicial problem,' İkmen said.

'Damn straight,' Martha concurred. 'Almighty God knows, if I could find who killed my boy I'd want to beat the life out of him. But knowing that he was probably a kid and almost certainly an addict, part of me also wants to help him too.'

'She's a good, good person, Inspector,' Ezekiel Goins said to İkmen. 'I ain't. All I wanna do is take revenge for my boy.'

'You should know who killed your children, both of you,' İkmen said. 'The pain of my own loss is sometimes more than I feel I can bear. But at the very least I have the knowledge of exactly how my son died, why and by whose hand. I would be lying if I said that those facts were of comfort. But I do feel that Bekir can rest now, even if I cannot.'

They drank their coffee and smoked their cigarettes in silence for a few moments then, each one of them focused upon his or her individual grief. But after a few moments, İkmen's thoughts turned back to Zeke Goins again. With Diaz dead, the old man had to be feeling that all his connections with the past, as well as the small amount of support that the lieutenant had given him, had gone. Now he had to wonder whether anyone would ever get to the bottom of what had happened to Elvis.

The words 'Got him' came back into İkmen's mind yet again. What worried at him was the notion that somehow Diaz had found a connection between Grant T. Miller and the death of Elvis Goins. If that had indeed happened, then there was no way that such information

116

should be allowed to die with the lieutenant. Detroit PD were dealing with Diaz's death, but were they factoring in that text İkmen had received?

'So when you off back to Turkey?' Martha asked as she poured some more coffee into İkmen's cup.

'At the weekend,' he said.

'Don't give you too much time left here,' she replied.

'No.'

Silence washed in again. When it was finally broken, it was by the old man. 'Can't say I'm looking forward to that,' he said.

İkmen didn't reply. His mind was too busy trying to find some way whereby he might be able to stay. When he didn't find one, he resolved to speak to Officer Addison and ask for her help. He knew that it could very easily be a dead end.

Going back to the hotel to a no doubt recumbent İkmen was not Mehmet Süleyman's idea of a good time. But there was no three o'clock lecture as usual, and so delegates had what they called 'free' time in the city.

An officer from Mexico City and the British officers were going off to the Motown Museum and had invited him to go along with them. But Süleyman had never really got into the Motown sound, and so the idea of spending a few hours looking at old recording equipment and listening to the Supremes didn't appeal.

What he had to do was get to some shops and find something uniquely American to take back home for his little boy, Yusuf. Apart from wanting to buy something for him, he also didn't need the disgust he'd no doubt get from his ex-wife should he return empty-handed. But what he could buy apart from a baseball cap, a T-shirt or some sort of computer game, he didn't know. Unable to interest the lovely Donna Ferrari in any extracurricular activities, he eventually gave his cousin Tayyar Bekdil a call. Tayyar was working on a rather complicated financial piece about some new development money that was going to be awarded to the city from Washington, and needed a break. He came and picked Süleyman up from the Cobo Center and took him to a restaurant in Greektown called Kleopatra.

'I don't know whether you're going to be eating with Çetin later, but they do a fantastic meze here,' Tayyar said, 'and I had no lunch.'

Süleyman had only really played around with the, to him, rather tasteless hamburgers they'd been given for lunch, and so he was very pleased to have the opportunity to eat something more familiar. Greektown, as the name implied, was where immigrants to Detroit from Greece had first settled. Both the menu and the surroundings, if not the bouzouki music, were familiar and welcome things.

'They make excellent falafel here,' Tayyar said as they sat down at a table beneath a large picture of the Acropolis. He called out his order to one of the waiters and poured a glass of water for his cousin. 'I've been thinking about you, actually,' he said to Süleyman. 'Or rather, Çetin İkmen and his interest in the Goins family.'

Süleyman told Tayyar how Diaz had warned İkmen off, and also how Diaz himself was now dead. Tayyar frowned. 'Gerald Diaz?'

'Yes. Did you know him?'

'No, but I knew of him,' Tayyar said. 'Very involved with community organisations. I heard something about an officer being shot, but I didn't know it was him. Was it a drive-by?'

'I don't know.'

'Mmm.' Tayyar shook his head. 'You know, after you and Çetin left the other evening, I looked up the Goins family in our archives. I interviewed Sam Goins, Ezekiel's big-wheel councillor brother, just after I came to Detroit. He doesn't buy the whole Turkish connection, or indeed any other supposed Melungeon ethnicity of origin. His whole thing is about achieving equality for his people.'

'That's a very good aim.'

'Of course, the Melungeons, just like the blacks, have had to put up with discrimination in all areas of their lives since they came to this country. By rising to become a councillor, Sam Goins has proved to his people that it can be done. I don't know the story of how he pulled himself up out of the rank and file, but it must have taken some guts.'

'Absolutely.'

The waiter brought them long glasses of sherbet and told them that their meze would not be long. When he had gone, Tayyar said, 'How Sam got to where he did, I have no idea. He came to prominence, as far as I can tell, in the early 1980s. When his nephew died, he was still just a grunt working the line.'

'Oh well.' Süleyman was not greatly interested in the Goins family, mainly because İkmen had gone on about Ezekiel and his dead son so much. He had also, it had to be remembered, almost got them both shot in pursuit of Ezekiel Goins' old adversary Grant T. Miller.

'Personally, and not detracting in any way from Sam's achievement, I think that someone in that family must have had money,' Tayyar said.

Süleyman looked doubtful. Ezekiel Goins was virtually a vagrant. 'Really?'

'Yes,' Tayyar said.

'How do you know?'

'When Elvis Goins died, his funeral took place at Woodlawn Cemetery. It's where the great and the good get buried,' Tayyar said. 'Not the place you'd expect to find a backstreet hoodlum like Elvis Goins. A Mafia boss, yes, but much as Elvis may have fancied himself one of those, he wasn't. Very expensive funeral, very expensive monument, and Sam Goins, as far as I can tell, was no one at the time. So where did the money come from?'

Süleyman looked blank. But then their food arrived, and for a while they talked of other, more pleasant things. Halfway through their meal, however, Tayyar returned to the subject one more time. 'Regarding Elvis Goins,' he said, frowning again as he spoke, 'tell

119

Çetin about that elaborate funeral he had, won't you? I know he's supposed to leave all that alone now, but tell him anyway.'

Süleyman said that he would.

Officer Addison was in the hotel lobby, apparently waiting for Çetin İkmen. She looked tense, and as soon as she saw him, she walked over to him and asked if she might come up to his suite. This caught İkmen unawares. He wasn't accustomed to women asking to come to his room. 'Oh, well, er . . .'

Not that he thought for a minute that Addison had designs upon his body. He knew that he was no Mehmet Süleyman, or even, for that matter, Gerald Diaz either. But Rita Addison put her head down close to his ear and said, 'It's about the gun that Grant T. Miller shot at you with.'

It was nearly five o'clock, but Süleyman still wasn't back, which was, İkmen felt, probably no bad thing. The younger man was still a little touchy on the subject of their recent adventures outside Miller's house in Brush Park. İkmen led Officer Addison over to what counted as their living area and ushered her into one of the plastic armchairs.

'Inspector İkmen,' she said, 'can you confirm to me that the weapon that Lieutenant Diaz took off Grant T. Miller was a Beretta PX4?'

İkmen too sat down, and after asking Rita's permission, he lit up a cigarette. 'It was certainly a Beretta,' he said. 'Why?'

Even though she knew that the hotel suite was entirely private, Rita Addison looked about nervously. Once she was entirely satisfied that they were alone, she told him all about the missing Beretta, and how it hadn't turned up, as she had expected, at Grant T. Miller's home.

'He had a little Glock 18,' she said. 'That was it!'

İkmen frowned. 'The lieutenant said to me that he imagined that Mr Miller had a lot of weapons. I think it was because he was once a man of substance, who lived quite alone.'

'Diaz wouldn't have held on to the Beretta for no reason,' Rita said, ploughing her own furrow of thought. 'Miller called him after he confiscated the weapon. Asking for it back? Who knows? The lieutenant sent it to ballistics, where it was checked out against our records by Dr Weiss.'

'And?'

'And at that time there was nothing wrong with the piece; it wasn't on any wanted list.'

'Was it old?'

'Old?'

'In light of the text that the lieutenant sent to me, I wonder if the Beretta was the weapon that could have killed Elvis Goins. I imagine you still have evidence from that crime, including maybe the bullet that killed the boy?'

'I don't know,' Rita said. 'But that could make sense.'

'It could.'

'What doesn't make sense, though, is that there are no records on the system of Miller ever having owned a Beretta. Now if Diaz had discovered that Miller didn't have the right documentation for the gun, he would never have given it back to him.'

'But you said that Miller didn't have it,' İkmen said.

'No, he didn't. He just had the Glock,' Rita said. 'We've taken that in, but . . .' She shrugged. 'A Beretta PX4 certainly passed through ballistics on Diaz's orders. Now it's disappeared. Diaz took it from Grant T. Miller and you witnessed him doing it.'

'I did.'

'And it was certainly a Beretta.'

'The lieutenant said so, yes. I didn't get a close look at it myself.'

'But it existed!' Rita said.

'Of course.'

'And yet if you look on Diaz's computer records, there's nothing about it. That gun is not registered centrally, there's no paperwork, apart from the Glock in the name of Grant T. Miller.' She leaned forward. 'Diaz would have confiscated an illegal piece. The only way

121

that wouldn't have happened would have been if he was in Grant T. Miller's pocket, and that I don't believe for a moment! But that doesn't mean that no one in the department is on the take. Erasing records on computer can be easy if you know what you're doing.'

İkmen, who knew absolutely nothing about that, kept his counsel.

'Inspector İkmen, I don't know what any of this means, but what I do know is that a slug we took out of an old house in Brush Park that killed a kid called Aaron Spencer came from that Beretta. Our ballistics guy is a hundred per cent on that,' Rita said. 'But if we're not careful, all knowledge about the gun that fired it is going to disappear. Would you be willing to sign a statement to the effect that the weapon existed?'

İkmen thought for a moment, then he said, 'Officer Addison, of course I will. But there may be something else I can do as well.'

It was going to be the easiest thousand dollars Kyle had ever earned. He'd put the gun on the front seat of the big old Chrysler he was about to crush, and that was that. Problem over for his customer, a thousand big ones for him, everybody happy. It wasn't the first time Kyle had done something a little bit to the left-hand side of the law. Once, long ago, there'd even been what he imagined from its size was a dead body, all wrapped up in plastic. Five hundred dollars had secured that crushed inside an Oldsmobile. When you wrecked cars for a living, sometimes shit happened. He wasn't a rich man, and so when opportunities came along, he tended to take them.

At first, Kyle put the weapon on the front seat of the Chrysler, but then he took it out again. Guns, if used correctly, could be worth a *lot* of money. If someone was willing to pay him a thousand bucks to get rid of this one, then it had to be in a way a sort of embarrassment to them. They wouldn't want it to resurface some time later. Crushing would avoid this.

What crushing wouldn't do was make Kyle more money in the future. Only using the theory of insurance, in other words hanging on to the gun, could do that. After all, if its owner really did want it gone that much, another thousand or so when Kyle's next alimony payment came up wouldn't be here or there. Kyle went to pocket the gun when a voice behind him said, 'What are you doing?'

It was him. Suddenly afraid, Kyle turned and began very slowly to move the gun back through the Chrysler's front window again.

'You were going to keep it? As insurance?'

On reflection, blackmail had been a bad idea, but Kyle was now too terrified to say so. Christ, he'd been watching him! But then Kyle might have guessed that he would. He told him to get inside the cab, start the crusher and get the Chrysler, and the gun, destroyed immediately. Kyle didn't need to be asked twice. He climbed into the machine and did the job while the man looked on. Kyle was sweating. All he could hope was that the man didn't go back on the deal and withhold his thousand bucks.

Once the Chrysler was crushed, Kyle got out of the machine and walked across the yard to where the man stood. Although it was dark by this time, he didn't want to receive money out in the open, and so he told the man to come to the small Portakabin that was his office. Kyle wasn't a small man, and he had to squeeze his gut in to get behind his desk. As he did so, the man put one hand on his shoulder while he stabbed him with a knife held in his other hand. No one was due to come to the yard that night, and so the man had all the time in the world to wait and watch while Kyle bled to death on his little office floor. Afterwards, he put Kyle's body into his own crusher and squashed it down quite flat. Then he set fire to the Portakabin.

Chapter 15

The final day of the conference was, in effect, one big plenary session albeit subdued due to Diaz's death. It was a case of reviewing what had been presented and what had been learned. To İkmen, the most valuable part of the course had been the visit out to Antoine Cadillac Project. That, if nothing else, had inspired him. Official police engagement with community organisations was a new concept to him. Of course he'd always had his informants, his little networks of people he knew he could always call on to give him information. But this was different; this was by way of being a partnership between police and public. How the concept would transfer to the booming, ancient city of İstanbul, he didn't know, but he could certainly vouch for its utility in one of the USA's most troubled cities.

The previous evening he had agreed to give a statement to the Detroit PD about the missing Beretta. If what Officer Addison believed was true, Grant T. Miller might well have killed a young black boy, although quite why he would have done so was very unclear. The old man was a known racist, but that didn't necessarily mean he killed people who were different from himself. On the other hand, did this now mean that Gerald Diaz's text made sense? Although 'Got him' still referred to Grant T. Miller, did it relate not to Elvis Goins but to this dead child Aaron Spencer? The ballistics evidence certainly pointed in that direction, but without the Beretta itself, there was as yet no concrete proof. However, İkmen knew that if what he'd suggested to Rita Addison went to plan, there could be another way to catch Mr Grant T. Miller that did not directly involve the weapon itself.

The Chief of Detroit PD was due to officially close the conference at four p.m., but İkmen noticed that he also attended the final luncheon too. That was useful. A powerful-looking black man, probably, İkmen thought, in his forties, the Chief was surrounded by city dignitaries as well as by a coterie of his senior officers.

'This food is terrible again,' Süleyman said as he laid his knife and fork on the side of his very full lunch plate.

İkmen looked over at him. 'Not much longer now.' He'd thought that his friend and colleague would have been more curious and excited about visiting an unknown American city. But he'd been by turns alarmed and bored by Detroit ever since they'd landed. İkmen imagined that in reality he'd been in the wrong frame of mind to go anywhere. Recently ejected from what had been his marital home, he was back with his parents and his widowed brother. It wasn't easy. Although Süleyman rarely talked about it, his father was clearly becoming confused, while his mother, a lifelong social climber, was still refusing to accept that her family could not financially support her excessive clothes and accessories habit.

'I'm going out for a cigarette,' Süleyman said. 'Are you coming?'

İkmen wanted to, but as the senior Turkish officer at the lunch, he felt he was duty-bound to stay and have yet another go at a meal that was, apparently, some sort of roasted meat dish.

'No, but you go.' He smiled. Süleyman left, and İkmen looked back at the Chief of the Detroit PD once again. If he was not very much mistaken, the Chief was talking very earnestly now to someone who certainly was not a senior officer. It was Rita Addison. That was good.

It was completely and utterly irrational, but just the thought of İkmen's return after the weekend made Ayşe Farsakoğlu feel reassured. Whatever Ali Kuban and his fan club might be planning, just having İkmen back would, she knew, give her confidence. Stupidly, she'd told this to İzzet, who had then looked a little bit crestfallen. He'd been thinking that just his presence was not enough for her, and in that, in a way, he'd

125

been right. Over the years, Ayşe had come to appreciate İzzet much more than she had done when she'd first met him. Both he and she had mellowed over time. But İkmen was in a different league altogether. Solid and utterly dependable, he was like the father she'd lost only three months ago. Haluk Farsakoğlu had been devoted to two things during the course of his life: his family, and his job as a guard on the railway. His death had affected both of his children enormously, but Ayşe was particularly bereft. Her father had never earned much money, had never been out of Turkey and had hardly ever done anything that was just specifically for his own pleasure. But he'd been a happy and generous man, and she missed him horribly.

Without her very sympathetic superior, it would, she knew, have been so much worse. İkmen had given her as much time off as she felt she needed, and had made sure that she wasn't over-taxing herself ever since. In a way, although he would never have presumed to give voice to such a notion, he was a kind of surrogate father to her. In reality, he always had been.

Ayşe put her paperwork in the top drawer of her desk and locked it. She was taking one last look at the Ali Kuban fan site when İzzet Melik knocked on her office door and she beckoned him in. 'I'm going to the Black Sea pide place, if you'd like to join me,' he said. The Black Sea Pide Restaurant was where some officers liked to have lunch from time to time, but it was also open in the evenings. 'Pide, I find,' he added, 'is very warming now that the nights are drawing in.'

'Yes, it is.' She smiled.

'And so . . .'

She'd had a very nice evening with him in the Kaktus earlier in the week, but her brother was back from Azerbaijan and so she was expected to cook for both of them. İzzet, though disappointed, said that of course he understood. She smiled, bade him good night and then looked back at her computer screen again.

İzzet Melik had just opened her office door when she called him back. 'I want you to see this,' she said as she led him back to her

126

desk and sat him down in front of her screen. 'Just in case I might be imagining it.'

İzzet read it out loud. '*An event for all of you to appreciate is happening Saturday midnight. Guess where!*'

There was nothing to indicate where the message had come from. As İzzet told Ayşe later when they were both sitting in the Sultan Pub over half-litres of Efes Pilsen, it could have come from Kuban, or from one of his fans, or even from someone wanting to taunt and tantalise visitors to the site.

'Kuban and the people we've identified from the site so far are being monitored,' İzzet said.

'If it is Kuban, the "where" he speaks about could be Sulukule,' Ayşe said. By now she'd called her brother and told him that she'd had to work late and that he'd have to get his own supper. He hadn't been pleased, but Ayşe didn't care. 'I wish I could say that I didn't feel as if something terrible were about to happen, but I can't.'

'You sound like your boss,' İzzet said, referring to İkmen and his occasional and often very accurate feelings about situations and people. 'We don't know that it's Kuban. It could just be a sick joke. I'm sure that Vice will take care of it.'

'Saturday is tomorrow,' Ayşe said.

'Yes, but if you know, then Vice . . .'

'I'm calling the Commissioner,' Ayşe said. 'If there's going to be some sort of operation mounted tomorrow, then I want in on it.' She rummaged in her handbag for her phone.

'I know that you feel strongly about this . . .'

'If you were a woman, you would too,' Ayşe said as she pulled the phone out of her bag and began to search through her directory for the Commissioner's office number. 'İzzet, the fact that internet sites like this exist at all means that far too many men get off on the notion of hurting women. And if women won't do anything to try and change that, then who will?'

* * *

127

Çetin İkmen couldn't remember exactly where he'd been when Grant T. Miller had shot at himself and Mehmet Süleyman.

'We both hit the ground quickly,' he said to Rita Addison and her companion, the ballistics expert Rob Weiss. 'I think I may have actually been in the middle of the road.'

With absolutely no regard for either his clothes or the fact that the ground was still covered with snow, İkmen lowered himself until he was lying face down in the road. Turning his head to one side so that he was looking at Miller's house, he said, 'Yes, about here.' He got up again. 'It was good there was no traffic that day.'

'There's very rarely much traffic up here, Inspector,' Rob Weiss said. 'This part of northern Brush Park is a house graveyard.' He looked sad. 'Used to live here myself.'

Rita Addison looked surprised. 'I didn't know that.'

'Back in the day, Brush Park was all lumber barons, auto bosses and Jewish doctors like my father,' Weiss said.

'Did you know Grant T. Miller, Dr Weiss?'

'Oh yes.' He gave a wry smile. 'Everyone knew Grant and his mother, Rose. A regular Blanche DuBois that one, all southern manners, big hats and church on a Sunday. Right up until the late seventies, Grant T. used to take her out in that massive old Packard Pan American of his. Man, that car was like his child! All fussing over it and shining it like a mother hen! But Gustav, Grant's father, he was something else. Couldn't read or write in any language, but he made great suits.'

'For Henry Ford, I believe,' İkmen said.

'Weirdly, yes,' Rob Weiss said. 'And for my father, too. Gustav would come to our house sometimes and he and my dad would speak Yiddish together. He was a lonely man. His wife didn't love him and his son found him an embarrassment.' He looked down the road and pointed to an empty lot about two hundred metres away. 'That was where our house used to be.' It was a melancholy moment, made all the more poignant by the fact that darkness was falling.

The conversation that Rita Addison had had with the Chief of the Detroit PD at the conference lunch had not been the first one. As soon as she'd left İkmen's hotel the previous night, she'd gone straight back to headquarters and requested to see the Chief as soon as possible. She'd been offered all sorts of other officers higher up the chain than herself and lower than the Chief, but she had insisted. If paper and computer records were missing from Diaz's desk and his system, it was possible that someone in the department was to blame. The Chief finally became free for a few moments in the early hours of the morning, and it was then that Rita told him about the other bullet from the missing Beretta.

'Grant T. Miller fired at the Turkish officers, İkmen and Süleyman,' she said.

The Chief did, of course, ask what the hell the Turks had been doing out in Brush Park, so Rita told him what she knew about that, including the foreign officers' involvement with Ezekiel Goins. Although still at high school at the time, the Chief remembered the murder of Elvis Goins.

'As Inspector İkmen, the senior Turkish officer, put it, sir, if the bullet used to kill Aaron Spencer is from the same gun as the bullet Miller shot over the heads of him and his colleague, our need to find the actual Beretta becomes less important,' she said.

The Chief had concurred. But in that second conversation with Rita at the conference lunch he'd added, 'But remember, Officer Addison, whether we find this bullet or not, we need to know where that Beretta is, and if you're right about missing paperwork and computer records, we need to look at that situation too.' She'd been just about to go when he'd called her back and said, 'Oh, and that senior Turkish officer . . . If he's been as involved as you say, he might need to stay with us here in Detroit for a while longer. You should warn him. And I'll need the name of his superior back in Turkey.'

They all knew that now that night had fallen, and because the

129

street lamps had all been knocked or shot out, there was no point in their looking for the bullet until the following morning. Rob Weiss had just taken them out there so that İkmen could at least point him and any subsequent search teams in the right direction.

'I've no idea where the bullet went,' İkmen said, 'but . . .' he looked over at the silhouette of a large rotting pile of real estate directly across the road from the Windmill, 'that house, if that's what it is . . .'

Rob Weiss followed his gaze. 'The old Johnson house,' he said, and his face visibly fell. 'Old man Johnson was a dentist back in the fifties. He killed his wife and cut her body up with a kitchen knife. Then he went back to his surgery as if nothing had happened.'

There were people outside the Johnson place. He couldn't see who they were, because it was too dark, but Grant T. Miller didn't like them on principle. Only nuts and cruising gangsters came up to Brush Park these days, and he wasn't keen on either of those. Urban explorers, some of the youngsters who clambered in and out of the old wrecked buildings called themselves. What did they want to do that for? Nice middle-class kids? It beat Grant T. Then there were the ghouls, any age they could be, always looking for the house where the dentist cut his wife up with a kitchen knife and then buried bits of her all over the garden. He remembered Hiram Johnson well. He'd quite liked him. But if asked, he always told the ghouls that the Johnson place was miles away. For all he knew, they might start digging up the garden, looking for Mary Johnson's left foot. That had been the only part of her the cops had never found. There was so much the cops never found.

Back in the fifties, most of the houses had still been inhabited. That was one of the reasons why the Johnson case had been so shocking. Mary Johnson had been murdered by a 'good' neighbour while the local children played in their gardens, had their piano lessons, went off to church. Hiram's evil was of an ordinary type, but then that was how most evil was. Mundane.

130

Not that there had been anything mundane about what happened after all the nice normal (and evil) people moved out of Brush Park. By the 1970s, the place was full of nigger drug-dealers cruising the streets in convertibles, shooting the windows out of mansions that had once sheltered the great men who had built the motor industry. All the hillbillies, the spics, the wops, the Muslims, the so-called mixed-race abominations were let loose by that bastard Mayor Young and infected every part of the city. Bleating about being laid off from their jobs and having no money, they soon found cash for the drugs they all shoved in their arms or into their lungs. Then all of Detroit became a marketplace, and one of the little traders in it had been young Elvis Goins. A nothing, a nobody and a punk, but a punk who'd had a big mouth.

Grant T. Miller looked out into the street again, and this time it was completely empty.

Chapter 16

'Has Ardıç agreed to this?' Süleyman asked.

'Yes.' İkmen sat in one of the plastic armchairs in the living area while Süleyman packed his suitcase on his bed. 'If this bullet is found and it can be proved to have come from the same gun that killed the young boy who died while exploring Brush Park, then my statement that it was Grant Miller who fired the shot at us will be of importance. Ardıç said that the request came straight from the Chief of Detroit PD.'

'He fired at me too!' Süleyman said.

'Yes, I know, but would you want to spend any more time out here?' İkmen asked.

'No.' Süleyman walked out of his bedroom and over to İkmen. 'Çetin, I know that old man Goins . . .'

'Lieutenant Diaz sent me that text message for a reason,' İkmen said. 'Like Ezekiel Goins, Diaz always believed that Grant Miller killed Elvis. He never said so in as many words, but it was clear that he at the very least had suspicions.'

'You can't convict a man of an old crime with no evidence!' Süleyman said.

'But you can convict a man of a new crime with some evidence,' İkmen responded. 'Grant Miller may never serve time for the killing of Elvis Goins, but he might well have to serve a sentence for the murder of the young black boy.'

'If he did it.'

'Indeed.'

'I mean, I don't know why he'd kill a boy for just messing around in an old house,' Süleyman said.

'The boy was black and the man is a racist,' İkmen replied. 'As you know, he fired on us just because he thought we might be Hispanic. Albeit much better these days, this is Detroit, where racial tensions can still run high.'

Süleyman sighed. 'But I don't know why they need you to stay here,' he said. 'You could just give them a statement, couldn't you?'

'I could,' İkmen said. 'But they prefer that I stay.'

Süleyman went back into his bedroom and continued packing. They'd known each other long enough to recognise when nothing more needed to be said. Süleyman knew that İkmen was staying on in order to pursue the Elvis Goins mystery. Whether Detroit PD had really pushed him to remain or whether İkmen had actually volunteered, he didn't know. But Ardıç had approved it and so it was happening. İkmen, for his part, was glad, although he did feel sad about not being able to go home to his family. Also, being alone in a place that was so far from Turkey was not going to be easy. But as soon as Ezekiel Goins had approached him that first time back on Antoine Cadillac, he'd known to the very centre of his bones that he had to try to help him. Whatever his real ethnic background might be, it was one Turkish father appealing for help to another, and that was something İkmen could not resist.

He looked down at his watch and saw that it was nearly nine o'clock. 'I have to leave now,' he said to Süleyman.

The younger man turned and walked out of his bedroom. 'Where are you going?'

'To Brush Park, with Officer Addison and the ballistics people,' İkmen said. 'We have to find that bullet.'

'Of course.'

'I don't know when I'll be back. Might not be until the evening. You leave for the airport at . . .'

'Five,' Süleyman said.

'Right.'

They stood and looked at each other for a moment. Letting Süleyman go like this was not easy for İkmen. He had always thought that as well as going to the USA together, they'd go home together too. He opened his arms to take his friend in an embrace. Süleyman walked forward, kissed him on both cheeks and then hugged him.

'Going home alone will be dull,' he said.

'You slept most of the way over here,' İkmen replied.

Süleyman broke away from his embrace. 'Çetin, when you get home, please speak to someone about Bekir.'

İkmen, smarting a little at this interference in his private life, even by Süleyman, nevertheless smiled and then said, 'I must go. Travel safely.'

'İnşallah,' Süleyman replied.

İkmen left the suite and took the lift down to the lobby, where Rita Addison and Dr Weiss were waiting for him.

It had been a full twenty-four hours since the fire at Kyle Redmond's wrecking yard had been put out. It had started, the fire department reckoned, in Redmond's office. It had spread to a couple of sheds and some cars waiting to be wrecked, but had otherwise been quite localised. It was definitely a fire that had been set deliberately.

However, straightforward as the fire may have been, locating the owner of the business was proving rather more problematic. Kyle Redmond was not at the house he apparently shared with a load of green budgerigars over in Mexicantown. He worked for himself and alone, and so there were no other employees the police could contact. According to a neighbour, Redmond had an ex-wife somewhere, as well as money troubles. This same neighbour seemed unsurprised that his wrecking business had ended its life in flames.

'I'm not saying that Kyle set the fire himself, but at the same time, I can't see him crying over it either,' the man said.

According to Detroit PD records, Kyle Redmond had no criminal

134

convictions and his business was legitimate, if far from solvent. In other words, he wasn't 'known'. Or rather, he wasn't known for criminal activity. The investigating officer, Lieutenant Devine, felt that there was something familiar about the name Kyle Redmond, although he had no idea what that might be.

'Trouble is,' he told Sergeant Ferrari as they watched the forensics team continue their search of the site, 'I'm so damn old, I've met just about everyone.'

Donna Ferrari didn't comment. Devine was coming up for retirement, and she knew that it was something he feared. He went on about his age a lot, but in a nervous sort of way, as if he were both pleased and upset about his advancing years at the same time.

'If the man were here, I might be able to tell,' Devine continued. 'But there's something buzzing at the back of my head.' He put a strip of nicotine gum into his mouth and chewed. He'd given up smoking five years before; now he had to try to tackle his addiction to the gum he'd used to quit cigarettes. Life, the lugubrious Devine thought, was a 'valley of trouble', just as his grandma back in Georgia always used to say. Unlike him, old Grandma Bette had had the Lord to pull her through; he just had a vague thought about going off to Canada to fish when he retired.

The jaws of the wrecking machine were closed. They'd been like that when the fire officers had arrived. Presumably Kyle Redmond had shut the thing down either when he left as usual for the evening, or before he set the fire in his office. An investigator climbed into the machinery and set about assessing its condition.

Donna Ferrari, looking on, frowned. 'You know, if Redmond did set his own yard on fire, it's weird to me that he didn't torch the crusher. Surely it's the most valuable part of the set-up.'

'Maybe he was going to do that but someone disturbed him,' Devine replied. 'Until we find him, how can we know?'

The crushing machine was started up. A low whine at first, followed by a clanking sound as the jaws of the automobile eater slowly came

135

apart. Both Ferrari and Devine could see that there was something inside the mechanism, but they couldn't tell what it was. The investigator down on the ground beside the machine, however, could. He immediately called up to his colleague inside the cab: 'Switch the fucking thing off!' He sounded, to Devine and to Ferrari, more than just a little agitated.

Ayşe Farsakoğlu had been told in no uncertain terms that anything to do with Ali Kuban, his 'fans' and/or his possible plans were nothing to do with her. The relevant officers were fully aware of everything that was being posted on Kuban's site and would act accordingly.

It was Saturday afternoon, and in the normal course of events, Ayşe, if not at work, would be out and about in Beyoğlu meeting her friends and shopping. Her brother had gone to see his new girlfriend, and so she was alone in the flat and theoretically free to do as she wished. But she just couldn't seem to rouse herself. What she'd seen in Ali Kuban's file when she'd first read it on his release from prison haunted her. All his victims had been so ashamed, and that particularly applied to the gypsy girl Fındık. He'd actually penetrated her three times, as well as forcing her into acts of oral sex and beating and cutting her body. The hours she was held captive by him must have passed so slowly for poor Fındık. He'd pulled her behind a pile of wood planks that leaned up against the old city wall and then just brutalised her.

At some point, according to the girl's statement, another man had put his head around the planks, but Kuban had told him to mind his own business and the man had disappeared. Ayşe wondered whether Fındık had had hopes of being rescued at that point; she thought about how crushed she must have felt when she realised that no help was coming. By the time he abducted Fındık, Kuban was, by his own later admission, feeling invincible. He'd dispensed with the balaclava mask he'd worn when he'd raped the other women. He'd been so

136

sure that the gypsy girl wouldn't report the incident or try to identify him. But she did tell the police, and eventually she did identify Kuban. Two years later, she killed herself, but not until she'd made sure that her attacker was in custody. The whole story made Ayşe feel humbled, and also in awe of Fındık's courage. Now, if either Kuban himself or one of his fans was planning to replay Fındık's ordeal with another girl, that was just obscene.

The Commissioner, of course, had a point that any action should be performed by officers already involved in monitoring Kuban, and İzzet Melik could well be correct in his assumption that it might all be just a hoax. But Ayşe wasn't convinced. What if the monitors decided that Kuban and his friends were not going to do anything? What if they just weren't in the right place at the right time?

She began to chew her fingernails. It was something she only ever did when she was extremely stressed. In spite of feeling weary because of her anxiety, she knew she wouldn't sleep. Thoughts about Kuban had kept her awake all the previous night. How was she going to cope with the idea of Ali Kuban and/or others stalking girls and raping them during the course of the night to come?

Not a sound or even so much as a flash of rotting-slipper-clad foot had been detected coming from Grant T. Miller's house since they'd arrived. The team searching for the bullet had now entered the front garden of the old Johnson house, while İkmen and Addison continued to scan the broken pavement and the road in front of the building. The defunct street lamp to the left of the property had already been climbed, and nothing had been found embedded in it.

'I was thinking,' İkmen said to Rita as he lifted up a loose paving stone, cleared some snow away from it and looked underneath. 'Even if we find this bullet, you only have my word for it that Miller had the gun at all.'

Rita was aware of this. 'I know,' she said. 'Without the Beretta, and with no paperwork to attach it to Miller, he can get his attorney to argue that it has nothing to do with him.' She sighed. 'I know it's too late now, but why didn't you and your colleague press charges against him when he fired on you?'

İkmen put the paving stone down, kicked away the body of a dead rat and then straightened up with some difficulty. 'I think because we are foreigners, we didn't want to get involved.'

'But you were already involved,' she said. 'If not your colleague. You came up here because of Zeke Goins, didn't you?'

'Yes. But Inspector Süleyman was not of the same mind. I brought him up here. He did not want to come. He is going home today and would not have liked to have been detained any longer.'

'Detroit not appeal?'

İkmen felt embarrassed. He didn't want to cause offence. Also, he actually quite liked the city himself. 'Inspector Süleyman comes from a very . . . a part of İstanbul that is like Grosse Pointe,' he said. 'I am more a downtown man myself.'

She smiled. 'Well, that you have in common with me, Inspector,' she said. 'You, me and Lieutenant Diaz.'

'Have you got any closer to knowing who might have killed the lieutenant, and why?' İkmen asked.

Rita shook her head. 'Now that I'm involved with this, which is a kind of side issue to the lieutenant's death, I'm not around Lieutenant Shalhoub and the rest of his team all the time.'

'Shalhoub is in charge of the investigation?'

'Yes.'

İkmen had had little to do with the Christian Arab policeman since that first meeting back at the Cobo Center. But he remembered him as a pleasant, if rather world-weary middle-aged officer, not unlike himself. Unlike Sergeant Donna Ferrari, whom he had met for the first time on the same occasion, Shalhoub was not what İkmen would have called aggressively American or what Shalhoub himself described as 'ballsy'.

Although it wasn't even midday, it was getting dingier and colder by the minute. Rita looked up into the sky and said, 'It could snow.'

İkmen followed her gaze. 'If that is the case,' he said, 'we all must work as hard as we can.'

Rubbing her hands together for warmth, Rita said, 'I just hope the damn bullet is here.'

'Surely it must be.'

'Maybe. But if Grant T. Miller has any knowledge about what has been going on around his Beretta, and I suspect that he most certainly does, then he'll want that slug to disappear.'

'But how would he do that?' İkmen asked. 'In spite of his bravado, he is an elderly man.'

Rita laughed. 'Oh, don't be too taken in by all that frail old man shit,' she said. 'He ain't half as breakable as he'd have the world believe. And anyway,' her face fell and became grave, 'Miller got friends even now, and believe me, Inspector, there are some think he got them everywhere. People say the Black Legion is still alive and well, and that Miller is, as he has always been, at the heart of it.'

It began to snow. Just a few small, wet flakes at first. But then it came on thicker and stronger. 'We got to do what we can,' Rita said as she put the hood of her padded jacket up. 'This looks like it's going to be a shitload.'

İkmen silently gave thanks to no one in particular for his thermal vest.

Grant T. Miller had phoned as soon as Officer Addison, old Weiss, one of the foreign cops and a whole load of others descended upon the Johnson house first thing. Not that calling for help at this point was going to do him any good. No one would or could come with all of them poking around outside. His call had been more an imparting of information – not that he thought for a moment that other parties didn't know what was going on. Other parties always did; that was their function.

Standing well back behind the drawing-room window, so that he couldn't be seen, Miller watched a cop climb up the broken lamppost outside the Johnson house and then shake his head. The bullet he'd fired at the foreigners wasn't there. Old Weiss the doctor's son seemed to be in charge. Miller remembered when he'd gone to college to study medicine. Some Ivy League place, where for some reason he'd become entranced by pathology and later ballistics. The study of death. Maybe the Johnson murder had piqued his interest as it had everyone else's in Brush Park. Then he'd worked for the cops, and continued to do so, even though, Miller knew, he had to have enough cash put by to retire.

Elsewhere, in other more distant parts of Brush Park, streets were being renovated and revived. Project housing and niggers with money mostly. But not for several blocks around his street. Miller smiled. He looked outside again and noticed that it was snowing. Contented now, he left the drawing room and went to his kitchen to make himself some coffee.

Chapter 17

The district of Sulukule was not what it had once been. When Ayşe had started her career, it had been a bustling, raffish place where men sang in the streets and the gypsies ran houses in which scantily clad women would dance for money. Although nominally Muslim, the gypsies generally went their own way, and so women might or might not cover their heads while the men drank alcohol, or not, as they pleased. Secretive and insular, they had been resident in Sulukule for over five hundred years, which made the current state of the district all the more melancholy.

In preparation, it was said, for İstanbul's elevation to European City of Culture status in 2010, certain city slums had been 'cleared'. Sulukule, with its unlicensed drinking and dancing houses, as well as its reputation for crime, which not everyone agreed was actually deserved, had been an obvious target. Depending, like so much in the city of İstanbul, upon one's political and sometimes religious beliefs, opinions were divided as to why Sulukule in particular had been pegged for demolition. Those of a generally republican, secular mind put it down as yet another example of the ruling AK Party, an organisation that proudly owned its Islamic roots, trying to 'socially engineer' Turkey's biggest city. Gypsies' morals, they said, were not good enough for AK. Those who supported AK, however, took the view that Sulukule was a slum that needed to be dealt with. Ayşe Farsakoğlu was not sure where she stood on the issue. All she knew was that the district was now a sorry shadow of what it had once been. When the bulldozers had moved in to demolish shacks where sometimes families had lived for generations, the gypsies had left not just for the alternative housing the state had offered them, but for places all over the city. Deprived of their usual ways of making money by entertaining, they were now a disparate group, scattered around making money in any way they could, up to and including by begging. One of the few exceptions to this was the famous gypsy artist Gonca and her family, who lived in Balat. Once mistress to Mehmet Süleyman, Gonca had been a hate figure for Ayşe Farsakoğlu for a long time. In recent years, however, that had changed. As the result of a shooting in Balat, Gonca had been wounded and had nearly died. After that, she and Süleyman, for reasons best known only to them, had parted. Now Ayşe, if anything, felt only sympathy for the gypsies who had moved on as well as for the few that remained. In between the many vacant lots that today characterised Sulukule, the odd shack, often covered only with a roof of clothing fabric, provided scant shelter to the worn-out-looking people who continued to try to eke out a living there.

When Ali Kuban's victim Fındık had been raped all those years ago, Sulukule had been a vibrant, exciting, music-filled district. There had been so much going on that no one had noticed when the young girl went missing. These days, the overwhelming sound of Sulukule was silence, particularly at night, which it was now.

Faint candlelight from the few shacks that remained on rough lots facing the great Byzantine city walls were all that illuminated Ayşe's progress. It was in the lee of this section of the wall, behind a stack of wooden planks, that Fındık had been raped and brutalised all those years ago. Instinctively Ayşe put a hand inside her coat and felt for the pistol underneath her arm. What she'd come to do, if anything, was unclear even to her. With the exception of one small shack that still clung like a lover to a litter-infested pit at the bottom of the wall, there was nothing to investigate. But Ayşe couldn't let go what she'd seen on that Ali Kuban fan site. It was nearly midnight, and as far as she could tell, there were no other police officers in the area. So much for the Vice officers supposedly being on top of the situation!

That said, she had a very strong feeling, which she'd experienced ever since she'd entered the district, that she was being followed. That was very likely. The gypsies, those that remained, were deeply suspicious of outsiders, and she knew that she was very obviously out of place in the area. But it was still a shock when, just moments later, she turned around quickly and found a huge man with a thick black beard standing right behind her.

'Çetin's staying in Detroit? Why?'

Süleyman told his cousin about Miller and the possibility that he had shot the young boy Aaron Spencer up in Brush Park.

'But of course a big part of the reason why he was so keen to take Detroit PD up on their request for his assistance was because of that old Melungeon man,' he added. 'Because of his own son's death, I think that Çetin now feels he has to help all the other bereaved fathers in the world.'

Süleyman had checked his suitcase in at City Airport and was waiting for the departures sign to light up and tell him when his flight was boarding. Tayyar had come to see him off.

'I'll offer him a bed at my place,' Tayyar said. 'If he doesn't know how long he's going to be here, he can't keep on staying in that awful hotel.'

'The Lakeland Plaza?' Süleyman smiled. 'It wasn't so bad in the end,' he said. 'I heard of worse. Three British officers were staying in some motel where rooms could be rented by the hour and there was an underwear vending machine in the lobby.'

'Yes, Detroit has a few of those,' Tayyar replied, unfazed. 'Mehmet, did you tell Çetin about Elvis Goins' elaborate funeral?'

'No, I didn't. I forgot.'

'I don't know if it means anything in the context of his death,' Tayyar said. 'I'll tell him.' He paused as they both looked up at the departures screen and saw that Süleyman's flight still wasn't ready for boarding. 'You didn't really like it here, did you?'

'No.' Süleyman smiled. 'I think I'm an old-world person, Tayyar. I could never settle in a new country.'

'The Melungeons had to.'

'So they say, if you believe them,' Süleyman said.

Tayyar grinned. 'The most Ottoman of the Ottomans.'

'Me?'

'Yes!' He laughed. 'Why can't they be Turks, even if they're not?'

'Well . . .'

'The reason people come to America is so that they can reinvent themselves,' Tayyar said. 'They can start again. Even in poor old Detroit.'

'You have.'

'Yes.'

Some members of Süleyman's family had speculated for some years about why Tayyar had gone to live in America. He'd had a good job in İstanbul, but when the Detroit post had come up, he hadn't thought twice. A few rather more perceptive members of the family had alluded gently to the fact that Tayyar had been less than pleased with the girl his parents had chosen for him to marry. A rather unworldly creature, she had been horrified by the thought of living in a violent American city.

They sat in silence, Süleyman wishing he'd had just one last cigarette outside the airport when he could. Then suddenly the notice that his flight was ready to board came up on the screen. He stood up. 'I must go.'

Tayyar stood too, and embraced him. 'It's been good to see you,' he said. 'May Allah protect you.'

Süleyman picked up his hand luggage and began to walk towards security. Just before he got to the barrier, he turned and said, 'Tayyar, look after Çetin for me, won't you? Just check on him from time to time. He can get himself into some insane situations sometimes.'

144

Tayyar Bekdil smiled. 'Consider it done,' he shouted back in English. 'No problem at all.'

Samuel Goins put his coffee cup down on Martha Bell's table and said, 'Of course I'll do what I can.'

'With Diaz gone, we got no real big-hitter supporters in Detroit PD,' Martha said. 'Chief likes what we do, or so he says, but he ain't got the time to get real involved down here.'

'Of course I have no influence over DPD,' Sam said, 'but I know a couple of people, including the Chief. You know I've always been in your corner, Martha, and not just because you look after Zeke.'

Sick of trying to stay warm on such a bone-cold day, Ezekiel Goins had gone to bed long before his brother arrived.

'How is he?' Sam put a hand into his jacket pocket and pulled out his wallet. 'Do you need any money?'

Martha smiled. 'That's a bit like saying does a fat man need to exercise,' she said. Then she pushed his wallet back across the table. 'Nah. Zeke don't cost me nothing. Keep it for your boys.'

Sam Goins, though divorced long before, had two sons currently studying at Ivy League universities.

He took two one-hundred-dollar bills out of his wallet and put them underneath one of Martha's hands. 'Well buy something for Keisha,' he said.

'Nah, she—'

'Little girls always need things,' Sam said. Then he changed the subject. 'Martha, how is my brother?'

She shrugged. 'Agitated.'

'The usual thing?'

'Course. Not made no better by the appearance of those Turkish cops. Thinking like they can do something about Elvis!'

'Yes, but they've gone now,' Sam said.

'One of 'em has.'

Sam looked shocked. 'One?'

145

'The older one, Inspector İkmen, he's still here,' Martha said as she tried and failed to give Sam back his money. She lit a cigarette. 'Called on the phone here this afternoon to say he'd be in town a while longer and would be over to see Zeke again.'

'Do you know why?'

'No.' Then she smiled. 'But in a way, it ain't no bad thing. The Turk lost a son hisself, and so it's someone else, apart from me, for Zeke to talk to about that.'

But Sam looked doubtful. 'Provided his presence doesn't embolden Zeke to go back to agitating Grant T. Miller again,' he said. 'We can all do without any more of that.'

'As long as Zeke don't get hurt or in trouble, it's no problem to me,' Martha said. 'Miller's a shit bag, always has been.' She frowned. 'Sam, I never asked you before, but do you think Miller killed Elvis all them years ago?'

'I don't know,' he said. 'When it happened, I was, I'm afraid, far too busy with my own life. When I look back now, I . . .'

'The boy was wild,' Martha said. 'No one blames you, or even his father.'

'I had to take advantage of the fact that Coleman Young was giving blacks and other ethnic minorities a say in the affairs of the city! I had to seize that moment!'

'I understand that, Sam. Everyone does.'

The 1970s, when Detroit got its first black mayor in the person of Coleman Young, had been a time of great fiscal hardship, but for the minorities it had also been a period of opportunity. Non-whites had been able to take some control and actually begin to affect law enforcement, public policy and wider political life. Sam Goins had been an early and very enthusiastic supporter of Mayor Young. The fact that some of Young's political dealings later became mired in controversy and allegations of corruption in no way ever either involved Sam Goins or dented his admiration for Detroit's first black mayor.

'I just wish I'd been there for Zeke when it happened,' Sam said. 'You know, I was so caught up with myself, the first time I saw Zeke after Elvis died was at the boy's funeral. I think that one of the reasons Zeke went hobo for all those years was because he felt that no one really cared.'

'Elvis was Sheila's son too. His momma cared.'

'Not as much as my brother,' Sam said. His face was white now, haunted by the recollection of old and painful events. 'Elvis was driving her crazy, selling drugs, taking them, leading that gang that everyone used to call "the rejects".'

'The Delta Blues.'

'Melungeons, Native Americans, gypsies, all the rejects of society! Boy, was he and his buddies giving us a bad rep!' He sighed. 'But they're all dead now, and so . . . You know, Martha, in a way I think Sheila was relieved when Elvis was shot.'

'Ah, now, Sam . . .'

'I know it sounds wicked, but that woman was at the end of her wits.' Now he just looked sad. 'All the stress of never knowing where the boy was, it was over. If only Zeke could have accepted what happened and settled in to a life with Sheila again afterwards.'

'He was too hurt.'

'Which is so, so bitter for me. My poor brother, who I love.' Sam's eyes had filled with tears. 'When Sheila died, I tried to have her buried next to Elvis in Woodlawn, but her family insisted on taking her body back to Alabama to their family plot. Zeke was who knew where. I would've paid for it myself.'

'And that ain't no cheap gig up there amongst Aretha Franklin's kin and all,' Martha said. 'I always thought what a great thing that was for a poor man like Zeke to do for his boy.'

Sam didn't answer.

The man with the big black beard hadn't even had a chance to speak to Ayşe Farsakoğlu when he felt the muzzle of a pistol against his head.

147

'What are you doing?' İzzet Melik hissed into his ear.

The man, struck dumb by the rapidity of what had just happened, said nothing. That he had one hand on Ayşe's breast spoke volumes.

'Were you planning to assault this lady?'

Ayşe couldn't imagine where İzzet had come from. She was grateful that he had come at all, but how?

Eventually the man spoke. 'Who are you?' he asked.

'Who are *you*?'

'I don't have to tell you . . .'

'Police, and so yes, you do have to tell me who you are,' İzzet said.

The man's identity card gave his name as Rıfat Özkök. He was forty-two. 'The woman was walking alone; what was I to think?' he said. 'This is a rough part of town where men have always come to . . . well, to seek . . .' He shrugged. 'I made an assumption that . . .'

'I too am a police officer,' Ayşe said, 'and you, Mr Özkök, are going to have to come with us to answer some questions.'

'Oh, no.' Rıfat put his head down in frustration and misery while İzzet Melik cuffed his hands behind his back.

'What are you doing here?' Ayşe mouthed to İzzet. 'What?'

But he didn't reply.

Rıfat began, 'I was just—'

'Sssh!' İzzet, still holding on to the big man's wrists, was now looking behind him. He shook Özkök quiet.

Ayşe, who was trying to see what İzzet might be looking at, peered into the darkness. 'What is it?' she whispered.

'Over there!' he whispered back. 'That shack at the bottom of the wall, something moved!'

Chapter 18

It had been quite impossible to even take a guess at who the human soup inside the car crusher had once been. But Ed Devine was pretty convinced that it was the owner of the yard, Kyle Redmond. He was, after all, nowhere to be found, and as Devine pointed out, the soup in the crusher was very intimately connected to what looked like a great deal of old, oil-stained denim.

'Simplistic, I know,' he said to Donna Ferrari once he'd had the remains photographed and arranged transport to the lab, 'but wrecker men always wear the same things. Jean dungarees, just like freaking hillbillies. It's a kind of uniform.'

Ferrari slipped into the passenger seat of his car. 'I don't know,' she said. 'Why would someone kill Redmond and torch his yard?'

'That's what we have to find out,' Devine replied. 'Maybe his financial worries led him to take out a loan with the wrong people. And if he didn't pay . . .' He started up the engine and put the gear lever into drive.

As they headed out of the yard, Ferrari said, 'Bad week.'

'Anything new on the Diaz hit?' Devine asked.

'Not that I know,' she answered. 'Shalhoub's pretty tight with his team when he's working a case.'

'You mean he don't blab like an old woman like me!' Devine laughed.

But of all the assets that Donna Ferrari possessed, humour was not amongst their number. As they turned into the road outside the yard, she said, 'I imagine Diaz was a drive-by hit. Maybe an ex-con with a grudge.'

'Some people are saying that maybe there's a connection with that old horror Grant T. Miller.'

'There's some possible connection between Miller and a drive-by in Brush Park,' Ferrari said. 'But not to Diaz. Why would Miller kill Diaz? He wouldn't. That won't fly.'

'Pity.'

She looked over at Devine and frowned. 'Why?'

He laughed. 'I'm a black man, Miller's a racist. It's in my genes to hate that man, Sergeant Ferrari.'

'I guess.'

She turned back to look at the road once again, and for a couple of minutes neither of them said anything. When Devine did speak again, this time it was he who had a troubled tone to his voice. 'You know, I'm still sure I've come across something about Kyle Redmond somewhere before,' he said. 'You heard of him before today?'

She shook her head. 'No. He'd no record.'

'Mmm.' Devine shook his head impatiently. 'Wish I could remember where I know him from! Old age! It drives me crazy!'

Because İzzet was holding on to Rıfat Özkök, and because Ayşe didn't get to them quickly enough, the two figures standing at the entrance to the shack beneath the city wall ran off into the darkness before anyone could stop them. As she walked up to the battered open door, Ayşe took her gun out of its holster. As far as she could see, there was only one entrance to the shack, and the whole structure backed on to solid Byzantine wall.

'Police!' she shouted as she moved into the wreck, her weapon held out in front of her.

Nothing moved. The shack was deserted save for a few old packing crates and some empty bottles of rakı. It smelt of mould and mice and piss.

'What's in there?' asked İzzet, still restraining Rıfat Özkök.

'Nothing much,' Ayşe said as she began to move forward into the narrow but tall space in front of her.

'Be careful!'

İzzet must have guessed what she was going to do and either had followed her to Sulukule or had been waiting for her to appear in the district. Knowing how he felt about her, it was creepy, but it was comforting too. Neither of them knew what Rıfat Özkök would have done had he been able to grab Ayşe with impunity. Given the size of him, it was not certain whether she would have been able to get to her pistol before he did.

Outside, she heard İzzet say to him, 'What do you know about this place?'

'Nothing! I swear!'

There was another smell now, and it was like old sewers in hot weather. Warm human waste. It was strong, too! Ayşe put her free hand up to her mouth as she felt herself begin to gag. Those characters who'd run off when she approached them must have been using the place as a toilet.

İzzet called out to her again: 'Are you all right?'

'Yes.' But then she felt something touch her face. It was heavy, and it tapped against her cheek twice before she managed to get her torch out of her pocket and shine some light on to it. It turned out to be a shoe, on a foot that was attached to the figure of what looked like a man hanging by his neck from a beam across the ceiling.

Çetin İkmen was about to get into the lift and go back to his suite when he heard a voice call his name. He looked around, and across the vast wastes of marble that graced the lobby of the Lakeland Plaza Hotel, there was Tayyar Bekdil.

'I thought you were seeing Mehmet Süleyman off at the airport,' İkmen said as he walked towards him.

Tayyar took İkmen's hand and smiled. 'I've just got back. Mehmet

151

told me that you were staying on in Detroit. I thought I'd come and take you for a drink.'

İkmen had had a long and fruitless day. They'd found a few bullets out at Brush Park, but according to Dr Weiss, none of them was the right one. The snow hadn't helped. Working on through it had been hard going. Now it was nearly eleven o'clock and he was exhausted. 'I'm really tired,' he said, 'but if you want to come up and join me in something from the minibar . . .'

They got into the lift together, and only had to stop once on the way to floor fourteen. On floor eight, the doors opened to reveal a young woman quickly putting her knickers into her handbag. When they arrived at İkmen's suite, Tayyar said, 'Now the conference is over, there's no need for you to stay here. There's a clean bed, TV, DVD, a full refrigerator, your own bathroom and a garden at your disposal at Grosse Pointe.'

'That's very kind.' İkmen lit up a cigarette and then took two miniature whisky bottles and a couple of glasses out of the minibar. 'But I don't really know what's happening yet. I've been asked by Detroit PD to stay on, and this room is paid for tonight. What will happen tomorrow, I don't know.' He handed Tayyar a bottle and a glass. 'Doesn't appear to be any ice. Sorry.'

Tayyar sat down. 'Mehmet told me that PD have kept you because Grant T. Miller shot at the both of you. Some connection to that supposed drive-by up in Brush Park.'

'Yes,' İkmen said. But he was tired and didn't want to go into it. Besides, for all his friendliness, Tayyar was still a journalist, and so İkmen didn't want to tell him too much. But when Tayyar launched into his story about Elvis Goins' elaborate funeral, he began to feel rather more alert once again.

'It was reported,' Tayyar said. 'There are even photographs. Colleagues of mine I've spoken to about it reckon it must have cost a fortune. Like a Mafia don's send-off!'

'Maybe the gang that he was with paid for it,' İkmen said. 'Some of these gangs have a lot of money.'

'Not the Delta Blues, by all accounts,' Tayyar said. 'They were like a ragbag of the dispossessed. The big white and black drug gangs at the time wiped them out. It's believed Elvis Goins was a victim of that conflict. Others came later. Now they're all dead.'

'Are they?'

'So everyone says.'

'Mmm. What about the boy's uncle? He's prominent, isn't he?'

'He wasn't back then,' Tayyar said. 'Just a grunt like everyone else in 1978. The father, Ezekiel Goins, was working, but it was well known he had some serious debts. Intriguing, isn't it?'

'Yes.' İkmen offered a cigarette to Tayyar, who declined. He lit one up for himself. 'I will try to help Mr Goins as much as I can while I'm here. So I will be seeing him again. I'll ask him.'

'About Elvis's funeral?'

'Why not? He wants me to get to the bottom of what happened to his son. In order to do that, I have to have as much information as I can. I will ask him when I see him.'

Tayyar only stayed for the one drink. He too was tired and wanted to get home. As he left, he said, 'Çetin, if you need anything, anything at all, you will let me know, won't you?'

Çetin İkmen smiled. 'I see that your cousin has asked you to look out for me.'

'Well . . .'

İkmen put a hand on the younger man's shoulder. 'It's all right,' he said. 'I've worked with Mehmet for many years. I know what goes on.'

Tayyar smiled.

'The best thing you can do for me is to find out which – what do the Americans call it? Funeral home? – performed the funeral. Find out if they're still in business. A big funeral like the one you describe will not be an event easily forgotten, even after thirty years have passed.' He smiled. 'And of course there is someone else I could ask too,' he said.

Dr Sarkissian the pathologist declared that life was extinct and also definitively identified the corpse. Ayşe had thought it was Ali Kuban; she'd hoped. Now she was rewarded.

'One never forgets a face like that,' Dr Sarkissian said as he pushed the head up slightly in order to see the rope burns that circled the neck. 'Of course I remember seeing Kuban on the television when he was arrested, but I also saw him in person too. My predecessor Dr Koksal was acquainting me with the intricacies of police head-quarters when they brought Kuban through. A lot younger then, of course, but he looked a mess. I think that perhaps he'd been given a rather enthusiastic reception down in the cells.'

He didn't say by whom, but Ayşe knew. Some officers remained overzealous in their interrogation of prisoners, but back in the 1970s, police violence had been endemic. Few had stood out against it. One of those who had had been Ayşe's boss, Çetin İkmen. Not that the young İkmen had had anything to do with Ali Kuban. Back in the early seventies, he'd been out pounding the streets, running after kids trying to steal sweets from grocers' shops.

Sarkissian, focused again on the face, said, 'I think it's probably suicide, but I won't be able to say with any degree of certainty until I've examined the body and the scene has been investigated.'

'Some people, men I think, fled the scene just before I gained entry,' Ayşe said. 'Maybe they strung him up. This is where he raped his last victim.'

'Mmm.' The doctor frowned. 'I don't know. Nearly all the gypsies have gone.'

'And yet the fact if not the details of his release was publicised,' Ayşe said. 'People knew he was out. Maybe the gypsies didn't kill him; maybe it was just people who thought he'd be better off dead, that the world would be safer without him.'

'Maybe.'

They both looked down into a face that was bloated and mottled and which looked sightlessly back at them with bulging, bloodshot eyes.

'Looks like he struggled,' the doctor said.

'Good.'

'Maybe if it was suicide, he changed his mind.'

Ayşe shook her head. 'On the Facebook site his fans dedicated to him, an unspecified event was advertised. I surmised it would or could happen here. I imagined it was going to be some sort of replay of his most notorious crime.'

'Somewhat obvious, don't you think?'

Ayşe felt a little offended by this. What did he know about detection?

'As I understand it,' the doctor continued, 'Kuban's apartment was being monitored by officers from Vice. But somehow he got out undetected and came or was brought here. Why?'

Ayşe, still looking down at the battered, bloated face of Ali Kuban, said, 'It's where he committed his most brutal crime.'

'Yes, when this area was teeming with girls. Did you see any pretty young ladies in swirling skirts dancing in the streets of Sulukule when you arrived, Sergeant?'

Of course she hadn't; Sulukule wasn't like that any more. 'But someone posted details about an event,' she said.

'If it was Kuban himself who posted it, maybe it was notice, as it were, of his own demise.'

'But there were people, other men, looking into . . .'

'Well maybe I'm wrong and they killed him,' Sarkissian said. 'Sulukule is not a safe place to be at night. But . . .'

'What?' She looked up at him.

'If Kuban did die here by his own hand, maybe, given the possibility that he issued a statement in advance that something was going to happen . . .'

'Yes?'

'Well, maybe suicide, as a sort of warning to others, if you will, was always his intention. Perhaps by attracting like-minded people to a place where they thought an assault was about to take place, he was showing them how a life like his ended. With constant surveillance by the police, with a prison sentence only curtailed by ill health, and with suicide.'

Ayşe frowned. 'Sort of a last decent act on his part?'

Arto Sarkissian shrugged. 'Maybe. Maybe.'

What she was doing took guts, patience and some very efficient winter clothing. Luckily Rita Addison had all three in abundance. When Dr Weiss and his team and İkmen left the scene, Rita, her car parked way back in the part of Brush Park that was being redeveloped, stayed behind.

The old Johnson house was all shades of black inside. The night, it seemed, got in there and just intensified itself, distilling its darkness to a treacly essence. Walking in through what had once been the back door was hazardous. The floorboards had rotted, leaving holes wide enough for a big guy like Ed Devine to rocket through. Rita moved slowly and with her flashlight held low to prevent its beam from being seen from outside. There was a smell like compost, undercut by what could be the reek of human faeces. Rita thought about what had happened in that house back in the 1950s, and tried not to picture the dentist's dismembered wife. Local legend had it that everything had been found except the woman's left foot. That had to be just a load of bones by this time, but it would still, Rita felt, be a very unpleasant surprise should she inadvertently put her hand on it. Not that such a thing was likely.

Slowly Rita found her way to what had been the Johnsons' front parlour.

Across waves of heavy snow outside she could see the light from Grant T. Miller's house shining in tiny points through the branches of the thick bushes that surrounded his garden. She sat down on what felt like a paving slab and switched her flashlight off. Now it was just a waiting game, a fight with herself to stay awake and alert. She put one gloved hand into the pocket of her puffa jacket and pulled out a plastic flask. Hot black coffee with plenty of sugar. She drank about half and was pleased with the results. The hot, thick caffeine hit both warmed her up and made her feel very alive, if a little bit weird. Some of those high-strength South American blends were like speed.

Rita hadn't told anyone about what she was going to do. Officially the Johnson house and its environs were not even a crime scene. But if she was right that Grant T. Miller had owned the Beretta that had killed Aaron Spencer, then he would be keen to recover the bullet that he'd fired from the same gun at the Turks. He might not have been worried about that bullet before; now, if she was right, he had to be. They'd been twice to the Johnson house looking for it, and Miller would have to have been both blind and stupid not to have noticed that. He was neither. As Lieutenant Diaz had once told her when she'd asked him about Miller, 'He knows everything and everyone. Never, ever underestimate him.'

She'd taken that to heart. His words had especially come back to haunt her since all of his records linked to the Beretta seemed to have disappeared. Miller had to be at the least concerned. But in spite of that, he made her wait, and it wasn't until almost two hours later that he finally made an appearance. Wearing his customary tattered dressing gown, his thin bare legs flashing purple-white below, he trudged with difficulty through the snow towards the Johnson house. A cell phone at his ear, she heard him yell, 'Of course no one can hear me! Nobody but me lives in any direction for three blocks. You should know that!'

Rita sank down closer towards the floor and pulled her hood over her head.

'Who comes through here except the odd punk in a Hummer!' the

157

old man said. 'Crack-dealers! What are they gonna do? Call you?' There was a pause while he listened for the reply, then he said, 'Yeah, well it has to be here somewhere, doesn't it!' Another pause. Rita heard him rattle what remained of the window frame right next to her head. Then he got angry. 'Oh well, you come and look see yourself!' he shouted into the cell phone. 'I'm up to my nuts in snow here! Oh, you won't? Well that's what I've come to expect from you, isn't it! And don't try to get on my good side or any shit like that. You should know by now I don't have one!'

Miller terminated the call after that. As he moved about outside, puffing and panting, his slippered feet shuffling into and out of the thick snow, the phone rang one more time, but he switched it off without answering.

With the temperature well below zero, there was a limit to the amount of time Grant T. Miller could spend out of doors, and within twenty minutes he was back inside the Windmill once again. Rita gave it another half-hour before she moved, just in case the old man came back wearing more snow-friendly clothes. But he didn't.

When she eventually got back to her car and put the heater on full blast, Rita thought about the things she'd seen and heard up at the Johnson house. Principal amongst these was what Miller had said about crack-dealers. He had said to the person on the other end of the phone that crack-dealers wouldn't 'call you'. Call who? To Rita, the logical response to that was 'the police'.

Chapter 19

In spite of the heavy overnight snowfall, the following day was bright
and the sky was blue. Çetin İkmen knew that Dr Weiss, Officer
Addison and the team would be out in Brush Park searching for the
missing bullet again, and part of him wanted to be with them. But
he was not required to attend, and so instead he fulfilled his promise
to Zeke Goins and went over to Antoine Cadillac to see him. There
was an ulterior motive too, but he knew that he'd have to approach
that most cautiously.

Martha Bell was out when he arrived, taking her daughter to dance
class and doing some shopping, and so the two men spent some time
alone. They naturally talked about their boys.

'Bekir was a delightful boy until he reached puberty,' İkmen said.
'Then, it seemed like overnight he became a problem. All teenagers,
of course, want to be grown up and respected as adults, but this went
beyond that.'

'With Elvis, it was the dope as came first,' Zeke said. 'Caught him
smoking at eleven, and then it was just way on downhill all the way.'
He shook his head. 'Me and Sheila, we done what we could short of
having him arrested, but it weren't no good. Some kids just born to
go bad.'

İkmen disagreed. 'I can't believe that anyone is born bad,' he said.
'I think that sometimes circumstances make a person behave badly.
My son was one of so many. Nine children. All the others, they . . .
well, they blended in together, you know. But Bekir was different.
Bekir needed more individual attention, which I did not give him.'

He hadn't wanted to dig so deeply down into Bekir's life and death when he came to Antoine Cadillac. But somehow that had happened as Zeke Goins too shared his sorrow.

'We only had the one child, Sheila and me,' he said, 'but I was working the line all time just to keep us fed. Lot of people didn't feel good about working with our kind, not whites nor blacks. I had to keep my head down and my nose clean to hold on to my job. Folk like Grant T. Miller always on your case! Then when things had to get better for the blacks, the white bosses misused us all the more. I worked like a dog every day of my life until the day that Elvis was laid in the ground.'

The subject of Elvis's funeral was now just a sniff away. But for the moment İkmen felt too sad and also a little too ashamed to do what he knew he had to. He waited in silence for the old man to speak again.

Zeke Goins finished rolling the cigarette he'd started making when İkmen had arrived, and said, 'I think, in a sense, when I took off after Elvis died, it wasn't just because of the grief. I think I was tired, too, of working the line, of automobiles, of the trouble that being what I am always brings. The only proud thing I have is the notion that my brother Sam has made things so much better for our kind now.'

'That's good.'

'Folk don't have to hide being Melungeon no more,' the old man said. 'If other folk don't like it, then they can have the problem and not us.'

He didn't say exactly how Samuel Goins had achieved this miracle, but İkmen imagined that because he was a city councillor, he had drafted and pushed through legislation aimed at protecting his community. But now they were a long way from Elvis's funeral again, and it took quite some time for their conversation to move back in that direction. When it did, there was no prompting from İkmen required.

'There was flowers everywhere for my boy,' Zeke said. 'Back at

160

our old home by Eight Mile, in the chapel, took to the graveside itself. Had Minister Hamilton to lay him to rest. Best preacher in the state. Voss Funeral Home, they put on some show.' He smiled. 'That was a day. That was some day.'

İkmen made a mental note of the name Voss, and though he wanted to push the old man for further details, he decided on a gentler approach instead.

'In my culture, bodies are usually buried within twenty-four hours of death,' he said. 'Arabia, where the first Muslims came from, is a hot place, and so for reasons of hygiene the dead have to be interred quickly. But of course because Bekir had died violently, there had to be an investigation, and so we could not bury him for some time.'

Zeke looked pained. 'That must've hurt you and your family.'

'It was not good.'

'So you have a big send-off for him when the time come?'

İkmen smiled. 'No,' he said. 'Big funerals are not really approved of in Islam. The dead return to the earth. That's it. I think in your religion more of a . . . a show is required?'

Zeke shrugged. 'Sometimes. I think we done all right by the boy for his funeral,' he said. And then suddenly he changed the subject. 'Do you like a drink, Inspector İkmen?'

'A drink?'

They had coffee. Did he mean an alcoholic drink? It wasn't much past eleven a.m. The old man, smiling now, went over to the kitchen sink and rooted about in the cupboard underneath. When he stood up again, he was holding on to two bourbon bottles. 'What's your poison, Inspector, Jack or Jim?'

Rita had already decided that she wouldn't tell anyone except the Chief about what Miller had said. But when she went to find out whether she could get in to see him, she was told that he was unavailable for the rest of the morning. Apparently he was in a meeting with the Mayor, and there was no way he could be disturbed for anything less than a national emergency. Temporarily deflated, Rita went back up to Brush Park to join the search again.

'There's a limit to the amount of time we can spend on this,' Dr Weiss said when she saw him. 'This is a city, not some backwater where nothing ever happens. We all have other things to do.'

'I know.' The existing snow was very thick, and just after she'd arrived, it had started snowing again. 'But the Chief ordered it himself.' At her request, she failed to add.

'I'm aware of that,' Dr Weiss said tartly as he pulled his coat tight around his body. 'But he isn't out here looking for a needle in a haystack, in the snow!'

Rita didn't reply.

Dr Weiss sighed. 'But I suppose if we must get on with this fool's errand . . .'

He walked back towards the Johnson house and went up the steps to the empty front door. 'Does anyone actually own this place now?' he asked no one in particular as he stood and looked up at the once elegant facade.

He wasn't actually expecting an answer, but some woman forensic investigator piped up and said, 'Think it's some real-estate company, Doctor.'

'Real estate?' Weiss shook his head in what looked like despair. 'When we sold our old house here back in the sixties, it was to the family of a successful haberdasher.' He threw his arms in the air. 'Real-estate company! These houses were built for families!'

Rita, still tired from her stakeout the previous night, went around the side of the house to begin to shift snow from the garden. As she walked, she glanced over the road at the Windmill, where she saw that Grant T. Miller was standing outside his front door looking right at her. On reflex, she turned away immediately. Heart thumping and mouth as dry as death, she wondered whether he'd seen her the night before. In his own search for the bullet, he'd come very close, and if it hadn't been dark at the time, he would most certainly have spotted her.

Maybe he had. Miller, she knew, had a reputation as a prankster, a player of games. It would be well within his abilities to know that she had been in the Johnson house the night before and keep it to himself. It was said that one of the ways that he had been able to retain his freedom, his money and his independence for so long was because he fully understood the adage *knowledge is power*.

Rita shivered, and not just because it was snowing again.

Devine walked over to John Shalhoub as he was getting into his car.

'How's it going?' the older man asked.

Shalhoub closed his car door and leaned on the roof. 'Diaz?'

'Uhuh.'

'One shot to the head killed him, straight between the eyes. Instant.' He looked tired and drawn. It was always difficult to work on the homicide of a colleague. So much was expected. 'Only bright spot in the whole thing.'

'He'd've felt nothing.'

'No.'

'Ideas about the perp?'

'*Only* ideas at the moment,' Shalhoub said. 'Corktown's not such a bad place these days, but people still don't see much, say even less.'

Ed Devine shrugged. 'Detroit ain't gonna stop being Detroit just because a few middle-class people decide to go and live on the east side. But look, you need anything, you just ask. Diaz weren't no life and soul, but he was one of us.'

'I hear you.' Shalhoub was just about to get back in his car when suddenly he stopped and said, 'You working that car-wreck case?'

'Yeah.' Devine shook his head. 'Thought it was a straight insurance job until we found that . . . mush in the crusher.'

'The owner.'

Devine nodded. 'Kyle Redmond. Forty, divorced, in debt, was five eleven. It was nasty.'

'Must've been.' Shalhoub's brow furrowed and he said, 'I may be completely on the wrong track with this, but you know that Diaz had some informant called Redmond.'

Devine leaned forward. 'You sure?'

'I don't know whether it was Kyle Redmond,' Shalhoub said. 'I don't even know what he used him for. Diaz was particular to keep his informants close.'

Devine shook his head as if he were trying to recall something. 'Because you know when I first heard about this Kyle Redmond, I felt I'd known that name before.'

'Maybe you heard Diaz talk about him?'

'Maybe.' He shrugged. 'Now that Diaz is dead, it ain't easy to ask. But maybe we should try, figuratively speaking. I mean, first Diaz is shot dead, and then this Redmond rocks up in an auto crusher. There could be a connection.'

'Or not.'

'But then again, there might be,' Devine said. Suddenly he laughed, and slapped the other man on the back. 'Come on, Shalhoub, man, don't shoot down the only lead I got!'

Rıfat Özkök, the man who had tried with staggering lack of success to assault Ayşe Farsakoğlu, had been taken in for questioning by İzzet Melik. Come the next morning, however, it was very obvious that he had had nothing to do with the death of Ali Kuban. He did have a police record for groping women, as opposed to girls, but nothing more serious than that. There was no connection with Ali Kuban, and Özkök was one of the few people in İstanbul who wasn't on line.

'I drive my taxi, and when my wife lets me, I go to the coffee house,' he told İzzet Melik as he left the station. 'When do I get time to look at computers? When do I get time to have a life?'

'You seem to make time to grope women,' İzzet responded sharply. 'Get out of here and give thanks to Allah your behaviour didn't get you in even more trouble!'

İzzet hadn't slept. In the wake of the discovery of Ali Kuban's body, the whole area had to be searched and any possible witnesses questioned. No one had volunteered information and none of the men they had spoken to had admitted to being anywhere near the city walls. Both time and exact cause of death were still elements that were being investigated by the pathologist. Ayşe Farsakoğlu, he knew, had opted to accompany the body to the laboratory so that she could be the first to know. No one from Vice had so much as made an appearance. But then they had, in effect, allowed this to happen. Not for the first time, İzzet wondered why some of his fellow officers were in the job at all. Unfortunately people like Çetin İkmen, people like İzzet himself, were not the norm. There were far too many officers who just drifted along doing only what they had to in order to qualify for their pension. It had always been like this to some extent, but in the twenty-first century it really was no longer acceptable. He wondered if people living in European Union countries had to put up with such sloppiness. But then he knew they certainly did. Italy, his spiritual home, had one of the most chaotic law-enforcement systems in the world.

'Sergeant Melik?'

He turned around and saw Ayşe Farsakoğlu, looking tired and drawn. But she smiled, and so he smiled back at her.

'Dr Sarkissian is of the opinion that Ali Kuban killed himself,' she said.

'Ah.'

'If he is right, which he must be, then it had to be Kuban himself who put that notice of an "event" up on the fan site. He'd planned to be dead by midnight, when his fans would, hopefully, be in Sulukule; doctor reckons he died before eleven o'clock.'

'But why kill himself?' İzzet said. 'And why in Sulukule? Why not in the comfort of his own apartment? It must have taken at least some effort to give the Vice boys the slip.'

'He was sick.' She shrugged. 'Maybe in pain? But then Dr Sarkissian did suggest another motive.'

'Which was?'

'A final act of decency. He invited his fans to come and witness his dead, swinging body. He made sure he was dead by the time of the "event". Maybe it was his way of saying that his was not a life to be admired and copied.'

İzzet looked doubtful. 'Dr Sarkissian said that?'

'It was a theory we came up with together,' Ayşe said. 'When Çetin Bey gets back tomorrow, I'll ask him what he thinks.'

'Ah . . .' İzzet had heard that İkmen wasn't returning from Detroit just yet.

'What?'

'Çetin Bey,' he took her arm and began to walk with her down the corridor towards their respective offices, 'he isn't coming back just yet. Inspector Süleyman is on his way home, but Çetin Bey, apparently there are some things he needs to do in Detroit . . .'

Ayşe looked both disappointed and appalled.

Getting properly, horribly drunk wasn't something Çetin İkmen had done for many years. But then he was unaccustomed to American bourbon, and so the two big shots of Jim Beam he had at the start of the session were enough to get him tipsy. His grief, which had just kept on coming, albeit in a low-level fashion, since he'd first met Zeke Goins, made sure that he carried on drinking.

The old man, matching him drink for drink, had to keep on going to the toilet. 'Waterworks ain't what they were,' he said on the third occasion he had to get up from the table and head for the bathroom.

While Ezekiel Goins was doing what he had to and while İkmen could still think straight, he called Tayyar Bekdil. 'The funeral home that buried Elvis Goins is called Voss,' he told him. 'Do you know it?'

'No,' Tayyar said, 'but I can find it. Do you want me to get the address? Meet you there? We can see what kind of a place it is.'

'No.' İkmen had just heard the front door shut, which meant that Martha had come back. 'I'm with Ezekiel Goins. To be honest, we've had a few drinks . . .'

He heard Tayyar laugh.

'I'm going to try and get him to tell me some more, if I can.' There were footsteps in the hall. 'I have to go.'

He put his cell phone back in his pocket just as Martha Bell entered the room. She looked at the bottles and the glasses on the kitchen table and said, 'I see.'

İkmen put his head down like a naughty schoolboy.

Chapter 20

According to the current owner of Voss Funeral Home Inc., death had become 'funky'.

'Look at that TV show *Six Feet Under*,' he said to Tayyar Bekdil. 'This industry is cool. If I had a nickel for everyone who wants to work here, I'd be a rich man.'

Richer, Tayyar thought, as he wondered whether it was actually possible to find an undertaker who wasn't rich. As for people wanting to work at Voss, in a city with high unemployment men and women would do almost anything. But he didn't say any of that, and just smiled.

'Only last week we buried a man who wanted to be interred in an Egyptian sarcophagus,' Ricky Voss said. He was not much over thirty, blond, with an LA smile, and although he sported a very conventional suit, he wore gold sneakers on his feet. 'Not only did we source the craftsmen who could make it, we also sourced the musicians who played at the ceremony too. Did you know that Egyptian Christians still use musical instruments that were played in ancient Egypt?'

'No, I didn't.' Tayyar took notes. His editor was fond of local wealth-creators, and so Tayyar's suggestion that he should contact one of the city's most prominent funeral homes had gone down well. What he hadn't expected was that Voss's MD would invite him over that very day. With the temperature so low, he had imagined that it would be a busy time for funeral homes. But then Mr Voss obviously had employees to do the actual day-to-day work. From what Tayyar could gather, 'Ricky' spent a lot of his time in his office, which was a cross between a conventional wood-panelled affair, complete with employee photographs on the walls, and a gathering place for numerous electronic gadgets. As far as he could tell, Voss had three cell phones, one laptop and one desktop computer, some sort of games console, two iPods and a Dictaphone. All the time they talked, he sent texts to someone.

'So what do you want to know, Tayyar?' It was strictly first-name terms at Voss.

'Stories, Ricky,' Tayyar said. 'The *Spectator*, as you know, likes to highlight local wealth-creators. We want to promote an image of Detroit as a city that is coming back to life. Your organisation generates wealth and employment, and we'd like to tell your story.'

'The history of Voss?'

'And maybe some anecdotes about your family's long association with Detroit and its people.'

Ricky smiled. 'Sure,' he said. 'I think I can do that. But do you mind if I go get my great-uncle? He's a Voss original, helped my grandpa found this company back in the thirties.'

This great-uncle, Tayyar thought, could very possibly have been present at Elvis Goins' funeral. If he was lucky, he'd get a story for the paper and a lead on who had paid for Elvis's funeral all in one hit. 'I'd be delighted to meet your uncle, yes,' he said.

Rita had heard something about some guy's body being disposed of in an auto crusher out on Eight Mile. But she hadn't paid it too much attention. Shit happened all the time, so quickly sometimes that people didn't even get a moment to grieve. She still hadn't really cried for Diaz. Sometime soon she knew the flood barriers would burst, probably when she least expected them to. In the meantime, although the search for the bullet had been called off for the time being, Grant T. Miller had far from been forgotten. She'd finally got in to see the Chief at two p.m. and had told him about the one-sided conversation she'd heard Miller have on his cell phone while he searched for the bullet in the dark. She'd told no one else, she said to the Chief. No one.

Ed Devine was leaning on Diaz's desk when she went back out. 'Hey, Addison,' he said when he saw her. 'You worked with Diaz more than most. You know anything about his informants?'

'Why?'

All Diaz's records had been taken by Shalhoub's team, looking for some sort of clue to who might have killed him and why.

'You ever hear him talk about an auto wrecker called Kyle Redmond?' Devine asked.

'That the guy crushed up on Eight Mile?'

'You always gonna answer a question with a question? Yeah, it is,' he said. 'Lieutenant Shalhoub reckons he could've been one of Diaz's informants.'

Rita stopped and thought. Diaz had had quite a few informants, all of whom he guarded jealously. She didn't remember him ever using their names; he'd just referred to them in terms of what he thought they were like, or what they did. She remembered a woman called 'the book store girl' and a man he called 'Baron Samedi' after the voodoo deity. Like Diaz himself, his system had been obscure and arcane, and Rita had never even thought about asking him questions that related to it.

'I don't remember any Kyle Redmond, Lieutenant,' she said. 'But you know that Lieutenant Diaz never actually called his informants by their real names.'

'He use numbers? Initials?'

'No, he used to make names up,' Rita said. As she explained, she thought of something else. Diaz had been an obscure law unto himself. He always did what he was supposed to with regard to official paperwork, but he sometimes had his own way of recording other information, like the names of his informants. Maybe he'd done the same with the missing Beretta. It would have been typical of him, as well as expedient in terms of who he was dealing with. Grant T. Miller

170

was still suspected of having eyes and ears everywhere, even inside PD. Diaz had never made a secret of his hatred for the old man. Had he coded what he'd found out about him just in case someone in the department tried to take those details from him and destroy them?

'I've heard of couple of names he used in the past, although none of them ring any bells with Kyle Redmond or auto wreckers,' she said. 'But maybe if I worked alongside Lieutenant Shalhoub I could see if anything in Diaz's files might relate to the man.'

'Mmm.' Devine nodded his head. 'Ain't a bad idea.' Then he frowned. 'You finished out at Brush Park now?'

'For the moment,' Rita said.

'Find anything?'

'Nah.'

'Shame.'

She smiled. 'Yeah.'

Unlike with Donna Ferrari, he didn't have to explain to Rita why he was sad that Grant T. wasn't getting his.

'So the man in the crusher,' Rita said, 'what do you know?'

'The man had money issues. Looked like a straight insurance job, until we found him squashed flatter than a Frisbee.' He chewed on his gum and then cleared his throat. 'No enemies beyond his ex-wife, but she was way out in Baltimore when Kyle bought the farm. There's so much over at that yard it could take weeks to sort through it all.' He looked down at the floor and sighed. Then he looked up at Rita and said, 'If Shalhoub okays it, you all right looking through some of Diaz's paperwork? See if anything relates to a wrecker up by Eight Mile?'

'Yeah, I can do that,' Rita said. 'No problem.'

Mr Stefan Voss had been born in Vienna, Austria, in 1920. When he was nine years old, he'd emigrated to America with his parents and his older brother Rudolf, Ricky Voss's grandfather.

'My father worked for an undertaking business in Vienna,' the old

171

man said. 'But the director was a gambler and the business died. My father couldn't get another job. So we came to America, and my father, and later on myself too, worked for Ford for a while until he got enough money to start Voss Funeral Home with my brother Rudi.'

Tayyar nodded. 'Was it hard? At first?'

'It wasn't easy,' Stefan said.

'Because of competition from established funeral homes?'

He smiled. 'In part.'

Tayyar cocked his head as if inviting the old man to say more, but he didn't. He just sat in a small, crooked heap in front of him, smiling with his watery blue eyes.

Tayyar looked over at the modern face of American undertaking, who smiled back brilliantly, and said, 'Ricky has told me stories about some of the more unusual services you've provided . . .'

'The sarcophagus, those Goths from Grosse Pointe who wanted their mother to have that escape mechanism in the coffin, the guy with the Lynda Carter fixation,' Ricky reminded his great-uncle.

'Americans are so self-consciously eccentric,' the old man said as he looked at Ricky with affection. 'Everything is some Hollywood musical. Your brains have been quite turned by such things.' He glanced back at Tayyar. 'You too are a foreigner in this country, Mr Bekdil; what do you think?'

'About elaborate funerals? I'm a Muslim, Mr Voss. We don't do them.'

'Don't you?'

'No.'

An awkward moment followed. The old man seemed to be indicating that he didn't know anything about Muslim funerals. Did Voss not offer a service to Muslims?

'What about high-profile funerals?' Tayyar said. He was very aware of the fact that with the old man he was pushing against the grain. Stefan Voss was an intensely measured, almost unknowable individual.

172

Two of Ricky Voss's cell phones went off at the same time, and he picked them up and walked outside his office with them pressed against the sides of his head. 'Hi.'

When he'd gone, the old man said, 'We've laid a few prominent people to rest over the years. But you understand that I can't tell you who. That would breach our clients' confidentiality.'

'Sure.'

Silence crashed in as Tayyar tried to think about where he might go with this conversation now. If the old man wouldn't tell him about any famous funerals they had conducted, he would certainly baulk at any sort of allusion to who might have paid for Elvis Goins' service and interment. But as a good reporter, he knew that there were ways and ways of getting information.

'What about notorious funerals?' he said. 'Detroit was once the murder capital of America.'

'You mean gangs?'

'Gangsters, bank robbers, murderers . . .'

'The black people don't use this funeral home as a general rule,' the old man said. 'There are black funeral homes.'

Even given the history of segregation in America, as well as the bitter race conflicts that had taken place in the 1960s, the old man's bald equation of black people with crime caught Tayyar off guard. He'd been around such things as equality training and positive discrimination for a long time. Also, he lived in nice, wealthy Grosse Pointe, where people just didn't talk about race, at least not to him.

'White people commit crimes too.'

The old man didn't answer. He just kept on with that infuriating smile.

Ricky Voss returned, sat down behind his desk and said, 'So, where are we?'

Tayyar didn't know what to say.

'Mr Bekdil was asking about whether we've ever buried any famous gangsters,' the old man said.

173

'Gangsters? Not many,' Ricky said. 'Not really our vibe.'

'But some?'

'Oh, sure,' Ricky said. 'Especially during the 1970s, when all the drug turf wars were going on. Before my time, of course.'

'We buried no one prominent, though,' the old man put in. 'A few street soldiers is all I remember.'

'Right.'

'Oh, but there was, so Dad told me, one gang boss,' Ricky said. 'Some mixed-race—'

'Mixed-race?' The old man shook his head. 'No, Richard, that's not possible.'

A look passed between them that Tayyar found unsettling. For the first time since they'd met, Ricky Voss wasn't smiling. Tayyar looked away and found himself contemplating the photographs of Voss employees on the wall. They were all white.

'Tayyar, we operate a fully racially integrated ship here at Voss,' Ricky said, now smiling broadly once again. 'If black people don't choose us, then that is their right, you know. The funeral I was talking about, the mixed-race affair back in the seventies, was for the leader of a gang who used to call themselves the Delta Blues.'

Tayyar looked out of the corner of his eye at the old man's face. It was bright with what looked like rage.

'A lot of allusions to the old Deep South here in Detroit,' Ricky said. 'But then so many of the auto workers came from places like the Mississippi Delta, Alabama and the like. I remember my father telling me what an elaborate funeral that Delta Blues affair was. Dad was always open to all kinds of different people. He said those mixed-race types who set up that funeral wanted every service we offered to the very highest degree. Best casket, best plot, everything. At the time, he said, he couldn't imagine where poor people like that had got so much money. Later, of course, folk realised it had to have come from drugs.'

174

Chapter 21

Lieutenant Diaz had been less than tidy both on and off his computer system. Sifting through his paper and virtual files, Rita Addison could only cope with looking for Diaz's informants by writing down any names she didn't understand. It was neither scientific nor even particularly practical, but it made her feel as if she was doing something. Everyone else in the department had always shared information to some extent; why hadn't he?

His ex-wife and his son had come in to see the Chief earlier on in the day, and it was said that they had both been in tears. The rumour mill had it that Carmen Diaz had been heard to say that she still loved Gerald, always had. She just hadn't been able to carry on living with him. Rita could so relate to that. For the past eight months, Diaz had supposedly been her partner. But he'd never really let her in. He'd liked her, she was sure, but he'd used every opportunity he got to do things on his own.

'OK?' Shalhoub's voice broke through her thoughts.

She looked up. 'Yes, Lieutenant.' Then she said, 'Lieutenant, did Lieutenant Diaz ever talk to you about Kyle Redmond by name?'

Shalhoub frowned. 'I can't really say,' he said. 'All I know is that I know that name, and I know that it's connected to Diaz.'

He smiled down at her and then moved away. Rita turned back to the screen. It was then, for the first time, that she saw the word *Rosebud* appear in the text. Apparently Rosebud was, to quote Gerald Diaz, 'a pernicious pain in the ass'. Who or what Rosebud was was unclear. But there was venom behind Diaz's allusions, and so she performed

175

a search for other references. There weren't many, but they were all negative. She still couldn't work out whether Rosebud was a person or an organisation, but whoever or whatever it was, Diaz had had his eye on it. Rosebud was something that obviously gave him grief, that bugged him. At one point he even referred to it as 'evil'.

Rita thought about bringing this to Lieutenant Shalhoub's attention, and then thought again. In reality, Shalhoub knew less about Diaz than she did, and besides, as she'd told the Chief, even assuming that the missing Beretta documents had gone back to Grant T. Miller, the fact that Diaz's record of them had disappeared was worrying. The Chief hadn't wanted to accept that anyone in the department could be protecting Miller, but he admitted that it had to be a possibility. Even allowing for Diaz's sloppy paperwork, he'd always had issues with Miller, and so he would have noted anything that could have possibly incriminated him. Deletion had to be a possibility, and she knew that the tech nerds were booked to come and look at the system some time soon. But if Diaz had deleted any references to Grant T.'s gun on his system, why had he sent İkmen that text that could only refer to Miller? 'Got him' had been celebratory, and implied that Miller would soon be behind bars. Why destroy evidence that backed that up?

Now that it was almost dark, he knew the police wouldn't be back. The weather had worked in his favour. Not that he had anything to worry about anyway. Not any more. Grant T. Miller moved back from his rotten front door and shuffled to the kitchen. Time for a cup of coffee and maybe even a cigar if he could find one. Then he'd call the bank. If there was one thing that never failed to bring a smile to his face, it was moving money around. He had a lot of it. He knew that people talked about 'Grant T. Miller's *reduced* fortune', but what did they know? Shit all! He laughed. All those years his father had spent building up the Windmill into a mansion worthy of a European Jewish industrialist. His mother had always known that it was an exercise in bad taste. To deliberately let it rot gave Grant T. pleasure.

176

It also served to give the impression that he, like his father had been, was something he was not. Poor. Poor and eccentric and needy, an old man not worth punishing or robbing because he was nothing and had even less. Not everybody had always been fooled, of course. Not everybody had needed to be.

Çetin İkmen hadn't been required to sober up quickly for years. It was well over a decade since he'd been what anyone could reasonably describe as a drinker. But with Ezekiel Goins, another man who had lost his son, he'd disappeared into a couple of bottles of bourbon. How he'd got back to his hotel suite, he had no idea. But since returning, he'd been sick twice, drunk well over a litre of water and taken a lot of aspirin. He'd just been drifting off into a sleep he hoped might sort his symptoms out when first Tayyar Bekdil had called, and then Officer Addison. The latter had wanted to come over and see him, and had refused to take no for an answer. Sitting on his bed, looking and feeling like death, he was waiting for her now.

Tayyar had spent much of that afternoon at the funeral home that had arranged Elvis Goins' burial. He hadn't managed to find out who exactly had paid for the service; apparently undertakers worked to codes of ethics like doctors and lawyers. But he had found the owners of Voss, or rather Stefan Voss, unsettling. It had been clear that whatever Ricky Voss said, the funeral home preferred, at the very least, to cater for white clients only. Although there was some indication that the younger man was not entirely comfortable with that, the older one had been quite clear on it. He'd also been visibly furious when his great-nephew had talked about Elvis Goins' funeral.

'Ricky Voss said that he believed the money for the funeral came from the sale of heroin,' Tayyar said. 'He said his late father, who had organised the funeral, had been surprised that a family like the Goinses could afford such an elaborate affair. Then, apparently, he'd realised just who Elvis Goins had been, and surmised that the money must have come from narcotics.'

'But the Goins family actually paid?'

'As far as I could tell, yes,' Tayyar said. 'Ricky Voss gave the impression that he was of that opinion, and I've no real reason to doubt him. It was the old man who really didn't want to talk about Elvis, who pulled all the confidentiality stuff.'

'You think the old man knows something different about who paid for Elvis's funeral?'

'I think it's possible, yes. He certainly creeped me out.'

'And this Ricky?'

'I don't know. He appeared to be very nice, very liberal. But he didn't actually answer any of my questions relating to the Goins family in a direct or concrete way.'

Rita Addison arrived later.

As he let her in, İkmen said, 'Have you found the bullet from the Beretta yet?'

'No.' She took her coat, hat and gloves off and sat down in one of the plastic chairs. 'Inspector,' she said, 'the Chief of Detroit PD is very keen to nail Grant T. Miller if he can. That's why you're still here. But with all references that Diaz must have had to the owner-ship of the Beretta gone, I'm in a real fix as to who I can trust. I just don't know!' She put her hands up to her head in frustration. İkmen sat down next to her. 'The only person I know I can definitely be sure of is you,' she said. 'Can I run all this by you again?'

İkmen reiterated how keen he was to help, and so they talked about Diaz's computer records, about Tayyar Bekdil's interview with the Vosses and, of course, about Grant T. Miller.

'Years ago, he had this city pretty much sewn up the way he wanted it,' Rita said. 'Some people believe he still has. Diaz, I think, was one of them. I think he sent you, specifically, that text because he knew that since you were outside of the situation, he could trust you. Without that text to you, I wonder whether the whole thing about Miller shooting the kid Aaron Spencer would have just disappeared.'

'But why would Miller shoot a child?' İkmen asked.

178

'Because the boy was black?'

'But that's ridiculous,' İkmen said. 'I know he is a racist, but surely to kill and put one's own freedom at risk for a dislike . . .'

'Prejudice goes deep here,' Rita said. 'In all directions. But I take your point that to kill Aaron was excessive. And yet Diaz thought he did, and Diaz was no fool! If we had the bullet Miller shot at you, or better still the gun itself, we could prove it.'

Rather unsteadily at first, İkmen got to his feet, went over to his suitcase and took out a pen and a notebook. 'We need to write things down,' he said.

Rita looked confused. 'You don't have a laptop, a BlackBerry?'

'I have a computer in my office in İstanbul and a mobile telephone that isn't a BlackBerry,' İkmen said. 'I'm an old man, Officer Addison; there is a limit to the amount of technological information I can absorb. Now, let us consider, step by step, everything we know about Elvis Goins' death, about Grant T. Miller and about Lieutenant Diaz.'

As Rita spoke, İkmen wrote down salient points, as well as adding some of his own.

'As far as I can tell,' he said, 'the fact that Elvis Goins was a gang leader and a drug-dealer has to be significant. Whoever killed him probably did so as part of a drugs war. Other gangs? Other dealers?'

'At the time, there were rival drug gangs, yes,' Rita said. 'Black gangs, white gangs, Hispanics. I think the Delta Blues were the only mixed-race, Melungeon crew.'

'Melungeons who, as I understand it,' İkmen said, 'were derided by everyone.'

'They were just making a play for some sort of recognition back then,' she said. 'Mayor Coleman Young was doing his best to get black people a fairer deal. Other groups were hopeful too. Eventually Sam Goins came out of all that and really shook things up. But back in the seventies, the Melungeons were still nowhere.'

İkmen wrote it down. 'Also, Miller was involved in drugs, was he not?'

179

'So it's said. But there's no proof. Diaz, I think, believed it. Zeke Goins of course does. The basis of his belief that Miller killed his son rests on the idea that Elvis and Grant T. were rival dealers. The Delta Blues were small-time, just started out.'

'So you wouldn't expect the money Elvis had then made from drugs to pay for an elaborate funeral?'

'No.'

İkmen told her about Tayyar Bekdil's experiences with the owners of the Voss Funeral Home.

'Sadly and stupidly, I got quite drunk with Mr Goins earlier today.'

'Oh.'

İkmen shrugged. 'Sometimes the death of my own son is difficult to bear. When bereaved people talk, such things can happen. But what I do remember him saying is that part of his guilt revolves around the fact that when he left his wife, after Elvis's death, he left her without any money.'

'Could've spent it all on Elvis's funeral,' Rita said.

'Maybe. When I have asked him about it, he always intimates that he paid for it himself. But he never actually says that he did.'

'So . . .'

'So maybe whoever did pay was protecting himself or someone else,' İkmen said.

'Hush money?'

'In a way.'

'But if that was the case, and maybe Miller paid for Elvis's funeral, then it didn't work,' Rita said. 'Zeke Goins attacked Miller . . .'

'Who didn't press charges.'

'And then he hit the road. After he came back, he has been accusing Miller of Elvis's death ever since,' Rita said.

'Diaz met both Miller and Ezekiel Goins when Goins attacked Miller, didn't he?'

'Yes, with his then partner, John Sosobowski.'

'Do you know anything about him?' İkmen asked.

'I know that he's dead,' Rita replied. 'The two of them went out to Brush Park in response to a call from Miller saying he was being attacked by Goins. They broke it up and then took Miller to the hospital. He didn't want to press charges.'

'Do you know why?'

'No. Maybe like you he didn't want the trouble of it.'

'Mmm. But perhaps we should ask him,' İkmen said.

Then they talked about Diaz and how, so far, no one was definitively in the frame for his murder.

'I was looking on his computer system just this afternoon,' Rita said. 'A guy who could have been one of Diaz's informants was found dead in a car crusher out on Eight Mile. Lieutenant Devine, who's working that case, asked me to look on Diaz's system to see whether there were any references to the dead man, Kyle Redmond.'

'And were there?'

'Not obviously,' she said. 'Diaz was very cautious, as you know; he used pseudonyms for his informants. Nothing jumped out that seemed to suggest a car wrecker from Eight Mile.' She frowned. 'What I did find, though, were some references to something or someone called Rosebud.'

'Rosebud? Like the sledge in the film *Citizen Kane*?'

Rita nodded. 'Hadn't thought of that, but yes.'

'What about Rosebud, then?' İkmen asked.

Rita shrugged. 'Hell knows!' she said. 'Mystery to me. All Diaz said about it was that whatever it was, it was bad.'

Rita didn't leave İkmen's suite until nearly midnight. They'd talked for hours and discussed all sorts of scenarios that might pertain to the recent deaths of Diaz, Aaron Spencer and Kyle Redmond. But they'd come to no firm conclusions apart from the fact that a visit to John Sosobowski's widow was something they needed to do. Sosobowski had probably been the closest person to Gerald Diaz.

Maybe he had told his wife things he hadn't told anyone else. Maybe he had known who or what Rosebud was.

Rita was aware of a man standing in the hall talking on his cell phone when she left, but as she got into the elevator, she didn't think about that. The man didn't get in with her. Even when the elevator stopped before the lobby, she didn't think anything about it. Elevators did that all the time.

The doors opened at floor eight and two young white men walked in. They were, Rita reckoned, probably on welfare. Baseball caps pulled tight over their eyes, their baggy jeans down round their asses and the laces undone on their big white sneakers. 'Welfare chic', Diaz always described such a look. Rita herself preferred 'dealer duds'. She made to move over so they could stand together, but she didn't get the chance. Before she could even think about reaching for her gun, they pulled her out of the elevator and threw her to the ground. Wordlessly, the taller of the two sat on her while his companion took his sneakers off and put them tidily down by the wall.

'What do you want! You want my purse? Take it!'

But they didn't want her purse. The one who had taken off his sneakers put on one steel-toecapped boot and kicked her with all his power square in the face. Rita screamed, and he kicked her again. Then she lost consciousness.

By the time someone had called for an ambulance, Çetin İkmen, six floors above, had gone to bed and instantly fallen asleep.

Chapter 22

'You have a problem,' İkmen said as he flicked the ash from his cigarette out of the window. No one had smoked in that office for years, but İkmen was not prepared to even begin to talk unless he was allowed to do so. Details of the attack on Rita Addison had left him shaking with fury.

The Chief of the Detroit Police Department sat behind his desk looking smaller than he usually did. 'I know,' he said. 'Officer Addison . . . she was looking into things at my behest. What she was appearing to unearth made it difficult to trust . . .'

'Someone in your department did not want Lieutenant Diaz's evidence about what I know was Grant T. Miller's Beretta to be discovered,' İkmen said. 'Unless that gun or the bullet he fired at me are found, there can be nothing to connect him, without doubt, to the murder of the young boy Aaron Spencer.'

'There's you.'

'Which was why you wanted me to stay on here?'

'Yes.'

'So you thought, sir, that you might well have a problem in your department, with Mr Miller.' İkmen drew heavily on his cigarette and then completely failed to blow the smoke out of the window.

The Chief sighed. 'People like Miller – and in recent years he's had his black equivalents too – have had undue influence over this city since the beginning of the auto industry. Where there's money, there's bad smells, and even when the money moves out, the stench can remain. Some of these people have influence in Detroit, and if you look, you can see it. They're dealing drugs, running protection rackets, buying up cheap real estate. But we can't connect Miller to any of that. So what's his game?'

'Does he have to have a game?'

'Unless he shot Aaron Spencer for nothing except the colour of his skin,' the Chief said. 'And you know what? I can't believe he did. He's bad, but he's no fool.'

İkmen put his cigarette out on the metal windowsill and then lit up another. 'He shot at my colleague and myself.'

'He didn't kill you.'

'No.'

'So why kill the kid?'

İkmen shrugged. 'Why has Officer Addison had her teeth kicked out, her head stamped upon? Why is Lieutenant Diaz dead? Sir, I am not from this city, and I know only that it has many problems but that the will to bring it back to life is here, is real. Lieutenant Diaz thought in a different way. It was an inspiration to me.'

'His involvement with Antoine Cadillac and other community initiatives was a passion of his,' the Chief said. 'I'll tell you, that's where my head is too, in part. But when shit like hits on kids and cop-killing happens, what can I do but give in to the baying for blood that breaks out across Detroit? This city, Inspector İkmen, has had an ongoing battle with cronyism and corruption since before I can remember. I've always liked to think my officers were above that. Maybe I was just delusional.'

'I think we can assume that Officer Addison is not corrupt,' İkmen said. 'But you know that. You instructed her to work to find that missing bullet. You have to think now about others you know or feel you can trust.'

The Chief put his head down and shook it from side to side. 'According to Addison, she was attacked by two white males in their twenties,' he said. 'Dressed like a hundred thousand other street punks.'

'Did they say anything when they attacked her?'

'Not a word.' He looked up just as İkmen put his second cigarette out on the windowsill. 'But then if it was a hit . . .'

'If.'

'If.'

Both men became silent then until eventually İkmen said, 'Do you know about a person or an organisation called Rosebud?'

It was an odd feeling not to be knocked back by Ayşe Farsakoğlu, especially now that Mehmet Süleyman had returned. Maybe she was disappointed that İkmen hadn't come back with him and wanted someone to talk to. But whatever the reason, she seemed to be quite happy to be sitting opposite İzzet Melik in the upstairs room of the Black Sea Pide Restaurant.

It was lunchtime, and the place was buzzing. There were local tradespeople, a lottery-ticket seller, a smattering of police officers and a small bunch of tourists who looked as if they might be Scandinavian. İzzet and Ayşe had ordered food as soon as they'd arrived, and were now eating.

'Dr Sarkissian is now certain that Kuban took his own life,' İzzet said. He'd heard Süleyman having a conversation with the Armenian earlier.

'Yes,' Ayşe said.

'An end to the matter.'

'For us, yes,' she said. 'But Vice should follow up on the men who admired him.'

'If they can.'

'If they have the will.' It was said bitterly. That absolutely no Vice officer had been in Sulukule on the night of Ali Kuban's suicide still appalled her. Men, she felt, still mostly failed to take the threat of crime against women seriously.

İzzet quite deliberately ignored her. He didn't want to have a conversation he'd already had with her several times already. 'Mehmet Bey didn't like Detroit,' he said. 'Apparently it's a mess.'

'Çetin Bey has other opinions,' she countered. If briefly, she'd spoken to İkmen just after she'd arrived for work. He'd apologised to her for not returning, but had said that what he was being asked to stay on for was important. 'He says Detroit is fascinating.'

İzzet smiled. İkmen always liked a challenge. 'I've heard there's a lot of corruption in that city,' he said.

'There's a lot of corruption everywhere,' Ayşe replied.

Although she'd come along with him happily, her spikiness was unsettling, and İzzet almost wished that he'd opted to have lunch on his own. He didn't say anything more and just waited to see if she'd open conversation with him again. It took several minutes, but when she did speak, her tone had softened.

'I miss Çetin Bey,' she said. It wasn't exactly an apology for her earlier, sharp tone, but he knew that it was as much as he was going to get from her.

İzzet knew that it had only been a few months since her father had died. He knew that Çetin İkmen had helped her, as much as he could, to get through that.

'I'm sure he'll be back as soon as he can,' he said. Then, on impulse, he moved one of his hands across the table and put it gently over hers. At no point did Ayşe look up at him, but she didn't withdraw her hand from underneath his either.

Marie Addison was in the kind of shocked state that turned a person to stone. She'd been in to see her only daughter Rita just the once, and had looked at her terrible smashed face with a mixture of numbness and curiosity. While Rita's older brother Frannie, an attorney, raged and threatened and cried, Marie just sat outside her daughter's side room and stared at the floor. Detroit PD had provided Rita with round-the-clock security, and so there was a uniformed officer at the door to her room, as well as Ed Devine, who had come to visit. Sitting next to Marie, he put a hand on her shoulder and said, 'Rita was conscious when they brought her in. That's a good sign.'

'You think?' Frannie Addison was furious. He walked up and down the corridor, agitatedly waving his BlackBerry around and rubbing a hand compulsively across his bald pate. 'My sister has no teeth, Lieutenant. Her head has been smashed! If she ever wakes up again, who's going to make that right, huh? Detroit PD?'

'Mr Addison,' Devine began, 'we'll do whatever—'

'Whatever what?' Frannie Addison was a tall, very slim man, who nevertheless found fronting up to the much larger Ed Devine no trouble at all. 'What was my sister doing in a shithole like the Lakeland Plaza in the middle of the night, Lieutenant? Can you tell me that?'

Marie looked up and said, 'Frannie, please . . .'

'Please what?' He stared down at her with total fury in his eyes. 'Please what, Momma? Shut up and go away? Just ignore the fact that my kid sister looks like the fucking Elephant Man?'

'Mr Addison, Rita was visiting a colleague who was staying at the Plaza,' Devine said.

Frannie shook his head. 'What? You got cops on welfare now?'

'No, sir, he's a foreign officer. He was at a conference at the Cobo. But while he was in the city—'

'What? He having a thing with my sister? What's this? Some Italian stallion?'

'No, I am Turkish.'

The two men turned around. Ed Devine had seen İkmen before, but Frannie Addison had not. He looked shocked. 'Did someone send for Columbo?' he said. He stared at Devine. 'Did you send for Columbo?'

'My name is not Columbo, it is Çetin İkmen,' İkmen said. He nodded at Marie, 'Madam,' and then walked towards the men. 'Officer Addison came to the Lakeland Plaza to see me. It was police business. Nothing of a romantic nature took place.'

Frannie Addison had a look on his face that seemed to suggest that anything in the slightest bit romantic between İkmen and his sister was impossible. Rita could sometimes be unpredictable in her

187

choice of boyfriends, but he felt she probably drew the line at middle-aged Turks who looked like scruffy TV detectives.

'I am a police inspector in İstanbul, Turkey,' İkmen said. 'I came to the conference here in Detroit and . . .' He didn't know how to even begin to tell the story of why he'd stayed on in the city. 'I have come to see Officer Addison if I can, and also you, Lieutenant Devine.'

'Me?'

'I was told by your Chief that I would find you here,' İkmen said. 'He suggested that we talk.'

The Chief hadn't known anything about the mysterious Rosebud, but he had told İkmen the name of the one senior officer he felt he could trust completely. Devine had just months left in the job, and if for no other reason, he had an investment in being clean because of his police pension. After thirty-five years of service to Detroit PD, he had a lot to lose.

'Talk about what?' Devine asked.

İkmen shook his head. 'I need to speak with you alone,' he said. 'How is Officer Addison?'

'She's alive,' Devine said.

'Just,' Frannie Addison added.

'You are her family?'

Marie stood up. 'I'm her mother,' she said. 'That's Francis, her brother. You didn't see . . .'

'No, no,' İkmen said. 'If I had been with Rita, Mrs Addison, maybe things would have been different. I am ashamed to say that I allowed her to take the elevator on her own. I should not have done that.'

'No, you shouldn't,' Frannie said.

'Ah, hold on now.' Ed Devine tapped Frannie's chest with one long finger. 'How do you think Rita would've taken to a man, any man, offering to protect her in an elevator?' he said. 'Think about it, Frannie, and ask yourself whether she would or would not have laughed at such an idea. Man or woman, Detroit's finest pride them-selves on being able to take care of themselves.'

'And yet clearly that failed in this case,' Frannie said. 'I know that Rita spoke before she lost consciousness, Lieutenant. Tell me, did she say anything about her attacker, whether he was old or young, white or black?'

'Oh, and how does that matter, Francis?' said Marie, suddenly roused to anger. 'White? Black? What's that matter? Too much of all that in this city. People are people!'

'Momma, you know—'

'Somebody tried to kill my daughter for some reason,' Marie said. 'Don't care what or who done it, I just want him caught!'

'I can't tell you any details yet anyhow,' Devine said. 'I'm sorry, that's just the way it has to be.' He turned to İkmen. 'So . . .'

'Çetin.'

'So, Çetin,' he said, 'you want to go in and see Officer Addison? I think the doctor should be finished with her in a little while. Afraid she ain't conscious right now.'

It had been a sadly familiar and characteristically ugly little story. It was one that Samuel Goins seemed to have been listening to for the whole of his life.

'Mrs Jay . . .'

'Your employer?'

'Yes,' the woman said. 'She said that she wanted to take care of William herself.'

'William is the baby you were engaged to look after?' Sam asked.

'Yeah.' The woman, Tabernacle Piper, was the very image of what people thought of as a typical Melungeon. Short, dark, dressed in cheap clothes, a slight look of reserve tinged with nervousness in her eyes. Not one of life's winners.

'Then she tells me I have to go, and so I go,' Tabernacle said. 'Said she wanted to look after William herself. I said fine.'

'So what is your complaint, Mrs Piper?'

189

'Councillor, that woman, Mrs Jay, she didn't look after William herself after I went.'

'Who did?'

'Some foreign woman!' she said. 'She took on some blonde girl from Europe!'

'How do you know this?'

'Because I went up there,' Tabernacle said.

'To Palmer Woods.'

'Mrs Jay said I could always come back and see William if I wanted!'

But as Sam knew, Mrs Jay hadn't really wanted her old nanny to come back at all.

'No other job'd come along, and so I went to see how they was getting on,' she said. 'Saw this girl with William in the garden. I said, "Hi, who are you?" and she said, "Oh, hi, I'm little William's nanny!" Not her fault, the girl. I never said nothing bad to her.'

'You saved that for Mrs Jay.'

'When she drove back in there, I followed her and asked her straight why she got rid of me,' Tabernacle said. 'She give me a lot of stuff about how she'd treated me so well, how she didn't owe me nothing and all that. I said that yes she'd always been good to me but why did she take my job away? First off, she didn't answer, so I run around to stop her getting in the house and I ask her again.'

Sam Goins could imagine the look on Mrs Jay's face, the expression of disgust at this hillbilly, this gypsy woman confronting her in front of her own million-dollar mansion.

'Well, she says that's her business, and if I don't go away she'll call the cops. I told her I was unemployed now and how would she like to try and raise three kids on welfare? Then she just takes her phone out of her purse—'

'Which you grab from her hand.'

'I didn't want her calling the cops! I would've give it back! But then she's "dirty hillbilly" this, "half-breed" that! I said, how come I was good enough to look after William when he was a real tiny baby? Then she says, "Oh, when babies are real tiny, they only need love and comfort, it don't matter where that come from." Mr Goins, William was getting older, starting to talk. She didn't want him to know me because of what I am!'

Back in the sixties and seventies, prejudice had been vicious and obvious and there for all the world to see. A lot of things had changed in the intervening years. Sam's people had, in some cases, moved out into wider society, become educated, sometimes even got good jobs. But what was behind who they were, the sneaking taint of black or Native American, Middle Eastern or gypsy blood in their veins, still meant that those who lived in the fancy burghs and boroughs sometimes openly discriminated against them. Melungeons always had been and remained cheap labour.

It was at times like this that Sam Goins wondered what his own struggle had actually been about. If attitudes had changed so little, why had he put himself through night classes, the hell of competing with his 'betters', in order to put in place an apparatus that felt like a straitjacket to keep him where he was. Tabernacle Piper was as uneducated and stupid as any of Sam's illiterate grandparents. In order to try to get her old job back, she'd abused and frightened her employer, giving the woman a hundred different reasons for not changing her attitude towards Melungeons.

'So you got arrested.'

'Because she give my job to some fancy foreign woman, yeah!' Tabernacle said. 'That ain't right! I told everyone! I said, "It ain't right, but if there's any man as can fix it, then that man has to be Councillor Goins."' She smiled.

Samuel Goins frowned. He'd had thirty years of this, almost without let-up. Complaints and prejudice, discrimination and violence. Would it ever end? Would Melungeons ever be anything more than half-breed trash? Had his Martin Luther King Jr style mission to free his brothers and sisters just been a total pointless fantasy? It wasn't even as if there were millions of them, especially not in Detroit. Sam suddenly felt desolate and weary, and when he spotted a letterhead with a familiar floral pattern on the top of his in-tray, he had to ask Mrs Piper to leave just in case he threw up over his desk.

Chapter 23

'I've no idea about any Rosebud,' Ed Devine said to Çetin İkmen. 'Only as the sledge in *Citizen Kane*.'

'Officer Addison found references to Rosebud on Lieutenant Diaz's computer system,' İkmen said. 'She told me that Rosebud, whatever it is, was something that Diaz found frightening and sinister.'

'Don't know why?'

'No,' İkmen said. 'Even your Chief of Police didn't know anything about it.'

'Diaz, you know, he kept himself to himself.'

They stood outside police headquarters, in the snow, while İkmen smoked and Devine chewed on nicotine gum.

'Lieutenant Diaz, I think, had many secrets,' İkmen said.

'I don't know about many . . .'

'He had secrets.'

'Sure. Who doesn't?'

Devine was being defensive; maybe he felt loyal to his fallen colleague. İkmen could understand that. Police officers everywhere felt a kinship with those also in the job. But in this instance, such loyalty wasn't helping. Even now that Devine had spoken to the Chief of Police himself and he knew full well what İkmen was doing, he remained protective.

'Lieutenant Devine, Lieutenant Diaz is dead,' İkmen said. 'To find out who might have killed him, we need to uncover some of these secrets, I believe. I think we have to do this as soon as we can before anyone else gets hurt.'

'You think whoever was behind Diaz's murder attacked Rita Addison?'

'I don't know,' İkmen said. 'What I do know is that a young boy was killed in Brush Park just as my colleague and I arrived in Detroit. Then I met Ezekiel Goins, who asked me, as a fellow Turk, to solve his son's murder, which took place back in the 1970s. Through Goins, Grant T. Miller came to my attention, and when my colleague and I went to see where he lived, he shot at us. It appears that Lieutenant Diaz managed to get the bullet that killed the boy matched to the gun that Miller used to shoot at me. Then he was killed. At some point, records relating to Miller's gun seem, according to Officer Addison, to have gone missing. To me this implies that someone in your department may have taken those records. Then Officer Addison was attacked.'

He stopped, looked up at Devine and shrugged.

'Seems that Grant T. Miller is quite a prominent feature in all this,' Devine said. 'Cool with me.'

'But not a done deal exactly,' İkmen said. 'Why would Miller kill the child? He wasn't trying to break into his house. Also, we don't know that Grant T. Miller killed Elvis Goins. Ezekiel thinks he did, but as far as I know, there is no actual evidence to prove that. If Grant T. Miller didn't kill Elvis Goins or the child, then why would he kill or get someone else to kill Lieutenant Diaz? Why has Officer Addison been attacked; was it in connection with these events?'

'Who knows?' Devine said. 'I been working on a case involving a man got murdered by his own car crusher.'

'Officer Addison told me about that,' İkmen said. 'The victim was one of Lieutenant Diaz's informants, wasn't he?'

'Could've been,' Devine replied. 'Still not sure. Diaz always disguised his informants behind nicknames only he ever knew.'

İkmen frowned. 'What happened when Lieutenant Diaz went on leave?'

'Vacation? He didn't take vacation,' Devine said. 'You know that just days after Elvis Goins was shot, Diaz and an old cop called John Sosobowski were called out to Grant T. Miller's house because Zeke Goins was trying to bite Miller's arm off.'

'I've heard that, yes,' İkmen said. 'Officer Addison suggested that we try to find out some more about that by visiting Officer Sosobowski's widow.'

'Why's that?'

'Because she may know how and why the two officers managed to persuade Grant T. Miller not to press charges against Mr Goins.'

'Well can't you ask old Zeke about that?'

'Martha Bell, the lady who cares for him, said that once Diaz and Sosobowski had pulled Ezekiel away from Miller, they just threw him out into the street. He'd know nothing. Would Lieutenant Diaz's wife know anything about it?'

'He weren't married to Carmen back then,' Devine said. 'No, Addison was right. If anyone, it would have to be Marta Sosobowski.' He shook his head and whistled. 'She is a scary woman.'

'In what way?'

'You and me'll take a trip over to Harbourtown and you'll find out,' he said. 'Marta and John, when he was alive, were not exactly easy people.'

The whole city was alive with the news that a second police officer had been attacked and, if not killed, then gravely injured. Some officers who had been working on the investigation into Gerald Diaz's death were seconded over to work with a Detective Ryan, who had been assigned to Rita Addison's case. The whole eighth floor of the Lakeland Plaza Hotel was alive with cops and forensic teams looking for clues to the identities of two young white men wearing very white trainers. Unfortunately there wasn't any CCTV evidence on account of the fact that none of the hotel's cameras worked.

The eighth floor was one of those allocated to people on welfare, and so officers made visits door to door. But as usual in these situations, no one had heard or seen anything. Even the woman who lived closest to the elevator and who admitted she must have been at home when Addison was attacked claimed not to have noticed anything. But someone had to have called the emergency services and therefore saved Rita's life.

'They had a double bill of old *Cheers* shows on the TV,' the woman said, and then she smiled. 'I loved them old things. But I have to have the TV up loud now on account of being old and deaf.'

She didn't appear to be lying; she was old and, to Officer Zevets, she seemed to be deaf. He looked around at the stained carpet that barely covered the old woman's floor, and at the tattered blinds up at her one window. What a place for a senior citizen to end up! Both of his grandmothers lived such different lives from this lady! One was in a good care home out at the Points, while the other, Grandma Monica, led what his father darkly described as a 'helluva life' down in Florida.

Zevets was about to leave the room when the old woman, Winnie McGrath, beckoned him back towards her.

'You got something else to say, ma'am?'

Winnie kept on beckoning until Zevets was near enough to be able to see every coarse hair on her chin. 'Come close,' she whispered, 'so they don't hear!'

'Ma'am?' Her thin lips were painted a wild shade of vermilion and her breath smelt like dirty socks.

'Like I said, I heard nothing and saw nothing,' she said. 'But I know that there's evil in this city, Officer.'

Zevets felt his heart sink. The last thing he needed was a religious nut with an evil complex. As soon as she'd said it, the old woman stood back from him as if she had to get out of the way while the shock settled.

'Evil? What kind of evil, ma'am?'

This time she leaned forward to put her head close to his. Then she said, 'Devils!'

'Devils?'

She began to shake. Whatever delusion she was suffering from was nevertheless very real to her. 'They come all hearts and flowers first off,' she said. Tears came into her eyes. 'Then they took everything!'

Zevets frowned. 'Took what?'

Exhausted by the emotions that were clearly taking their toll on her body, the old woman sat down on her bed and closed her eyes. In spite of the fact that he was certain she was insane, Zevets persisted. 'Mrs McGrath? Mrs McGrath, I don't know what you mean. Took what?'

As quickly as they had shut, her eyes snapped open again and she said, 'They took my home, fool! They come in, gave me a handful of dollar bills and they took my home!'

'Now you just sit down there and I will get you a nice glass of tea,' Marta Sosobowski said to Çetin İkmen.

She was a thin, small woman, probably in her early sixties. She was extremely well preserved. This she didn't of course allude to. But what she did go on and on about were her many foreign holidays with her sister Stella.

'Me and Stella've been all over Europe and to Turkey twice,' she said. 'We liked that Grand Bazaar you have in İstanbul very much. Stella bought a lot of purses there, but I went for the tea.'

When she'd left the vast living room with its fabulous riverside view to go and prepare the tea in her equally vast kitchen, Devine turned to İkmen and whispered, 'Marta Sosobowski is what we call an "iron butterfly".'

Çetin İkmen looked confused.

'A southern, generally white woman, all ice tea and home-cooked cakes and standing by her man on the surface, while underneath there's a heart so hard you could cut a diamond with it,' Devine said. 'Mrs Sosobowski is from Texas, which just makes it all the worse.'

'Why?'

'Texans have an attitude, know what I mean?' Devine said. 'Because they come from the biggest state in the union, they always have Old Glory up their asses.'

İkmen didn't really know what he was talking about, but then Marta Sosobowski came back in again carrying very authentic-looking tulip glasses full of tea and what looked like a plate of baklava.

'I am always shopping for groceries in Greektown,' she said. 'Of course, I know you're not Greek, Inspector İkmen, but I know that Turks, just like Greeks, do love these sticky pastries.'

She put their drinks and the plate of baklava down on the coffee table in front of them. İkmen took a sip from his glass and just about managed to avoid pulling a face. It was that disgusting powdered apple tea! So sweet it made your teeth hurt! Sold mainly to tourists, it was something that was in no way to his taste. Mrs Sosobowski, on the other hand, seemed to be enjoying her glass immensely.

Ed Devine put his glass, untouched, down on the table and got straight to the point. 'Marta,' he said, 'I know it's still not easy for you to talk about John, but with Gerry Diaz dead, I didn't know who else to come to.'

Her eyes appeared to moisten. 'That's just fine,' she said through a small smile. 'What do you want to know?'

'It's a long time ago now, and I can't tell you why we want to know about this or nothing, but . . .' Devine swallowed hard. 'Marta, do you remember when John and Gerry hadn't been partners for very long and they were called out to Grant T. Miller's place in Brush Park? Councillor Goins' brother Zeke had attacked Miller because he thought he'd killed his son. It was back in 1978.'

For a moment she didn't speak. She'd heard him all right, but she was, or appeared to be, considering what he had said very carefully. Beautifully made up and also, İkmen reckoned, enhanced by some

198

plastic surgery, Marta Sosobowski was a pretty if rather expression-less woman. Eventually she said, 'I do recall that time, Lieutenant. Not always with affection.'

'No.' Devine chewed hard on his nicotine gum. 'Wasn't a good time for any of us. But that incident, when John and Gerry went out to Grant T. and pulled Zeke Goins off of him, I wondered what you knew about that?'

She shrugged. 'Why would I know anything? John never brought his work home.'

'Just that that incident was famous,' Devine said. 'In the department.'

'Was it?'

'Yeah. Because after John and Gerry pulled Zeke Goins out of there, Grant T. dropped all charges against him.' He smiled very broadly at her unmoving face. 'Not like old Grant to give a break to anyone, much less a guy he considered to be trash.'

'I don't know anything about it.'

Her tone had a finality about it that seemed to rule out any sort of argument; at least that was how it sounded to Çetin İkmen. But Ed Devine, still through a smile, persisted. 'Word at the time was that John and Gerry had done some persuading on Grant T., although I never did believe it myself,' he said. 'Gerry maybe, but not John. Why would he?'

There was some movement in her face, but it was minimal and it made her look slightly cross. 'I hope you aren't implying anything by that remark, Lieutenant.'

Devine shrugged. 'Implying what?'

Her eyes peered up from under her false lashes with what İkmen could only describe as malevolence. 'You know,' she said. Two words imbued with such menace, they made the Turk shudder.

'John's . . . associations?' Devine said.

Marta Sosobowski said nothing.

'Given John's . . . associations, it has always seemed strange to me that he didn't encourage Miller to pin Goins' butt to the wall,' he continued. 'Goins is what John would have called "mixed", a half—'

'Maybe it was Gerry as persuaded him,' she said.

'John?'

'Maybe.' She kept on looking at him, now apparently completely oblivious of Çetin İkmen's existence. 'There is no way of knowing.'

'Because Gerry is dead.'

'And because John's work was a mystery to me.'

'But not his associations?'

Not once did her gaze falter, although it was clear to both Devine and İkmen that there was plenty going on behind the scenes. Her right eye just very slightly squeezed partly shut. 'Lieutenant Devine,' she said, 'the beliefs that John had . . .'

'That you shared.'

She ignored him. 'The beliefs that John had did not, as you know, *ever* affect his application of justice. If he thought that Mr Miller shouldn't prosecute the Goins man, then that had to be for a good reason. My husband was a good person.'

'He was always cool with me, Marta,' Devine said. 'Personally I have no complaints. But I knew of John's beliefs, which was why I could never really square him letting Zeke Goins get off like that.'

'Well maybe it was Gerry who persuaded him,' she said. 'He, after all, would have a . . . sympathy . . .'

'As a Hispanic, or "spic", as I think—'

'We don't use words like that in this house, Lieutenant,' she cut in coolly. 'Opposing views are one thing, bad manners are quite another.' She very quickly and suddenly stood up. 'Now if there's nothing more . . .'

She wanted them to go. İkmen, with some relief, put his glass back on the coffee table and rose to his feet. Devine, suddenly apparently interested in his tea, drained his glass first and then stood up.

'Thank you for your time, Marta,' he said. 'It's appreciated.'

She led them out into the hall and opened the front door for them to leave. When she closed it again, she did so with some force.

Once they'd got into the elevator to take them down to the ground floor, İkmen said, 'Mrs Sosobowski was not pleased to see us in the end, I think.'

'Ah.' Devine chewed his gum and shook his head. 'John Sosobowski, rest his soul, was a man who believed himself to be racially superior to other folks. Don't get me wrong, he never targeted blacks or other non-whites unfairly, as far as I could ever tell. He was always cool with me. But away from work, he hung with some dubious characters.'

'Like Miller?'

'Like him, but not him, if you know what I mean. At the time, back in '78, nobody could work out why he'd been responsible for in effect protecting a Melungeon. Zeke should have been done for attacking Miller.'

'Maybe Lieutenant Diaz . . .'

'Maybe.' He shrugged. 'Although he was very much the junior partner in those days. If John had said "Jump", Gerry would have asked him "How high?" And then there's all the wealth and privilege.'

İkmen frowned.

'You don't get an apartment in a place like this on a police retirement pension,' Devine said. 'It's said that years ago Marta's father was in the Black Legion. There are some who believe that those bastards never disbanded as history would have it. The Legion included a lot of people with a lot of money. It's been said they'd pay cash for those in some kind of authority to do favours for them, know what I mean?'

'Yes.'

'Problem is, a favour for Ezekiel Goins don't exactly fit what John Sosobowski was.'

İkmen said, 'If you knew that Sosobowski was a racist, why didn't you say something before we came here?'

The elevator doors opened.

Ed Devine smiled. 'Because in this city,' he said, 'these days, no one talks about race unless they have to. We all want to move on, Inspector, whatever colour we may be.'

Chapter 24

Çetin İkmen's wife Fatma had already been in to see Ardıç; now she was in Süleyman's office, a large plastic bag full of vegetables at her feet.

'But Mehmet,' she said to him, 'if you were both shot at by this lunatic old man, why has my husband had to stay on in that terrible place and not you?'

Fatma had not been at all happy about her husband going to America. She'd seen a lot of Hollywood movies over the years, and as a consequence of this, she didn't trust Americans. 'Remember that movie *Con Air*?' she asked her husband not long before he was about to leave. 'Terrible convicts who have worn dead people's severed heads as hats flying around in planes! And then *Beverly Hills Cop*! All that swearing, and girls wearing virtually nothing . . .'

'But those are just films,' Çetin had replied, exasperated. '*Just* films!'

Mehmet Süleyman had known Fatma İkmen for years, and to some extent he knew how to handle her fears. 'You know how Çetin Bey always puts himself forward for any kind of duty in a very selfless manner . . .'

'In Turkey, yes.'

'And also abroad,' Süleyman said. 'Look how he volunteered to go to London.'

İkmen had indeed volunteered to work undercover in the British capital some months before. But Fatma knew that at least in part, that had happened because they as a couple had not been getting on.

Disagreements over Bekir's death had led her to tell Çetin to leave. But all that was now very firmly in the past and she just wanted her husband back again. Fatma sighed.

'The bullet that was fired at us has still not been discovered,' Süleyman continued. 'There are problems, Fatma Hanım. I cannot go into those, but in summary, if the Detroit police do not have the evidence from Çetin Bey's eyes, then they have nothing against the man they suspect might have killed a young boy.'

'But if you too were shot at by this man, why couldn't you stay?'

Süleyman smiled. 'Oh, Fatma Hanım,' he said, 'you know your husband better than anyone alive. As soon as we arrived, we were confronted by a mystery. How could you possibly expect Çetin Bey to leave that alone?'

'What are you doing here?'

'What are *you* doing here?' Zeke Goins said to his brother.

It was freezing cold and the early hours of the morning in Brush Park, and the battered, rotting landscape looked like a black-and-white photograph of some wrecked French village during World War I.

As promised, the old man had stopped yelling outside Miller's place in the daytime, but he still turned up to lurk around the Windmill, silently, at night. He knew that Miller didn't sleep. It pleased him to think about him in his cold ruined house, haunted by his own ghastly past. He hadn't expected to see Sam coming out of Miller's place.

'What you doin' goin' in there?' he asked as he pulled his brother away from Miller's front gate and began to drag him down the broken and pitted road.

'My car's this way!' Sam hissed as he pulled his arm free from Zeke's grasp. 'Come on, I'll take you back to Antoine Cadillac.'

But Zeke held on to him. 'No,' he said. 'You're stayin' here until you tell me what's goin' on!'

Sam stopped and shrugged. 'It was business,' he said.

'You do business with . . .'

'Not me, the city!' Sam said. He took hold of Zeke's shoulder and pulled him. 'Come to the car, I'll tell you then.'

When they got inside Sam's Audi, he said, 'You know Miller lives in that wreck by choice? He's salted away millions of dollars over the years.'

'So he *is* still a player in this city.'

'Of course he is!' Sam had always despaired of what he took to be his brother's slowness, his stupidity. 'What do you think happens to people like him? They don't just go away, do they!'

'People like him, people who makes others' lives a misery, who kill people . . .'

'Oh get real, Zeke!' Sam said. 'Haven't you ever heard of the expression "holding hands with the devil"?'

Ezekiel Goins looked over at his brother with what he felt were fresh eyes. What kind of business could Sam possibly be doing with Grant T. Miller on behalf of the city in the middle of the night?

'So, you holding hands with this Miller devil, then?' he asked. He couldn't wipe the disgust off his face and he was well aware that his brother could see it.

Sam turned in his soft leather seat and looked squarely at Zeke. 'You know what the score is, don't you?' he said. 'Look around you. The city's fucked.'

They could both remember when Brush Park had been a district that people aspired to live in. Zeke could easily recall when the local women had employed nannies and some of the men chauffeurs. Now there were junkies' syringes in the bushes, and great open pits were all that remained of people's once well-stocked cellars.

'I know that what Martha and all her workers do is marvellous,' Sam said. 'But Zeke, that is small-scale. To bring Detroit properly back to life, we need big money.'

'From Grant T. Miller?'

'He's just one of a number of possible investors,' Sam replied. 'He's got no heirs. If I can get him to give at least some of what he's made from this city back to it, then that will be something, won't it?'

'Dirty money!'

'Who cares!'

Zeke looked at his brother with what Sam interpreted as suspicion.

'What?'

'What?' You say "what", Sam?' He shook his head. 'Don't make no sense.'

'What doesn't?'

'That they send you to do business with Grant T. Miller! You, being what you are. There's white people on the city council; why didn't they send one of them? And why you do this at night? Why?'

Samuel Goins was tired. After being in with Miller for an hour in the middle of the night, the last thing he'd needed was an argument with his brother. Uncharacteristically, he lost his temper.

'You know what, Zeke?' he said as he leaned in closer to the smell of old tobacco and soil that was his brother. 'It's none of your fucking business! I work for the city authorities and what they ask me to do, I generally do. And don't give me any of that Melungeon shit either! Completely alone I have raised awareness of our illiterate, superstitious, thoughtless people to a level where at least we are listened to now. Although why, I don't know! I had a woman in my office yesterday, one of our people, who'd got herself arrested for threatening her previous employer. Illiterate and stupid, she couldn't understand why her employer had replaced her as a nanny with a highly educated European girl!'

'Well that's just plain wrong!'

'What? Replacing the stupid woman with a bright one, or threatening an employer?'

For a moment Zeke looked confused, and then he said, 'Well, both.'

Sam, now spent after his outburst, put his head down on the steering

206

wheel and shut his eyes. For a moment there was complete silence, then Zeke said, 'So did I get that wrong, Sam, or what?'

For a few seconds Sam Goins didn't answer. When he did, he lifted his head slowly from the steering wheel and said, 'Let me drive you home. We're both tired now.'

Zeke looked back at him and said, 'Sam, I'm just worried that if you're doing business with Miller, he's gonna cheat you.'

Sam started the ignition. 'Don't worry about that, Zeke,' he said. 'No one's going to cheat either me or the city of Detroit. Not even Grant T. Miller.'

Lieutenant Devine hadn't told him that he was moving out of the Lakeland Plaza until they had returned to the hotel at the end of the day. He'd been even more surprised when Devine had told him that rather than moving to another hotel, he was for the time being going to be staying with the lieutenant at his apartment in Greektown. The irony of a Turk staying in that particular district was not lost upon him. And neither was the motive behind the move. Two officers who had been involved in the investigation or possible tracing of a significant weapon had been attacked; one had died. İkmen alone in the US was the one person who could and would swear that the gun that had fired at him had been a Beretta that had belonged to Grant T. Miller.

İkmen turned over in the vast and very comfortable bed Devine had shown him to and tried not to think about home. In reality, Süleyman could just as easily have stayed on instead of him. But then not only had the younger man not wanted to, he didn't have the same investment with regard to Ezekiel Goins as İkmen had. He thought that all Melungeons were delusional nuts and was also, İkmen felt, rather offended at the idea of a load of uneducated Americans calling themselves Turks. To İkmen, although he'd used the 'helping a fellow Turk' line of reasoning with Ardıç, it didn't really matter either way. If Goins was a Turk, then fine; if he wasn't, that was OK too. That he was a grieving father was the only thing that meant anything.

He'd had a pleasant evening with the lieutenant. Devine's wife was away visiting her family in Georgia, and so Ed, as he insisted İkmen call him when they were off duty, had cooked a very nice meatball and pasta dish. After that they'd had ice cream and had then settled down to watch TV with a couple of beers. It had all been very civilised, and İkmen had even been able to smoke indoors, provided he stood by an open window. But in spite of all that, he couldn't sleep. As well as seeing Fatma's disappointed face over and over in his mind, he also couldn't get Ezekiel Goins and his son out of his head either. Then he started wondering why he'd never seen a photograph of Elvis Goins, and began creating a picture of what he might have looked like in his head.

The more he thought about it, the more he began to realise that Zeke, as well as so many other people he'd met in Detroit, was hiding something from him. True, he clearly had absolutely no idea about why he hadn't been prosecuted for his attack on Grant Miller, but he did know who had paid for Elvis's funeral. What was more, İkmen knew to his marrow that whoever had paid for the boy's funeral knew who had killed him, and why.

The receptionist at the Lakeland Plaza hadn't noticed two white men wearing hoods and white trainers exiting the building any time during the night when Rita Addison had been attacked. Just like Diaz's neighbours over in Corktown, she was deaf, dumb and blind. That said, if the two men had had accomplices in the hotel, they could have got out via the service entrance. Since none of the hotel CCTV cameras worked, there was nothing to stop them doing that completely undetected. Apparently the cameras hadn't worked for months.

What was clear, however, was that somehow the men who had attacked Rita had either been following her or had been tipped off about her whereabouts. Zevets couldn't sleep for thinking about it.

He got out of bed as quietly as he could so as not to disturb his partner and went down the corridor to the kitchen. Even though what he really, really wanted was a cigarette, he made himself a cup of coffee instead and stood at the breakfast bar to drink it. There had been just one thing that the receptionist at the Lakeland Plaza had said that had been interesting, and that was about the old woman he'd interviewed on the eighth floor, Winnie McGrath. While he'd been with her, Winnie had become very upset about having lost her home some time before she'd come to live in the Plaza. But when he'd asked her where her home was, she hadn't been able to tell him. She couldn't remember. But the receptionist had known. 'Oh, Winnie lived in a big house in Brush Park for years,' she'd said.

Remembering Winnie's story about devils coming and taking her home from her, Zevets had asked the receptionist whether she knew how the old woman had lost her home.

'I think from the sound of it it was one of those companies who come in and offer you money, you know. Sort of like a cheap way to buy property. She was confused and took it and it was virtually nothing,' she'd said.

'When was this?'

'About five years ago.'

'Do you know which company?'

She hadn't. But when he'd got back to headquarters, Zevets had done some research into who had bought property up in Brush Park over the past few years. There were basically three commercial companies involved. Two had already started on programmes of redevelopment, while the third, an organisation with the unlikely name of Gül, owned all of the wrecked and blasted land that surrounded Grant T. Miller's house – with the very glaring exception of the Windmill itself.

Chapter 25

'Martha!'

'What?' She had been vacuuming the living-room carpet. Now she'd switched the carpet sweeper off and was looking across the room at Zeke. His face was grey and he was troubled. She went over to him. 'What is it? You feel sick or something?'

'No.' He sat down on one of her large orange sofas.

'Then what is it?' It was like having another child, which was probably why Martha Bell put up with it. She missed her sons, both the living one and the dead.

'You know when Inspector İkmen come and he ask me to tell him everything I could remember about Elvis's death?'

'Yes. You did that,' Martha said. 'I heard you.'

Zeke took a deep breath in. ''Cept what I left out.' He lowered his head in shame.

Martha looked confused. 'What's that?' she said.

'About my payin' for my boy's funeral,' Zeke said. 'I never had that kinda money.'

'Then who did pay for it?' Martha sat down next to him and took one of his hands. Silly old fool, he was probably just rambling in his mind, like he did sometimes.

'I don't know,' the old man said.

'You don't know?'

'The cops took my boy's body for some time to look at it for evidence,' he said. 'I couldn't arrange no funeral until they gave me him back. Before that happened, I had a visit from Mr Stefan Voss from the funeral home.'

210

'Mmm, mmm!' Martha shook her head wearily. 'Don't the vultures always gather!'

'Oh, he didn't want my business, not as such,' Zeke said. 'No, he come to tell me that if I went with his company, then anything that I wanted would be paid for.'

'By who?'

'He wouldn't say.'

'Did you ask?'

'Course I did! But he just clammed up! Said it was a "well-wisher". Someone heard about Elvis and wanted to do what he could. First off, I didn't know what to do! Me and Sheila had just about enough for burying the boy, but nothing fancy. If I went with Voss, I could have him buried with respect out at Woodlawn, big memorial, everything!'

'Without knowing who was paying, or why?'

'Old man Voss wouldn't say. What could I do? Over the years I've thought all sorts. Maybe it was someone with money in our community . . .'

'Back then your people didn't *have* money!' Martha said. 'Even now, beyond your Sam, how many mountain people you know with that kind of cash?'

He shrugged.

'Why didn't you say anything about this before, Zeke?' she said.

He was quiet for a moment, and then he said, 'Because I was ashamed. There's only so much failure a person can stand. I couldn't hold down my job after that, couldn't stay and try to keep my wife, couldn't even bury my own son with some kind of dignity.'

Martha walked over to the stereo and put a Stevie Wonder CD on. She always thought better with Motown in the background. 'Maybe you should ask this Mr Voss about it now,' she said.

But Zeke just shrugged. 'Lord, he was about a hundred then. He must be dead and gone by now.'

* * *

Donna Ferrari didn't know whether or not she should speak in front of the Turk. That he was still hanging around the department was not something she could really understand. So old Grant T. Miller had shot at him and his colleague! Why Detroit PD couldn't just take a statement off him and send him home, she didn't know.

Seeing her reticence in İkmen's presence, Ed Devine said to her, 'It's OK. If you've got something to say to me, you can say it in front of Inspector İkmen.'

She eyed the Turk a little nervously. Unlike his colleague, he was battered, skinny and in no way easy on the eye. His teeth were yellow! But she ploughed on. 'Lieutenant,' she said, 'the car wreckers up on Eight Mile. It seems that an old Chrysler was crushed not long before Kyle Redmond met his death. Forensics are pulling it apart to take a look.'

'Mmm. Radical, but if there's nothing else . . .'

'The wreckers' lot is isolated,' she said. 'Redmond had cameras just for show.'

'Like so many,' sighed Devine. 'You have these security cameras in Turkey, Inspector?'

'Increasingly,' İkmen said.

'Mmm.' It wasn't easy for Devine to work with his own team as well as trying to pick up where Rita Addison had left off. 'OK, Sergeant,' he said to Ferrari. 'Keep me posted about what, if anything, forensics find.'

'Yes, Lieutenant.' She moved away.

'So you and me, Inspector, up to Brush Park,' Devine said as he stood up and put his suit jacket on.

'We're still looking for the bullet?'

'Not yet,' he said. 'We're going to go and meet an Officer Zevets up at a place called the Royden Holmes House.'

When they'd left the squad room to make their way down to Devine's car, John Shalhoub came out of his office and took Donna Ferrari to one side. 'Where are they going?' he asked.

'I don't know,' she said. 'Lieutenant's working two cases now; he's all over the place.'

'I have no idea whether any of this means anything, Lieutenant,' Mark Zevets said as he walked over to Ed Devine's car and got inside. 'If the receptionist at the Lakeland Plaza hadn't confirmed what the old lady had said, I would have thought it was just crazy rambling.' It was only then that he noticed İkmen. 'Oh . . .'

'This is the Turkish officer that Miller shot at,' Devine explained. 'He was staying at the Lakeland Plaza until yesterday.'

Zevets leaned across the back of İkmen's seat and took his hand. 'Sir. Officer Addison talked about you.'

İkmen asked after Rita Addison and was told that her condition was slowly improving. But it was not because of Rita, or even because of the missing bullet, that Zevets had suggested meeting outside the house where Aaron Spencer had been killed. 'I did some research last night,' he said, 'and what I discovered was that all this property round here, with the exception of Grant T. Miller's place, is owned by one property development company.'

'Uhuh.'

'If what old Mrs McGrath and the Lakeland receptionist told me is true, then they're the kind of organisation who march into old folk's places, offer them a few dollars for their damp, rotting property and then promptly ditch them out on the street,' Zevets said.

'Unfortunately there's no law against the practice of buying and selling property, unless duress can be proven,' Devine said. 'And as you know as well as I, Officer, that is no mean task to accomplish.'

'No, Lieutenant, except that Mrs McGrath was apparently turned out of this part of northern Brush Park five years ago. Now do you see any property development going on around here?'

The view outside the car consisted of potholed roads, empty, litter-strewn lots and houses in either moderate or advanced states of decay.

'In the streets where this company doesn't own property, to the south, regeneration has been taking place for some time. But these people . . . Not a thing.'

'Maybe they're waiting to get old Grant T.'s place before they flatten the whole burgh,' Devine said.

'They must've tried.'

'Yeah, or not.' Devine smiled. 'Can you imagine anyone forcing Grant T. to do anything he didn't want? Chances are they were more afraid of him than he was of them.'

'Perhaps they're waiting for him to die.'

'Wait a long time,' Devine sighed. 'What's that saying about the devil looking after his own?'

They all laughed. Then for a moment they stopped and looked at the desolation around them. What remained of mansions in styles that ranged from the classical to the gothic poked out like sinking ships from ground littered with old furniture and the detritus of drug use. Even the litter was old; even the junkies had moved out years before.

'Lieutenant, I think we should go talk to Miller, see what he knows about these people.'

'Why's that? Company's buying old property, badly, but legit as far as anyone knows,' Devine said. 'If they've been hassling Miller, then he's enough money and influence to look after himself.'

'Maybe,' Zevets said. 'But there's something else.'

'What?'

'I don't know, but I think that Lieutenant Diaz had some sort of notion that there was a witness to the murder of Aaron Spencer.'

'How you know that?'

Zevets cleared his throat. 'Because when Officer Addison and I were looking for the bullet that killed the boy in the Royden Holmes place, Diaz asked us if we'd seen anyone around apart from the couple of kids we'd interviewed on the day of Spencer's death.'

'He didn't say exactly why?'

214

'No.'

'No idea who he might have been talking about? Who he had in mind?'

'No.'

'And had you seen anyone?'

'No,' Zevets replied. 'No one. He asked Addison, Lieutenant Shalhoub, who wasn't there that day anyway, and me. We saw nothing. Don't know who or what could have given him that notion. But so few people come up here now, when I heard about this property company I wondered if maybe it was one or more of them. I'm not saying I believe that they're involved or anything, but . . .'

'You think maybe they were viewing their real estate that day?'

'It's not impossible,' Zevets said. 'And there's something else too, Lieutenant. This company, Gül Inc. . . .'

'Gül?' For the first time İkmen spoke. 'How do you spell that word, Officer?'

'G, U, L,' Zevets said. 'Based down south, Savannah.'

'Stylish.'

'Turkish, if I am not mistaken,' İkmen said. 'You know, gentlemen, that *gül* in Turkish means rose.'

Ayşe looked at her own reflection in her bedroom mirror. She was still good for a woman in her thirties. Not exactly beautiful any more, but very striking. She moved her head closer to the glass and looked at herself in more detail. Twenty years of smoking and the strong İstanbul summer sun had put some lines on her face, but they weren't deep. She'd used moisturising cream since she was in her early twenties and so her skin was still supple.

At one time she had considered having Botox injections, but had then decided against it. Not only were they expensive, she wasn't sure that she liked the frozen-faced look it gave some people. Besides, it didn't seem appropriate somehow for a police officer. A lot of the rich women in places like Nişantaşı did it, and they had plastic surgery

215

too. But she wasn't one of them. She didn't fit with the covered religious women who would consider such vanities sinful either. When she felt the time had come to have some physical 'augmentation', she'd have it, provided she could afford it. Not that that was a real possibility. She was a single woman who earned a no-frills living wage; there was just about enough money for clothes, perfume and make-up.

Ayşe threaded a pair of gold and turquoise earrings through the piercings in her lobes and sprayed her throat with Prada perfume. It was clearly fake; she'd bought it from a rough little man with lots of similar bottles in a suitcase in the street. His brown countryman's face had reminded her of her father. She missed him so much! She was a modern, independent woman, but the warm feel of the presence of a man in her life was now missing, and she hated it. There was her brother, but he had a new girlfriend with whom he was besotted and so he really didn't count, Çetin İkmen was thousands of miles away in America, and Mehmet Süleyman was now entirely off her radar. Some men, however fascinating, were just too complicated and difficult.

Apart from a few acquaintances, that left only one man of any significance in her life, and he looked for all the world like a *maganda*, a brainless macho man. Except that he wasn't. İzzet Melik, appreciator of art and speaker of Italian, only looked like a *maganda* on the outside. But that, sadly, was a problem.

He'd asked her out and Ayşe had agreed to go. Dinner at a new and apparently exciting international restaurant in Beyoğlu. She loved to go to places like that! İzzet was very knowledgeable about food and would not do or say anything that would in the least way embarrass her. But with that awful moustache and those terrible man-made-fibre shirts he bought from the cheap market stalls down by the Yeni Cami . . .

Ayşe looked in the mirror again and asked herself seriously who she was fooling. İzzet clearly adored her. He was intelligent, cultured,

216

kind and honest. He wasn't hideous, and although he still smoked heavily and ate too much, he was far from being gross. She could do worse, especially for a woman of a certain age with lines on her face. And yet as she finished getting herself ready for her date, she found she couldn't, not even to preserve her carefully applied make-up, stop just one tear from sliding down her cheek and on to her lip gloss.

Chapter 26

Details regarding Gül Inc. were few and far between. Based in Savannah, Georgia, their offices appeared to be not much more than a post pick-up point. The company had no direct internet presence, and all telephone calls went straight to answerphone.

'Outside Turkey and the Turkic nations, few people speak Turkish,' Çetin İkmen said once they'd returned to PD headquarters and were sitting around Ed Devine's desk.

'Yeah, but Inspector,' Devine said, 'Grant T. don't have to know what the word means to know that a company with that name has bought up all the property around his house. Whatever he is, Miller ain't no fool, and so he was lying when he said he'd never heard of Gül.'

They'd been to visit Miller while they were in Brush Park, and he had admitted to no knowledge about anything, least of all a property company called Gül Inc.

Zevets, who at İkmen's suggestion had been looking at Diaz's computer, came back into Devine's office and shut the door behind him.

'I can see what Addison meant,' he said as he sat down beside the Turk. 'There are references to going to visit Rosebud, to the increasing influence that they are having, but then there's some stuff about Rosebud ultimately "playing ball", whatever that means.'

Devine raised his eyebrows.

'The last thing I'd ever say is that Lieutenant Diaz was on the take or anything like that.'

'But not saying don't mean you ain't thinking it,' Devine said.

Zevets said nothing.

'I knew Lieutenant Diaz only a little,' İkmen said, 'but he seemed in no way corrupt to me.'

'No.' Devine, if not Zevets, was, İkmen felt, dead set against the idea of Diaz being caught up with anything he shouldn't have been. İkmen himself was not, in reality, so sure.

'Unless it can be proved that Gül is in fact a Turkish company, then whoever named it did so either because they know what it means, rose or rosebud, or because it means something quite different to them, maybe in another language,' he said. 'If we assume that it is Turkish and that the Rosebud that Lieutenant Diaz talks about in his records is one and the same thing, then we have to look at not just local Turkish people, but also some of these Melungeons who believe they are descended from Turks.'

'Some of 'em speak Turkish?'

'According to my superior in İstanbul, some of those who have visited our capital, Ankara, have taken it upon themselves to learn,' İkmen replied. 'Maybe Mr Ezekiel Goins' brother would know of any such people in Detroit.'

'Sam Goins? Maybe.' Devine leaned heavily on his desk and chewed his nicotine gum thoughtfully. 'But rather than go to Sam yet, I think I want to get as full a financial work-up on this Gül company as I can. I don't like it when property developers turn people out of their homes, however bad those homes might be. Where things like that happen, you also find things like tax evasion and money-laundering too, in my experience.' He picked up his landline telephone and punched in a number that he obviously knew by heart. 'Let me talk to some people, get a view.'

İkmen looked out at the squad room, where members of John Shalhoub's team were eyeing Devine's office with looks of anxiety on their faces. No one ever liked even the vague suspicion that a fellow officer was corrupt, and Gerald Diaz, for all his maverick awkwardness, had been liked.

*   *   *

219

Once he'd made a few telephone calls, Grant T. Miller felt better. Everything had been taken care of; the cops were just poking around in response to a few facts they'd come across that wouldn't make any sense to them. Everything that needed to be in place was in place, and so nothing, for him, was going to change.

He sat down in front of some crazy talk show on the TV, but he couldn't get into it. His mind went back to Elvis Goins. Sometimes it just did. Little punk had thought he was king of the world when he'd formed his gang of misfits and got his hands on some gear from immigrants over in Greektown. One bunch of foreigners going into business with another bunch of foreigners. It had disgusted him! And the kid had been good at it too! Grant T. put a hand up to his chest and tried to control his breathing. Even though all of that had happened over thirty years ago, it still rankled. Elvis Goins had been so full of himself in his new, big drug-dealer persona!

Grant T. shuffled around amongst the boxes of pills on his coffee table until he found those things the doctor had given him for his blood pressure. He didn't generally take them, but now he could feel his heart pounding and so he swallowed one. After that he necked a shot from a bottle of Jack Daniel's, and then tried to forget about Elvis and his dad and John Sosobowski and Gerald Diaz and all the shit. But it wasn't easy, mainly because he couldn't get away from the idea that all this police sniffing around was something he'd brought upon himself. Because it was.

The car had been a Chrysler New Yorker from sometime back in the 1980s. How the forensics people could tell that from an almost completely square hunk of mangled metal, Donna Ferrari didn't know. But then a lot of them were nerds, and she knew that at least one was a crazy automobile nut.

They'd taken the New Yorker to a lot they used to test cars just up beyond Six Mile. Donna Ferrari watched as three investigators began to gently remove any pieces of metal or fabric sticking out from the periphery of the block.

'What are you looking for exactly?' she asked.

No one said a thing. It was always the same with these nerdy, academic types. In their own worlds, up their own asses.

'Hello?'

A guy who was somewhere in his thirties but looked about twelve glanced up. 'Can I help you?'

'What you looking for?' Donna Ferrari asked.

'Don't know,' he said. He was called, she remembered, Dr Harris. Doctor!

'So . . .'

'This vehicle was beside the crusher when we found Redmond's body in the machine,' Dr Harris said. 'It could be that it was the last automobile Redmond ever wrecked. Maybe if we can find out who it belonged to, we might be able to get some kind of lead on this.'

'You think the owner of this car could have killed Kyle Redmond?'

'It's a possibility,' he said.

The two other investigators were almost gleefully beginning to tease the cube apart.

'As far as I know, you've no other lines of inquiry on this case, have you?' Dr Harris said as he looked away from Ferrari and attended to the block once again.

'No.'

He pulled a strip of metal forwards with one plastic-gloved hand. 'Then let's see what she gives us, shall we?'

Donna's cell phone rang, and she took the call while walking over to the far side of the lot. It was Lieutenant Shalhoub.

'Thought you'd like to know we've had a break in the Diaz investigation,' he said.

She hadn't agreed with Gerald Diaz about much, but she had always admired him and had been quietly distressed when he was murdered.

'A white guy called Clifford Kercheval,' he said. 'A record for small-time misdemeanours going back to when he was a juvenile.'

'He killed Diaz?'

'It's possible.'

'Why?'

'Same gun, couple of pictures of Diaz obviously taken without his knowledge. Also a pair of bright white sneakers. Addison was hit by a young white guy wearing bright white sneakers. Remember?'

'Yeah, but Addison was just beat up,' Ferrari said. Rita Addison had been savagely attacked by people whose motives were unknown. Diaz, on the other hand, had been a prominent local detective with any number of potential enemies.

'So what's this Kercheval's connection to Diaz?' Ferrari asked.

'Don't know, as yet,' Shalhoub replied. 'But we'll find it.'

'You gonna make him talk?'

'Unlikely,' Shalhoub said.

Ferrari didn't understand. 'Why?'

'Because he blew his own brains out,' Shalhoub said. 'A neighbour called in the shot a couple of hours ago.'

'Hey, you.'

'Hey.' Rita Addison spoke with difficulty, her words spilling out of her mouth on a froth of saliva. Eight of her front teeth had been completely destroyed, while all her side and back teeth just hurt like hell.

Mark Zevets, with Çetin İkmen in tow, walked over to her hospital bed. He took one of her bruised hands and squeezed it. 'How you doing?'

'I guess I'm OK for a toothless hag.' She smiled, but kept her lips closed as she did so. In spite of the damage to her mouth and the bruising and swelling on her face, she was still a lovely young woman. She also realised, along with everyone else, that she was very lucky to be both alive and out of the coma she had been in just twelve

hours before. 'You still with us, Inspector?' she said to Çetin İkmen.
İkmen smiled.

'Fortunately he is,' Zevets said. 'This Rosebud thing you saw on Diaz's computer system? Inspector İkmen found what could be a connection to a property company name of Gül, which is Turkish for rosebud.'

Rita looked up at İkmen. 'Diaz was involved with Turkish people?'

'We don't know,' İkmen said. 'Maybe I am wrong about Gül, maybe I am right. Lieutenant Devine is trying to find out more details about this company now. Perhaps it is a coincidence.'

'Gül owns all the land around Grant T. Miller's place,' Zevets said. 'Block after derelict block.'

Rita raised her eyebrows.

'Even if he's not involved with Gül, Miller has to know about them,' Zevets said. 'They're his neighbours. But he denied all knowledge.'

'That's Grant T.'

'And there's something else too,' Zevets said as he put a hand inside his jacket and took out a photograph. 'Can you look at this and see if you recognise this guy?'

'Sure.'

A photograph of the man who might have killed Diaz, Clifford Kercheval, was handed over. Rita frowned. 'You have him in custody?'

'Kind of,' Zevets said.

Rita looked up.

'Kercheval is dead,' İkmen said. 'It was apparently suicide.'

'Do you recognise him?'

Rita stared at the photograph for another few moments, then said, 'Sort of. But I couldn't swear to it. There's something about him, but . . . Why'd he commit suicide? Not over me, I don't imagine.'

'We don't know,' Zevets said. 'But Lieutenant Shalhoub has recovered some evidence that could suggest he may have had something to do with Diaz's death.'

'You think?'

'I don't know. We just found out,' Zevets said.

'A lot has happened,' İkmen said. 'Many things that may or may not be connected.'

'But if connections do exist, it's up to us to find them,' Zevets said. 'At the moment we have a dead kid called Clifford Kercheval and a real-estate company with a Turkish name, but there's still no sign of Grant T. Miller's Beretta. What it all might mean is anyone's guess.'

Gül Inc. was registered in the state of Georgia under the name of someone called R. Lacroix. There were apparently two R. Lacroix in Savannah, Georgia. One, Ronald Lacroix, was eighty years old and in a care home, while the other one, Renee, was a child of five. That said, the name was well known in Savannah. From a once influential French family, they had owned vast lands in Georgia upon which they built a huge antebellum mansion and employed thousands of African slaves.

Detective Katz, who had been investigating the profile of Gül Inc., told Ed Devine that the family had hit hard times just after the turn of the twentieth century. 'The Lacroix clan split up,' he said. 'The family that remains in Georgia aren't rich. Current head, Laurent Lacroix, grandson of Ronald and father of Renee, teaches high school. No one in the city has even heard of Gül, apart from the landlord of the building where the mail gets delivered.'

'What's he or she say?'

Katz rubbed his eyes wearily. He'd been on this Gül thing since early that morning. Now it was dark.

'Once a month, some smart-looking man with a northern accent comes and collects the mail. Once a year, this same man pays the landlord rent for twelve months in cash.'

'He's no idea who the man is?'

'The guy pays in cash,' Katz said. 'What's not to like? Savannah

PD say that the address is in a part of town where most men drink Bud all day long and a lot of women earn their bread dancing around poles.'

'Classy. What else?'

Katz looked down at the notes he'd taken. 'It's definitely Gül of Savannah that owns the lots up in Brush Park,' he said. 'There's a business account with the Bank of America that contains just under a million dollars.'

'Not rich for these days,' Devine commented.

'No, sir. But as far as we can tell, it all belongs to this R. Lacroix, who would appear to be a northern guy somewhere in his middle years.'

Devine laced his fingers underneath his chin and frowned. 'What about Lacroix in Detroit?'

'I'm on it, but it'll take time,' Katz said. 'Lieutenant, is this about wrongful appropriation of land up in Brush Park?'

The financial guys didn't need to get mixed up in homicide cases, or indeed in the investigation into the death of a fallen homicide officer. Devine had decided to keep much of the reason he wanted to know about Gül to just himself and his own team for the time being.

'Yeah,' he said. 'Found out about it when Officer Addison was beaten up in the Lakeland Plaza. One of the residents alleged certain things about this company Gül.'

'Including homicide?'

Devine smiled. Katz was no fool; he knew that there was more to Gül than just some harassment complaint.

'Maybe,' Devine said. 'Thanks.'

'I'll keep digging on this Lacroix thing,' Katz said as he rose from his chair to leave. 'Most of the old south came up here for work at the beginning of the twentieth century. I'd not be surprised if the odd Lacroix was somewhere in town.'

* * *

Dr Steve Harris, known to his friends on Facebook as 'the Docster', found the remains of a small firearm in the very deepest part of the New Yorker in the early hours of the morning. He couldn't even begin to make a guess as to what kind of gun it was. Firearms were not his thing. But he bagged up the twisted, tortured object and put it to one side with all the other detritus from the crushed car. Then he updated his Facebook status from 'overworked but happy' to 'totally jazzed'.

Chapter 27

To begin with, Çetin İkmen wondered why and how someone with such a strong southern American accent had got hold of his mobile phone number. Then, as his brain began to emerge from the fog of sleep, he remembered: of course, this was Ezekiel Goins.

'I apologise for calling so early, but I had to talk to you, Inspector,' Goins said.

İkmen looked at his watch. It was just six a.m. He wondered if the old man had been awake all night waiting to call him when the time arrived at a 'reasonable' hour.

'What do you want, Mr Goins?' İkmen heard Devine stir in the next bedroom. He lit a cigarette and leaned back on his pillows.

'Martha said I should tell you,' Goins said.

'Tell me what?'

'That I never paid for my Elvis's funeral,' Zeke said.

This was, of course, no surprise. 'Oh?'

'When Elvis got shot, Mr Stefan Voss of Voss Funeral Home come to see me and he told me as how there was money at his company for my boy's funeral.'

Dragging hard on his cigarette, İkmen asked, 'You mean Voss paid?'

The old man cleared his throat. 'No!' he said. 'They way too close to do that!'

'So who did pay, then?'

'Can't tell you,' Zeke said. 'Don't know to this day who done it.'

'You have no idea?'

227

'No!'

'But how could you do that?' İkmen asked. 'How could you not know? It could have put you in debt to someone unpredictable or dangerous.'

'I don't know,' the old man said. 'Whoever done it never come back to ask me for nothing. Stefan Voss, he said it were an anonymous donor. Some rich person felt sorry for my boy in all likelihood.'

'But I still don't know how you could take it.'

'It ain't my concern you never been too poor to not take no handouts!' Zeke Goins sounded angry now. 'Some of us don't have the luxury of questioning where things comes from and what folks do and why!'

The old man slammed the receiver down and İkmen quickly moved his phone away from his ear. A knock on the door immediately following the call had him up and in his dressing gown to answer it.

'Problems?' Ed Devine stood at the door with cups of coffee for both of them. 'Heard you on the phone.'

'It was Ezekiel Goins,' İkmen said. He told Devine what had passed between them.

'A friend, a relative of my colleague Inspector Süleyman, is a journalist here in the city,' İkmen said. 'He's called Tayyar Bekdil. Partly for his newspaper, but I admit, partly for me, he went out to see the Voss Funeral Home.'

Ed Devine, who was now sitting on a chair beside İkmen's bed, said, 'Right.' He knew full well that the Turk had been sniffing around on his own ever since he'd met Zeke Goins. It was part of the reason why the department was keeping him close.

'Richard Voss, the present owner, led Tayyar to believe that the money for Elvis Goins' funeral had come from drug deals,' İkmen said. 'Richard Voss was just a child at the time and so could not possibly remember such a thing. But his great-uncle, Stefan, was also in the room, and he said nothing. Whose story is the truth?'

Devine frowned. 'I can get a warrant to force the Vosses or their accountants to divulge their financial records,' he said. 'That is, if they still exist. It's real financial mining, but PD has the resources, if necessary. Problem is, though, *is* it necessary?'

'I think so, yes,' İkmen said. 'Ever since I met Ezekiel Goins, things have been happening. The reason I am here at all, to attest to the fact that Grant Miller did shoot at myself and my colleague with a Beretta that was then confiscated by Lieutenant Diaz, is connected to all of that . . . that past.'

'Inspector, we have to solve homicides that are happening now,' Devine said. 'With respect, we ain't got time for the past, if you know what I mean.'

İkmen, beginning to feel agitated, lit another cigarette and said, 'But the past is always relevant. In my city, I have worked on crimes that have their origins not just a few years ago, but over a hundred years in the past.'

'You come from a very ancient country, Inspector.'

'And I believe that the deaths of the young boy, Aaron Spencer, Lieutenant Diaz and Elvis Goins are all connected.'

'If you're fingering Grant T. Miller, then that is dangerous . . .'

'Miller is the common factor,' İkmen said. 'But I don't know whether he killed any of those people. He's only a link at the moment. A link who for some reason is lying to you about a mysterious property company that he must know about.'

Ed Devine sat in silence and chewed hard on his nicotine gum. He hadn't even had a shower yet, but the gum was already in. 'I don't know,' he said. He thought some more. Miller, for all his quirky ways and rotting mansion, had a lot of money and a lot of powerful friends. Taking him on on any level was going to be difficult, and if so much as a foot was put wrong, Devine would find himself in a world of attorney-laced shit.

'What if Grant Miller paid for Elvis Goins' funeral?' İkmen said.

'What? Why would he do that?' Devine said. 'That old racist paying for some mixed-race kid's funeral don't make no sense at all!'

'No, it doesn't,' İkmen said. 'I agree. But someone with a lot of power and a lot of money did pay for it, and that person would probably have been known to Mr Miller. We spend all our time looking at little people and what they may or may not know when so often it is the big people who do know.'

'It's the big people who have the power to come and get you!'

'The same is true in my country, too,' İkmen said. 'But occasionally we just have to close our minds to that.'

The two men looked at each other through the strengthening light of the morning for a few moments. Then Devine rose to his feet, and İkmen thought that he was going to leave the room without further comment. But then he said, 'I'll get a warrant for the Voss Funeral Home, and after that maybe I'll think about what to do with Grant T. Miller. In this city, Inspector, railing against old racists is one thing; bringing them in is quite another.'

Intellectually, Ayşe Farsakoğlu knew exactly what had been going on. İzzet had taken her to a new, very smart restaurant called Topaz, which was very near to her apartment in Gümüşsüyü. Not only did its vast windows give diners a wonderful panoramic view of the Bosphorus; the food had been excellent too.

İzzet, all clumsiness, nylon suit and coarse face, had ordered the house speciality, the Ottoman degustation menu, for both of them. Twelve small, exquisite courses each matched to an expensive and delicious wine. Knowledgeable about both the food and the wine, he had nevertheless not bored her about either. They'd talked of many things, including the job, and he had even made her laugh on several occasions. Nothing had been too much trouble, too expensive or too gracious. Whenever she got up from the table, he stood too and pulled her chair out for her. When she returned, he made sure that she was seated comfortably before he sat down himself once again. Only at the end of the meal did he go outside for a cigarette, even though she knew he had to be absolutely desperate by that time.

He had, of course, escorted her back to her apartment, where they had parted with a handshake and he had just very lightly kissed her once on the cheek. There and then he'd said that they really had to do that again, even though she knew that his bank account would probably not be able to take such punishment a second time that year. What he had meant, of course, had been that it would be nice to go out together again. And she had agreed.

It had been very pleasant to spend an evening with a man who was not either her brother or some Neanderthal who just wanted to get her into bed as quickly as possible. But then as Ayşe knew only too well, İzzet loved her. As he left her putting her key into her door, he even called out, 'I like this courting, it's nice.'

Courting, as in the chivalrous wooing of a lady by an admirer, was such an archaic concept, like something from a fairy tale. Courting was asexual, at least it was in fairy tales, but also electric with passionate potential. İzzet was such a strange person to court anyone, and yet Ayşe was finding that in spite of herself she was flattered. He loved her. He was kind, considerate, solvent and intelligent, and he loved her. For a very brief moment, Mehmet Süleyman's handsome features swam into her mind, but she dismissed them. She was getting far too old to play the sort of games he wanted to play.

'Dr Harris tracked down the owner of the New Yorker,' Rob Weiss said as he placed his own report into Ed Devine's hands. 'Some grocery store owner from Dearborn. Licensed for a firearm but not a Beretta PX4.'

'It's definitely the Beretta that Diaz gave you just before he died?'

'The serial numbers are incomplete on this weapon,' Weiss said. 'Automobile crushers take no prisoners; it's a miracle any of it survived. But from what I can decipher, it would seem to be the same piece that Diaz brought to me, the one we think came from Grant T. Miller.'

'So this was in an automobile crushed by a man who's now dead who could've been one of Diaz's informants.' Ed Devine shook his head and then looked behind him at Çetin İkmen. 'Connections, huh?'

'But Lieutenant, do such connections exist between the crushed man and Mr Miller?' İkmen asked. 'Because if not, then why would Grant Miller's gun be in a car that belonged to a grocery shop owner? Did the grocery shop man know Mr Miller?'

'It's doubtful,' Weiss said. 'The grocery store man is black.'

'So where's the connection?'

'Through Diaz, possibly,' Devine said. 'Diaz was always obscure about who worked for him in the community.'

'But why would Diaz dispose of Mr Miller's gun, unless . . .'

'He was bent as a horseshoe,' Devine said.

There was a moment of both embarrassment and horror at what had just been said.

Dr Weiss cleared his throat. 'I always found Gerald Diaz reserved and a bit odd, but not rogue, I don't think,' he said. 'He loved this city and always wanted to protect it from people like Miller – or that was the impression he gave me, and that was over a long period of time, thirty years.'

Silence rolled in again, and then İkmen said, 'Officer Addison was concerned that maybe someone in your department, not Lieutenant Diaz, could have not only disposed of the Beretta but also wiped all records of it from your systems. Rita Addison was attacked, and we still don't know why.'

'Except that Shalhoub now has his white-sneakered suicide,' Devine said.

'If Kercheval did in fact kill the lieutenant and attack Rita,' İkmen said.

'Addison didn't positively ID the photograph Zevets showed her.'

'Even if she had, the man is dead,' İkmen said. 'Such a person was probably only a hired thug. Who sent the white-sneaker man, and why did he kill himself? If indeed he did.'

Weiss and Devine looked at him, both fostering their own feelings of growing disquiet.

'Your Chief of Police,' İkmen said, 'has not just kept me in the city because I am a witness to Mr Miller handing the Beretta over to Lieutenant Diaz. I am also here because, like Officer Addison, I think your Chief feels that not everyone in your department is to be trusted. As an outsider, with no knowledge of this city and its people, he knows that I can if necessary come to dispassionate conclusions. At home in my own city,' he smiled, 'that would be very difficult for me indeed. I know this must be hard to hear, and I am sorry.'

There were no real set hours for working in a funeral home. Richard Voss was accustomed to people calling after dark. He was even inured to the sight of a bunch of police officers at his door. Often when death came calling the police were involved. What he hadn't been expecting, however, was a warrant to search his records.

'If you ask me what you're looking for, then maybe I can help,' he said. He was very clearly panicking.

'Mr Voss, we need to know who paid for a particular funeral back on January third 1979,' Ed Devine said.

'I was just a—'

'Yeah, you were a kid,' Devine said. 'But that's what I need to see, Mr Voss. Funeral of one Elvis Lorne Goins, buried up in Woodlawn. A fancy funeral for a boy whose folks were dirt-poor mountain folk from the south. Funeral, I heard, fit for a senator.'

Richard Voss, now rather less full of bonhomie than he had been when Tayyar Bekdil visited him, said, 'What's this about?'

'I can't tell you that, sir,' Devine said. At his back were İkmen, Zevets and a female officer called Diana Birdy.

'Only we had a reporter here,' Voss said, 'a foreign guy. He asked about what I think must've been the same funeral. Mixed-race drug-dealer, a gang boy.'

Devine didn't answer. Then he said, 'Mr Voss, I need to see your financial records from 1978 and 1979.'

'That'll take a bit of organising. We don't keep records that old here.'

'Where do you keep them?'

'All the old records are in my basement,' an elderly, time-cracked voice said. Stefan Voss had come into his great-nephew's office quietly and completely unnoticed. But now all eyes turned to him.

Ed Devine smiled. 'Mr Stefan Voss?'

'Yes?' The old man viewed him with what looked like amusement.

'We need to see your financial records,' Devine said, 'relating to one Elvis Goins' funeral on January third 1979.'

'Why?'

'Need to find out who paid for his funeral,' Devine said.

'Why's that?'

'Can't tell you, sir.' The old man looked down at the floor. Devine said, 'You know who paid for Elvis Goins' funeral, Mr Voss?'

Stefan Voss looked up again and smiled. 'I'm an old man. My memory isn't what it was.'

Tayyar had told İkmen that old man Voss had given him the creeps. He could now see why. Even if he didn't actually know anything about Elvis Goins' funeral, Stefan Voss was taking far too much delight in gently goading Devine.

'Well, sir, your memory doesn't have to be,' Devine said with a smile, 'provided you've kept all the records you should. Now I believe that the antebellum-style house down the way is yours, isn't it.'

'You want to go and look now?'

'As I told your great-nephew,' Devine said, 'we have a warrant, Mr Voss. It allows us to search all properties that house Voss financial records, which, as you said, includes your home.'

For a moment, Stefan Voss didn't say a word. He appeared to be thinking very hard about something. Then he said, 'OK then,

234

gentlemen. Shall we go?' He stretched one thin arm out towards the office door.

'Thank you,' Devine said. 'After you.'

The old man led the way. As he walked past Richard Voss, İkmen saw that the younger man was sweating very heavily.

It was just a short walk to the vast mock-antebellum mansion where Stefan Voss lived alone. An elderly black man in a very smart morning suit opened the door to them and looked at Stefan Voss questioningly. 'Sir?'

His accent came from way down south, and he bowed just a little as he spoke. To Devine it was like looking at an old photograph of an ancestor. To İkmen, the man was just another rich man's servant.

'Nothing to worry about, Nathaniel,' Stefan Voss said. 'These officers just need to look at some of our records.'

The servant let them in while Stefan Voss offered coffee, tea or brandy.

'I'd rather just get to work so that we can move out of your hair for the night, Mr Voss,' Devine said.

The old man looked a little disappointed that his attempt to stall proceedings had failed, but he smiled anyway and led them all down through a small door underneath his wide marble staircase.

Beneath the modern house was a large, poorly lit chamber that was much, much older. Clearly there had been a structure of some sort on the site way before any Voss had ever set foot in the New World. As the smell of damp hit his nostrils, Devine turned to İkmen and whispered, 'If he's keeping paper down here, I sure hope he's covered it in plastic or some such.'

But İkmen doubted that. Had he been hiding something it was possible to find, the old man would have been much more nervous than he was. Only a short pause before he'd agreed to take them to his house made him doubt that a little. Then, for a moment, Voss had looked concerned.

235

The cardboard files that comprised the Voss Funeral Home's audited financial records were housed on racks constructed on row upon row of free-standing wooden shelves. Each shelf was labelled with a number that corresponded to the year the paperwork related to. Behind Officer Birdy, İkmen could see Richard Voss's face, which was white with what could have been fear.

'As you can see, I like to keep tidy records,' Stefan Voss said.

'Yeah.'

Without really pausing to look, he took them straight to the racks that related to the year 1978/9. 'It's all chronological,' he said. 'The records for January third will be quite far on.'

Ed Devine opened up a large cardboard file and watched as dust puffed up from it and then subsided on to the floor. İkmen, looking over the lieutenant's shoulder, saw piles of yellowing invoices and correspondence, some of which bore the Voss yew tree logo. Devine shuffled quickly through the paperwork until he came to something that interested him and bent down low in order to look at a document more closely. In that moment, İkmen's view was completely obscured. Then Devine stood upright again and looked at Stefan Voss with a smile on his face. 'Mr Voss,' he said, 'do you have any idea who R. Lacroix might be?'

'R. Lacroix? No. Why?'

Devine held up an invoice that had apparently accompanied a large amount of cash. It had been signed, in a very unsure and rather spidery hand, by someone called R. Lacroix.

'Mr Voss, you ever heard of a property company called Gül Inc.?'

Stefan Voss frowned. 'No. Why?' he repeated.

Devine looked at the paper in his hand and said, 'Because someone called R. Lacroix is involved with them.'

'Really?' Now it was Stefan Voss's turn to smile. 'I've no idea,' he said. 'But then if you look at the paperwork closely, Lieutenant, you will see that none of it is signed S. Voss. It's all R. Voss, which means it must have been dealt with by my brother Rudolf.'

Only İkmen, or so he thought, heard Richard Voss almost choke at this point.

'Sadly Rudi died in 1989,' Stefan said. 'So unfortunately we can no longer ask him.'

'Mr Voss, we have a witness who claims you actually organised this funeral,' Devine said.

Stefan Voss smiled. 'Well, he or she is mistaken,' he said. 'It was definitely my brother Rudolf.'

Chapter 28

Mark Zevets had what he felt was an investment in finding out who had attacked Rita Addison. Not only did he like her, she was one of the few people who knew that he was gay. She was the only officer in the department he'd told. Rita was discreet and sympathetic, and he could always talk to her. So Mark wanted to know a bit more about the man, Clifford Kercheval, who had supposedly attacked her. Rita hadn't, after all, definitely identified Kercheval, and his death was rather too convenient from Mark Zevets' point of view.

Shalhoub, who was still working on Diaz's murder, for which Kercheval was in the frame, was of another opinion. 'The stuff he had on Diaz in that hovel he called home!' Shalhoub had said. 'He hated cops!'

'Then why target Diaz? Addison?'

Shalhoub had said that he didn't know but that he was certain they'd find out. Zevets wasn't so sure, and so he went to Kercheval's apartment building and made a few of his own enquiries. The block was uniformly poor and white, and several of the outside walls were covered with artless graffiti.

Mark, in his skinny jeans and leather jacket, looked far too prosperous to be a resident, and so as soon as he arrived, even at such a late hour, people were looking at him. But he didn't hide who or what he was.

'Detroit PD,' he said as he held his badge up to the face of a young boy he found leaning against the wall outside Kercheval's apartment.

The boy said nothing.

'Want to find out about Clifford Kercheval,' Zevets said.

The boy shrugged. 'You and all them other cops.'

'Other cops say that Clifford was a cop-killer,' Zevets said, 'but I'm not so sure. You think he was a cop-killer? What was he like?'

The boy shrugged again, but this time he said nothing.

'We know he'd been charged with misdemeanours. He a player or just a small fish?'

'No player.' The boy smirked.

'So a small fish?'

'Who ain't round here?' The boy looked at him with straight, accusing pale blue eyes. 'You see any made men around these parts, Officer?'

Zevets didn't reply, on the grounds that the answer was self-evident. The boy began to move away and Zevets let him go. Kids like that were hardened to most things. He was seventeen at most, but had the eyes of a forty-year-old who'd been in prison at least twice. There was no point pursuing anything with him. The door to Kercheval's apartment, still taped over, was black and grimy and pitted with what looked like pellets from a BB gun. According to Shalhoub, Kercheval had lived an idle life, sitting around taking welfare payments, smoking joints and occasionally ranting about white supremacy. The latter activity, in this particular building, Zevets knew, was a very common pursuit. Just like back in the sixties, to these people everything was the 'niggers' fault' – the fact that they were poor, the fact that they couldn't get jobs, the fact that so many of them were on drugs. It was so much easier than blaming economics they didn't understand, or City Hall, or their own legacy of white, usually southern, poverty. They were blind to the black poor, just as the black poor were often blind to them. So little had changed, and yet so much had too. That Mark Zevets, a rich Jewish boy from a good family, should be walking Detroit's streets as a police officer – and a gay one at that – was certainly some kind of progress. But with people like these, still so needy and hostile, was it enough?

'Hey.'

Zevets looked round and saw a tiny girl standing behind him. At first he thought, through the gloom, that she was a child, but then he realised that she was actually a red-headed dwarf. Looking at him with such open hostility it almost made him flinch, the girl said, 'You all about Cliff again?'

Her use of Kercheval's shortened name made Zevets wonder if she had known him well. If she had, then possibly she had liked him too. He decided to change tack very slightly. 'I'm not convinced that Clifford killed my colleague,' he said.

'The Latino?' the girl said. 'Nah.' Then she laughed. 'Woulda beat up on the nigger, though.'

Zevets sucked down on his disgust at this reference to Rita's attack and the girl's dismissal of her as a 'nigger'.

'Cliff was a clean boy,' the girl said. 'Only liked clean girls.'

By that he imagined she had to mean white girls. She'd taken more than a shine to Cliff herself, he suspected. 'You knew Clifford well?'

She looked at the ground in a coy way. 'Maybe.'

'How?' Zevets leaned down so that his head was on the same level as hers and smiled. 'How you know Cliff?' He saw that she had a bag with a name very roughly scrawled on it in silver paint. He took a punt on it being her own. 'Misty?'

She giggled. Then, as quickly as the laughter started, so it stopped. 'We used to hang,' she said.

'Here?'

She shrugged.

'Here?' Zevets asked again.

'Sometimes.'

'Anywhere else?'

For some reason she was hostile again. He couldn't fathom why, and when she began to move off and away from him, he felt his heart sink.

But then, just before she went out of sight, she said, 'We'd go round old Brush Park sometimes, with Artie.'

Zevets ran over to her and just stopped short of grabbing one of her arms. 'Artie? A friend of Clifford's?'

She looked at him with contempt. 'Yeah.'

'Artie who?'

'Artie Bowen,' she said, as if everyone would and indeed should know who that was.

But Mark Zevets didn't have a clue. 'A friend of Clifford's?' he repeated.

'Went off somewhere when Cliff disappeared,' Misty said.

No one as far as Zevets knew had mentioned this friend Artie Bowen before, or Misty for that matter. 'Do you know where?' he asked.

She sighed. 'Probably making money just for hisself now,' she said.

Zevets frowned. 'Did he used to make money for other people?'

'He give it to me and Cliff. Cliff used to score for him sometimes.'

'Dope?'

'Mainly.'

'So what sort of work does Artie Bowen do?'

'What Cliff wouldn't never do.' She smiled. 'Cliff weren't like that.'

'Like what?'

'Like a man who sucks another man's dick for money,' Misty said.

Only a very distant cousin was prepared to come and claim Ali Kuban's dead body for burial. Even he would only do that provided the staff at the mortuary listened to his rants about how much he had despised his relative.

'The only reason I'm doing this at all is to make sure that he at least has a decent Muslim funeral,' the man said as he watched the orderlies load Kuban's body into an unmarked van. 'Pity he couldn't have led a decent life too, but there it is. Kismet.'

Ayşe Farsakoğlu had listened to Dr Sarkissian's account of the cousin's visit with interest if with little real attention. Mehmet Süleyman was in her office, and his presence was distracting her. She was unhappy that it could still do that.

'And so Kuban's last, probably most sensible, act in terms of the safety of the city pulls the curtain down on a miserable and seemingly worthless life,' the Armenian said. 'I imagine he'll be safely in the ground by the end of the day.'

'Thank you for letting me know, Doctor,' Ayşe said as she watched Süleyman pick up items from İkmen's desk, smile, and put them down again. Though thinner than he had been, he was still a stunning man, and she wished that he would leave.

'Thank you for telling me, Doctor,' she repeated into the phone.

'Pleasure.' He laughed a little. 'If you know what I mean!'

'Yes. I hope you have a good day, Doctor.'

'And you.'

Ayşe put the phone back on its cradle and said to Süleyman, 'Yes, sir?'

He looked up and smiled. How he managed to keep his teeth so white when he smoked so heavily, Ayşe couldn't imagine. Maybe he had cosmetic dentistry.

'Sergeant, I need to speak to you about some practical procedural issues,' he said. 'Because Inspector İkmen is going to be in the US for an as yet unspecified length of time, your duties as his professional partner will need to be temporarily reassigned.'

She'd known that this was bound to happen, but had thought that notification would come from higher up. But then she didn't know what discussions Süleyman had had with his superiors since his return. 'Sir.'

'I'd like to fix a meeting with you at four-thirty this afternoon,' he said. 'Is that convenient for you?'

She was, it had to be said, engaged in nothing beyond some non-urgent paperwork. 'That will be fine, sir,' she said.

It was still odd that, even when they were alone, she called him 'sir'. In the past she'd slept with him, they had kissed each other, seen each other naked, made love.

'Good.' With yet another smile he took his leave of her and left. Ayşe was due to go for a drink with İzzet Melik after her shift finished at five. What, she wondered, would he be doing while she talked to his boss?

Americans had the weirdest things for breakfast. Ed Devine had made up a great stack of thick rounds he called pancakes. As far as İkmen was concerned, these bore no relation to the pancakes he had back in Turkey. There they were thin and could have either sweet or savoury fillings. Here they seemed to be simply drowned in maple syrup. Great big doughy discs covered in stuff that had only to make contact with a tooth to dissolve it. But he was nothing if not a trier, and so, between puffs on his cigarette, he managed to get one of the pancakes down. Devine, a contented expression on his face as he sat down to his breakfast, made short work of five.

After a few moments of silent chewing, the American said, 'So about what we were saying last night . . . how you know you can trust me. I mean, if Diaz was bent . . .'

'I don't,' İkmen replied. 'I just have to take the word of your Chief, who seems to think that you are trustworthy. Also, er, Ed, you are, er, well, you are black . . .'

'You think that Grant T. Miller hasn't never bribed a black man?' Devine said. He laughed. 'Where big money is involved, anyone can be in the frame. And Miller, for all his white-power craziness, will use anyone to further his aims. White, black, grey, green – he don't care. Use friggin' men from Mars if he had to.'

243

'So are you saying, Ed, that I can't trust you?'

Devine laughed again. 'No. And yes,' he said. 'One's fact, one's theory. In fact, I could never do anything for that old vulture, money or no money. In theory? Well, like most folks I have a mortgage to pay, a wife to support, kids going through college. I'm vulnerable as anyone else.'

'As Diaz?'

'Maybe more,' he said. 'Diaz, as far as I know, didn't have debts. He was pissed about his marriage breaking down, but then that's just part of the American condition. We like to commit, you know? Then we get bored. Even I've been married twice, and I been with my wife for over twenty years. The Chief been married twice too, Diaz once, but divorced, Shalhoub three times . . .'

The doorbell rang. Devine got up and said, 'Who can that be?'

While he was gone, İkmen shovelled half of his second pancake into Devine's cat's bowl underneath the table. Very soon afterwards he heard the sound of heavy purring. Meanwhile there were voices out in Devine's hall, and a few moments later the lieutenant came back in with Dr Weiss the ballistics expert in tow.

'Good morning, Inspector İkmen,' Weiss said as he leaned across the table and shook the Turk by the hand.

'Good morning, Doctor. Have you come to join us for breakfast?'

He smiled. 'I know Ed makes a mean pancake,' he said, 'but no. I came because I worked very late last night and bumped into someone who got me thinking.'

Devine first offered Weiss some coffee, which he declined, and then sat down to his breakfast again. 'Who?'

'Lionel Katz,' he said.

'The fraud guy?'

'Yes. Through connections I won't bore you with, I was at his bar mitzvah twenty or so years ago,' Weiss said. 'The diminishing Jews of old downtown Detroit.' He smiled again. 'You know that synagogue in Griswold Street does get a fair congregation on high holy days,

244

but . . . beside the by. Katz said he was working for you, Ed; something about a property company buying up from vulnerable people in Brush Park.'

'Called Gül,' Devine said. 'What about it?'

Weiss cleared his throat. 'Katz told me he was having trouble finding out who owned this company. Registered, he said, sometime in the 1990s in Savannah of all places. I thought nothing of it until he dropped a name at me.'

'A name?'

'Lacroix,' Weiss said.

'R. Lacroix,' Devine elaborated. 'You know an R. Lacroix?'

'Sort of,' Weiss said. 'But she died sometime in the nineties.'

'Oh.' Devine was momentarily deflated. Then he said, 'She?'

'Rose Lacroix,' Weiss said, 'was Grant T. Miller's southern belle mom, and she came from the beautiful city of Savannah.'

'Why would Grant T. Miller buy up all the housing and land around his place? At the moment, it's worth squat,' Devine said. Now in his office in police headquarters, he was addressing İkmen, Weiss, Shalhoub and Katz.

'In the southern part of Brush Park, developers have been buying up old houses and empty lots for some years,' Katz said. 'There's a level of redevelopment there. You can make money.'

'But not a lot?' Devine asked.

Katz shrugged. 'Depends whether you've got confidence,' he said. 'If the D takes off one of these fine days, then prime sites like that could be worth a bundle. If it doesn't . . .'

Devine looked briefly at his computer screen. 'Says here Rose Lacroix Miller died August eighth 1999, aged ninety-eight,' he said. 'This Gül company started . . .'

'Ninety-one,' Katz said.

'So old Rosie was still alive when it was formed, maybe cognisant of its purpose . . . You know, I didn't realise that Rose was still alive then. I mean, that place of Grant T.'s was in a helluva state years before that.'

'If I remember correctly,' İkmen interjected, 'there was also the issue of someone called R. Lacroix paying for Elvis Goins' funeral.'

Devine frowned. 'Yeah, you're right,' he said. 'Think that was old Rosie too?'

'The handwriting looked as if it could have come from an old person,' İkmen said. 'Maybe if her son had killed Elvis Goins, she felt some guilt about that which manifested as a desire to pay for the boy's funeral?'

Dr Weiss looked very doubtful. 'Unlikely, I would say,' he said. 'To my recollection, Rose was not a woman easily given to sentiment, unless it was over her son.'

'Whatever may be the truth, we need to speak to Grant T. anyway,' Devine said. 'Apart from anything else, I think he probably needs to know that a weapon has been found that belongs to him.'

'Possibly,' Dr Weiss interjected. 'It possibly belongs to him.'

'Does it?' Devine stood up from his desk and winked at Weiss. 'Oh, and there's me thinking it was all cut and dried and everything. What a shame!'

'So what do we do now?' Shalhoub asked.

'I think that someone needs to visit Mr Miller. And someone else should visit the Voss Funeral Home.'

Chapter 29

Mark Zevets wasn't afraid of east side Detroit. OK, it had a bad reputation for drug-dealing, drug-taking, prostitution and all sorts and varieties of crime, but he was a realist, he knew that wasn't the whole picture. Most people, whatever their addiction, their status, their race, religion or whatever, were just trying to do what people everywhere did and get by. It wasn't easy, and Mark had a lot of sympathy for their plight. That said, there were spots that did make his skin creep. One of the worst ones was on the corner of Chene and Ferry. Even as he approached, he could see the rocks of crack passing between the windows of cruising cars. Some black women stood in slippers in the snowy slush, completely inured to the cold, totally wrapped up in their need.

Although Misty hadn't told him much, Zevets had learned from her that Clifford Kercheval's old friend Artie Bowen had a bit of a rock habit. As well as buying dope for the others, his little blow-job enterprise probably funded quite a few crack pipes, and word was that some kid had been forced to go down on a group of gangsters in a crack shack somewhere in this area. Some folk liked sex when they were high. A lot of them didn't give too much thought to who they did it with or details such as issues of consent. That said, a willing participant had to be a lot easier than some terrified kid who could fight and scream and make trouble. A white boy who'd do the business for the price of a couple of rocks would have some sort of appeal, if only that inherent in apparently degrading a person who belonged to a race who had been oppressors in the past. And Bowen, according to the mug shot Zevets had got off the computer for him, wasn't a bad-looking man. The Chene/Ferry crews would not, he felt, say no to a bit of Artie.

Ignoring the desperate addict women on the corner, Mark Zevets made his way to the only Chene/Ferry crack shack he knew he stood some small chance of getting out alive from. If the place was full, he wouldn't have a prayer, but it was midday, and so with luck, most of the inhabitants would be downtown hustling. That, hopefully, would just leave old Mel.

The so-called shack had originally been quite a nice house. It was a detached wooden place that had once had windows and doors. Now it just had flaps of chipboard that could be pulled across in bad weather, opened in good – if of course anyone even noticed what the temperature was. Mark banged on what passed for a front door while looking down at the bodies of several baby mice as they oozed through the remnants of the floorboards. 'Mel? Mel, you in there? Mel!'

For a while, nothing happened at all. But then Mark didn't expect it to. If Mel was in, which was almost certain, he was probably dealing with a comedown, which meant that he was probably on smack. A lot if not all of the crackheads Mark had come across used heroin to help calm down after a crack binge.

'Mel!' He hammered on the door again. Only after just shy of five minutes had passed were his efforts rewarded.

'Where the fuck's the fire, boy?'

The tiny gap between the chipboard slab and the door frame revealed a small black man wearing nothing but a hat and a string vest. He had grizzled grey hair and a small but unkempt beard, and could have been almost any age from forty-five up to eighty. Ageing a crack addict was a difficult task, as Mark knew only too well. Mel Cooper, however, was a person whose age, due to his many previous arrests for possession, Mark was well aware of.

'You know seventy is not a good number to still be living in a shit shack at, Mel,' Zevets said as he entered the vaguely smoky interior of the frigidly cold building.

'You think?' The old man laughed, then coughed, then spat out a load of phlegm on to the floor. 'So what you think I should do about that then, Jew-boy?'

Zevets shrugged. 'I don't know, Mel,' he said. 'Maybe move in with Zita?'

The old man pulled a face.

'She's clean now,' Zevets said as he followed Mel into what passed for a living room. It stank of piss and damp and semen.

'I know,' the old man said. 'Last thing she needs is a junkie in her life.'

'You're still her dad.'

'I'm a junkie,' Mel said as he sat down and pulled a filthy sheet from the floor over his withered penis and balls. 'Anyway, what do you want, Jew-boy? I'm on a date with some smack.'

'I appreciate that.' Zevets bent down and gave Mel the printout of Artie Bowen's mug shot. 'Just want to know if you've seen this dude.'

The old man held on to the picture with shaking hands, moving it up and down in his field of vision in an attempt to focus. Eventually he just said, 'Nah.'

'His name's Artie Bowen,' Zevets said. 'Lives in a nice apartment over by Lafayette Park that belongs to his brother.'

'So why you looking for him up here?' Mel asked. 'In case you ain't noticed, we don't have too many rich white boys here.'

'Artie Bowen, who his brother hasn't heard from in he thinks about two weeks now, wasn't at home when I called,' Zevets said. 'But then he mixes with the wrong crowd. A couple of dope kids over on Cass. A girl, and a boy called Cliff Kercheval who we think might have killed himself. We need to talk to Artie about it. They were close.'

The old man shrugged. 'Nothing to me, boy. Why you here with this shit?'

Zevets picked up the photograph and pushed it back into the old man's lap. 'Because Artie has a bit of a rock habit,' he said. 'The kid doesn't have a job, and so he funds himself by sucking dick.'

'Who don't!' The old man pushed the print out to one side and stared vacantly into space.

Zevets pushed it back and made him look at it. 'To this kid, sucking dick is a business,' he said. 'Look again, old man, and tell me whether this white boy ever been up here offering head for rocks.'

With a sigh, Mel looked again. He shook his head and looked up at Zevets. 'We don't get anything like that down here. Class like that . . .' He shrugged.

Mark Zevets hardly saw Artie Bowen as 'class', but in terms of the lower depths that was the Chene and Ferry intersection, he probably looked like Johnny Depp.

'OK.' Zevets leaned forward and took the photograph out of the old man's clawed hands. He was just pulling it away when he felt Mel's long, filthy fingernails suddenly bite into the flesh around his wrist. 'Ow!'

'Why don't you ask your rich white buddies about your dick-sucking boy?' he said fiercely. 'Boys like that, they don't have to come down here. Lots of rich white folks pay good money.' He smiled, showing blackened, snaggled teeth. 'I know. Many years ago now, young man, black as my ass is, I had more'n my share of white dick in exchange for rocks.' He laughed. 'The great and the good, so they say! The great and the good!'

The old man's eyes rolled. There'd be no more getting anything out of him for hours. Zevets, feeling both cold and bleak, put a twenty-dollar bill into one of Mel's clawed hands and left.

It was the smell that hit them first. It wasn't like the usual old man/damp smell that Devine and Weiss at least associated with Grant T. Miller's home; rather it was a far more ripe and meaty aroma.

'It's sweet,' Çetin İkmen said as he waded through the oceans of newspaper, unfinished meals and broken furniture that lay all over the floor of the main reception room. 'Rather like . . .' He stopped himself from going any further. If he was wrong, he would have caused unnecessary anxiety; if he was right, they'd find it soon anyway. The smell was strong.

Dr Weiss looked closely at a broken baby grand piano and said, 'Rose Miller used to play the harmonium mainly. You could always hear it going past this house.'

Devine, agitated, scratched his head. 'Miller never goes out,' he said. 'Only to the end of the block. Where can he be?'

İkmen, still tuned into the smell, thought that it was unlikely that Miller would have died and begun to decompose so quickly. The weather was, after all, still very cold.

'Maybe Lieutenant Shalhoub will discover more up at the Voss place,' Weiss said. 'If Rose Miller did indeed pay for Elvis Goins' funeral, she must have trusted the Vosses on some level. Not that I've ever heard anything white supremacist about them.'

Devine, casting around the shattered room, almost in despair, said, 'Neither me. But that doesn't mean that old Mr Stefan won't deny everything and just pin whatever happened on his dead brother.'

'He was the one who signed the paperwork for the funeral,' İkmen said.

'True. But that don't get Stefan off the hook,' Devine said. 'It's a family business, meaning they should all know about everything to do with it, Stefan included.' He shrugged. 'Where is this old fool?'

It had been a shock to discover that Grant T. Miller was out. As far as anyone knew, he never went beyond the end of his block. A store out in Royal Oak delivered all his groceries. But when the police officers had knocked on his front door, it had swung open and they'd found themselves in what appeared to be a completely empty house. It wasn't easy to tell, because the place was so full of junk, but it felt uninhabited.

251

'I'm gonna go check upstairs,' Devine said. 'I don't know whether the old man still sleeps up there or not.'

'I'll come with you,' Çetin İkmen said. It was pure curiosity that led him on. There was no need for him to follow Devine up that broad, rickety staircase to possibly a world of broken and hazardous floors up above. But he was compelled.

As he put a foot on the first step, he heard Dr Weiss exclaim from the kitchen, 'Oh God, there's something vile on these curtains!'

İkmen followed Devine, and as he did so, the sweet smell of death and decay grew stronger and stronger. At the top of the stairs, Devine sniffed and pointed in the direction of a closed wooden door in front of him. 'Just in case,' he said to İkmen, 'I'd cover your mouth. I find it helps a bit to prevent vomiting when we find the stiff.'

There was no question but that he was coming on to her. She sat in front of his desk, in the chair he had led her to, while he perched on the edge of the desk, casually and very close to her body. He smiled an awful lot, which was not at all like the man he had become in recent years.

'Sergeant Melik will be absent on vacation as from this Saturday,' Süleyman said to Ayşe Farsakoğlu.

This was nothing she didn't know. İzzet himself had told her that he was going back to İzmir for a few days to see his mother and visit his children.

'Yes, sir.'

'So for a few days, at least, we'll both be alone,' he said. Again, and unnervingly, he smiled. 'It is therefore expedient that when Sergeant Melik goes on leave, should the need arise, you and I will work as a team.'

Quite who had decided that this was 'expedient', Ayşe didn't know. No one else had mentioned anything to her. But he was her superior, and so how could she argue?

'Yes, sir.'

'Good.'

She saw that he was looking at her legs and had to resist the temptation to pull her skirt down further towards her knees. She was fully aware of the dichotomy between her earlier and her present feelings about him. It was truly strange to feel creeped out by a man she had once fantasised about marrying. What a disaster that would have been! He had cheated on his wife not only with the gypsy Gonca, but also, it was rumoured, with any other woman who casually took his fancy! That he was clearly so sexually insatiable used to be, she had to admit, rather exciting. His appeal had always been that he didn't appear to have a clue as to how attractive to women he really was. But all that had gone. Since Ayşe's brief affair with him years before, Mehmet Süleyman had acquired a large dose of self-knowledge. Now he was a sensual, cocksure, if charming, playboy. True, he was still good at his job, but unlike İkmen, it was not his life, and so his many women could, and did, sometimes, come first.

Unwilling to get up out of her chair with him so close to her, Ayşe stayed where she was. She hoped he couldn't see that she was sweating – such a thing made her look star-struck and weak. But then he got up, moved around to the other side of his desk and sat down.

She stood up. 'If that's all, sir . . .'

'Yes.' He looked down at the papers on his desk and Ayşe began to walk towards his office door. İzzet, she knew, was waiting for her downstairs in the car park. All she'd have to do was tidy up her office, switch off her computer and leave.

But then Süleyman's voice brought her to a standstill. 'And I would really use Sergeant Melik's absence to think about whether or not a liaison with him is a wise course of action,' he said. 'Affairs of the heart in the workplace can be problematic, as I know you are aware.'

Stung and appalled, she wheeled around quickly to see that he was still looking down at the papers on his desk.

'If my recollection is correct,' he said, without looking up, 'the last time you engaged in an affair in this station, it all ended rather badly.'

253

He wasn't lying. The last time she'd had an affair at work it had been with an officer called Orhan Tepe, and it had indeed ended badly. Prior to that, she'd been with this stranger who now sat in front of her, this judgemental man who was making her feel angry and dirty.

'But nothing has happened between İzzet and myself!' she blurted. To her horror, it was as if she needed him to know that fact, as if she were still, somehow, under his spell. Every bone in her body seemed to squirm away from the idea, but still she couldn't entirely prise herself from it.

'Well make sure that it stays that way,' Süleyman continued. Then he looked up into what she knew was her red and maybe even puffy face. 'It would be most unprofessional.'

She was so tempted to say something! But she didn't. She just stood there for a moment, feeling appalled at how, quite suddenly and maddeningly, she desired him once again. Then she left to keep her date with her new, very courteous beau, İzzet Melik.

Chapter 30

Quite who the corpse in Grant T. Miller's bed had been was impossible to tell. The only things that were certain were that it was male, and it definitely wasn't Miller.

'Thirty-five at the outside,' Ed Devine said as he looked carefully at the smooth, if greying, torso. Not that actual identification was possible at this stage, the man's head having been almost totally destroyed.

Dr Weiss, who had now joined İkmen and Devine in Grant T. Miller's cold and reeking bedroom, said, 'I don't want to cast aspersions, but you know, years ago I wasn't the only one around here who reckoned that Grant T. had a fancy for his own gender.'

Ed Devine, who had never heard such a thing in his life, narrowed his eyes. 'You think Miller's gay?'

'Well and truly closeted,' Weiss replied. 'But think about it, Lieutenant, can you ever recall Grant T. Miller with any woman apart from his mother? I can't.'

'You think this could be a lovers' argument gone wrong?' İkmen asked as he made himself look again at the ghastly, pulped head of the man on the bed.

Devine sighed and then said, 'No.' He looked at Weiss. 'But if what you say's true, then maybe we could be looking for a missing rent boy.'

'That's the road I think Grant T. probably travelled, yes,' Weiss said.

Grant T. Miller's bedroom reminded İkmen of a room he'd been

255

in years before when Mehmet Süleyman had still been his sergeant. A deluded old woman called Maria Gülcü had lived at the top of a house in Beyoğlu, convinced that she was the only surviving daughter of the last Tsar of Russia. Like this room, Maria Gülcü's chamber had been dark and vermin-infested, and once glittering fabrics had been overtaken by mould. He looked down and saw a pair of damp, battered slippers that had originally, by their appearance, probably been red. Ed Devine saw them at almost the same time. 'Mmm,' he said, 'didn't know that Grant T. *had* any shoes.'

'Why?'

'Well known he always wears house slippers,' Devine said. 'Can't see him going out with nothing on his feet. Can't see him going out period.'

'Unless someone came and took him out,' İkmen said.

Both of the other men considered this for a moment, and then Dr Weiss said, 'But who?'

'Miller still has influence in this city,' Devine said. 'We know he has a lot of money. He could well own this Gül property company.'

'Which remember, gentlemen, is apparently administered by a man who is most definitely not Grant Miller,' İkmen said. 'The landlord of the Gül mail box in Savannah reported that a middle-aged northern man came to empty it from time to time. If Gül and Mr Miller are one and the same, then he has to be using at least one other person to help him.'

The other two men were silent.

'And if we assume that Mr Miller did indeed use rent boys considerably younger than himself, then a middle-aged man would not fit that profile. Mr Miller has therefore to be involved with someone else, someone who maybe is helping him even as we speak.'

'Could even be someone we know, too,' Devine said. 'Grant T. didn't know that we were coming. Rather convenient that he's out now, just at this precise moment, don't you think?'

* * *

There was a sound he recognised! An acetylene torch. He could hear it fizzing and spluttering above his head. Scrappers had to be in – the homeless, the addicted, the desperate – in search of metal to sell, especially copper. Copper made good dollars. Grant T. Miller hadn't survived all these years without knowing what made top dollar, what one could barter with and how.

It was cold and damp underneath the old plant, but it had still been a good idea. His own, of course. That people – junkies, scrappers, kids, urban explorers – came to the plant all the time was no bad thing. It was far too obvious! Folk'd think he'd have to be mad to go there. But the junkies, the scrappers, the kids and the urban explorers wouldn't bother him even if they did happen upon him. Who was he anyway? They wouldn't know. He just looked like any old bum. They certainly wouldn't call the police. Not doing what they did. Breaking into places like this was technically illegal.

Grant T. sat down on what looked like an old junction box and wished that he still smoked. Leaving in a hurry meant that he hadn't been able to grab anything to eat or drink, and so he was hungry and bored. When he had smoked, years ago, he'd done so to help while away the many weary hours he'd spent supervising the line. Five dollars a day was what those grunts from Fuckarse, Alabama, or whatever shit shacks those hillbillies he'd had to oversee had come from, got back in the day. Good money for people whose momma and poppa were brother and sister. White trash. At least the niggers didn't inbreed – or didn't seem to.

His sense of calm, given his predicament, came as a surprise to Grant T. Miller. Technically, he'd lost everything – his home, his money, his liberty. The whore Bowen had had to die, unfortunately, simply because he wasn't content with what he was given and was threatening to blab his mouth. Funny that a kid who gave blow jobs for a living couldn't keep his mouth shut! Grant T. laughed, softly. Then he wondered what Canada would look like after such a long time. He hadn't, he reckoned, been over the border for at least thirty years. Not that he was going to stay in Canada for very long. There was another, final destination that he had in mind. It was somewhere his hated father had known very well. Given that fact, in reality, Grant T.'s predicament wasn't so bad after all.

Only a cigarette would do. Ayşe thought about just making do with the glass of water that İzzet brought her, but it wasn't enough. So when he offered her a smoke, she took it and then felt awful about herself. How weak she was! In all sorts of ways!

But then if Mehmet Süleyman hadn't expressly forbidden her to take her relationship with İzzet Melik any further, would she actually have slept with him at this point? Ayşe didn't know; she was totally confused – about everything. She turned on to her side, pulled the duvet up over her naked breasts and looked at the man in her bed. İzzet was overweight, had monstrous bags underneath his eyes and reeked of tobacco. On the other hand, he'd made love to her with such tenderness and yet such passion that just simply recalling what had passed between them made her want to take him in her arms and cradle him like a child. Oddly, there was a side to İzzet that was child-like and which came to the fore when she was with him – or so it seemed to Ayşe. She liked him. He was a nice man, a clever man, and now he was also a considerate lover too. But still her flesh refused to be set on fire by his. This disappointed her, and it must have shown on her face, because İzzet took her chin in one of his hands and said, 'What's the matter?'

She made herself smile. 'Nothing.'

'Everything . . . it was . . .'

'Everything was, is, fine,' she said, and then she leaned forward and kissed him on the cheek. 'Everything's wonderful.'

He took her face in his hands and kissed her on the mouth. Just touching her aroused him. But then for him, what they were doing was the fulfilment of a long-held fantasy. When she'd first suggested they go back to her apartment, he'd been so stunned he'd just babbled. She'd had to take him by the hand and lead him to her bedroom. And now her brother was not, apparently, returning home that night, and so theoretically they had the apartment to themselves until the morning. Ayşe wondered what Süleyman would make of it, should he get to know, and then she felt guilty for even remembering his name. Here she was with a kind, passionate man who would marry her in a heartbeat, and all she could think about was a shallow, spiteful philanderer. But then the philanderer's face reared up in her mind, and she saw, as always, just how handsome and charming he was. Just for a second it made her pull away from İzzet.

Looking wounded, he said again, 'What's the matter?'

Yet again, she made herself smile. 'Nothing,' she said, and then she put her arms around his neck and kissed him until he forgot all about her tiny moment of oddness.

As the crime-scene team moved in, so İkmen, Devine and Weiss moved out of Grant T. Miller's bedroom and went downstairs and outside. They all needed to clear the smell of death out of their nostrils, and İkmen wanted a cigarette.

Chewing hard on his nicotine gum, Devine shook his head and said, 'You go out to talk to a man about a suspicious realty company and you end up with a dead body with a pulped-up head.'

'I don't see how a frail old man like Mr Miller could do such a thing,' İkmen said as he smoked as hard as Devine was chewing.

'Maybe someone helped him,' Devine replied. 'Maybe the kid was drunk or drugged when Miller smashed him.'

They both watched for a moment as Dr Weiss moved various fronds of snow-encrusted vegetation aside at the back of the property.

'Rob? What you looking for, man?' Devine asked.

For a moment he didn't answer. İkmen for his part, and not for the first time, wondered what the mutilated body had been doing in

Grant T. Miller's bed. Had he killed the man after having sex with him, or maybe . . .

'You know I think that if I'm not mistaken, this is what remains of the Millers' old garage,' Dr Weiss said as he pulled away branches and bindweed from a slowly emerging wooden structure. Ed Devine shrugged his shoulders helplessly at İkmen, as if to signify that this was not unusual for the slightly eccentric academic.

'He had a car to die for – if you'll pardon the pun,' Weiss continued as he carried on clearing twisted vegetation. 'An early concept car, a Packard Pan American. Two-seater convertible, it was beautiful. I was just a kid when he got it, and I used to run out of my house to see him drive it down the road, usually with his mother beside him. I badgered the life out of my poor father to get one too. Of course he never did. God, if that's here . . .'

As Weiss carried on hacking his way through urban jungle, Ed Devine took his cell phone out and called John Shalhoub. 'He'll need to know what's happened here,' he said to İkmen before the officer at the other end picked up.

Part of and yet not part of the unfolding scene, Çetin İkmen watched his colleagues go about their business, then turned and looked out into the street. Beyond the wrecked Johnson house opposite, there was little but ruins for at least three blocks all around. This was the land owned by Gül. Back towards the city, he could see a few turrets that belonged to the last remaining derelict mansions to the south, then Brush Park became what the Americans called project housing.

Even if he had been a rent boy, what had brought the dead man to such a place as this? And if Grant T. Miller was indeed the sort of man who would pay for sex, then was he maybe famous for that in some quarters? Although it seemed unlikely that anyone else could have killed the man in Miller's bedroom, they couldn't assume, as yet, that it had been the old man. That Miller himself was missing could be viewed in two ways. Firstly, that he had indeed murdered the dead man and then run away; or secondly, that the murderer had been a third party, who had then taken Miller to somewhere unknown for reasons equally unknown. His mind turned to Ezekiel Goins, and he was disquieted that it did so. There had been so much hatred between those two for so long! Had Goins finally had enough and maybe kidnapped Miller? Had he followed the dead man to Miller's house and, catching him in the act with the old man, killed them both? But if that were the case, then where was Miller's body?

'Inspector İkmen?'

He looked around and, shocked out of his reverie, put a hand over his heart as he regarded Mark Zevets. 'Officer,' he said, 'you caught me dreaming.'

Mark Zevets smiled. 'No problem.' Then he said, 'Inspector, is it right that a body has been found here?' He looked up at the old house and sniffed.

'Yes,' İkmen said. 'A man. But not Mr Miller.'

'You know who?'

'No,' İkmen said. 'Miller is not at home. When we arrived, the house was empty. Dr Weiss thinks it possible that the crime could have a sexual element.'

Zevets raised his eyebrows.

'Mr Miller, Dr Weiss believes, could possibly have had an interest in young men,' İkmen said.

'Really? Rotten old creature like him?' He looked appalled for a moment, then said, 'You don't think there's any chance that the dead man was a rent boy, do you?'

'As a matter of fact,' İkmen replied, 'that is a theory. The body is . . . mutilated . . .'

'What colour is he?' Zevets asked.

'Colour?' It wasn't a question İkmen was often asked back in Turkey.

'Yeah, the rent boy, was he black or white?'

'Oh, white, er, or rather the man we think may be a rent boy. Why?'

Mark Zevets pushed open Grant T. Miller's rickety gate and entered his garden. 'Because I'm looking for a missing rent boy called Artie Bowen,' he said. 'A crackhead who funded his habit by going down on men. Some of them may well have been old white guys.'

'Why are you looking for this man, Officer Zevets?' İkmen asked.

'Because apparently he was best buddies with the guy Lieutenant Shalhoub believes killed Gerry Diaz.'

Chapter 31

Night was beginning to fall over the Motor City, and those skyscrapers that weren't bursting into bright electric light were fading into the darkness like fictional spies. Only at night did one really get the measure of just how many Detroit skyscrapers were now empty. Çetin İkmen turned away from the window and looked back into Ed Devine's office, which except for him was empty. The identity of the dead man in Grant T. Miller's house had been established as one Arthur 'Artie' Bowen, a rent boy from Lafayette Park, the man that Officer Zevets had been looking for.

Artie, it seemed, had been best friends with the man who it was still thought had killed Lieutenant Diaz. That said, apparently the forensic investigators were throwing doubt on whether Clifford Kercheval, Diaz's supposed killer, had actually taken his own life. Devine, amongst others, was currently in a meeting about that.

İkmen had little to do beyond sinking into his own thoughts. Lieutenant Shalhoub had returned from the Voss Funeral Home with news that Mr Stefan Voss had persisted with his story that he knew nothing about Elvis Goins' funeral. His brother Rudolf had done 'all that', apparently. It seemed strange, but then with only Rudolf's signature on the paperwork, it was just possible that he was telling the truth. Although why hide an innocuous thing like that anyway? Unless it was because those who'd been involved at the time were somehow still involved now. İkmen shuddered as he thought about Grant T. Miller lying beside the rotting corpse of Artie Bowen, maybe even using it for sex . . .

The door to the office swung open and Devine put his head through. 'Inspector,' he said, 'we're going out after Grant T. Miller – if he's still alive, that is. You want in on that?'

İkmen stood up. Finding Miller was now the only way to get answers to so many things, not least of which could still involve who had killed Elvis Goins. 'Yes.' He put his coat on. Then he said, 'Where are we going to look?'

Devine first smiled, and then let his face settle into a grave frown. 'Everywhere,' he said.

Grant T. Miller and his mother had paid for Elvis Goins' funeral, and Ricky Voss's great-uncle Stefan knew it just as surely as Ricky himself did. The Millers had given Voss a blank cheque! It was the only time that had ever happened, and Zeke Goins, completely unaware about where the money had come from, had spent like a wild man. The incident was legendary even if, as his grandfather used to say, discretion had to be upheld at all times. One did not want to upset the Millers. It was generally held to be unwise.

But Ricky hadn't been comfortable about effectively lying to the police. They'd all been fully aware, since before Ricky could remember, of the fact that Grant T. and his mother Rose had paid for Elvis's funeral. His grandfather had taken payment, that was true, but the whole family had known.

What if the issue about whether or not the Millers had paid for Elvis's funeral was crucial to something that maybe threatened someone's life or liberty in the present? It was easy for Stefan to say that it didn't matter! But what if it really did?

Stefan had gone back to his house and everyone except Ricky had left for the day. If he made up some shit about how his uncle was getting senile and how he'd been embarrassed to show him up in front of the police, maybe . . . Ricky looked at his vast array of telephones and other gadgets and wondered whether he should just e-mail. But then if the cops really did need the information quickly, that wouldn't be any good! Some people, even some big companies, took for ever to read their e-mails. No, he'd have to call, and he'd have to get the right guy too. There was no point talking to anyone but the right guy. Ricky Voss breathed in deeply and picked up his cell phone.

'As far as we can tell, Miller didn't leave town on a bus,' Ed Devine said as he motioned for İkmen to get into his car. 'And seeing as he don't have no car . . .'

'Not one that works,' İkmen said.

Devine, smiling now, sat in the car and fired up the engine. 'Thought old Rob Weiss was gonna pass out when he saw that Packard Pan American in Miller's garage,' he said.

'The car was . . .'

'Beyond reasonable repair? Sure! But I've not see Weiss as jazzed as that for years!'

They pulled out of Beaubien Street and on to the wide boulevard known as Gratiot.

'It's my hunch that if Miller did kill that Bowen guy, his best bet would be to try and get across the border to Canada,' Devine said. 'That's what I'd do. And knowing Miller as we do, we know he has money and possibly the help of others too.' He looked across at İkmen. 'So we're stopping everything going under the Detroit–Windsor Tunnel.'

'Which we're going to now?'

'Yeah.'

İkmen looked out of the car at the streets of downtown Detroit. They were just leaving Greektown and the huge new casino, headed now for the river and the complex of buildings that littered the shore in front of the tunnel.

'We're taking over from Regine and Ferrari,' Devine said, naming a couple of officers, only one of whom İkmen knew. 'We got a good complement of uniforms, which we'll need.'

To stop every vehicle travelling from Detroit to Windsor, Ontario was clearly not going to be an easy task.

'Shalhoub and just about everyone else is searching the metro area,' Devine continued. 'Miller could just lay low for a few days and then try to cross.'

'Do a lot of criminals try to cross the border into Canada?' İkmen asked.

Devine laughed. 'Is the Pope a Catholic? Sure,' he said. 'They get our scum, we get theirs. Cosy, huh? Tonight we just oversee, though. Rookies can get their hands dirty with the search.'

It was still going to be a long night. Devine's cell phone, which was on hands-free mode, began to ring. He pushed a button to answer it. 'Devine.'

'Lieutenant, just had a call from a guy called Richard Voss, very anxious to talk to you,' a shrill and distorted voice said.

Devine mouthed to İkmen that it was headquarters.

'Did he say what he wanted?' Devine asked.

'He said he'd like you to call him back about an old funeral,' the voice said. 'Mr Voss said to tell you that they all knew. He said you'd understand what that meant.'

Devine and İkmen looked at each other, and then Devine said to the cell phone, 'Give me Voss's number, will you.'

In spite of needing to be down at the tunnel almost immediately, Devine pulled the car over to the side of the road, picked up his phone and called Ricky Voss. When he finally got finished with that, he turned the car around.

'But I thought we were going to the border?' İkmen said as Devine executed a very rapid U-turn in the middle of the road.

'Change of plan,' Devine replied. He pressed a button on his phone to bring up speed-dial and called Mark Zevets. 'Hey, Mark,' he said as İkmen sat in some confusion beside him, 'where you boys at now?'

'Just coming up on the old Packard place,' Mark Zevets' crackly voice replied. 'Gonna take a look. You down at the border?'

'Yes, we are,' Devine said. He put his foot down hard on the accelerator. 'Mighty busy.'

'You drew the short straw!' Zevets joked.

'Sure did.' Devine accelerated even harder. 'You boys stay safe,' he said, and cut the connection.

İkmen, who was no great fan of really fast driving, said, 'Can I be allowed to know what's going on, Lieutenant?'

Devine looked across at him and said, 'Where Miller is, I don't know. But I know a man who may well do.'

'Who?' İkmen asked.

But Devine was already back on the cell phone, telling Sergeant Ferrari that she and Frank Regine were going to have to hang on down at the border for a little while longer.

'I ain't been scrappin', no,' the kid said.

'Bo, don't try and mess with me,' Mark Zevets said as he made the boy take him over to a big pile of metal in one of the old offices upstairs. 'There's enough scrap here to keep even you high for at least a week.'

The old Packard plant was one of the biggest ruin sites in the city. Mark Zevets often wondered if the mile upon mile of what had once been one of the most prestigious factories in America was in fact the largest ruin site in the world. People on the run had been known to hide out there in the past. Searching through its endless empty factory floors, offices, bathrooms and car parks for Grant T. Miller was something he knew had to be done, but it was a laborious, eerie task. Especially at night. Urban legend had it that homeless people lived in the old Packard, and there had at one time been some evidence for this. But in reality, most of those found lurking in the building were actually people like Bo Tara, drug addicts seeking to make a quick buck stripping the place of its metal.

'But I'm not here to bust you for scrapping,' Zevets said as he held his torch up to the boy's vaguely sleepy-looking face. 'Bo, have you seen an old man around here? White, eighty-odd years old, filthy pyjamas?'

'Some old junkie?' Bo sucked his teeth dismissively. 'Man, this place teems with folk like that, you know what I'm sayin'? People pass through, sometimes high, sometimes—'

'This old man isn't a junkie,' Zevets said. There was no point giving Bo Miller's name; he was far too young to know about him.

'So why you looking for his ass?'

Zevets was considering whether to tell him that the man they were looking for could have murdered someone when he heard John Shalhoub shout up from outside the building.

'Zevets!'

Dragging Bo with him, Mark Zevets walked over to one of the empty spaces where a window had once been and pointed his flashlight down towards the ground. 'Hey!'

John Shalhoub, standing on a small pile of brick and litter, looked up and said, 'Anything?'

Zevets directed the flashlight's beam at Bo's face. 'Only Mr Tara,' he said.

Shalhoub groaned and shook his head. 'Christ, Bo,' he said, 'can't you leave this fucking place to rest in peace?'

'I wasn't doin' nothin'!'

'Yeah, right, and I'm Barack Obama,' Shalhoub said.

'Lieutenant, with respect, we're not here for scrappers,' Zevets cut in. 'Bo says he's seen no one we'd find of interest.'

'He high?'

Bo Tara, furious, leaned over the windowsill and said, 'Would I be out scrapping, as you have it, if I was high?'

Shalhoub looked up at his partner. 'Zevets?'

'He's a little spaced, but . . .'

'Bo, go back to whatever crack shack you call home these days,' Shalhoub said. 'Zevets, get down here. I wanna take a look at the tunnel that runs underneath this place.'

Mark Zevets began to move off towards the exit to the ground floor of the plant, dragging a clearly reluctant Bo Tara with him. When they got outside, he told the boy, 'Just go now, Bo. Come pick your scrap up some other time.'

Bo Tara pulled the hood of his jumper up over his head and began to slouch off towards East Grand Boulevard. Amazingly, on the side of the road he saw a car that was clearly not abandoned. It wasn't a cop car. Maybe it had been stolen? But then the headlights from another car passing through the desolation of Packard temporarily blinded him, and so he just stumbled off into the wasteland in the general direction of the place he called home.

Ed Devine switched the car's headlights off and took his gun out of its holster underneath his jacket. Then he turned to İkmen and said, 'You stay here.'

İkmen was appalled. 'No!'

'Man, I can't issue you with a weapon! You're a foreigner! Stay here, get in the driver's seat, and if anyone tries to jack the car, just get the hell out!'

Devine started to open his door, but İkmen caught him by the wrist. 'Lieutenant Devine, are you going to tell me what is going on?'

For a second, Devine appeared to wrestle with himself, then he pulled his door shut and said, 'Listen, Çetin, it could be a colleague who's involved with Miller . . .'

'I guessed that!' İkmen said. He was angry that Devine apparently thought he was so stupid. Not to have realised what his tense silence meant would have been stupid. Besides, as they both knew only too well, Miller had enough money to be figuratively everywhere. 'Who is it?' İkmen asked.

Ed Devine wiped sweat from his brow. 'I can't tell you until I'm certain,' he said.

Zevets and Shalhoub were the only officers İkmen knew for certain were at the great ruin that loomed three storeys high on each side of the car. It was only eight p.m. but in this deserted and unlit part of the city it already looked as if it was dead of night.

'It's a terrible thing to make accusations against brother officers unless you're sure,' Devine continued.

'So can't you wait . . .'

'If I'm right, someone else could get hurt!' Devine said. Suddenly apparently galvanised into action again, he got out of the car. 'Stay here!'

İkmen got out too.

Devine stamped one foot on the ground. 'Man!'

İkmen walked over to him and put a hand on his shoulder. 'Ed,' he said softly. 'You know that back in my country we are obliged to carry guns too. But I find that I rarely do that.'

Devine looked at him as if he were insane.

'You know why?'

Devine shook his head. 'I can't even begin to . . .'

'It's because I have a brain as well as a trigger finger,' İkmen said. 'And my brain, and yours, is much cleverer than that finger will ever be. Lieutenant, if I can't reason my way out of trouble, then maybe I am in the wrong job. This is my philosophy. It has kept me free from bullet holes for over thirty years.'

'In İstanbul,' Devine replied. 'Çetin, with respect, this is Detroit! Car-jack central, murder capital of America, junkie—'

'Detroit is a city of people just like İstanbul,' İkmen cut in. 'You think we don't have killers in my city? You think you are unique?' He buttoned up his coat to show that he meant business. 'Come on,' he said. 'Let us go and find what you are looking for.'

Chapter 32

To feel this way was not only destructive, it was also irrational. But Mehmet Süleyman couldn't help it. In his absence, somehow, Ayşe Farsakoğlu had taken up with İzzet Melik. A colleague, Metin İskender, had told him. He'd seemed to find it quite amusing.

'Remember that Disney film, *Beauty and the Beast*?' he'd said. Then he'd mumbled something about if Farsakoğlu and Melik were both happy, then who was he to criticise? But then İskender was happily married. He had also never so much as had lunch with Ayşe Farsakoğlu, much less an affair.

It was two o'clock in the morning, and İzzet Melik still hadn't left Ayşe's apartment. Süleyman sat in his great white BMW outside and fumed. What on earth was a woman he had bedded doing with a creature like İzzet? Ugly, lumbering, when it was hot very sweaty, he was an absolute oaf of a man! Except that Süleyman knew full well that he wasn't. Unattractive and ungainly were only aspects of İzzet. He was also intelligent, sensitive, perceptive, and in addition he loved Ayşe with all of his heart. If a man like that committed to a woman he really loved, then it would be for ever. Ayşe would be cared for, on all levels. They could even have children! Oh, that was a ghastly thought!

But then was it? Really? Only for him. To some extent he'd always been like this. If he had something, then no one else was allowed to have it too. As a child, his brother Murad had readily let little Mehmet play with his toys. But little Mehmet did not reciprocate. What was his remained his, and that included people. And yet he'd dismissed

Ayşe Farsakoğlu from his life years ago! Surely he didn't still have feelings for her after such a long time?

Of course he didn't! She was still lovely, but he rarely, if ever, thought about her in a sexual way. No, he was just plainly and simply jealous that his ugly inferior was having sex with a beautiful woman while he was all alone. What a spiteful, ungenerous man he was! Mehmet Süleyman felt his face colour at the thought of it, hot red blood running to his cheeks in the moonlight. Shameful! And he'd threatened to expose her if she didn't get rid of İzzet, and had followed them from the station to a restaurant and then on to her apartment! What an awfully sad man he was.

Süleyman looked up again at the window he knew was her bedroom and saw that the light was still off. He put the key in the car's ignition and turned it. In the morning he would, he promised himself, have Ayşe into his office and make it all right with her once again. What he'd said before had not been kind and it hadn't been fair. As usual, it had been mostly about him.

Mark Zevets had known that there was some sort of tunnel system underneath the Packard plant, but he'd never been down into it before. The entrance that he and Shalhoub had used had been accessed via a scrubby slope that led to a break in one of the tunnel walls. Moving carefully with their flashlights held out in front of them, both officers wore plastic gloves to protect them against any stray hypodermic needles that might be down there. Junkies were keen on dark places to shoot up.

Zevets went to the right while Shalhoub went left from the break in the wall. 'You're younger than me,' Shalhoub said as he pointed Zevets towards the more rubble- and junk-filled arm of the tunnel.

'Yeah, right.'

Where Shalhoub was going, Zevets noticed, if not exactly clean, was a darn sight more wholesome-looking than what he himself was facing. It was only when he'd climbed up on to a great pile of wood, stones and plastic flex that it occurred to him that if he was having a problem getting around in this environment, how would it be for a man of over eighty? Unless the tunnel led somewhere much more accessible, there was no way that Miller was in there. Using the spaces where mortar had fallen away between the bricks on the tunnel roof, he pulled himself forward until he came to a void, and then, at last, he lowered himself on to the floor. Moving his flashlight around, he could see that he was in fact at a dead end. He called out to Shalhoub: 'Lieutenant, there's nothing here!'

But Shalhoub did not reply.

'Lieutenant?'

Liquid was coming in from somewhere. At first he thought it might be dripping down from the roof. To begin with, he thought it was water. He was wrong on both counts. The liquid was actually coming from the woodpile he'd just scrambled over, and it wasn't water either. Mark Zevets bent down and put his fingers into a pool of gasoline.

'Lieutenant!'

He hurled himself forward on to the woodpile and his escape route just as the whole thing burst into flames.

'What's that?' Çetin İkmen pointed to a flare of light that came from the part of the plant that was across Grand East Boulevard.

Ed Devine ran back and shone his flashlight in the direction İkmen was indicating. 'Could be almost anything,' he said. 'Acetylene torch; some of the addicts that hang here sometimes light fires in the winter.'

'Should we look?'

Devine sighed. 'I guess,' he said. 'But if it's a whole heap of junkies, I'm just gonna let them go. We have, as the saying goes, bigger fish to land.'

They walked across Grand East and underneath an archway that led through into a vast masonry- and vegetation-choked lot. Built to a design by arguably Detroit's greatest architect, Albert Kahn, in

1903, even in ruins what remained of the building still looked modern-istic to İkmen. Mr Kahn had been clearly a man well ahead of his time. But Ed Devine wasn't looking at the building, rather at a fire that had apparently started down one of the slopes that led to the tunnel running underneath the whole plant.

'Fucking junkies!' he muttered as he switched on his flashlight and removed his gun from his jacket once again.

Çetin İkmen saw two figures emerge from the slope, both of them shrouded in smoke.

'Police!' Devine shouted. 'Freeze!'

There was some movement in the smoke.

'I said, freeze!' Devine reiterated.

A voice yelled back: 'That you, Ed?'

Devine, his gun still in his hand, moved in front of İkmen and said, 'Yeah. Who's that?'

'Shalhoub!'

It sounded like his voice, but Devine still didn't put away his weapon. 'You got a junkie fire down there, John?'

'Yeah.'

'Zevets with you?'

'We're trying to put it out,' Shalhoub said. 'Can you come and give us a hand?'

'Yeah, we can do that,' Devine said. He turned to İkmen and whispered, 'I got a bad feeling here.'

'About Shalhoub?'

'Çetin, John Shalhoub never went out to Voss Funeral Home earlier today,' Devine said. 'I don't know where he went, but he was off the rader. Stay behind me. Hear?'

İkmen nodded.

'Ed? You coming?' Shalhoub yelled.

'I am.'

Devine and İkmen moved down the slope and into the smoke. But then suddenly Devine's body just slumped down in front of the Turk,

274

and he found himself looking through a thick ball of black and grey smoke at John Shalhoub and Grant T. Miller, both carrying guns. From what appeared to be a fire on his right, he could hear what sounded like someone screaming.

John Shalhoub took Ed Devine's gun out of his hand and frowned at Çetin İkmen.

'Not your day, Turk,' he said as he and Miller moved out of the smoke and began to walk towards him.

'Where is Officer Zevets?' İkmen asked. He was scared, and yet at the same time he couldn't ignore those screams. 'Is he in the fire?'

Shalhoub shrugged. 'Shame I couldn't get to him when a load of crazed junkies decided to set him alight,' he said. 'There were just too many of them.'

İkmen said, 'Get him out of there! He will burn to death!'

Shalhoub said nothing, but Miller, a ghastly vision in pyjamas and work boots, said, 'John, we need to go now. We need to meet—'

'You are a police officer!' İkmen yelled at Shalhoub. 'What are you doing?'

'I'm earning some real money,' Shalhoub replied. 'I'm taking care of business. You try living with my debts. Try being an Arab in this fucking country! Don't judge me!'

Down on the ground, Ed Devine began to come around from the blow that Miller had dealt to his head with his weapon. In the tunnel, Zevets could be heard pleading for someone to end his misery and shoot him. But no one possessed of a gun was willing to do that, and no one unarmed was able. A ghastly smell of cooking meat filled the air, and İkmen knew that it was far too late already for the young officer. He also knew that it was probably too late for himself and Devine too. Suddenly and unexpectedly calm, he dispassionately wondered how long it would take the US authorities to repatriate his body back to İstanbul.

'So you were removing Mr Miller to a safer location when you were supposed to be over at the Voss Funeral Home,' İkmen said.

'Oh, Ricky Voss been in touch, has he?' Shalhoub smiled. 'I wondered how and why Devine came to be here and not at the border.' To Miller he said, 'You'll have to chastise your old friend Stefan. His great-nephew contacting the police. What's that all about?'

'You killed a man called Artie Bowen,' İkmen said to Miller.

'A rent boy. A greedy rent boy.'

'A person you could not risk the lieutenant and Dr Weiss and myself discovering,' İkmen said. 'How many other people have you killed, Mr Miller? Were they all just inconvenient, or . . .'

'We have to go,' Grant T. Miller said to John Shalhoub. He lowered his gun and aimed it at the once again recumbent body of Ed Devine, shooting him without a word and without any small flicker of emotion. Çetin İkmen reeled at the barbarity of it. Miller had behaved as if he were putting down a rat.

'John? Oh, I wouldn't be too ready to leave yet,' İkmen heard another voice say. Although still gasping for breath after the shock of Devine's shooting, he managed to look up and see that on the top of the grass-covered tunnel lay a man with a gun aimed at Grant T. Miller's head.

'This all stops tonight,' Samuel Goins said. 'No arguments, no bribes, no excuses.'

Nobody spoke. From inside the burning tunnel there was no more noise, and the flames were now beginning to abate. Çetin İkmen hoped that Mark Zevets had been overcome by fumes. He hoped that he was dead. He hoped that Ed Devine, however, somehow remained alive.

'Inspector İkmen? That your name, right? Get up here, will you?' Sam Goins said.

For just a moment, İkmen hesitated. Who was this man?

'Yes?' he said.

'You don't go anywhere!' Shalhoub barked as he raised his gun level with İkmen's head. Then he said, 'What are you doing here, Sam Goins?'

Sam Goins? Zeke Goins' brother? İkmen both heard and saw Goins take his safety catch off and then push his weapon in closer still towards Grant T. Miller's head. 'I'll kill him without a thought!' he growled. 'Inspector İkmen, get over here!'

Without taking his eyes off Shalhoub, or Miller for that matter, İkmen made his way slowly up the slope. As he drew near, Sam Goins said, 'There's a gun in the pocket of my coat. Take it!' Then, to Miller and Shalhoub, 'Put your weapons on the ground! I'm not bluffing. I'll kill you.'

Confused as he was, İkmen had to assume that Samuel Goins was a good guy. He also had to, if shakily, take that gun and look as if he meant business with it. Devine, he thought briefly, would have been horrified.

'Now let's have your weapons, boys,' Goins said. 'On the ground. Steady now.'

Slowly, Miller and Shalhoub bent down to put their guns by their feet. İkmen staggered down the slope and picked them up. He stuck them both in his pockets. He felt, he thought, a little like the Terminator.

'What brought this on then, Sam?' Miller asked.

'Sickness,' Sam Goins responded.

'Sickness?'

'Sickness with you, Miller,' he said. 'With what you do, what you've done, what you are. Sickness at seeing my own brother still tearing his heart out thirty years after his only son's death.'

'And whose fault is that?' the old man said. No answer came, and so he continued: 'Sam, you know where I'm going and you know full well that there'll be a big fat cheque at the end of it for you and your hillbillies. What's it gonna benefit you if you shoot me? Let's revert to the original plan, shall we?'

'I don't want to shoot you, Grant,' Sam Goins said. İkmen could see that he had tears in his eyes. Still with his gun pointed at Miller's head, Goins stood up. 'I going to turn you in,' he said.

'To the police? I already have an officer right here.' Grant T. Miller smiled.

'I've called 911,' Goins said.

'Why don't you come to Zurich with me, Sam,' the old man said. 'We can buy chocolate and cuckoo clocks and I can introduce you to my banker.'

'I thought you were taking Shalhoub with you.'

'Jealous?' Grant T. Miller smiled. 'I'd rather you came than him.' He looked over at Shalhoub with disgust. 'Shabby little Semite!'

Çetin İkmen saw John Shalhoub wrestle with his fury; even through the fire-tinged darkness, he could see the Arab American's features flooding with blood. What were the relationships between these three, and how did they work? All he knew was that whatever the situation was, Miller was, or had been, in control.

'Sam . . .'

The sound of distant sirens cut Miller off.

Samuel Goins looked quickly over his shoulder, and then said, 'There isn't long.'

'They've burned a man in that tunnel,' İkmen said as he flicked his head towards the now dying wood fire. 'We have to see if he's still alive!'

'The cops'll be here soon.'

'And Lieutenant Devine . . .'

'They'll be here!'

'To arrest you as well as myself and Shalhoub,' Miller said. He was so calm, so idly, mildly amused. İkmen aimed at his head and hoped he'd try to make a break for freedom. Not that such a thing, given Miller's age, was realistically possible.

'Things need to be said,' Samuel Goins continued. 'Inspector, you're all I have. You gotta listen now.'

The wail of the sirens was getting louder.

Sam Goins bit his bottom lip nervously. Then he said, 'Miller didn't kill my nephew Elvis; I did.'

278

İkmen was speechless. Why?

'The boy was a punk,' Miller said.

'Shut the fuck up, Miller!' Sam Goins rammed the pistol hard against the top of the old man's head. Miller held his arms up in a gesture of submission and duly held his tongue.

Goins looked again at İkmen. 'It takes a lot of money to become a politician in this country,' he said. 'Back in the day, I worked the line at Ford, my daddy was an unemployed drunk, and all those who'd left the mountains with us remained as stupid and as poor as they had ever been. I wanted to change that.'

Grant T. Miller looked as if he was about to speak, but then appeared to change his mind.

'I knew I could be a good politician,' Goins said. 'I believed in myself that I could change things. Maybe I have, maybe I haven't. But I needed money, I needed someone to sponsor me. I knew that Mayor Young was in the market for helping minorities like us, but I couldn't get to him.'

İkmen, in spite of the fire, began to feel cold.

Sam Goins glanced down at Miller. 'You'd always wanted me, hadn't you, Grant?' He looked back at İkmen again. 'In exchange for sums of money that were nothing to him but something to me, I became his bitch.' He curled his lip in disgust. 'Twice a week, usually in some rat-infested, ruined house. Couldn't go to his place, couldn't have his southern belle ma knowing that Grant was a faggot. I hated him and I hated myself!'

The old man laughed. Sam Goins ignored him. 'But then all of a sudden, I hit the big time,' he said. 'I was offered a deal by the devil and I took it. That was my mistake.'

'Mistake? I thought it had all been worth it in terms of your "people",' Miller said.

Goins ignored him. 'It was the 1970s, the heroin years in Detroit,' he said. 'Some of Grant's white-rights buddies were getting in on the action big-time. Competition was fierce. White gangs against black gangs against Hispanics . . . And then there was my stupid junkie nephew Elvis and his crew. A small player by anybody's measure, but he managed to piss off one of your old southern white yacht-club associates, didn't he, Grant?'

Miller did not reply.

Shalhoub, his voice trembling, said, 'This has nothing to do with me!'

'No. You're just his latest police whore.'

'I'm a fucking straight man . . .'

The sirens stopped and they heard car doors open and close, and then voices.

Sam Goins bit his lip again. 'Elvis was a selfish little prick. I begged him to stop dealing. I told him he was in danger. But he just laughed. Meantime, my brother and his wife were falling apart because of the boy. I saw Zeke cry that many times over Elvis . . .' He swallowed back his own tears and then sighed to control his nerves. 'Miller told me, Inspector İkmen, that the boy was as good as dead.' Then he added with a bald simplicity that was so emotionless it was shocking, 'I figured if Elvis had to die, it was best that I did it. Quickly. These people with a racist agenda, they can enjoy torturing folk.'

'Hands up in the air! Weapons where I can see them!' Orders were barked out by a man in a black helmet, Kevlar-padded and aiming an automatic weapon. İkmen flung his arms upwards.

'Inspector!'

He saw Sam Goins begin to raise his arms too, but then he said, 'All I ask is that my brother never finds out.' And he stuck his gun against the side of his own head and pulled the trigger.

Chapter 33

It was impossible to know what to say, and so Martha Bell opted for saying nothing. Somehow Samuel Goins had been shot and killed and Zeke was weeping fit to cry his eyes dry. For want of anything else to do, Martha just kept making more and more coffee. So far she'd made him three, none of which he'd drunk, and herself four, which she had mindlessly consumed. Her head was buzzing and she felt vaguely sick.

Becca, Sam's ex-wife, had called at around two in the morning. Martha had thought it had to be about Marlon. Her heart had nearly jumped out of her chest as she'd lifted the phone to her ear. She'd been both appalled and relieved when it was Becca Goins. She was at police headquarters and Sam was dead.

Even when she'd told him first off, Zeke hadn't said anything. He'd just cried as he was doing now. He wasn't even smoking. Martha wondered if he would or could ever stop, or whether he'd just end up crying himself to death.

She'd put the radio on for the local news at six. She rarely if ever listened to that, especially not first thing in the morning. Sam's death was reported. They said that in the same incident, two DPD officers had been wounded too. They were both at Detroit Receiving Hospital and one of them was critical. They weren't named. The only detail the station gave was that whatever had happened had occurred out at the old Packard plant on East Grand. Martha wondered what on earth Sam Goins had been doing out in that godforsaken place.

Keisha had only just got up and was in the bathroom. When she came out, Martha knew she'd have to tell the girl that her friend Councillor Sam was dead. It was going to upset her. She was just a kid; it wasn't right that she'd seen so much death in her little life.

Çetin İkmen was being interviewed by a detective called Bains. A middle-aged African American, he was the antithesis of Ed Devine. Bains was thin, dry and cold, but he was also sympathetic to İkmen's rather strange predicament. İkmen told him everything he knew about Sam Goins, Grant T. Miller and John Shalhoub.

'Lieutenant Devine got a call from Mr Richard Voss of Voss Funeral Home,' he said. 'That was what made him turn the car around and take us to the Packard plant. Mr Voss told Lieutenant Devine, or it came up in conversation, I don't know which, that Lieutenant Shalhoub had not been to see him that afternoon.'

'Shalhoub led Devine to believe that he had?'

'Yes. When we arrived at the Packard plant we discovered that instead of going to Voss, Shalhoub had actually gone ahead of our party to Grant T. Miller's house to take him away before we arrived. We found a dead body . . .'

'Artie Bowen, yes,' Bains said. 'In Miller's bed.'

He shuffled through a sheaf of papers. İkmen, in spite of the knowledge that he was in no way a suspect, sweated. He was in a foreign interview room, speaking in a language that was not his own about his involvement in a terrifying and violent incident. And he hadn't slept or had a cigarette.

'How are Lieutenant Devine and Officer Zevets?' İkmen asked. That either of them had survived at all was miraculous. But try as he might to shoot Devine in the heart, old Miller had only succeeded in smashing up his shoulder. Devine had played dead at first in order to prevent the old man from taking another, more successful shot at him. Then he'd passed out. Zevets had been badly burned and had not been breathing when they'd got to him, but he'd still been alive – just.

'Ed Devine will be fine,' Bains said. 'Zevets?' He shrugged. 'He's critical.'

'That's terrible. I'm sorry.'

'You did your best.' Bains gathered his paperwork together in a pile. 'Shalhoub wants to cut a deal,' he said. 'Should be illuminating.' He stood up. 'The Chief wondered if you'd like to join him in the observation room.'

'Yes.' İkmen rose wearily to his feet. In spite of his tiredness, he wanted to know what Shalhoub was going to say. Miller had so far refused to so much as open his mouth.

Bains pulled a tight little smile and said, 'I'll take you through.'

'I'd only heard about Grant T. Miller when John Sosobowski first spoke to me about him,' Shalhoub said. 'I'd never met him.'

His interrogators, Lieutenant Joe Fortune and Detective Dianne Scott, looked across the table at Shalhoub without a shred of sympathy in their eyes. A bad cop, a corrupt officer, was a pariah and an embarrassment, and Çetin İkmen could relate to their hatred all too easily.

'What did Sosobowski say?' Scott asked.

'John knew I was having money problems,' Shalhoub said. 'Alimony and . . . He was retiring. He said that I could make good money for doing very little.'

'For Grant Titus Miller?'

'Yes.'

'What sort of things?'

'Looking out for him mainly,' Shalhoub said. He looked, İkmen felt, remarkably fresh for a man who'd been up all night watching men get shot, burned and threatened. 'Miller has a predilection for rent boys. Sometimes they wanted to take advantage of his position in society.'

'To demand more money.'

283

'Yes, or maybe threaten to blackmail him. John had been taking care of that business for Miller for years. A friendly cop who'd scare punks away, basically. That was how it was put to me. It wasn't until later that I realised it wasn't as simple as that.'

'Why not?' Fortune asked. He was a pale, thin Italian American in his forties. He had eyes that had seen and been affected by a lot. İkmen knew such eyes well. Mehmet Süleyman had them too.

Shalhoub, for the first time, began to show signs of faltering. 'Well, er . . .' He put his head down and scratched his cheek. He seemed paler than he had a few moments before. 'John Sosobowski first got involved with Miller back in 1978,' he said. 'He and Gerald Diaz were called out to Miller's house because Ezekiel Goins was attacking him. He was accusing Miller of killing his son.' He took a deep breath in and then let it out on a sigh. 'Diaz pulled Goins away from Miller and took him outside the house to cool down. He had some sympathy with Goins because the guy was bereaved, you know, and so he didn't cuff him, just made him promise not to move. Meantime, Sosobowski did what he could for Miller's wound. When Diaz came back in again, he found Sosobowski and Miller talking about what an animal Goins was and how Miller was going to enjoy putting him behind bars. John had Black Legion leanings, you know. Anyway, Diaz said that Goins' accusations against Miller would have to be investigated. And that was when Miller said that he knew that in fact another Goins family member had killed Elvis, and that he had the evidence to prove it.'

'Did he?'

'So he said.'

'What was that evidence?'

'A gun,' Shalhoub said. 'A Glock. He said the family member had given it to him for disposal, but he'd hung on to it.'

'Did Miller tell Sosobowski or Diaz who that family member was?' Scott asked.

'Not then,' Shalhoub replied. 'But of course later, when Councillor Goins did some serious work for Mr Miller, they got it.'

'Serious work? What do you mean, serious work?' Fortune asked.

'Councillor Goins made sure that a company set up by Grant T. Miller and his mother Rose could purchase all the land around their property in north Brush Park.'

'Why did Miller want to purchase that real estate?'

'Because he didn't want it to go like south Brush Park.'

'South Brush Park is developing.'

'Exactly,' Shalhoub said. 'He didn't want to live next door to anyone, least of all the kind of people who live in project housing.'

'Black people?'

İkmen looked over at the Chief of Police, whose face was entirely impassive. Inside, he felt, he had to be reeling. His own officers, involved with a creature like Miller!

'Anyone,' Shalhoub replied. 'Miller likes to be on his own, with the exception of an occasional rent boy. Councillor Goins made sure that he got that land, firstly because Miller was primed to blackmail him, and second because Miller agreed to leave the property to the city of Detroit on his death.'

'He has no heirs? As far as you know?'

'No. But I also know that recently he's gone off the idea of leaving the land to the city.'

'Why?'

'I don't know. Life's a game to Mr Miller. He changes with the wind. But I do know that Councillor Goins took it seriously, and that he had been working hard to try and get him to change his mind.'

'OK.' Fortune turned to Scott, and for a few seconds the two of them whispered between themselves.

İkmen turned to the Chief of Police. 'Sir, if I remember correctly, a Glock pistol was found at Mr Miller's house, was it not?'

The Chief looked at him. 'Yes, Inspector, it was,' he said. 'You know, I am so . . . I can't tell you how I feel . . . Like all my nightmares about this department have come to pass!' İkmen saw him shudder briefly, but then he smiled. 'I have to thank you, in part, for this, Inspector. If you hadn't been so anxious to help Mr Ezekiel Goins . . .'

'John . . .'

Both İkmen and the Chief looked back into the interview room as Scott began to speak once again.

'John,' she said, 'we'll come back to just how Sosobowski became involved with Miller in a little while. For the moment, though, we need to focus on four separate deaths. What can you tell me about the deaths of Lieutenant Gerald Diaz, about an auto wrecker called Kyle Redmond, a small-time player called Clifford Kercheval and a rent boy with a crack addiction called Artie Bowen?'

İkmen's mouth fell open. Were they really going after Shalhoub and possibly Miller for all those deaths? Even through the one-way glass, he saw John Shalhoub's face turn white.

Sam Goins' death still didn't feel quite real. To kill himself like that had been excessive! He had to know that he had only been teasing about not leaving the Rosebud land to the city. Grant T. chuckled to himself. Stupid half-breed! Sam had taken power in the city back in the 1980s and still his people were plug-ugly and pig-ignorant! It was a shame; as a young boy, Sam had been a looker.

Grant T. Miller surveyed his cell, which mercifully he had all to himself. If things had gone to plan, he would have been either in Canada or on his way to Zurich by this time, about to visit his Swiss bank account. But for all his flaws Miller was a realist, and he knew that everything that had happened had done so because of his own actions. Or rather one action, that had set everything else in train. If only he'd not seen that kid messing around in the old Royden Holmes place! A nigger, on Rosebud land! Of course they came and went in cars down the road just like anyone else, but they never stayed, there was nothing for them! Not that kid, though.

Aaron Spencer had been in a world of his own, talking to himself in some sort of fantasy game, when Miller had first seen him wandering past the Windmill. Fearful that the kid might try to break in, he took his Beretta and went to make sure that he left. He followed him as far as the old Royden Holmes place, and then watched in horror as the kid went in. He'd been about to follow him when the kid came out again and saw him, gun in hand. There'd been something else too, something hanging limply outside of Grant T.'s pyjama bottoms. The boy had pointed and said something like 'Old pervert!' or some such, and it was then that Miller had fired. Given that people seemed to take the word of stupid kids so seriously in the modern age, he'd had no choice. Aaron Spencer, a child he'd never seen before in his life, could have finished him. Gerald Diaz, still bent on revenge thirty years after Elvis Goins' death, would have made sure that Spencer was listened to just as surely as he had been in the process of burying him with the evidence from the Beretta. Shooting at the foreigners with the same gun he'd used on the kid had been a mistake too. Grant T. was getting old, losing his touch. He began to feel a little depressed. But then a few minutes later his attorney, one of the best in the state of Michigan, arrived, and he regained his bonhomie.

'I haven't killed anyone,' John Shalhoub said. 'Kercheval killed Diaz! He was working for Miller! He and Bowen beat up Rita Addison!'

'Meaning to kill Officer Addison too?'

Shalhoub put a hand up to his head. 'I don't know! You'd have to ask Miller, you'd have to ask Kercheval and—'

'They're dead,' Fortune said baldly. 'Can't ask them anything. What we do know, in spite of your "evidence", is that Kercheval didn't kill himself. He was murdered.'

Shalhoub's face creased in what could have been pain. 'No!'

'Yes,' Scott said. 'He was asleep when he was shot. Neat trick to kill yourself in your sleep, but completely impossible too.' She leaned forward on the table and looked him in the eyes. 'John, if you want to cut any sort of deal, you have to tell us the whole truth. Now I'm going to ask you again: what can you tell us about the deaths of Gerald Diaz, Kyle Redmond, Clifford Kercheval and Artie Bowen?'

'I just told Miller when Diaz found the bullet in the Royden Holmes House. That was all!' Shalhoub yelled. 'I swear!'

Chapter 34

Night had fallen by the time they got around to Grant T. Miller. İkmen, who again was invited to observe, was no longer exhausted, having got a second wind once he'd been able to go outside and smoke for a while. He'd also managed to speak on the phone both to his wife and to Mehmet Süleyman. He hadn't been able to tell either of them when he was coming home, but just speaking to them both had felt good. Everything in İstanbul was apparently 'good', although it was generally agreed that it would be better if he were home.

Miller's attorney, according to the Chief, who again sat next to İkmen in the observation room, was a hotshot, an expensive celebrity lawyer who had his suits made to measure in London. He was called James P. Masterman, and he looked very confident and very relaxed. But then so did Lieutenant Fortune and Detective Scott. For the time being, they had finished with Lieutenant John Shalhoub.

Fortune began. He looked into Miller's eyes and said, 'Tell us about your company, Gül.'

Miller turned aside to whisper to his attorney, and then he said, 'How does that relate to what happened last night?'

Fortune looked through his notes. 'Gül, a Turkish word meaning "rose" – your mother's name also, I believe – is a real-estate company owned wholly by you. Previously jointly owned with your mother, it was apparently serviced occasionally by Councillor Samuel Goins, who would travel down to Savannah to retrieve the company mail and pay the rent.'

'Lieutenant, my client has been in custody for coming up to twenty-four hours now,' James P. Masterman said. 'Can we concentrate on the events of last night? That is why we're here, isn't it?'

Fortune looked at Scott and raised his eyebrows. She shrugged her assent. 'OK,' he said. 'So what's your version of last night's events, Mr Miller? I'd urge you to remember that two of our officers who were involved in that incident are still fighting for their lives.'

'Sadly,' Masterman put in.

'Yes.' Grant T. Miller suddenly looked small and old and vulnerable. But then it wasn't just Çetin İkmen who thought that that was entirely the impression he wanted to create. 'Officers,' he said as he looked from Scott to Fortune and from Fortune to Scott. It was at this point that İkmen noticed that Fortune had an evidence bag on his lap. 'I know it's difficult to hear, especially when you have two of your fellows in the hospital,' Miller continued, 'but you have to know that an officer called Lieutenant John Shalhoub, an Arab of all things, has been blackmailing me for years.'

'Really?'

'Planting evidence in my home . . .'

'Evidence of what?'

Miller had a brief confab with his attorney, who then answered for him. 'Lieutenant Shalhoub used his knowledge about my client's sexuality to extort money and favours. When my client refused to pay him any more, Lieutenant Shalhoub killed a male prostitute called Artie Bowen with whom my client had been involved in the past and then put the body in my client's home in order to incriminate him. As you can see, my client is an elderly gentleman who couldn't possibly remove said corpse on his own.'

'So if Shalhoub wanted to incriminate your client, why did he make it his business to go and collect Mr Miller before Lieutenant Devine and his team arrived yesterday afternoon?' Fortune asked.

Mr Masterman smiled. 'Because he was desperate,' he said. 'Shalhoub had only sought to threaten my client with Bowen's body.

Now that it was about to be discovered, he faced having his revenue stream cut off. So with the ultimate intention of both escaping abroad and extorting money from my client overseas, he kidnapped my client and effectively buried him underneath the Packard plant on East Grand Boulevard.'

'To go pick him up later?'

'Yes.'

'Weird that Officer Shalhoub thought he could evade Interpol. Him being a cop himself . . . Maybe he panicked.' Fortune sighed, then said, 'You do know, sir, that we have a witness to last night's events.'

'A foreign gentleman, yes,' the lawyer said. 'My client informs me that in the past this gentleman has attempted to speak to him on behalf of a man called Ezekiel Goins, a character apparently obsessed by the erroneous notion that my client killed his son.'

İkmen felt strange hearing himself discussed in this way. He said to the Chief, 'Does this lawyer actually think this story can work?'

'Mr Masterman has supreme self-confidence,' the Chief said. But he smiled as he spoke.

'Mr Miller,' Fortune continued, 'I want to go back to your company, Gül. Why'd you name it that?'

Grant T. Miller smiled. 'Because I liked the sound of it.'

'Not because Councillor Samuel Goins suggested it?'

'Why would he?'

'As a little joke, maybe,' Fortune said. 'Using a Turkish word he learned from his Turkish-obsessed brother as a way of both flattering and getting back at you? Rose was your mother's name; surely rendering that into Turkish was a little offensive?'

'No.'

'So you admit that it was Turkish, and it was Sam Goins' idea.'

'No!'

'My client merely admits that the connection between his mother and the Turkish word for rose is not a thing he finds offensive,' Masterman said. 'Councillor Goins . . .'

291

'Councillor Goins made sure that your client got the real estate around his house,' Scott said. 'That is fact.'

Investigators had been to Goins' house and had found all the documents they needed neatly laid out on his desk. For how long he'd been planning to kill himself it was impossible to tell, but that he had meant to do it when he did was easy to see.

'OK,' Scott said, 'let's go right back to the beginning, shall we? When John Sosobowski and Gerald Diaz came to your house for the first time in December 1978 to remove Ezekiel Goins, who was attacking you, you, Mr Miller, entered into a sort of negotiation with those officers.'

The lawyer frowned, while Miller just carried on looking straight ahead.

'She's going to let him have Shalhoub's version,' the Chief said to İkmen.

Scott continued. 'You could see that Diaz didn't want Goins prosecuted, while Sosobowski wanted him nailed to the wall. You'd wanted a cop in your pocket for years, and here was Sosobowski all nice and racist. Problem was Diaz. He was the rookie, but he made it quite plain that he wasn't frightened of Sosobowski, or you or anyone. He even had the gall to tell you that he was of the opinion, given your reputation, that maybe Mr Goins' beliefs had some substance. He was a firebrand back then, wasn't he, Mr Goins?' The old man's gaze didn't falter, even though his face had now darkened. 'So you did a deal, the three of you. You agreed to drop charges against Ezekiel Goins, while Diaz agreed to overlook the fact that Sosobowski was now gagging to work for you. Diaz was always a handsome guy, but he must have been really beautiful back then. Throwing in an expensive funeral, too. What was that? An enticement to the pretty little rookie to come back?'

At first Miller didn't speak, but then he said, 'What a marvellous fabrication. That Shalhoub?'

'Mr Miller, we've ordered an investigation into Marta Sosobowski's finances,' Fortune said. 'Think we may find some payments from a company called Gül? Mmm. You know John's pension wasn't really up to the apartment she lives in at the moment. But I may be wrong.' Now he lifted up the evidence bag he'd had on his lap and put it on the table. 'What I'm not wrong about is this.' He put his hand inside the bag and took out a twisted piece of metal. 'This used to be a Beretta PX4,' he said. '*Your* PX4, Mr Miller.'

This time Miller's face paled, and for the first time in the interview he averted his eyes.

'You know we found this out at a car wreckers on Eight Mile? One of Diaz's old informants, useless hick called Redmond. No obvious connection to you or your tame cop. Shalhoub had come across Redmond working with Diaz in the past, and he fixed him up with the little matter of disposing of this weapon. Not good enough for you, though, was it, Miller? You told Shalhoub to make sure of the job by killing the wrecker; said you'd make it go bad for him if he didn't.'

'This is bullshit!' Miller looked at his attorney. 'Shalhoub is framing me!'

'This gun is accusing you!' Fortune said. 'You shot at the two visiting Turkish officers with it, and as Diaz had just found out on the night he died, it was also used to kill Aaron Spencer. You know he even sent a text to one of the Turkish officers to tell him he'd finally got you!'

'Yes, but if Diaz had, as you say, finally "got" me, why had he let John Sosobowski be my creature for so long, eh?'

'You tell me? Loyalty to Sosobowski?' Fortune smiled. 'All I know is that maybe just like Councillor Goins, Diaz finally got pissed off with you, what you stand for and what you'd made him become,' he said. 'Two things set all of this in motion, Miller. A cop from a foreign country came, and quite by chance he listened to old Zeke Goins with fresh ears. He wouldn't let that mystery go. I don't know why. But it got Diaz looking for your blood again. And you killed a kid.

Diaz suspected it, and it disgusted him. He was going to call time on you, and so you had him killed.' He leaned across the table. 'Whichever way you swing it, we've got you for Aaron Spencer at the very least. We're working on the others.'

The lawyer shook his head. 'Lieutenant,' he said, 'my client—'

'Grant Titus Miller,' Fortune cut in, 'I am arresting you for the murder of Aaron Reginald Spencer . . .'

Sophie Devine, Ed Devine's wife, came straight back to Detroit as soon as she heard about her husband. Çetin İkmen first met her at the Detroit Receiving Hospital. Ed was now sitting up and even taking liquids, while Sophie, a tall, well-built white woman in her fifties, sat beside him stroking his forehead.

On Detroit PD Chief's orders, Donna Ferrari had driven İkmen to the hospital. She too was happy to see Devine almost back to his old self again. Neither she nor İkmen wanted to tell him about Mark Zevets, but they were both fully aware that the lieutenant would want to know of little else.

And so when the inevitable question came, Ferrari dealt with it immediately and without ambiguity. 'I'm afraid Mark Zevets died just over two hours ago, Lieutenant,' she said. 'His injuries were too bad for him to survive.'

Devine shook his head in disbelief. His wife said, 'That poor boy! His poor family!'

Zevets' condition had been grave from the start, and so his family had been alerted to the possibility of his death and had consequently been with him since his arrival at the hospital. As far as anyone could tell, he had died without excessive pain. A small consolation for his family, as was the honour guard that the department had already pledged to provide at his funeral.

'Grant T. Miller has been arrested for the murder of the young boy Aaron Spencer,' İkmen told Devine. 'So far Lieutenant Shalhoub has admitted to killing the car-wrecking man on Miller's orders.'

294

'What about Diaz?'

'Neither of them are admitting to Diaz,' Ferrari said. 'But it's pretty certain that once the lieutenant had taken that Beretta off Miller, the old man knew he'd either have to somehow persuade Diaz to lose the forensics he knew he would perform on the weapon, or he'd have to kill him. We think that Diaz, although sick to the gills with Grant T., was conflicted. Shalhoub didn't fess up to removing those ballistics records from the system. There's a chance Diaz could've done it himself.'

'He must have protected John Sosobowski for years,' İkmen said. 'To finally arrest Miller could risk damaging his memory.'

Ed Devine shrugged. 'Weird! I never saw them as close.'

'Maybe they weren't; maybe they were just tied together by that encounter with Miller.'

'That was a shaker about Sam Goins,' Ed Devine said. 'I never saw that one coming!'

'How could you?' İkmen said. 'From what we can infer, Lieutenant Diaz had probably worked it out, but then he had access to Sosobowski and to Miller.'

Devine shook his head again. 'Terrible thing.'

'Goins didn't want his brother to know.'

'Chief's going to have to think about whether or not to open up the case on Elvis Goins,' Ferrari said.

'I hope he doesn't,' İkmen said. They all looked at him. 'What purpose would it serve?' he asked.

'But Inspector, ain't getting the truth for old Zeke Goins one of the reasons you hung around?' Devine asked.

'Yes,' İkmen replied. 'But,' he wiped a weary hand slowly across his tired features, 'maybe sometimes I am wrong. Maybe in this instance, in these circumstances, Mr Goins is better left without that knowledge.'

'Well someone's gonna have to explain to Zeke why Sam was at the Packard plant,' Devine said. 'How you think they gonna do that without telling him the truth about Elvis's death?'

İkmen didn't know. He was glad that Ed Devine was making a good recovery, but all he really wanted to do now was sleep. The department had booked him a room at the Hilton, but Sophie Devine wouldn't hear of it. 'All your things are at our apartment,' she said as she led İkmen out to her car. 'No need to move them. I'll take you home and you can do whatever you like, and that includes smoking cigarettes behind closed windows!'

Chapter 35

It was nearly time to get up for work, and still Ayşe Farsakoğlu had not slept. The previous day had been one of the strangest she could ever remember, and its echoes had kept her awake and agitated all night long.

When she'd gone to her office the previous morning, Mehmet Süleyman had been waiting for her. He told her he wanted to talk and she really feared that he had somehow found out that she had directly disobeyed his orders by sleeping with İzzet Melik. She had no idea what the punishment for such an offence might be, but she feared it would not be easy.

As Süleyman had shut the door behind her, he had looked very grave and she had felt her face flush with blood. But once he'd sat down with her, everything had changed. He'd smiled, asked her how she was and then, although he hadn't actually used the word 'sorry', he had apologised to her for attempting to interfere in her personal life. He'd said that, even as her superior, it had not been his place to do so and that she was to forget everything he had said to her the previous evening. He had offered no excuse in mitigation and had then simply left her office with a polite bow.

Ayşe had been stunned and upset. And in the evening, when İzzet Melik took her out to dinner and then proposed marriage to her, she had been even more distressed. Of course she had been flattered, and she told İzzet so, but she also told him that she would need to think about it for a while before she gave him her answer. At the back of her mind she could hear her late mother's voice urging her to accept immediately, 'while you still can!' But she just couldn't. She liked İzzet, she even found his company amusing and of interest, but did she love him? She didn't know. All she did know was that when Mehmet Süleyman had apologised for interfering in her life, she'd felt crushed. Finally and at last, or so it seemed, he had managed to flush her out of his system. There was now no hope for any sort of relationship with him ever again. Hard as she tried, Ayşe could not help the tears that ran down her face and on to the bedclothes.

With her mass of red hair and her tiny misshapen body, the girl looked like the Nain Rouge, the legendary harbinger of doom for the city of Detroit. It was said that the Nain or Red Dwarf had first appeared to the city's founder, Antoine Cadillac, just before he lost his fortune and became bankrupt.

'I heard Officer Zevets is dead,' Misty Rodgers told Lieutenant Fortune. 'I thought I'd better come in.'

She explained how and why Zevets had come to see her.

'Cliff Kercheval and Artie Bowen were friends of mine,' she said. 'But Artie weren't really a friend, not really.'

'Why not?' Fortune asked.

She shrugged. 'Too much crack,' she said. 'Artie had a big habit and it made him crazy. Sometimes the two of them, they'd do jobs for people, together.'

'Criminal jobs?'

'I guess.' She looked down at the floor. Then she looked up again, and this time she said with more certainty, 'Yes. Yes, just lately the boys had money.'

'Do you know where from or why?'

'No. Although Artie sometimes got other jobs from men he . . . guys he did the dirty with, you know.'

'Men he charged for sex?'

'Yeah.'

Artie Bowen had definitely had sex with Grant T. Miller.

'Did he ever mention the names of any of these men?'

'No.' She swallowed hard. 'But one thing I do know is that Cliff wouldn't never have killed hisself.'

They knew that Kercheval had not committed suicide, but who in fact had killed him was still unclear. Maybe this girl had a view on that.

'Why do you think Cliff wouldn't have killed himself, Misty?'

'Because he applied to Wayne State University and he got in,' she said. 'Art. He was studying art. "Start again, Misty," he told me. "I get my place and start my life over." Then some job come along. "Just one more job with Artie, Misty, and then I'm out." Then he was dead.'

Her eyes began to look wet.

'You've no idea what the job was, do you, Misty?'

'No,' she said. 'But I know it come from Artie and I know it frightened Cliff. I begged and begged him to tell me what it was!' She began to cry. 'But he wouldn't. He said he didn't want me to know nothing so I couldn't get in no trouble! It's my belief that Artie killed Cliff. I reckon he wanted his share and Cliff's too. He was always greedy, God rest his soul!'

Grant T. Miller had started talking to his mother Rose once again. Some of the prison guards reckoned he'd finally lost it, but Lieutenant Ed Devine disagreed. The old man was just trying to convince the world that he was crazy in order to enter a plea of insanity. Ed was not fooled. But then neither was Miller.

'Grant, dear,' Rose said as she sat on his prison cot and applied her trademark thick red lipstick, 'you know I am very distressed at how you have allowed the Packard to get into such a terrible state of disrepair.'

Grant T. lowered his head in shame. 'I'm sorry, Momma,' he said.

'How we going to go out touring if you allow that automobile to rust into the ground?'

299

'I don't know, Momma.'

Rose put some blue powder on top of her eyelids and said, 'I recoil from saying that you're just like your father, but ignorance is as ignorance does, and it is ignorant and disrespectful to cut off your own mother's only form of transport.'

'I know.'

Ed Devine, his shoulder still strapped up and painful, looked through the bars at Miller talking to his dead mother. 'Hey, Miller, motherfucker!' he said. 'Stop trying to pull a crazy stunt, man!'

But Miller neither replied nor even seemed to hear him.

'You know you should tell these folks about how you got those two boys to kill that Hispanic cop,' Rose said. 'That was spiteful, Grant, but I can understand it. I would have been disappointed if you'd had relations with a spic, but you didn't and so I'm content.' Her eyes glittered with malice. 'Spiteful, though. You should tell them about that, Grant.'

He turned away from her. 'No . . . Wasn't spite, Mother, I had to do it.'

'Did you?' Rose sprayed perfume, Californian Poppy, on her wrists and underneath her ears. 'Did you also have to kill Artie too? All he wanted was more money. You could've given him that, couldn't you? You have it.'

'Artie killed the other boy, his buddy,' Grant said.

'Oh, don't you go getting all moral on me now, Grant T. Miller,' Rose said. 'You didn't give a damn about—'

'All right! All right!' He dragged a shaking hand through his hair. 'All right, I killed Artie because, because the sex, it all got . . .'

'Your little sex game ended in poor Artie being suffocated to death,' Rose said. 'That's the truth, isn't it, Grant. Your little tryst went wrong and then you lost your temper and smashed his head in. I blame your father. He had no control over his emotions either. Crying it was with him. You know, Grant, you should really tell these people that you got those boys to kill Gerald Diaz.'

And then he lost his temper. 'No, Momma!' he shouted. 'I won't do it! My attorney says that if I keep quiet, everything'll be all right. You just want to get me into trouble, Momma! You always did!'

Rose's eyes hardened. 'Now that is a lie, Grant Titus Miller, and you know it.'

'No it isn't!' Miller yelled. 'Buying all that real estate around the house to stop the niggers getting nearby was your idea, Momma! You made Sam Goins set that up, you started Gül, you!'

And then, just like his father, Grant T. Miller began to cry.

Ed Devine turned to the prison guard behind him and said, 'He strike you as genuinely crazy?'

The guard shrugged. 'Who's to know. He talks to someone in there.'

'When did it start?'

'Soon as he arrived. Started yelling first when they cut that girlie old ponytail off of his head.'

Miller had been in prison awaiting trial for three days. It seemed very convenient that he began to break down as soon as he was incarcerated. It was not, however, a phenomenon that was unknown. And if it was genuine, then he seemed to be talking to Rose about killing the rent boy Artie Bowen. This only strengthened John Shalhoub's evidence about how Miller had accidentally killed Bowen and then continued to have sex with his body. Shalhoub had also told his interrogators that Miller had paid Bowen and Kercheval to kill Diaz and disable Rita Addison. Bowen, in order to feed his crack habit, had then killed Kercheval for his share of Miller's money. That had of course, at the time, been a gift to Shalhoub.

'Well I don't know about your momma,' Devine said as he began to move away from Miller's cell. 'But I'll still see you in court, Grant T.'

Miller glanced up just as his mother, a vicious pair of eyebrow tweezers in one hand, looked at Devine with reptile eyes and said, 'You keep your opinions to yourself, nigger!'

Chapter 36

Çetin İkmen's flight to Frankfurt wasn't due to leave Detroit until nearly eight in the evening, and so when Martha Bell invited him over to Antoine Cadillac for lunch, he was happy to accept. It also, of course, gave him a little more time with old Zeke Goins.

Martha had laid on quite a spread. The really cold weather had let up for a few days and so most of the snow had melted. This had revealed the famous vegetable patch, and now that the sun was out, Martha had put out a table laden with food right in the middle of the garden. When Çetin İkmen arrived, she kissed him on the cheek and pointed at the table. 'Now there's Coney dogs and French fries, my own coleslaw, corn bread and home-made chilli,' she said as she pushed a plate into his hands. 'You just get involved.'

İkmen looked at the vast, groaning banquet before him and said, 'That looks wonderful.'

'You want coffee?' Martha asked.

He sat down beside Zeke, who was slumped contentedly in his chair, and said, 'Yes please.'

'OK. I'll just go inside and bring a fresh jug.' Martha sashayed off back to the apartment block, her great tiger-print coat swinging in the gentle breeze behind her.

İkmen took a local version of the famous American hot dog, the Detroit Coney dog, and said, 'How are you, Zeke?'

The funeral of his brother Sam had only taken place the day before.

'I miss Sam,' the old man said. 'What do you think he was doing up at that old Packard plant, Çetin?'

302

The Chief of Police had decided not to reopen the Elvis Goins murder. Samuel had been at the site of the incident with Grant T. Miller and John Shalhoub and had shot himself, but quite why he'd done so remained uncertain – at least as far as Zeke was concerned.

'I think he was probably trying to get Miller to give that land back to the city,' İkmen said.

Zeke Goins frowned. 'Don't know how Sam, much as I loved him, could have done business with that old Black Legionnaire!' he said. 'You reckon he killed hisself because of that?'

'I don't know.' İkmen bit into the Coney dog and found it, unlike most hot dogs he'd tried in the past, spicy and interesting. 'We cannot know what pressures people have put upon them. Your brother did a lot of good work for your people in his life.'

In fact there had been some evidence amongst his papers that Sam was becoming increasingly frustrated with the Melungeons and the rate of their progress into mainstream life. He still railed at what he saw as their sometimes wilful rejection of education. Although whether they even now had the same opportunities as other groups, İkmen didn't feel qualified to say.

'I am proud of Sam, yes,' Zeke Goins said.

'And Grant T. Miller is behind bars,' İkmen said.

'But not for killing my boy.'

'No.' İkmen put what remained of his Coney dog down and lit up a cigarette. 'In that I am afraid that your Turk failed you, Zeke.'

'And Detroit PD.' He cleared his throat. 'Fancy that Shalhoub giving out information to Miller about the department all the time! An Arab too! Miller can't have liked that! Hey, is it right that Miller gone crazy in prison?'

'So some seem to think,' İkmen said. 'I can understand it. He wanted to spend his final years alone in his house, away from people he felt were inferior. Now he's surrounded by them.'

The old man turned towards him. 'You know it's OK that you never found who killed Elvis.'

İkmen frowned. 'Is it?' Surely that couldn't be so? If not to find out, ultimately, who had killed Elvis Goins, why had he stayed on in Detroit? Except of course that he did know who had killed Elvis Goins, and why.

'You know, Diaz said something to me just before he died,' Zeke said. 'He said that I was a lucky man.'

'Did he?'

'Yeah. He said that because of Sam and Martha, young Keisha and this garden, I had a lot. I had a sight more'n a load of other folks who just got the booze bottle, or crack, or some hole in the ground for a home.'

'Lieutenant Diaz was a very perceptive man,' İkmen said. 'And very right.'

Zeke Goins raised a couple of French fries in salute. 'Yes, he was. I guess that what I have is just my kismet, as you my Turkish brothers say. Took me many years to really understand that. Took me a lost marriage and a lot of bumming around and drinking to understand that.'

'But now you do? Understand fate?'

Someone was singing what sounded like the old Supremes hit 'Baby Love' somewhere. The old man looked over his shoulder and smiled. 'Maybe,' he said. 'But it don't matter none. Here comes Martha Bell singing Motown hits and carrying coffee and cigarettes.'

İkmen leaned across and saw her too, resplendent in her crazy tiger-print fake-fur coat.

'Motown is the heartbeat of this city, Inspector,' the old man said. 'Don't matter too much really who lives or who dies, Detroit keeps on going just like she always has. We used to make automobiles and sing songs here in the Motor City. Now we work the land instead. But we still sing songs. We still do that good.'

Detroit

Detroit is the largest city in the US state of Michigan and is a major port on the Detroit River, which marks the border between America and Canada. Founded in 1701 by a French officer called Antoine de la Mothe Cadillac, Detroit was owned first by France, then Britain and then in 1796 under the terms of the Jay Treaty it passed into US hands. In modern times Detroit has been famous mainly as the centre of the mighty US motor industry – it remains the home of Ford and General Motors – and also of Motown Records. During the Second World War, Detroiters made weapons to fight the Nazis and the city was known as the Arsenal of Democracy. But after the Second World War and with the coming of competition from motor industries abroad, the city began to decline. In 1967 rioting on the streets of Detroit signalled that black workers in the car plants were sick of being treated as second class. But in the eyes of many people the city's reputation was tainted and the decline accelerated.

Actual car production in Detroit finished in the 1980s. Only offices remain in the city and poverty and urban decline have replaced the largesse of the past. Now characterised by empty auto magnates' mansions and hectares of urban prairie, Detroit is nevertheless starting to come back to life, albeit in a very different fashion. Individuals and groups have set up city farms, art collectives, slow food restaurants, independent theatres and bookstores. Famous buildings like the Fox Theatre and the Fisher Building have been beautifully restored and even some of the fabulous old auto bosses' mansions in Brush

Park have been saved. Detroiters themselves remain a tough, no-nonsense group of people who love their city and will proudly show it to visitors with eyes to see beyond the 'murder capital of America' label. It's the best US city I have ever visited.

The Melungeons

The people known as the Melungeons originate from the Appalachian states of Georgia, North Carolina, Virginia and Tennessee. They are characteristically dark-skinned, sometimes with startling blue eyes, and are thought to be of mixed-race origin. However, just what this mixed-race heritage might contain is open to question. Some believe that they are gypsies, others that they have Native American or Spanish blood. The most famous group of Melungeons believe that they are descended from a group of Ottoman sailors who were shipwrecked on the US coast in the sixteenth century. Some genetic data exists to support this claim and deputations of Melungeons have visited Turkey and been most warmly welcomed in recent years.

However, what has generally characterised Melungeon life is prejudice. Neither white nor black, they fitted nowhere. Hidden for years in the Appalachian Mountains, they appeared to outsiders a strange and ignorant southern people. How many Melungeons went north to Detroit to work in the car plants is unknown. But like both whites and blacks from the south, many of them moved north for higher wages and a better, more equal life. Most got more money, but, albeit not officially, prejudice and segregation remained.

Acknowledgements

This book would have been poorer, if not impossible, but for the kind assistance of the following people and organisations. Firstly I'd like to thank Urban Adventures for their fine introduction to downtown Detroit. I'd also like to acknowledge my cousin Brian Mills. Invaluable support was also provided by members of the DetroitYes forum. I'd particularly like to mention Lowell Boileau, Sumas and Ron, Sumas's mum, Gannon, Stromberg, Bluidone and granddaughter Jessica. Long live Mark Covington and his mum Lorraine and all the wonderful people at the Georgia Street Community Collective. Keep growing, guys!

Kathleen and Dave Marcaccio and the fabulous Django took me to parts of the city that tourists do not reach and I thank them all so much for that. I thank them for being patient, kind, enthusiastic, and totally understanding what I wanted to do and why. Thanks too to Greg at Leopold's Bookstore.

My final thanks go to all the folk I just met on the streets of Detroit. Whatever your situation, you made this foreigner feel at home in your city.